HONG KONG

by Mona Gardner

HONG KONG

MIDDLE HEAVEN

THE MENACING SUN

Mona Gardner

HONG KONG

1958

Doubleday & Company, Inc.
Garden City, New York

SEVERAL HUNDRED years ago sailing ships coming up the China Sea often put in to fill their water casks at a small coastal island where a copious waterfall tumbled conveniently onto the beach from flower-scented ravines high above. When these Western sailors asked the Chinese name of the island, the few local fishermen—misunderstanding the question—spoke the name of the waterfall itself, which was Hong Kong and meant Fragrant Water. Thereafter navigators from Portugal, Holland, Spain, England, France, Denmark, and America wrote that name on their various sailing charts and maps. And so, to this day, the ineffably beautiful, upthrusting mass of granite and white ginger blossoms bears the name of Hong Kong.

HONG KONG

CHAPTER I

THE SUMMER PALACE—PEKING,
August 1838

THE SHALLOW skiff was shaped like a pea pod, and bobbed around as fitfully, as the Lady Yi nudged it gently between the lotus leaves that bent every which way in a tangle of clammy wetness. Her lantern cast too hazy a gleam to outline the thick-ribbed pads, but as she poled past them they trailed dew across her young cheeks and chaffed her arms with a ghostly grasp.

The two islands of lanternlight in the darkness beyond were the Lady Tan and the Lady Hsu poling their skiffs on the same purposeful errand. As they drew farther apart their laughing, gossiping communion subsided into silence; and for company there was only the croupy bark of frogs and the bronze-toned thud of the third hour echoing from the night-hung palaces.

The Lady Yi worked quickly, her nimble fingers grasping each pink bud, peeling it open, and plucking out the tiny packet inside. She'd wrapped them herself—a spoonful of tea leaves twisted into cobweb paper—and had put them into these flowers as they closed at sunset last evening. She was gathering a harvest of scent now, she hoped.

Pressing each packet against her button of a nose, she sniffed deeply. Had the bud lent elusive scent to the tea overnight? When she thought it had, she opened an oval hamper at her feet and laid the packet inside, where the wadded silk lining would trap the flavor until time for the Celestial One's morning brew. But if the lotus had been stingy, she tossed that packet into an open basket—it would do for the eunuchs. Not the Chief Eunuch, naturally, but for the thirty or forty senior eunuchs who had acquired the taste for lotus tea.

Gathering the dawn cup always made her wonder who'd be drinking it in His Presence. Not Third Empress! Not that wolf-eyed Manchu with thighs as muscular as the pony she rode. "Sat her horse like a man," everyone said. H'm-m, sat a silken couch as unseductively, it seemed—only pregnant once in four years. A wife, Yi reminded herself from a store of unpracticed dreams, must be tireless and fascinating, solicitous and flattering, soothing and delightful. Third Empress was none of these. No, Third Empress was neither a probable nor an enchanting prospect for this morning's Dragon bed.

Who then? Which Minor Star? Concubine Borgikit? Nui? Peony? Orchid? Jade Snow . . . yes, obvious as a pearl in the hand it would be that conniving, that silken fishhook of a Jade Snow who'd suck the lotus-scented brew. *Ai-yah*, in two whole years no one had budged Jade Snow from favorite's place.

Yi shivered, not at the tepid breeze, but at memory of Jade Snow's swift malice towards those who'd dreamed of supplanting her. Not pretty, those tales. Not pretty at all in this rustling blackness.

She turned to scan the skies, and then with little whinnying moans urged her fingers on, until they flew from rosy bud to rosy bud like weaving shuttles. All spring she'd schooled them to this task—rolling the same four marbles around and around in one hand, and then in the other, until the muscles were as hard and tenacious as eagle claws. That way they matched her resolve for this sublime Cause.

The pre-dawn hours, the echoing blackness of the lonely lake were nothing. It was consecrated office! It was supreme privilege! She—the inconsequential sixth daughter of an inconsequential mandarin of the ninth rank—*she* was achieving a delicacy for the Celestial One himself! That discerning palate—so civilized, so poetic! She smiled in dedicated happiness, humming a tremulous little melody of summer.

At midmorning the Celestial One paced the terrace with a quick testy step, his arched eyebrows arched still higher in the anguish of indecision. He had the tall, lean-hipped body of his Manchu father and the angular, flatly molded face of his mother's Yehonala clan, but the wide sensual eyes and the small miserly mouth were his own. So was his reign name of Tao Kuang—meaning Glorious Rectitude—for he had chosen the characters himself from a welter of high-flown prose. It suited him, he thought: it suited his appetite for accomplishment; and he often repeated it softly to himself as though it were a talisman—knowing full well he had need of a talisman if this appetite was to overreach the other two gnawing and tormenting appetites that were with him always: the one for refined food, and the other for refined gold.

The terrace was the double-tiered one—felicitous enough for this morning's cricket fights, perhaps, but not his favorite. Too many pillars and finicking porticoes. White marble every way one looked. Too dazzling a reminder of erudition. Why in the name of all that was windy had Grandsire not controlled his urge? What had tormented the Old One into writing poems by the tens of thousands year after year, even to the very day he ascended the Dragon? Not only had he scrawled them over every post, every wall in the hive of thirty summer palaces, but—at the age of eighty, mind you—he'd caused this marble fantasy at the lake edge to be run up simply so he'd have additional space for his interminable couplets.

Tao Kuang didn't dislike verse, nor yet apostrophe. He didn't condemn elegy, sonnet, or ode. It was writing them that made him bilious. It was the besetting grind of keeping up with the court fashion in poetry writing. Literary humbug—thinking up fresh subjects, fresh turns of phrase, fresh metaphor every day. Enough to curdle a man's stomach!

Stomach . . . ah! That reminded him. He must make the choice. Nothing to be gained by sending the odious bill back to the kitchen a third time. Cook insisted it was the barest minimum. But . . . five thousand dollars a month for another bowl of soup at dinner! Unthinkable! Under cover of his long sleeves of yellow gauze he wrung his hands, tugging at the finger joints until they popped like firecrackers.

Hovering in his wake were the five perpetual shadows who attended him always. Each swayed forward, inclined backwards, fluttered and oscillated, carrying either a stool, a fan, a handkerchief, a fly whisk, or a cushion, in the expectation that he would undoubtedly halt and require one, or the other, or all.

The Celestial Being didn't halt, however. He stalked on to the last haven of shade under the gingko trees, and then pivoted so abruptly the pleats of his yellow gauze shirt swung out behind like a pheasant's tail. The five shadows scattered from his path, and a minute later re-formed in a solicitous half circle and then hurried after him along the marble lacework framing the lake.

There was the tangled scent of wild roses and jasmine and resinous pines. The lake was a sleek blue. The fragile green of willows hung like tassels over the little ornamental islands. But the Celestial heart wasn't wooed by these gifts of summer. They were merely further reminders that today's poem hadn't been written yet: that he hadn't even hit upon a subject he could announce to the court. H'm-m, what about tea scent? Sky tent? Summer bloom? Full moon? Lantern-in-the-Sky? No, no! Overworked. Stale. But what, then?

He paced on in a peevish stiff-kneed stalk, taking refuge behind a look of refined imperturbability. It denied the things he didn't wish to see—the stacked cricket cages waiting for the fights, court ladies twittering like rice birds over their wagers, eunuchs trading

rumors, two under-ministers restlessly fingering the beads of their
court necklaces as they waited for audience. H'mph, let those
two come another day with their report on the Canton muddle.
Plaguing foreigners from places of outer darkness called England
and America! Red-pated and perverse uncouths with their in-
fernal trade ships . . . drat them!

The Chief Eunuch, his ponderous mass a statue of somnolent
patience, stood back from the Imperial path. His soft amiable face
was creased in a perpetual Buddha-like smile of benevolence and
goodwill. He lived and breathed, the smile proclaimed, merely to
serve and alleviate: his sole aim on earth was to cradle, foster,
and contribute to the well-being of others.

Behind the curtain of benign lids, however, his little prying
eyes watched everything. They saw the Celestial ferment. They
measured and gauged it. They ferreted along the terrace for some
antic which would create a diversion. Nothing offered itself, nothing. Yet the danger point was near. He unclasped sausage fingers
and raised one in a scarcely perceptible signal. It was sufficient
for the two boy eunuchs over under the willows. They reached
down forthwith and opened the cage of the pigeon orchestra.

The birds went soaring up in a rush of sweet sound, the tiny
bamboo pipes on their tails fluting through the air as the flock
wheeled and circled and dipped in serenading flight. It was dulcet
cadence, the minstrelsy of distant lyres, and vastly beguiling. Especially to the Chief Eunuch. He doted on birds with all the
passion left him, and he tilted his head from side to side in cherishing pleasure as he watched each skimming surge.

The birds worked their charm on the Celestial body also. He
came to a halt, his grooved cheek lines relaxed, a portion of torment went from his eyes, and his thin lips parted in a smile.
Instantly a shadow approached and placed a stool. A second
plumped a cushion upon it. A third opened a summer fan of eagle
feathers, and waggled its crystal pendants until they shivered
together with the sound of splintering icicles. The Body sank onto
the stool.

Respite was momentary, though. The inner tug began again, and contentment drained away like water from a cracked gourd. The Celestial mouth snapped shut in bitter renunciation. A jeweled hand summoned the Chief Eunuch; and that mountain came bowing, smiling, holding his breath as he took a place slightly behind the Presence.

"I won't pay it!" Tao Kuang said harshly. "Tell Cook five thousand dollars a month is too dear for a third soup course at dinner. Even if it is such subtle, such savory . . ." He choked on saliva, and couldn't go on for tasting the spongy velvet of those noodles this very moment.

The Chief Eunuch held himself in immense suspense, not breathing even, only praying that the weakness of human flesh would assert itself quickly and save him his two-thousand-dollar *squeeze*. He licked watery lips and said as hoarsely as he could: "Lord of a Myriad Years, this epitome of soups contains many rarities . . . rejuvenating deer horn rendering one as powerful as a ram. Choicest man-root for longevity. A full ounce of each is in it. Pheasants' eggs in the dough, which is cooked in essence of week-old squabs. Herbs . . ." But his voice was neither mellow nor salty nor thick enough with luscious richness to evoke the soup.

Tao Kuang flicked his hand with finality. "No! I take deer's horn and man-root already. I shan't run up kitchen bills for more of *them*. Besides"—his mouth puckered waggishly as he glanced towards four pregnant concubines at a card table—"my ladies are busy enough."

The Chief Eunuch tittered, his moonface blissful and un-ruffled by greed; and though he moistened his lips twice in quick succession, no whisper of regret escaped them.

A whiff of honeyed sweetness blew by. Tao Kuang's nostrils flared. "I detect—ah, glacéd crab apples!" he said in pleased surprise, regarding the sweetmeat tray a shadow held before him. Ah . . . the tart tang of apples crusted with sugared walnuts! That is, *providing* the apples were astringently acid. Not sour! *Providing* the sugar was delicately crystallized. Not brittle! Merciful heavens, no. Not brittle!

"Ah . . ." He lifted a confection by its stick and examined it. Behind him a shadow brushed the air with a horse-tail fly whisk in whooshing circles to shoo evil spirits and flies away. Tao Kuang nibbled the sugared coating tentatively, rolling the morsel on his tongue, savoring it judiciously. He nodded his head in grave satisfaction while he considered the taste for another interval, then raised his thumb in approbation. "Today's subject for poems has come to me. Crab apples! They have the elegance of an ivory miniature. Their color has the bloom of Kang-hsi porcelain. They endow one with a pungent and vigorous taste."

A shadow detached itself and scurried off to relay today's poem theme to the court. Over his shoulder the Celestial One said to the Chief Eunuch: "I am reminded—I have yet to examine tomorrow evening's menu."

"Everlasting Lord, it is here . . . ready for your connoisseur's eyes," the Chief Eunuch breathed. "May it whet your juices." From the tentlike folds of his lilac gown he drew forth a roll of paper wrapped in yellow silk and held it forth on upraised hands as a priest would hold a votive offering.

Tao Kuang took the last bite of the glacéd apple, belched appreciatively, tossed the empty stick aside, wiped his fingers on the handkerchief a shadow purveyed, and then as leisurely took the paper and unrolled it. "H'm, tomorrow night the moon begins its wane. I would have something compensatory and elegant to distract me from contemplation of the summer's end. H'm-m . . ." He blew air through his nose as he read aloud: " 'Minced pheasant breast with olive pits. Lake shrimp cooked with water chestnuts in crab fat.' Yes, a teasing enough beginning. Then— 'Winter melon steamed with mushrooms, chicken and lotus seed' . . . yes, a haunting dish. Admirably suited to this lunar cycle." He belched again, and looked off contemplatively at the Western Hills dancing on a horizon of shimmering heat.

"Next—'Chopped partridge in lettuce. Beef sinews in gravy.

Chicken brains in custard.' Let me think, do I fancy chicken brains? I'm not certain. Of course, they *are* a tongue-dissolving smoothness, and that's a nicety near the halfway point in a meal. H'm, yes, I'll have chicken-brain custard. Then what have we? 'Peking duck with silver-thread wheaten bread, and duck-liver pâté.' Yes, good. Ah, 'Bird's-nest soup with squab essence.' Not very imaginative, but . . . 'twill do, I suppose. 'Carp, Szechuan style.' No! What's the clod thinking of? Carp is too soft-textured for the Szechuan crust! Certainly not. Use a fast-swimming river fish.

"Now, where was I? What's this . . . *'Pheasant-egg noodles in longevity broth!'* Strike it out! I won't have it, I tell you! Substitute something cheap like fried rice. No, that won't do. Too inartistic between crusty Szechuan fish and pear-dumpling pastry. H'm, the intermediate course must be slippery and elastic. Hah, onion noodles thin as silk. The very thing! Yes, I approve. Convey the order. It's elegant, yet simple. Neither too fiery for the blood nor the heart, and contains a good balance of the two 'hards' and the two 'softs.' "

He tossed the paper aside. A shadow caught it in mid-air and handed it to the Chief Eunuch, who continued to stand in rapt attendance since he hadn't yet been dismissed.

Tao Kuang shifted on the stool, easing one foot forward to rest a cramped muscle, and caught sight of the frayed satin soles of his slippers. Another pair gone—in two days! A hundred dollars for new ones! Expense, expense! Why should scraps of satin be so costly? "The gold dragons embroidered on them," the Chief Eunuch said. Everlasting *squeeze*, that's what it was. Everlasting *squeeze* that ran the bills up and up.

More revenue, more money, to shrink bills before *squeeze* caught up with them again, that's what he had to find. But where to put hand to it? Every tax device had been tried—even to collecting household taxes thirty years in advance. And this last scheme—assessment on pig butchering, pig intercourse, pig troughs—had the farmers rioting in Shensi and Shansi. No, further taxation wouldn't do. Nor asking for extra levies from the vassal states. Too many soldiers killed in ambush. Then where, where, *where* could dollars be found?

Ai-yah . . . those barbarians in Canton whining to have more ports opened for trade! Their petitions mentioned no money. But obviously they were waiting for the Throne to name a bargaining price so they could counter with less. Yes, by thunder! Those uncouth English and Americans might be turned into a mint. A mint to be tapped this year, next . . . oh, indefinitely.

"Summon the under-ministers reporting on Canton. Warn them, though—no long-winded harangue. We've cricket fights to see." He snapped his order over the shoulder to the Chief Eunuch and shook his sleeve in the dismissal gesture.

The Chief Eunuch withdrew backwards the proper distance, then turned and crossed the terrace in monumental majesty, singing a ravel of song as he went:

> *"With claws of an eagle, the heart of a kite,*
> *let falsehood, and cunning, and flattery unite,*
> *To deceive all above me and oppress all below."*

He sang it softly and sweetly, but he considered it a caroling tune.

The two under-ministers bustled forward, bending one knee and lifting both hands in supplication—the lesser *kowtow* permitted in the garden. Under-Minister Ho rose first and patted his handsome gown of duck-egg blue into becoming folds as he waited for recognition. He was Northern Chinese—big, broad-shouldered, and jolly, with drooping mustachios which waggled as comically as a horse's tail when he talked—which he was usually doing, and ached mightily to do now after having been corked this past hour.

Under-Minister Kan was an exact opposite. He hated laughter —it ate time; it distorted men's faces and minds, he said, and kept himself a stranger to it. In a dour and bitten face his eyes were as hostile as a hawk's. Even his clothes were somber stone gray, somberly cut, without pleats or embroidery. His belt buckle and jacket buttons were grudging necessities.

Tao Kuang recognized them with a tranquil smile. "You bring interesting tribute from Canton?" he queried.

Ho sailed in with gusto, unable to bear that Kan should be spokesman. "We do, Sire. Depend upon it. The Viceroy sends a stunning necklace of jewel jade. *Millennial!* Nothing its equal. Smite me with goiter if I don't speak the truth. A dinner service from the Governor. *Millennial!* The most complicated pattern the Shekwan kilns have ever made. Called 'Thousand-Flower-Pattern.' Unutterably new—dedicated to your name. It'll be famous for ten thousand generations! *Millennial!*"

He gestured expansively to show the scope of history, caught his breath for the ensuing installment, which trembled on his lips, and in rollicking laughter said: "The Customs Collector wouldn't be outdone! Never, Sire! Sends two pearls as large as plover eggs! Unbelievable, I said, even after I saw them. *Absolutely millennial!* Never before encountered on land or sea. As for your favorite stem—ginger in honey—the Cantonese mandarins sent a junk filled with it."

Tao Kuang fanned himself with the eagle feathers. The gift descriptions soothed and titillated. "And from the foreign devils?" he inquired.

Ho's eyes faltered; his beard waggled lugubriously. "Sire, it tears my bowels asunder to say it—the Vulgarians sent nothing."

Tao Kuang's lips pursed as though he'd bitten into a green persimmon.

Ho sprang into an attitude of incredulity. "Their ocherous-colored hair! Their eyes like tiger's!"

Tao Kuang shuddered involuntarily. He'd heard it before, but it was still repulsive.

Ho began to snicker. "They're upside-down men, these 'tiger's-eyes!' They worship callow youth, and run about on foot like coolies pretending they're young. Sit in chairs still warm from another's body! Instead of shaking his own two hands a man mingles the sweat of his palm with the sweat of another's palm! Do they eat with clean jade? Or clean ivory? No! They use the kitchen utensils our servants use—a pronged skewer and a butcher's knife to lift coarse chunks of half-cooked meat into their mouths! This renders them so dirty they must bathe every day!"

Nausea threatened Tao Kuang. He transferred his eyes to a marble bridge arching over its own pearly reflection and mused pityingly: "They're dazzled, poor bath-a-day creatures, by China's light and glory!"

Ho snickered. "Canton merchants call doing business with them 'child's play,' so childish are they at bargaining. Yet the Barbarians call it *trade.* They're doting fond of that word 'trade' —*trade between nations,* they say, *is progress. Ai-yah,* we can afford to let them call it what they choose. . . ."

Kan made a sudden spitting sound. "China doesn't require progress! *We are the Middle Kingdom!* The center of the universe. The ultimate in the world! We have nothing to learn. Our dearest wish is to maintain things precisely as they are—in accordance with Confucian doctrines." His voice was as numbing as sleet in a winter wind.

Tao Kuang was too startled to stop the ranter.

Kan's voice rasped on: "*Trade* with them? Why should we? We Chinese have the best food in the world—rice! The best drink— tea! We make the best clothing—with silk, linen, cotton, and Siberian furs. What is there to want? The Barbarians' tomfool tinkling little singsongs are novelties—but the Imperial City and the Great Within are already filled with these music boxes. As for chronometers—we have plenty, sufficient! The Grand Treasurer alone has collected more than two hundred pairs. Should we open ports to acquire more? No, I tell you—foreign devils have nothing to offer us! Nothing!"

"Except opium," Ho said slyly.

The Celestial One quivered perceptibly at the word, and glanced questioningly towards Ho.

That was invitation enough. Ho was off, telling how this "foreign mud" was coming into a thousand rivers, and winding creeks, and bays: brought by lorcha, lugger, junk, sampan, and those incredibly agile "fast crabs" with fifty oars . . . all, all despite the valiant, the ferocious, the superhuman effort of that naval genius, Admiral Ku, and his mighty fleet of war junks.

"Why?" Ho demanded oratorically, and hastened to answer himself in the same breath. "Because foreign-devil ships copy the anatomy of deep-sea fish. They swim fast and powerfully. Let us avail ourselves of this clever idea. Three million *taels* would buy enough swift ships and guns to put down smuggling!"

Tao Kuang frowned concentratedly. Opium traffic didn't bring a copper's worth of revenue to him. It benefited neither the Throne nor the populace—only fat smugglers, and they were those South China aborigines, the Hakkas. Not Manchus! But how to cope with the muddle? Spending three million *taels* on new ships was obvious nonsense. Something easier . . . The opium law itself—wasn't that the sore point? Why countenance an impractical, wasteful, extravagant law that cost money? If it couldn't show a profit, throw it out!

He cleared his throat. "Moral fragrance and wise conduct must guide us," he said experimentally. "We must give due consideration, always, to economic factors. Suppose . . . we open two additional ports to these 'bath-a-day' creatures? Suppose, simultaneously, we rescind the opium law . . . mightn't that increase our nation's revenue?"

Ho's bargaining blood surged high; his heart quivered with excitement. He saw himself departing southward on a second mission—heading it, undoubtedly, conducting parleys with Hong merchants, dissembling, feigning, outwitting. . . . *Ai-yah*, there'd be a quarter million in it for him, easily.

But before he could laud the acumen, the statesmanship, the utterly delightful deviousness of the plan, Kan was speaking. Not speaking really, but grinding and clacking his teeth, and croaking like a raven in heat.

"Rescind the opium law? Never! Open our gates wide to this contemptible breed? Never! They'd swarm like locusts in a wheat field—devouring everything. They're turbulent, disrespectful, fractious, unreasonable men. They bring disaster wherever they go. Propriety vanishes. Honest men turn into thieves, and black rebellions hatch. Consider their acquisitive history. They swallow every country they get into. Once in India, what happened? They intend swallowing you and the Dragon Throne the same way. No! Every precept in the Confucian code demands their exclusion."

His voice became an awl, piercing flabby consciousness, drilling into the core of being. Tao Kuang felt a stab of fear, and flinched. Could it be the goodly heritage was disintegrating? Nine million dead of the famine in Chili, Honan, Kansu, and Kwangsi! The hill people of Kwantung revolting again! That pseudo-religious murmur in the Yangtze delta! Another garrison required to control infuriated Formosans. Dare he brave another hazard—even though it promise prodigal dollars? His fingers plucked distractedly at his gold belt buckle, hooking and unhooking it, tracing damp tracks over its sapphire settings.

Travelers' tales from India crowded and pushed through his memory—indelible, graphic, obsessive tales! The Grand Mogul gone, an English Viceroy sitting on the Peacock Throne. . . . "Enough," he whispered to himself, banishing the horrid picture. Then to the air around him, to the four winds, he screamed: "Their destiny decides for them. Not I!" He raised trembling hands and clapped twice peremptorily. "A vermilion-pencil edict!"

A shadow bounded off like a startled hare, returning in a trice with two others—one carrying inkstone and brushes, the other rolled paper and writing board. With them came a scribe, flexing the muscles of his writing hand nervously as he ran. He'd barely warmed the brush in his mouth before the Celestial voice pronounced:

*"To Viceroy Liu in Canton—*include the usual salutations—

"In our opinion Outer Barbarians are uncouth beings. Their dispositions are depraved by the education and customs of those countries beyond the bounds of Celestial Chinese civilization, so they are incapable of following right reason. Their characters are formed, their perverse obstinacy untamable, and they are dead to the influence of our renovating laws and good manners.

"The size and wealth of China, its excellent institutions, are all immeasurably superior to the odd confused rules by which these red-pated barbarians are governed. Our glorious literature contains every noble, elegant, and profound idea: everything, in fact, from which true civilization can spring; and upon this we claim our national superiority. What is to be gained by permitting such uncouths to come and go at will in our glorious country and to partake of its sacred bounty?

"Therefore: Outer Barbarians are beasts, not to be governed on the same principles as citizens. To rule them by our great maxims of reason would tend to nothing but confusion. The true and best way to rule these barbarians is by misrule.

"A special edict! Tremble, and obey!"

The scribe twirled his brush in final flourish. A shadow snatched the paper up and held it aloft while the ink dried.

During the writing the concubine Jade Snow had come sidling nearer and nearer the Celestial One. It was very daring of her, not having been summoned. But then Jade Snow was a daring little trick. She had eyes the color of ripe mulberries, a pearl-tinted skin, and she was twenty. Moreover, she had given Tao Kuang a boy baby this spring. It was the first healthy one he'd fathered in many years.

The Celestial One was too cramped with fear of survival to

notice her immediately, but the sun shooting splinters of golden light from her hair ornaments diverted him. The golden dazzle suggested an idea, a splendid one. He directed: "Take another memorandum for Viceroy Liu."

The scribe moistened, sucked, and moistened his lips again as he effected each elegant stroke on a new sheet of paper. It was short and explicit.

> *"Whereas the custom in the civilized world requires vassals to render tribute in material form—let it be known to the foreign-devil merchants that I, the Son of Heaven, Ruler of the Universe and Ten Thousand Nations, am graciously inclined to receive a birthday present of $360,000 from these merchants prior to their departure upriver for the trading season in Canton.*
>
> *"Read and obey!"*

The official jade seal, rolled in yellow silk, was proffered to Tao Kuang. He dipped it into the jar of vermilion paste and stamped his signature on both papers. He had dispatched his business for the day. Ah no . . . one duty. He unhooked the embroidered purse from his belt, felt to make sure it was empty, and bestowed it on Ho. The eagle-feather fan went to Kan. There, he'd indicated gratitude. He shook his sleeve in dismissal.

Ho and Kan backed from the Presence, murmuring in devout unison: "The Son of Heaven is sole interpreter of the unknown power swaying the universe."

Tao Kuang turned to Jade Snow, who had not left, and queried her with soft eyes. She smiled full at him, lowering her head only slightly and looking at him with a quivering look in those entrancing eyes of hers.

"Ineffable One," she said softly, "I would see the cricket fight before the morning spends itself too far into afternoon."

But he knew she meant more. He knew that through the long hypnotic hours of the afternoon she would lie beside him, fondling

him with her exploring little fingers, until she released his body to
those other sweet transports of opium.

When the moon was exquisitely right that evening,
the Imperial barge drifted across the lake and stopped near Third
Island. There was neither lap nor gurgle of water, for the oarsmen
had suspended their blades, and only a gentle momentum carried
the craft on, nearer the vista, nearer the singers' platform built
over the water.

Third Island was a replica of Mo Kan-shan, but in miniature.
The exalted crag was there, its top-heavy cliffs, its tenacious
pines, its tumbled obsidian boulders, but in inches instead of
meters. Even the misty veiling waters were there—for as the barge
floated into perspective a plug was pulled and water came cream-
ing from the moonlit crag, tumbling and splashing and spraying
into the illusion of depths below. A hundred coolies had drawn
the lake water, bucket by bucket, throughout the day, and had
carried it up the crag to a hidden reservoir that this delicious moment might be created.

"Ah-h-h!" Tao Kuang sighed in quivering ecstasy, imprisoning
with his eyes the classic contours of a mountain which actually
existed in a distant province.

Jade Snow murmured a lesser "Ah-h-h!" from the deck near
him as she toyed with a pair of enameled watches he had given
her this afternoon while she prepared his opium pipe. She had
expected jade.

For months now, since her son's happy birth, she'd made what
she considered a subtle point of dressing to complement her name.
Her dozens of coats, gowns, slippers and boots were, in winter,
entirely of jade-green brocade. The gauze and shadow silk of
summer were just as invariably the same green, occasionally
embroidered in white. Her only other dress ornament was the
deepest, the most translucent of emerald jewel jade set in . . .
what else but pearls?

A lone lute trilled. The plaintive echoes of a woman's song

throbbed out, and the bright watching moon looked down on its floating ghost.

Tao Kuang searched for words elegant enough to express the pulsing elation he felt. When none came, he resorted to the classic poem for this classic August evening:

"To wait for the moon I am sitting in the Western parlor,
To greet the wind, I have left a door ajar.
When a flower's shadow stirred and brushed the wall,
For a moment I thought it was the shadow of a lover coming."

The Chief Eunuch—on the deck below with his favorite nightingale in a cage beside him on the bench—suffered the lute and the song in silence. It wasn't music to him. It wasn't the silvery-toned trill, the carillon, the joyous diapason of song this bird could pour from its miraculous throat.

He shrugged in adoring apology to the bird, tilting his head from side to side and pursing coaxing lips at it, and then reached into the cage with his hand to stroke the bird, faster and faster. . . . The bird took a couple of quick hops, preened, ruffled, and stretched prima-donna fashion, and the eunuch withdrew his hand in a spasm of tender suspense. The song, the mellifluous song, would come any minute now, any second.

The barge drifted beyond Third Island, and the rowers dipped their oars again, making towards the farther side of the lake. Mosquitoes were plentiful there, Tao Kuang remembered. He rose and went below to the sitting room, where silk gauze screened the windows.

Jade Snow trailed genteelly behind, lingered on the afterdeck, adjusting her hair ornaments, removing a crumb from her slipper, on the chance of a quick word with the Chief Eunuch. He'd taken too much *squeeze* on this morning's cricket fight, what with the percentage all under-eunuchs and ladies-in-waiting were obliged to pay him, plus his own winnings, plus the sum she'd paid him to make sure her crickets were their lively pugnacious

selves at fight time. Who, then, had put the doped cucumber in
her champion's cage?

But it was obvious as a pearl in the hand that he didn't mean
to let her speak now. He was wholly absorbed in the bird. After a
defeated moment she swayed on into the sitting-room in her
wagging little walk and settled herself, beautifully and exquisitely, on the divan.

By Fate's design the young and unknown Lady Yi had been
taken from her tea tasks and chosen for the Emperor's entourage
this evening. She had dressed herself in gauze the color of rainbow spray, and at this moment she was offering the Celestial
One a cup of hot almond milk. She held it in her two hands
worshipfully, lowering her lids to shield her eyes from the dazzle
of his countenance. She was very young, and very new to court
life.

Tao Kuang barely noticed the girl until he happened to
glimpse a folded slip of paper beneath the cup she was proffering
him. Whatever was it . . . a note? A warning? Some new com-
plication? He leaned forward, and contrived to receive the bowl
and paper together, adeptly palming the paper as he raised the
bowl to his lips.

Before he'd thought what he was doing, though, he'd drunk the
delicately warm mixture and was smacking his lips. "Excellent!
Delectable!" He looked around in gratified wonderment. "Who
has created me this favor?"

The Lady Yi made little sounds in her throat until the words
came. "This unworthy menial—I learned making it thus in my
father's house," she told him shyly, not knowing in the confusing
glory of having been spoken to by the One whether she should
now retire or stay.

Tao Kuang let a belch work its way up, and then in an excess
of gentility and wile he caught up an ivory paddle and held it so
as to deflect his breath from others. Behind the paddle he opened
and read the note.

It was a poem . . . a charming, well-turned little poem about the splendor of the big white sky lantern lighting the ramparts of Heaven and bequeathing the national treasure of tranquillity on all who viewed it. The rhyme was signed—of all things!— "Tao Kuang's poem" in brushstrokes amazingly identical to his own style of writing.

He sorted the puzzle in his mind for an interval. Then it came to him, and he comprehended the full of it. This new-found lady-in-waiting was bequeathing him a poem, making him a present of the lines themselves. The clever little pet!

He regarded her thoughtfully. H'm-m . . . virginally young, waist slender as a roll of new silk, eyes pure as autumn rain. H'm-m . . . composed facile little poems, signed them in his name, made succulent almond milk. H'm-m . . . easing back in his chair, he felt a pleasurable tide of expectation wash over him.

On the divan Jade Snow was splitting melon seeds between her sharp little teeth with heedless regularity, revolving the halves until her tongue had the wafer of kernel, spatting out the hulls, and then cracking another seed in rapid succession. All the while her unblinking opaque eyes were watching the Lady Yi. Who was this unknown thornbush? How had she got here? Chosen by whom? By that suet bag of a bird lover? Or had the little goose feather bribed her way into tonight's entourage? What was she conniving with that slip of paper? The sly, insinuating piece of turtle dung!

At that moment the nightingale began its hosanna.

CHAPTER II

MACAO,
September 1838

MACAO DISSOLVED out of the noonday haze and became a green ridge curving around a sickle-shaped bay. Pink and blue and yellow dots, sprinkled like confetti on the green shores, took shape and became houses. Square bell towers, butter-colored domes, and cathedral spires jutted above the rooftops; while gray smudges on the upper ridge materialized into the ramparts of four forts.

The *Seraph* had arrived—one hundred and ten days out of New York: one hundred and ten days of sea and sky and wind and anticipation that was merging into reality now. Macao—the back door to Canton; and Canton was Cathay—the quaint, ferocious, upside-down, bloodstained land of ten thousand fables and treasures.

The roadstead was as crowded as a city street. Every sort of craft rode the slow swell there—sloops, luggers, brigantines, clippers, India tea wagons, bulging-hipped carracks, frigates with two-decked gunports. Between the big hulls hundreds of little hump-backed sampans darted and skipped like scrambling beetles, and off on one side in a sort of outer channel there was a continual coming and going of big old high-pooped junks with sails as ribbed as a bat's wing.

Gill Bennett took stock of the spectacle from the *Seraph's* deck as she edged into the thronging roads, his shrewd, friendly, quick-moving blue eyes roving expectantly. His mouth grew dry with the excitement of it. He swallowed, licking his lips; and his sun-stained face glowed with eagerness. So . . . this lunatic jumble of heat and smell and color was Macao!

He felt lightheaded. Or maybe it was the newness within him —bred somewhere out there in the immensity of that wondrous blue desert of the Pacific—that he was feeling now. He was sure of only one thing: an indescribable freedom of mind and body, a sense of fitness and ease and power.

Captain Macy came hippety-hopping across the quarter-deck in that petulant stride of his, screeching orders to the men aloft in his scratchy Nantucket twang. Seeing his passenger pressed against the monkeyrail, he checked his headlong ferment long enough to flick a bony hand towards the town and say: "There it is, Mr. Bennett! Prettiest little sinkhole the Devil ever made. Help yourself. Go ahead, jump head-over-teakettle into its mucking opium business—along with all the other heathens!"

Gill smiled good-humoredly in the face of Macy's ranting glare and said: "Remember, Capt'n, I didn't come out to China to be a missionary."

"Fumadiddle!" Macy snorted. He swung away, calling back over his shoulder: "You haven't got there yet. Wait and see what China does to you. . . ."

It was familiar rant. Gill hadn't listened to it for weeks. He leaned out now on tiptoe from the crosshatch of shrouds to see the big junk sweeping by in the opposite direction. What a shindy aboard! Pigs, ducks, nets, poles, babies and grownups strewn every which way and two deep in a tangled mess. His eyes lingered on the men—the first living, breathing Chinese he'd seen. But these meager, small-boned creatures looked more like undernourished children to him!

Their frisky agility was childlike too, he decided . . . look how they raced back and forth on the narrow canting deck, grinning and chattering and gesturing at the *Seraph*. Those with babies strapped to their backs were women, sure enough—and yet, women and men alike, these comicals dressed in identical blue pantaloons and jackets, their ropy queues hanging down from identical cart-wheel hats. Made them look like a string of dolls cut from the same faded cardboard.

"*Fan kwae! Fan kwae!*" the animated dolls screamed in paroxysms of laughter at him, and the junk churned past.

It was only a minute later that another junk swung close in under the taffrail. This time when Gill leaned out on the rail he found himself staring directly into a pair of inky eyes glittering with malice and aversion. Instinctively Gill recoiled. The sailor, attributing the recoil to fear, threw back his head in contemptuous laughter. Between guffaws he screamed: "*Fan kwae! Fan kwae!*"

Gill tried the words softly. Were they casual oaths, he asked himself, or specific insult? Anyway, whatever they were, there was no mistaking the venom in them. Well, nothing inscrutable or impassive about these lads.

"Brail up!" the Captain shouted, and the *Seraph* slid forward, her momentum diminishing as the wind took her way off. She slowed, scarcely moving, and the land heat settled down upon her —a clogging, inert, pressing weight.

But the *Seraph* had no more dropped anchor than small boats were nudging in around her four and five deep. Howling figures were hopping up and down on them, waving arms, straw hats, matting, pantaloons, anything and everything; and all the while laughing in that strange hilarity which was neither welcoming nor predatory, and yet somehow was both.

Gill marveled that anyone so brittle and gaunt could manage hectic activity in such muffling heat. He sopped at his face with a handkerchief that was already wet, and moved out of the sun into the shade of the mizzenmast. But the heat followed. His shirt clung to his body like plaster, and the neckcloth he'd put on an hour ago was a soggy pulp. New York could be hot enough in July and August, Heaven knows, but this was far hotter, far heavier. This was hideous.

He moved away. Suddenly he wanted nothing so much as to get ashore and see Tad. To feel his brother's grip on his shoulders, to see Tad's deep-set brown eyes light up, hear that low voice with the strange burr in it. He set the cabin boy to moving his trunks and carpetbags out on deck; and with the last one gone, he struggled into his broadcloth coat. It was easier to wear the thing than try to carry it and his banjo as well, he argued with himself. But the dratted thing would probably give him heatstroke.

He settled it into place, smoothing the lapels. H'm-m, even in this heat it showed what it was—a banging fine job of tailoring. He leaned closer to the wall mirror to examine the set minutely . . . didn't exaggerate his broad shoulders too much, and fell smoothly over his flat middle, exactly the right length for his long legs. He wrinkled his nose with acute repugnance when he turned to take up his high castor. Lordy, lordy, *ne plus ultra* in New York, absolutely the glass of elegant fashion . . . but here, balmy. Completely harebrained.

Out on deck he looked around for Macy, and found the Captain fidgeting around the ship—cursing the multitudinous boats below that were scratching his paint, brandishing a peavey at a washer-woman trying to climb the anchor chain, dashing to the rail to estimate the *Seraph's* swing on the next tide. When Gill appeared with coat and hat on, Macy grimaced and snorted: "In a hurry, I see."

Gill nodded jauntily. "Can't wait to get ashore and make that first million, I guess."

"Off you go, then. I suppose you understand those boxes of yours in the hold can't be off-loaded now. They'll come ashore later with my specie, in right and proper time."

Gill nodded. "Yes, I understand. My brother will take delivery."

"You're off then." Macy flicked the air with his hand. "Use the main ladder there."

"You mean—I go ashore in one of *those?*" Gill asked, pointing to the litter below.

"Yup, a *tangka.* What else?"

Gill laughed at his own naïvete, and thrust out his hand. "Capt'n Macy, I want to thank——"

Macy interrupted impatiently. "Stow that! We're not parting for all time. Can't avoid bumping into each other here or Canton next month. Meanwhile keep your nose in tea, where it belongs!"

Gill mocked: "You never give up, do you? It's like having the force of gravity working on me."

Macy's reply was a rasping cackle as he mounted the quarter-deck steps. "Mind the ladder on the way down," he said. "See you don't drop that grand-elegant castor. 'Twould blight Macao entirely not to set eyes on it."

Gill turned and made a point of shaking hands with Chief Mate Trow, and the second as they hurried by. He waved to the men in the rigging, to the *Seraph* herself, and stepped up on the rail. The rope ladder swayed dizzily over opaque yellow water, and the bizarre little boats below churned and muddled. The spectacle was beckoning, and yet curiously repelling. It symbolized the very things he'd come for—adventure, risk, whirling chance, yet it filled him suddenly with unaccountable panic.

"I've come thirteen thousand miles for it—why should I hesitate now?" he chided himself resolutely, and started down into the calamitous din.

When he reached the bottom rung he didn't choose a sampan: he glimpsed inches of planked deck and stretched a leg towards it. But hands snatched at his trousers, twitching his legs to one side and away, completely unsteadying him. Only the grip of his own hands on the rung supported him while his feet dangled until an authoritative pair of wiry arms closed about both ankles and yanked them onto a deck.

He looked around to see a witchlike creature straightening up beside him. Her yellow face was as puckered as a wet rag, and as lifeless. Whatever dubious hair she had was hidden under a filthy skullcap, and her raisin-colored eyes flickered at him with calculating animation.

"Hi-yah! Hi-yah!" she cackled, baring livid gums. Then she jumped away in macabre activity, her skinny old shanks and fleshless bones parodying life, like a skeleton dancing in daylight.

She fended off an encroaching sampan, clutched the ship's ladder with one claw, motioned sailors above to lower Gill's duffel, and somehow managed in the same tumultuous moment to push Gill forcibly towards a bench under the hooded cover. But the hood was too low: his elongated hat bumped and toppled from his head. Gill grabbed, bouncing it on finger tips as it arched towards the water. Then the boat lurched, and Gill felt himself following the hat.

There was a scurry and a scramble. A pair of hands flashed out, scooped up the castor before it hit the water, and in the same fractional second caught Gill by the coat and settled him back on even balance. These rescuing hands were not the crone's claws, but firm young ones belonging to someone who'd been hidden under the canopy. Gill bent to look under an absurd cart-wheel hat and saw shy brown eyes looking up at him. They went with a comely girlish face and full red lips.

"Thank you," Gill said in profound gratitude, but somewhat louder than he meant to.

Three scarecrow urchins in the next boat mimicked in screams: "Tank-oo! Tank-oo!"

In quick confusion the boat-girl drew back under the canopy. Gill scowled at the magpie faces an oar's length away, which only set off hiccoughing laughter. "Tank-oo! Tank-oo!" the taunting chorus echoed from boat to boat.

Gill's trunk came bumping down from the *Seraph's* deck, and the crone pounced on it like a terrier, barking over her shoulder at the girl. Together they pawed the rope sling away, and together they tugged the trunk towards the center well. Gill set his hat on the bench and sprang to help.

But as he put his hand over the girl's wrist to disengage it from the trunk handle, she jerked erect, flung his hand aside, and jumped away from him, whimpering like a hurt puppy. The crone broke into scolding gabble, and gestured incomprehensibly at the nearby boats. Whereupon the two of them dragged the trunk in under the hooded canopy.

Gill looked on in complete bewilderment. Obviously they'd misunderstood. But why were they so nervous and afraid—afraid of what, in God's name? Not of *him!* He laughed and shrugged his shoulders.

The sling disappeared upwards, and in the interval before the second load began its bumping descent, the boat-girl ducked her head under the hood and whispered: "No this side. Plen-tee bobbery other mans!"

She was speaking English. At least, some of it resembled English. What in suds name did she mean? *Bobbery? No this side?* No this side—*what?* While he mulled the conundrum, his second box arrived, along with his carpetbags. This time he allowed the two women to stow the luggage without an offer of help.

In another minute the *tangka* was sliding out from the tangle around the *Seraph*, and was winding and twisting into open water as both women lay on their fishtail oars.

Gill settled himself on the bench, his mind busy with the prospect of his meeting with Tad. Dumfounded surprise first, of course. Then the hoot of laughter that would burst from Tad when he was shaken by surprise—because Tad had no idea he was aboard the *Seraph*, or that he even contemplated being there.

It was a long way to come to break the momentous news—to say the New York shop of Bennett Brothers was liquidated, finished, sold out. That there was to be no more pip-squeak joggling along in tea while others were galloping in silk—and opium. It was Bennett Brothers turn to do some galloping.

Gill said the words again to himself with a spurt of exhilaration. He got the same swelling throb of relief each time he did. And that night—that cleaving, severing, dividing night when he'd closed the wooden door of BENNETT BROTHERS, TEA MERCHANTS, for the last time and turned the large key, shutting out the big brown canisters, the tea chests, sealing up the odor of lapsang, congou, and oolong—he'd been overwhelmed by such an upsurge of relief that his feet had actually slipped on the brick pavement and he had fallen against the wall, with the rain pelting down from the old leak in the gutter above him. He even remembered how he'd let his breath out slowly, as though he'd been holding it for years—which, of course, was just what he had been doing. He'd got very drunk indeed that night and ended up in a room he'd sworn he'd never enter, but found marvelously engulfing and assuaging, and the lady—thank God—very willing. . . .

Probably it was the chronological fact of being twenty-seven years old that rankled Gill, even though he knew he was flexible, pliant, and bouyant still. Twenty-seven was crucial—in an age when men matured early. Amasa Dewing, for instance, third mate on the *Seraph* he'd just left, was a man at eighteen. Admirals got their braid at thirty-one. And in the hurly-burly of the Canton trade it was not unusual for a man of twenty-five to be senior partner in a mercantile house handling more than a million a year.

Galloping into trade here in Asia. How wonderfully easy it sounded. Silk, nankeen, porcelain, spices—every mercantile house in New York, every crossroad grocery in the country begging to get. And opium—the whacking starter to build up capital for quantity buying. The poor man's mint. Ten casks, sold just right —five thousand profit. Then twenty casks! Thirty! Forty! Each tumbling in beautiful foot-loose dollars. Cash *before* delivery— that was the opium business.

"Foreign mud" the Chinese called it, even though they'd been using it for twelve centuries . . . a commodity you bought and sold as you would sugar or molasses or coffee. Big American merchant firms took a realistic view of the trade, and applied the same economic formula of supplying demand for it that they applied to wallpaper or beeswax or liver pills. Moral principles? they scoffed. Who could bring up moral principles with slavery what it was in the South and indentured workers living the lives they did in the North? And what about saloons? Gin? Rotgut whisky?

They quoted eminent doctors who said opium did no more harm in China than the beer habit did at home, and certainly was twice as efficacious for colic and the cramps. They told you about De Quincey, Coleridge, and dozens of others who used it regularly.

All the substantial American houses in the China trade were in opium hand over fist this year, building, or buying every fast clipper they could lay hands on to increase their merchant fleets, and thus get ahead of the big British traders.

Gill wasn't arguing with himself. It was Tad he was hoping to convince with logic and reason. For already he could hear Tad saying—in that infuriating righteousness their father would have used—"But—it isn't *right.*"

God knows he didn't want to step off the *Seraph* after two years' separation and club Tad with *fait accompli.* But still there it was—the decision definitely and irrevocably made. Bennett Brothers, according to the bill of sale, were to stay out of tea business in New York for five years. He'd signed the verdict, he—*Gill*—because it was his turn to make a decision. Tad had had *his* way for five years. And for five years they'd been nobodies in a cubbyhole of an importing house puttering with black sawdust. Now—maybe—the way was open to get *somewhere,* quickly, with zest and flavor. Now they'd begin to live, by God—but strictly at eye level. Not indulging in cloud-capped gestures like this last grandiose notion of Tad's!

Gill ducked to look under the canopy, and saw they were heading into an embankment that was a continuous stone jetty which stretched the full curve of the shore. At intervals there were loading steps and ramps leading down to the water. Several boat lengths away the girl shipped her oar and let the crone swing them around stern-to for the approach, and it was then the girl came whipping in under the hood to grab up a carpetbag and whisper over her shoulder: "Nighttime my come your side! My sleep you! Yes?"

Gill's mouth dropped open. This shy, immature twit!

"You wantchee, yes? Number One good, my!" She nodded insistently, her large brown eyes close to his face.

Gill jumped to his feet, the absurdity of it flooding over him. "No, I certainly don't *wantchee!*" he laughed, and brushed past her onto the deck. He ought to smack her bottom soundly. What an introduction for a future merchant prince—bobbing around in an eggshell of a boat with a witch-faced crone and a maiden who wasn't a maiden at all, but an aggressive little trollop!

The girl studied his face; and then, grinning confidently, she lowered one eyelid in a slow lewd wink.

The arrival of a New York packet was event enough to bring out the whole community, Gill knew, and he expected to see Tad staring at him from the jetty as though he were an apparition. But now as he searched the patchwork of faces lining the embankment, he couldn't discover the familiar close-cropped head.

The crone brought the *tangka* against the steps and scrambled out to hold it while Gill stepped ashore. He stamped his feet, getting the feel once more of the absolute substantiality of land, then bounded up the steps to hunt Tad.

He found himself on a broad esplanade. What he'd taken for a jetty turned out to be a stretch of packed clay leveling back from the stone bulkhead for a hundred yards or so to the first tidy row of houses. Crowds of shifting and milling people drifted in every direction; while here, at the water's edge, pressing close around and staring at him, was a mingle-mangle of curious faces—white, black, brown, yellow, and sepia: all impassively non-committal and alien.

He felt a moment of strangeness, almost revulsion. Where was Tad, anyway? Surely he must be close by. Was Gill to plunge amongst this reeking mob? And if so—which way should he go?

Just then—as though they'd seen enough of him—the crowd broke up, shoving off along the jetty. Gill took off his hat and wiped his face. The noise was appalling, and the tide of heat constant. Ahead, in gaps between shifting sunshades and clerks tallying chests and flagons, he saw a group of naval officers—British, by their white starched uniforms—accompanied by two pink parasols. The ladies actually looked cool in their bombazines, and wonderfully isolated from the haze of dust. One of the men, noting Gill, bowed coolly; and Gill, recollecting himself, inclined his head. These people were as standoffish as New Yorkers!

He turned, and was moving quickly away when he felt a tug at his arm. "Best watch your duffel, sir, until it's ashore. These boat-women are magicians at disappearing." The voice was American, and so was the young, good-natured face.

"Why, thank you." Gill couldn't help smiling back at the friendly stranger. "You're mighty kind. In the excitement of being on land again, I guess, and looking for my brother, I'd clean forgot."

"*Brother?* I hadn't heard we were to have the pleasure of a relative in the community." The freckle-faced stranger was a tall, gangling weed of a man with big hands and straight sandy hair falling over his forehead. His clear blue eyes looked puzzled momentarily, then brightened. "If you've a brother in Macao, you can depend he's here. A New York packet is rare excitement for us exiles. And a brother aboard would be double measure." His voice rose to a shout on these last words, and he grimaced in comical helplessness as he tried to make himself heard above the measured chant of a coolie crew lugging hampers up the steps behind.

Gill warmed to the fellow immediately—taller by an inch or two than himself, and maybe six or seven years his junior. He said: "No doubt you're acquainted with my brother. Bennett is the name."

The stranger stiffened. His mouth opened ineffectually once before he stammered: "Bennett? You don't mean Thaddeus Bennett, the er . . . the tea man?"

A band of urchins in filthy pantaloons pushed between them; and until they and their sweaty bedlam had passed, Gill could only nod and wonder at the man's queer expression. Then he said: "Tad didn't expect me, as a matter of fact. I decided very suddenly to come out East. Since there wasn't a mail packet before the *Seraph* sailed, I couldn't get word to him."

"Oh. I see er . . ." The young man's eyes roved somewhere beyond, as though searching the multitude for someone he couldn't find. But when the pause lengthened, he turned back overeagerly, almost nervously. "Do allow me to help you, sir. The first thing's to get you fixed up. Er . . . allow me." He spun around and waved an arm at the loungers along the jetty.

A ruffianly collection lunged forward like an advancing army. From them the American selected a crew of twelve and motioned them down to Gill's *tangka,* saying: "Makee do this side. Chop-chop!"

The coolies surged down the steps. Immediately more faces

closed ranks about Gill and his acquaintance—the same inquisi-
tive, languid, grinning, numb faces as before. Gill's nostrils ached
with the reek of perspiration and garlic they exuded.

"*Fie-tee! Fie-tee!*" the American shouted vehemently at the
coolies tussling with the luggage below. Then with a quick dis-
arming smile he turned to Gill and said: "Don't ask me what
it means. I haven't a clue. They're forever screaming it at each
other, so I do likewise and hope for action. Seems effective. Oh,
er—my name's Stacey. Philip Stacey of Russell and Company.
Only a year out—so I'm as junior as they come."

Despite his boyish friendliness Gill had the feeling Stacey was
grabbing at words to fill in, to cover something. But this vertical
sunlight, the noise and dust were nauseating. How could anyone
think, or reason, in it? He felt a panicking urge. He must break
clear. Do something.

At that moment the boat-girl came bounding up the steps and
was at Gill's elbow in a flash, tugging at his sleeve. "Nighttime
you wantchee, I come! Yes? Yes?" she hissed at him.

Gill tried to focus on what she was saying, but his mind was so
occupied with fathoming the reason for Stacey's masking loqua-
ciousness that his tongue seemed made of lead.

Not so Stacey. He cried: "You little scrawn! Get back to your
tangka, and be damned!" And with the toes of his white shoes
he kicked her bottom so hard she sprawled flat on the stone stairs.

A laugh went up from the grinning audience. The girl scrambled to her feet, rubbing her behind, and with a baffled scowl
backed down to the *tangka.* Whereupon the crone launched an
obscene scold that encompassed the girl and everyone else within
reach of her gabble.

Gill was annoyed with Stacey, who seemed to guess it, for he
clapped a conciliatory hand on Gill's shoulder and said: "Seems
brutal, I expect. But it has taken me a year to learn that's the only
way to handle 'em. Otherwise they're over you like lice. Not that
one kick will stop that little hussy. She'll try her shenanigans on
you again, never fear. Otherwise dear old granny there will give

her hell. They're practical people, the Chinese, first, last, and every other time. You have to remember that always."

Gill ceased to be concerned with the girl and the essential characteristics of the Chinese race. Dust gritted on his eyelids, and flies swarmed about his head. He flicked his handkerchief before his face. "What about my brother, Mr. Stacey?" he asked. "Do you know where he is?"

Stacey's frank blue eyes clouded again, and he bit at his under-lip as he reached a tentative hand towards Gill and patted him gently on the sleeve. "Oh, forgive me. I *am* spouting, aren't I? You see, I thought we'd best get your gear ashore and safe. Then, er . . . Wait right here, will you? I'll just fetch Timothy Manning. He'd best tell you." Without waiting for Gill's reply Stacey disappeared along the embankment.

"Manning?" Gill repeated the name to himself. He'd heard it somewhere . . . Then it came to him in a rush. Of course, Manning was Number One out here—*taipan*, as the Chinese called it—of Russell and Company! The big tea house Tad had been such a damned fool over last season. The memory of it still had the power to set a flood of anger loose in Gill . . . rather than take commercial advantage of a friend's illness—this friend being Russell's chief tea buyer, that's all—Tad had bought the choicest half of the crop in that friend's name, thereby losing all chance of buying for Bennett Brothers on the first, and best, market! Oh, a pretty gesture of righteous nicety! It had lost Bennett Brothers exactly three thousand dollars in clear profit, and a dozen disgruntled customers, at least. So—now he was to meet Mr. Manning. Well, he could hardly wait.

Gill saw Stacey elbowing back through the crowd with a tall, imposing-looking man who was dressed in an immaculate white silk suit. The man stepped forward to greet Gill with an outstretched hand. "Welcome to Macao, Mr. Bennett. I'm Manning," he said gravely in a reticent and poised voice.

His green-gray eyes flicked quickly over Gill's face, and almost immediately he put his arm through Gill's. "Shall we just step out of this ruckus?" he said, propelling Gill gently past heaps of decaying cabbage leaves and out of the direct stream of traffic. Stacey made no move to accompany them; instead he busied himself with paying the boat-women and watching over the baggage coolies.

They'd gone a dozen paces when Gill disengaged his arm and turned to look questioningly at Manning, whose gnawed and incisive face struck him as anything but sympathetic. Manning pursed his lips somberly, and was about to speak when a young woman suddenly thrust her way between them. "Please, Uncle Tim," she said urgently, pushing Manning farther aside, "let me."

Manning frowned. "No, Lael. This is not——"

"But, Uncle Tim, I've already met Mr. Bennett. I *know* him," she insisted, her violet-colored eyes turning from Manning to Gill imploringly. "You remember that evening, don't you, at Delmonico's—the Tea Association's Annual Dinner—Christmas before last?" And then, without waiting for Gill's acknowledgment, she pushed gently again at Manning's arm. "Please, please, Uncle Tim," she begged compulsively.

Manning's shoulders went up in what seemed to be a deferential shrug. "Evidently my niece is not convinced, Mr. Bennett, that I am equipped with a heart," he said sardonically, stepping slightly aside. There was no telling whether he was nettled or joking.

Gill's mind registered that the girl—woman, really—was uncommonly attractive. How marvelously that yellow-sprigged dimity suited her fresh coloring—she looked so cool, so vestal. He was certain he'd have remembered anyone as lovely as she if he'd ever laid eyes on her before—and yet there was something vaguely familiar about that inexpressibly graceful way she held her head, and that pile of auburn hair atop it.

She couldn't be—no, impossible—not that gawky all-arms-and-legs youngster in her first evening gown that he'd tried to fortify with a laugh or two the night she mentioned before old Mrs. Whitcombe had borne him off imperially to an exceedingly uninfatuating dinner partner. He looked again with beginning recognition, but the sorrow and compassion he saw in her eyes made him forget everything but what she was about to say.

"I hoped——" she said earnestly, her voice trembling a little. "I hoped somehow that I could soften the cruel news. But how can I, really? You see, Tad died three months ago . . . of cholera."

Gill stood stock-still, unbelieving. His incredulous eyes sought the girl's, and then Manning's behind her, for some retraction, some disavowal of the words. "No," Gill whispered. "No, it can't be so."

Lael Manning's fine eyes went misty with recognition of the pain in Gill. "Oh, we do grieve with you—most deeply," she murmured. "Your brother had the affection of all of us in the community. He was excessively fine, and good."

Gill felt as though he were bleeding. A numbing sickness crept up his legs, through his body, into his mind. He couldn't think, he couldn't speak. He could only stare woodenly at incongruous coolie shapes passing and repassing.

Manning's precise voice cut through the miasma. "I wrote, telling you about this, but obviously you'd left New York before my letter could arrive. If it's any small comfort to you—your brother didn't suffer long. The 'chilly death' is hideously quick and decisive. His end came three hours from onset."

Lael made a sign for him to stop, and tucked her arm into Gill's as though she meant to lead a bewildered child. "Come," she urged softly, "we'll go immediately to Uncle Timothy's house, away from these people. You must stop with us until you've—got your bearings."

Gill disengaged himself slowly. He lacked the will to walk while he was struggling for a semblance of control. He'd never looked to others for support and sympathy before, and now he didn't want to inflict the burden of his grief on these two strangers. It took moments, though, for him to rally himself enough to force the struggle out of his voice so he could thank them both for their considerateness. Then he asked: "My brother had a house, hadn't he?"

Manning nodded. "Still has—on a year's lease, you know."

Overwhelmingly Gill knew he wanted to go there, away from strangers. He said to Lael: "I appreciate your kindness, ma'am, but if you'll excuse me—I'll go to my brother's house."

Lael looked swiftly at her uncle, as though asking him to intercede. Manning studied Gill thoughtfully for another moment before he said: "Suppose you send your trunks and duffel to Tad's place. Tad's boy will unpack it for you. The other question—housing with us for the first few nights—we'll leave open until after we've complied with certain technicalities the Portuguese require for newcomers."

Gill shook his head. "Please," he said. "I've decided."

Manning apparently saw that he had, and turned to beckon a short, obsequious Portuguese in clerk's clothing who'd been hovering within call on the fringe of the jetty crowd. The man came at a run. Manning gave directions about Gill's luggage, and in the same breath reached for the banjo hanging over Gill's shoulder. When Gill demurred and said he'd carry it himself, Manning became peremptory. "Certainly not!" he snapped with finality, and handed the banjo to the little dark-faced Portuguese, who nodded as though he'd been expecting it all along.

Lael didn't appear satisfied. She shook her head with a distressed little pucker on her face. "Loneliness is an additional burden you shouldn't try to bear now, Mr. Bennett. Please allow us to be your friends. We Mannings—Uncle Timothy and myself—are in Tad's debt, and always shall be, for his gallant gesture last season."

It was an added flick to rawness, and Gill drew his breath sharply. She reached over and took his hand in a firm positive clasp. "Please know that our house is open to you at any hour. I realize you've formalities to attend to now—but we shall be hoping to see you whenever you'll give us that boon." She turned away from them and went to join the group of pink parasols and bombazines.

It came over Gill that he'd never met a woman so absolutely natural and forthright. And she was generous of heart.

Manning made a move to go, but found their way blocked by a procession of coolies carrying hampers covered in white linen. Gill didn't take any notice of them, blinded again by emotion. When the sixth or seventh coolie had passed him at a jog trot, some impulse moved his feet, and he went blundering into the path of the next. Manning snatched him back at the same moment the laden coolie tried fending him off. But it was too late, and the bamboo shoulder pole struck Gill's jaw a grazing blow.

The impact snapped Gill into reality. He found the graze wasn't bleeding, and he looked along the line of laden coolies strung out to the landing steps. There were fourteen or fifteen of the same white hampers still to come.

At his side Manning said quietly: "You are witnessing one of the spectacles of Macao—bought and paid for with opium. It is the good Senhora Pinto's laundry returning from Goa."

"Goa," Gill repeated dully, not caring. "Isn't that in India?"

"It is. Thirty-five days' sailing from here," Manning said, permitting himself an incomplete smile that was more like a spasm of indigestion, and continued: "The good Senhora is the wife of Macao's foremost dealer in opium. Her only addiction, however, is ruffles ironed by experts. Experts, to her thinking, are those trained by grandfather-ironers appointed two generations ago to the Vice-Regal Court at Goa during the Portuguese heyday."

Manning coughed, watching two more hampers swing by. "The Senhora's washing goes regularly to Goa. It requires something of a wardrobe—allowing for the ten-week trip—I'm told. Her husband stocks his shirts by the dozen dozen. An impertinent footnote, isn't it, on the equality of man." He pointed ironically to a coolie whose one ragged shirt didn't begin to cover gaunt ribs.

Manning talked on casually and deliberately. Gill recognized that it wasn't heartless chitchat. The other, in his way, was tiding him over, getting him out of the crowd, across the hot beastly ground into the shaded avenue.

"We buried your brother in the East India Company cemetery," Manning said, "since it is the only plot of ground in all this Catholic colony where a Protestant body can find haven."

"It's good of you to tell me, sir," Gill said. And then before he knew it, "I was very fond of my brother." He looked straight at Manning, and saw that he had touched him momentarily.

"I'm sorry for all this." Manning lowered his head as though determined not to show any emotion. "Sorry."

They were on the broad avenue of banyans now which separated the waterfront from the candy-colored villas of the town. Gill's mind registered there was a juggler in crimson robes twirling a rod above his head, an itinerant barber braiding a man's queue, a dumpling cook with a kitchen slung over his shoulder, but he went on thinking that the wave which had suddenly seemed to wash over him and leave him so displayed, so open to his own eyes, was bound to sweep back again and cover him. There would not be time, probably, to suffer, or even realize his grief and loss. And in thinking this he nearly walked into the dumpling cook's steaming cauldron.

He shook his head ruefully and turned to apologize to Manning. "I'm sorry, sir, to be such a charge. I'll keep what wits I have about me for the rest of the way." And with that he stepped forward more resolutely, master of himself outwardly at least. Something Manning had said earlier recurred to him, and he asked: "You spoke about 'landing technicalities.' What are they?"

Manning wiped dust from his face before he replied. "All foreign residents are required to have a Portuguese sponsor vouch for them. It's an involved point I'll be glad to explain more fully at a better time. Meanwhile—if you'll be good enough to take my word—it's devilishly pressing since you're already ashore and no papers are in process for you. You're actually liable to deportation, or arrest, at the moment. However, I'm taking you directly

to a man who obliges—for a fee—our company. His name is Sur
Manoel Rozario. He's influential, and knows ways to cut red tape.
You'll find him er . . . accommodating, shall we say?"

Manning stopped before a birthday-cake villa of
rich raspberry with curlicue frostings of white plaster around the
windows and doorways. A pair of African guards, theatrically
dressed in sultan trousers and braided jackets, touched their fez-
zes in salute and opened the grilled gate. Two others, similarly
flamboyant, ushered them along a tiled portico, past a cool grotto-
like patio full of ferns and begonias, and then up a grand staircase
which divided midway, to become a pair circling the wall and
meeting above in a broad reception gallery.

A flunky stood bowing and motioning them into the drawing-
room at the far end. From the medley of voices and laughter drifting out, it was obvious Sur Manoel was entertaining. Manning
halted abruptly, indicated they wouldn't join the party, and sent
the man to fetch Sur Manoel.

The place was lavish with mirrors and velvet. Dresden, Meis-
sen, and Venetian bric-a-brac, in overripe colors, stood crowded
onto the tables, in cabinets and wall niches. It had a heavy-
handed, opulent air: the house, Gill reflected, of a man who put
infinite reliance in money.

It was a surprise, then, to see a submissively meek little man
come springing towards them with outstretched hands. "My dear
Manning, what an unearned pleasure!" he said softly, his doelike
eyes traveling amiably to Gill, and then as amiably returning to
Manning. His swarthy, pock-marked face was a mixture of Portuguese, Kaffir, and Chinese.

"*Mafaz o favor, senhors,*" he implored, "give us your company in the drawing-room! Our captivating newcomer, Senhorita
d'Almada, arrives momentarily to favor us with songs she brings
from Lisboa."

Manning declined with an urbane headshake, at the same
time presenting Gill and explaining he was just off the *Seraph.*

"Bennett!" Sur Manoel was quick to pounce on the name. Then he frowned, and looked at Gill in growing solicitude. "Let me welcome you, Mr. Bennett." He shook hands with nice punctilio. "You're not kin, I venture to hope, to our lamented fellow citizen, Thaddeus Bennett?"

"His brother," Gill said.

Sur Manoel's magpie face puckered dolorously. "Oh, my dear sir! My deepest sympathy. But why do we stand here? My library is at hand. Pray let us seek seclusion." He bustled them along the gallery and into a nearby room, tck-tcking with his tongue and making little sympathetic sounds as he closed the door.

He hovered courteously until Manning and Gill were seated in the red Spanish-leather chairs, and then sat himself in the thronelike chair behind the desk. Gill guessed it had been built on a step, or platform, to elevate it enough so the occupant wasn't lost behind that overcarved and overvarnished desk.

A Chinese servingman came bringing tea in covered bowls as yellow as jonquils and almost as fragile, which he placed on tea-poys at each man's right hand. Then he went the rounds with Manila cigars and a lighted taper. It was his placing of the teacup that drew Gill's attention to the intricate and infinitesimal carving on an ivory figure standing on the teapoy. In spontaneous admiration he picked it up to marvel over its delicacy; it was a quintessence of the beauty he'd expected to find in China.

Sur Manoel asked: "You are connoisseur, Senhor Bennett?"

"Not by a long shot," Gill hastily disclaimed. "It doesn't require a connoisseur's eye to appreciate a piece such as this, though."

Sur Manoel beamed as happily as though he'd carved it himself. "It is truly to your liking?" he wanted to know.

"It's superlative," Gill said, putting the piece back on the table.

Sur Manoel spread supplicating hands. "It is *yours!*" he exclaimed. "Honor me by accepting it."

Gill was flabbergasted. What was this, anyhow? Barely step foot in the house, and be given a treasure! "No! Of course not," he protested in confusion. "I but meant to convey admiration."

Woe dragged at the little man's face. "You consider me too presumptuous on short acquaintance?"

"Not that——" Gill tried to explain. "I . . ."

"I want you to take it." Sur Manoel's voice rose insistently as he hopped from behind the desk. Catching up the figure while Gill was still protesting, he thrust it into the servingman's hand, saying a quick something in Chinese and waving him from the room.

"The merest nothing," Sur Manoel deprecated touchingly as he climbed into his chair again. "There—we forget it. Already it goes to your brother's house . . . *Pu-tai*, his name is, a God of Felicity. Happy omen, let us hope, of your arrival."

Gill stammered thanks, his head swimming with such openhanded generosity. Through it all Manning had said nothing.

The incident was a gnat, the way Sur Manoel brushed it aside. He peered at one, and the other, saying softly: "May I venture to guess what brings you, gentlemen? Senhor Bennett has come off ship. He stands in need of a sponsor?"

Manning nodded, saying: "If you would be so good as to oblige."

"A privilege!" Sur Manoel turned to Gill. "Let me be entirely frank—even in the shortness of our acquaintance, I have the impression you are a type our colony urgently needs. Young, ambitious, farseeing, *sensitively artistic*. . . ." He chuckled softly and tapped a front tooth meditatively with a fingernail. "Ah— what I cannot guess, however, is whether Senhor Bennett bears any relationship to Russell and Company."

"None whatever," Manning replied brusquely. "Bennett is a stranger. I've offered assistance in lieu of his brother—to whom we of Russell and Company are indeed beholden."

"A most gallant act." Sur Manoel spread his hands in a gesture of homage.

Gill's stomach churned. More pious talk. As though pretty words would restore non-existent cargo and put three thousand dollars into Bennett Brothers' till! If only they'd stop being reverent about the lunacy.

Sur Manoel was saying: "I merely inquire in case the mandarins should want to know. It's barely possible they've heard talk. Gossip, my dear Manning, unmitigated gossip, I expect . . ." Sur Manoel paused discreetly for Manning to deny or affirm.

Manning did neither. Sitting as erectly and unbending as the big chair would permit, he looked levelly back at the Portuguese with only a small liverish smile twitching at his lips.

"Would you say a merger was likely?" Sur Manoel glanced quickly towards Gill with the same deprecatory smile he used for Manning. "That Russell and Company might absorb Bennett Brothers as an—adjunct, an enlargement, say, of their tea department?"

Gill caught his breath. This was getting near home. A merger? Absorb Bennett Brothers?

Manning's eyebrows arched urbanely. "Soothsaying is not in my line," he said, waving the question aside.

"Very well put." The dark little man chuckled under his breath until it was almost the sound of rustling leaves. Gill got the feeling the two of them were sparring, in wide circles yet, over something beyond his understanding.

Sur Manoel turned to Gill and shot the question: "Is it your intention to engage solely in tea?"

Gill was caught off balance. He hadn't expected a point-blank inquiry into his affairs. He couldn't very well tell these strangers, here and now, that Bennett Brothers had been sold expressly for that reason, so the brothers would have capital for opium. Yet some answer was expected. This business of obtaining a Portuguese sponsor was obviously vital or Manning wouldn't have brought him here.

Or would he? After all, what did he, Gill, know of Manning's real intentions? Certainly his manner was ambiguous enough at times. But surely, *surely*, this was pure kindliness in memory of Tad. And yet Gill had the uneasy feeling that somehow or other business rivalry was mixed up in it. Could it be opium?

He made himself answer before the pause was too noticeable.

"My brother's death has been so unexpected," he said, hesitating. "You see, I'm not the tea expert my brother was. I really don't have any definite plans yet. I'll look into any good opportunities I see."

Sur Manoel nodded sympathetically. "Very wise of you. A *good* opportunity—such as opium, perhaps?"

Gill heard Manning's indrawn breath. It was Gill's turn to dissemble. "Not necessarily," he said casually. "I understand there are other bonanzas here."

"But none so golden as opium, eh, Manning?" Sur Manoel asked with the candor of a child.

"You'd know better than I—being heavier in the market," Manning replied with the same suave gentility.

Sur Manoel raised compliant hands to show he was the plaything of circumstances. "My affairs *do* enlarge," he said modestly. Then his eyes suddenly shot to Gill. "Quite possibly, Bennett, you and I could have mutual interests to discuss—to *mutual* advantage."

Gill blinked. Even for him this was moving at a thundering rush. How could a man think, plan, weigh . . . ? He found himself saying: "I should feel honored—to *discuss* them."

"Excellent," Sur Manoel said quickly. "Today is Monday. Shall we say Friday at five? If you'll give me the pleasure here?"

"Friday at five," Gill agreed, feeling as though he were being jerked by a string.

"I felt I could intrude," Sur Manoel said softly to Manning, "since you assured me Russell and Company is without prior claim on Mr. Bennett."

Manning got quickly to his feet, his urbanity evidently sheathing some inner vexation as he stepped to the door. "Could it be you're forgetting our Macao weather, Sur Manoel? The mutual interests of our friend here will be with tailors, most likely, for the next week to ten days, until he's outfitted Macao style." Then he turned to Gill as though reminding him indulgently: "There'll be Tad's papers to tackle—accumulated orders, and so forth. I warrant you'll want a breather all of this week."

"I want anything but leisure." Gill was very definite. But he was much less definite in his mind about other things. Was Manning merely offering excuses? Or a warning? Anyway, it was too late to back out of the appointment now. Besides, he was curious.

Sur Manoel bowed them out, and then came springing along on his short little legs to keep pace the length of the gallery. "Have no concern whatever about your residence permit," he told Gill. "I shall arrange it immediately. I'm happy to be of service."

Three steps farther on he was saying: "If you're musically inclined, Mr. Bennett, you'll find Macao isn't isolated culturally. We've such a charming opera house where we foregather regularly. The San Carlos troupe comes from South America next month with the latest Italian opera, including a new Rossini. Perhaps you're not partial to Rossini? Some are: some aren't. We've gentlemen's clubs, fortnightly horse races, amateur theatricals, quartets, chamber music. How eagerly we shall welcome you into these . . . *when* your bereavement will permit you to mingle again, of course. We shan't intrude before then. Meanwhile promise you'll acquaint me if there is something I can do to make living more bearable for you?"

Gill was touched by the man's generous cordiality. A stranger far from home. Not even a fellow American. "I am indeed grateful," Gill said with feeling. "Tad wrote me about Macao's friendliness. I thought he was exaggerating then. But now I see he wasn't."

Sur Manoel's ceremonious leave-taking was interrupted at the grand staircase by arriving guests, and they were delivered into the keeping of the two Zouave guards. Manning appeared engrossed in thought as they descended the stairs and went along the tiled portico. It wasn't until they'd passed through the grilled gate and were out on the avenue that Manning pinched his nose contemplatively and said: "You've acquired a sponsor. What opinion did you form of him?"

Gill was surprised at so obvious a question from this man, but he answered: "An excessively kind gentleman, I thought."

Manning chewed at his lip, looking off into space. "Yes," he said dispassionately. "I was afraid you might."

Gill was on the point of asking what he meant, but at that moment Stacey came dodging and ducking long-leggedly between a line of sedan chairs to join them. Nor could Gill satisfy his curiosity about this merger gossip between Russell and Company and such an inconsiderable rival as Bennett Brothers. Stacey, it appeared, was there to conduct him to Tad's house on the ridge.

Manning said to Gill: "There's to be a meeting of foreign merchants—indignant foreign merchants, I should add—at my house tomorrow at five o'clock. I'd like it if you'd be present. It should be an illuminating session for you. Aside from a fine display of justifiable choler, it should indicate some of the obstacles we encounter in the course of business with self-styled 'celestials.'" There was emotion neither in his opaque eyes nor on his long saturnine face as he nodded composedly to them both and turned away in the opposite direction.

CHAPTER III

MACAO,

September 1838

By now the avenue—which Stacey called the Praya Grande—was a moving stream of sedan chairs and promenaders. Gill thought the swarms of silk parasols rising and tilting above the ladies' heads in the long curving line were like a canopy of shimmering butterflies. The chairs and an occasional horseman kept to the center; but drifting along in pairs and groups on either side was an elegant potpourri of townspeople—stylishly got-up Portuguese and their ladies, British naval officers, white-habited nuns in black wimples, flirtatious half-caste girls, Chinese gentlemen in philosopher's beards delicately airing caged birds —saluting each other, chatting, strolling on, and bowing again with European punctilio. Obviously it was the fashionable hour to see and be seen.

In his boyish way Stacey observed: "Mighty mannerly, eh? These *fidalgos* bobbing and bowing to each other quite as though they really were that—you know, 'son-of-a-somebody,' as they call it, instead of more than half of them being born on the wrong side of the blanket."

"I'm surprised to see so many blacks," Gill said.

Stacey nodded. "So was I. At first I thought a 'blackbirder' had lost his way into these waters. Then I found out these were Kaffirs—or part Kaffir—that is, descendants of the Kaffir slaves the Portugalers brought with them generations ago."

"How many Portuguese are there here?" Gill asked.

"About five thousand—but very, *very* mixed," Stacey grinned. "Part Kaffir, part Japanese, part Chinese, part Goanese, part God knows what. That leaves about two or three hundred pure Portuguese. But, great suds, even they have a touch of the Moor in them. So where does one draw the purity line?"

Between sentences Stacey had been bowing in friendly greeting to other promenaders, but he was careful not to stop and involve Gill in any introductions. Then abruptly he halted as a thin youngish woman came hurrying by. The green parasol she carried cast a sickly light on her already ravaged face. "Good afternoon, Mrs. Thomas," he called. "Should you be out in this heat?" His freckled face puckered with concern.

"The *Seraph* is in!" she told him in a querulous wail, nervously fingering her white coral necklace. "I must have my mail." Her disordered eyes roved from Stacey to Gill and back again. "What's a person to do without mail? Oh, poor me!" Her already anguished face twisted into new torture.

"Now, now. Just you go back and set comfortably on your veranda and let me bring your letters to you," Stacey coaxed. "I'll do it in jig time—immediately I've seen Mr. Bennett up the hill."

"Oh no, that would be an eternity. I couldn't endure it!" she whimpered. Dodging past them, she went hurrying towards the landing.

Stacey watched her with a scowl. "Suds," he muttered, "we'll be without a teamaster entirely unless someone controls her." He was too disconcerted to let the episode drop. "Just out of sickbed and running around in this heat to get a handful of letters not worth a tinker's dam. . . ." Stacey turned to Gill, but at the clouded look he saw on the other's face he recollected himself.

"Oh, I *am* a fool," he exclaimed contritely, "spouting this way! I guess I took it for granted you knew all about Thomas, he and Tad being such solid friends. Why—of course you know—he's the man Tad bought tea for last winter when he collapsed during one of Mrs. Thomas' spells. Banging fine, it was! Absolutely banging!"

Here it was again. Gill quailed inwardly. Obviously Stacey was keyed to go on and on, but he couldn't endure it. "No, Stacey," he said harshly. "No more."

Underfoot the brittle little banyan leaves crackled like scales until they left the avenue and turned into a small lane, quite empty of people, and began a gradual climb. They passed a milk-white church, and houses of mint green, azure, and pink with chocolate-colored and maroon shutters—as gay as a confectioner's window. Their elegant embellished walls were three and four feet thick, latticed with balconies and verandas and vines, vines galore—jasmine, chain-of-love, and bougainvillaea pouring torrents of blossom. Locusts rasped like files; and there was zither music, a Spanish guitar, and the soft contented voices of women.

Suddenly, without warning, a covered sedan chair swung around the corner of a wall, coming straight at Gill, the forward shaft on a level with his chin. Instinctively he flung an arm out, and the next instant he saw with dismay that he'd done more than fend off. He'd knocked the foremost bearer off balance. The man staggered to keep upright, but a flouncing movement inside the chair added crucial momentum and the chair fell sideways towards the cobbles.

Gill caught the shaft, bracing it on his own shoulder while the coolie picked himself up. But before Gill could shift the burden back, a hand yanked the curtain aside and a shrill soprano screamed: *"Hola! Secours! Help!"*

Stacey sprang forward to lend a hand, but that only made the woman scream again—louder, more penetratingly.

Gill was furious. In another minute the fool would fill the lane with a mob. "The only aid you need, ma'am, is in controlling yourself."

"Put me down instantly. Brigand!" the woman screeched, the face she thrust between the curtains so lively with rage it was difficult to make it out, except that it was young.

Gill glared at her, caught on the raw by her senseless tantrum. All his pent-up anger and despair burst forth. "Hush your mouth, you noisy shrew! Instead of thanks for saving you from a fall we're treated to hysterics! Keep still, I tell you!" He motioned the coolie into position while he and Stacey shifted the load.

The woman stared, wide-eyed; and in its momentary composure Gill saw a pale provocative face framed in curling black hair under a white mantilla.

After a moment the stare quivered into a small smile. Then, without a word of thanks, she motioned the bearers on and withdrew behind the curtains. The bearers shouldered the shafts and went jog-trotting down the lane until an abutting wall cut them from view.

"Great lack!" Stacey muttered, goggle-eyed, as though the heavens had parted and he'd seen a cloudload of angels. "Do you know who *that* was . . . ? Senhorita Zena d'Almada, the heiress!"

"Heiress to a powerful set of lungs," Gill growled, and then shed his outrage as quickly as he brushed his sleeves and straightened his waistcoat. He turned and continued uphill.

Stacey trailed a step or two behind. "She didn't remember me, of course," he mourned wistfully. "I'm just one of the horde she's met since she arrived a month ago. Old man Noronha left his shipping fortune to her—she was his ward."

He was silent for a hundred yards or so, and then snickered: "Macao's reigning belle—and you called her 'a noisy shrew.' Why, the Governor himself introduced her at the flossiest ball Macao's ever had. Since then everybody's in a swivet to fete her."

The cobblestones ended, and shelving steps began between baroque houses whose fretted windows were filled with tiny panes of shaved shell instead of glass. It gave the houses an aloof, opaque look.

Halfway up the first tier they paused for breath, and Gill said: "The puzzle is—when the lady was making all that squawk, why didn't it draw a mob?"

Stacey shook his head in emphatic negation. "Not out East, sir, it wouldn't. Not in Macao. You see, the Portuguese have so many offspring they take noise for granted. As for the Chinese— well, they won't lift a finger to save a dying man, *much less a woman! They* say—if you save a life, then you're responsible for it the rest of your days."

Gill whistled softly as they started up again. "That could deafen anyone in time," he said.

Tad's house was a modest two-storied stucco, on the crest of the ridge, with walls of terra-cotta plaster and maroon shutters. It was small in comparison with the rococo mansions Gill had seen on the way up, but was pleasantly arranged, with the entire living quarters on the upper floor, and kitchen, servants' rooms, and laundry together on the lower floor at street level. Out behind there was the merest patch of garden choked with cypress, bananas, orange trees, and a camel's-foot gaudy with purple bloom.

Gill discovered the real treasure of the place when he stepped out from the sitting-room doors onto a wide covered gallery. It ran the whole width of the house, and looked out for infinite miles over a glory of sea and islands and green hills.

In the slanting light of sunset the scene was as luminously yellow as an operetta curtain, and seemed as insubstantial. Macao spread in the foreground, clinging to its buttonhook of hills—an absurdly precarious speck of Europe, Gill told himself, for there beyond was a slender handle of yellow sand fastening the buttonhook to China.

Below where he stood, the spine divided, to step—on one side —from one piebald level of villa roofs down to the next, and end in the Praya Grande promenade; on the other side yellow clay hummocks shelved and rifted into a Chinese city hugging an inner harbor around behind the hook. This second city was more water-borne than earth-bound certainly, for junks by the thousands paved the shore in solid ranks until it was impossible to say where yellow land left off and yellow water began.

Gill walked back into the semi-darkness of the shuttered sitting room, and it was as though Tad were describing it as lovingly as in his letter ". . . quite an elegant little half-dome ceiling with plaster thingumabobs running up it. Floors of terrazzo, which, I find, the Italians do prettily out of chips of colored marble. Mine is a muted rose, admirably suiting the three wine-colored Persian rugs I got at a bargain from a Parsee homesick to return to Bombay. Chairs of Philippine mahogany, handsomely carved by a Spanish joiner in Manila, backed and seated in cane, naturally, for ventilation. What with lacquered tables, cabinets, and teapoys to help out, you'd never recognize that patched and darned Thaddeus Bennett you grew up with, who tended counter for Hodgett's Family Grocery on Saturdays. China has converted me to beauty. I enjoy, and gloat over, each tidy elegance I acquire. . . ."

Yes, Gill thought, his eyes traveling the room again, a far cry from their boyhood home. How good that Tad had had this for a little while, at least. There was that to be thankful for.

Gill went on to the bedroom and found Tad's clothes hanging

in the big wardrobe in tidy rows—washed, ironed, and creased, ready to be put on again any moment. He crossed to the desk to lay things out from his pockets, and there were tea bills in Tad's rounded script, receipted, carefully annotated . . . he was alone in the sanctuary of this house, and yet Tad was in every room.

Gill gripped the back of a wicker chair in a spasm of emotion, his fingers straining white. What earthly good was it all without Tad? Why in God's name had he come? What was to happen now?

Stacey was a reluctant witness. In tongue-tied nervousness over his own inadequacy he turned and went sidling down the stairs and out into the lane, only to return to the top of the stairs several minutes later—out of breath and ducking his head apologetically —and say: "I forgot to tell you, sir, supper will be got for you at the proper time. The caretaker has sent for your brother's Number One boy. Ah Lau, he's called. He'll take charge in jig time. He'll do everything that a mother'd do—whether you want it or just think you want it. I'm sorry I'm such a donkey. I don't seem to be able to do anything except talk when I shouldn't."

Gill reached out impulsively and took Stacey's hand in a strong clasp. "You *have* helped, Stacey, and I feel I've made a friend. But right now—you've sensed it—I'll do better alone."

With a stricken salute Stacey went thumping disconsolately down the teak steps and out the door.

Gill found a bathroom of sorts next to the bedroom where he sluiced himself off with cold water he dipped from a vast green crock. It was a cool, refreshing way to bathe in this climate, he decided, as he watched the water drain away from his body between wooden slats into a gutter which emptied outside.

In the bedroom, after an interval of staring abstractedly, then bathing, then staring again, he found the shutters opened, a mosquito net rigged over the bed, his bags opened, and clean linen laid out on a chair for him. But he'd got no farther than underclothes when he heard a rustle and, looking around, saw a Chinese in starched white gown standing beside him.

"My chin-chin you, Mas-tah. My belong Ah Lau," the man announced gravely.

"Good evening, Ah Lau," Gill said with matching gravity. "I'm glad you've come." He meant it. He was touched that Tad's man-servant was here to look after him. Tad had often remarked about Ah Lau's intuitive service and untiring devotion.

Gill looked with interest at this stranger who was to be an intimate part of the new life in this house. He saw a short, slender, small-boned man with quick-moving nimble fingers which tapered as fragilely and sensitively as a musician's. There were neither wrinkles nor lines in the hairless waxen face, nor any revealing signs in the braided black queue, to tell whether he was thirty or forty. He presented a tidy, impersonal exterior, but beyond that Gill could read nothing.

Ah Lau lowered his gaze behind half-closed lids and held out a long gown. "Moh bet-tah nightie-time," he said.

Gill saw it was Chinese style, of linen as sheer and fine as a handkerchief. It looked cool and airy and absorbent, but it was foreign, Chinese—he'd feel a fool in it. He motioned towards his own clothes. "I'll wear these," he said.

The lids flew open, and a curious look flicked across the eyes before they became opaque again. "Mas-tah suitee belong no proper. Moh bet-tah puttee so-so," he said flatly, and raised the garment over Gill's head.

Gill's immediate instinct was to resist; then he told himself not to be an ass, and raised both arms. The curious garment settled into place comfortably enough. Ah Lau fastened the cloth tabs which held it together in front, and stepped back. Gill supposed the thing had belonged to Tad, but he didn't ask.

Supper, instead of being a sandwich or a cold pork pie rolled in a napkin—as Gill had imagined it might be on such short notice—was a full-course dinner at a completely laid table under a punkah. It was tasty and satisfying, with both white and red Portuguese wines. Afterwards, out on the gallery with a fragrant brandy—also from Portugal—there was a long thin Manila cigar which the deft, observant, silent, but never obsequious, Ah Lau brought.

How blessed the quiet was, Gill thought, after the constant din of the *Seraph*—the whine and hum of wind, the staccato of blocks and the screak of straining timbers. There was no moon yet, but the stars gave the sky a milky radiance, and down below the sampan lights were like other stars floating on the water. An irresistible peacefulness settled upon him.

It was all incredibly far from Murray's dock at the corner of Wall and Front streets, from the cheering crowds who'd lined the Battery after the salute; and it was incalculably farther for the spirit. For, like the voyage, it came to him now how far he'd widened the distance between himself and the mean poverty of his apologetic and scrimping youth.

Even here—years and continents away from childhood—Gill felt the same hot surge of mingled affection and shame which always flushed through him whenever he remembered that staunchly righteous and infuriating putterer who'd been his father. Or when he thought of his flurried mother, who'd worked herself into an early grave because she couldn't bear saying no to anyone.

Kindly, good-natured, upright folk, the pair of them, but pathetically inefficient and pathetically without success. In this image they'd brought two sons through pinched years, which, in Gill's memory now, ceased to be a span of months and seasons and became instead an endless seesaw between skimping makeshift and momentary well-being, between a pallid sort of pride and the awful humiliation of submerged mediocrity.

His recollections were isolated bits and pieces of memory. The mean brick house, Tad, his mother, himself were all strung together like threadbare wash on a line, revolving around the man, Corwin Bennett. As though he'd called his father up from the China Sea, Gill saw him now, derby set straight across his head, gray hair curling under the brim, pince-nez low on his nose, bending in close concentration over a hummingbird feeder attached to the lone tree in their small grubby yard. Or he was shoveling symmetrical paths through snow to the street because he'd just been laid off from the office, the store, the factory, or wherever he'd been working that year. And there was Corwin Bennett again, in the same derby, the same shiny black suit, refusing to pick up a five-dollar gold piece on a deserted sidewalk. "It isn't *mine*," he'd kept repeating with infuriating patience at Gill's bewildered questioning. "The man who dropped it may come looking for it."

Gill had never known what his mother thought. There was no knowing whether love or ache or frustration lay behind those protuberant blue eyes. He'd come walking into the kitchen and toss his books on the dresser, ready to talk, wanting to talk and ask . . . But she'd always been busy with kind missions for someone else: taking a batch of gingerbread out of the oven for the church social; finishing booties for the new baby next door; or taking a basket of cupcakes to the bedridden spinster in the next block. She'd smile at his big yearning eyes, trim off a small sliver of gingerbread for him, and go hurrying off. The spiceful fragrance would linger for minutes, and then gradually the cabbage and onion and stew smells clinging to the wallpaper, the curtains, and the threadbare carpeting would exert their sourness again.

Strange how different they'd been, two brothers. Tad, matter-of-fact, quiet, plodding. Tad hadn't minded sweeping out *Mr. Spence's School*, emptying trash and burning it, or closing the school in the afternoon, or washing windows, or lighting the fire in the big coal stove. But Gill had done it only because the alternative was—no school. The two of them were always there when the other boys came in, stamping their feet, shaking snow from their coats in winter, or rushing for the stove to warm their hands.

Gill recalled the exact moment when Harding Seton had turned and flung his thick coat at Tad . . . "Hang it up, will you, Bennett?" And Tad's quiet nod and the look of his back as he went down the hall, the red lining of the coat bright on his arm.

Gill had stood pressing his shoulders into the banister while the other boys clattered up the stairs.

Then, rage and panic mixing hideously within him, he'd wheeled swiftly to pound his fists against the wall until Tad caught hold of him, finally holding him in his two arms, tight and hard. Twelve . . . he'd been twelve then. Now he was twenty-seven, and he could still feel the rush of rage in his throat. But Tad had said: "No sense taking on over a *mite*. Shucks, what was hanging up an old coat, anyway?" Tad had made it sound so reasonable that Gill, wiping tears from his face with his coat sleeve, hadn't known how to tell the wrong he felt.

When Gill had got his first job in a tea warehouse, it was Tad who came round the block at noontime from the shipping house where he worked and settled in with deep content to eat his scanty sandwiches in the scented shade, and who then went wandering up and down the long aisles in a bemused way, reading the queer foreign labels.

By and by, when the firm's teatasters came down to classify a new shipment, Tad and Gill had joined in, making it a sort of private challenge between them to see which, with his eyes blind-folded, could taste a dozen or so varieties and name each accurately, as the tasters did.

Tad would hold the hot tea in his mouth twice as long as Gill, spew it into a spittoon, sniff wet tea leaves still in the cup, and take an uncomfortable interval to decide. Then, his eyes aglow, he'd name the crop and year, and be right, invariably! Even the teatasters used to applaud and exclaim: "What taste buds!" and say his life work was certainly settled. Not that Tad had ever doubted it. Tea had become his one desire and aim.

He'd coaxed, exhorted, and striven with calm missionary zeal until Gill went into the tea business with him. Gill had fought it with laughter, with ridicule, with indifference, hating the very thought of being trapped in such a tame-cat business. But Tad had smoothed the obstacles away, until five years ago they'd opened their cubbyhole of a tea-importing business.

Gill felt his stomach churn and rumble at the memory. Well, anyway, he'd had his own way about one thing—they'd sold the mean little family house after their parents had died; and Gill had taken rooms on Front Street, where he had his evenings to himself to read and study, to shed his awkwardness and ignorance in the realm of the mind. Someday, he'd said to himself then, he meant to make a place for himself, to be accepted in the world of New York, or any other world, for that matter.

It was the Church Board Library that had given him the first little boost he'd needed. Happening in one night when the Council was meeting, he'd offered his services as secretary, the regular secretary, Miss Tillet having been taken suddenly ill. He'd continued the position through the winter, and by various other services—the annual lectures and musicals, where he'd been useful—had risen at last to a position on the Board itself, due, perhaps to Harding Seton's wife, who was particularly gracious to him.

There'd been other steps, but the longest one was coming here —to get his hand into the grab bag of Asia. He'd been certain that fortune lay here, and this certainty had put him aboard the *Seraph.* But now—now there'd be no explanation, no sharing, no partnership. The thought set Gill to pacing again aimlessly. What was his next step to be?

Tad was dead, and had been for three months. Nothing would bring him back, nothing. And yet mourning wasn't an allotted state in time and place; it wasn't a thing of the face. It was of the heart, and could be kept there.

He'd had the impulse to cut and run earlier—on the next outbound clipper for Manila, for India, for anywhere so long as it was away. But that was only a temporary solution, he told himself now. No, he'd dig in here. He'd start what he'd come to do. God knows he had everything to learn—the familiarity and knack of the market, the Portuguese themselves, the baffling Chinese, the way to speak even . . . in this place where there were twenty variations of how to say yes and mean no.

When Gill went into the bedroom an hour later, Ah Lau appeared without being called and helped him lay aside the Chinese gown and his soggy underclothes. Without a word, as though it were a ritual they'd performed together night after night, Ah Lau went into the bathroom and poured a basin of cool water so Gill could dip his perspiring face in it; and when that was over, the man held Gill's nightshirt while he got into it.

Gill stared dubiously at the white cage the big mosquito net made of the bed, not sure of the procedure in entering without letting man-eating visitors in with him. But Ah Lau anticipated that also. With a quick flip he held up a loose fold, motioned Gill to duck under quickly, and then tucked the fold under the mattress. He stood back, surveyed the finished job, blew out the lamp, murmured a respectful "Night-night, Mas-tah," and disappeared—evidently through the door to the sitting room because Gill heard it closing softly.

"One of the motherly attentions Stacey meant, I suppose—tucking me into bed at night," Gill said half aloud to himself.

It was hot under the net, too hot even to put a sheet over his body. And the pillow was soggy—acrid, really—with the odor of successive crops of mildew. Gill twisted and turned to get comfortable, only to find a damp puddle growing under one shoulder until he shifted to the other. He was tired, Heaven knows! Exhausted! And yet he lay staring, wide awake, into the darkness.

Some minutes later he heard a rustle on the gallery, another, and then a cautious footstep. Was it Ah Lau putting something to order there? He raised up on one elbow to look through the open French doorway. Against the radiance of the sky he saw a small Chinese figure creeping into his room.

"Who's that?" he demanded.

"Belong Su-ling," a girl's whisper told him.

Good lord, the boat-girl!

She ran soundlessly on bare feet towards the bed, squirming out of her jacket and standing bare to the waist. "My come makee lof pidgin."

Gill thrashed at the net, pushing it aside, and stood up. "You jade! I told you *no!*"

Su-ling smiled, putting her face close as she rubbed her body against his. "How fashion no? My very proper do. My Number One good!" she beseeched softly.

Gill wanted to smack her. The audacious little wanton. "I don't know how you managed to get in—but get out! Hurry!" He didn't actually strike her, but he raised his arm in threat.

Instead of falling back, though, the girl grabbed at his upraised hand and clutched it to her small breasts, whimpering: "No can! My olo mama plen-tee cross my no makee lof pidgin. She spank my. *Ai-yah! Ai-yah!* Must wantchee! Must!" And she rubbed more insistently against him.

Gill jerked away. What was he to do? Ring for the all-competent, almighty Ah Lau? If that factotum was so blasted omnipotent, why wasn't he here right now attending to this pest? Where the hell was the bellpull?

He shuffled into slippers, groped along one wall, bumped smack into the bureau, and felt the purse he'd laid there when he'd un-dressed earlier in the evening. Money! By God, he'd handle this for himself in his own way. At least once today he'd not wait for someone to jerk the strings for him.

He grabbed up two silver dollars and thrust them into the girl's sticky little hands. "There, get out! Damn quick!"

The girl shut off in mid-sob and wiped her nose on her arm. "*Hi-yah!* My chin-chin you! All same tank-oo. My go chop-chop." Clutching up her jacket, she darted out the gallery door.

Gill followed through the doorway to make certain she actually left. The place was empty: she'd already disappeared. No, there she was at the far end—climbing over the balustrade and letting herself down by the firecracker vine.

Next morning at breakfast on the gallery Ah Lau poured a steaming yellow brew into Gill's teacup and returned the pot and strainer to the serving table before he said: "Mas-tah no have talkee which tea wantchee morning time—Tit Kwan Yin? Hangchow bud? Dragon Well? Black congou? Kee Mun? Boo Yee?"

Gill looked out at the descending rooftops. He recognized only two of the names. Was Ah Lau testing his tea knowledge or talking bunkum? Gill passed the cup under his nose, sniffing the pungent bouquet, and made a wild guess. "Hangchow bud?" he asked negligently.

A flicker of approval crossed Ah Lau's face. "Mas-tah have savvee," he said, and disappeared towards the kitchen for fresh toast.

When he'd returned and cleared away the eggcup, put the hot toast and marmalade jar beside Gill, he busied himself with a bushy fly whisk—swishing it industriously, but working closer and closer to Gill. Evidently when he considered preliminaries were sufficiently advanced, he said quietly: "Boat-girl Su-ling no Number One. My can catchee moh for bet-tah. Moh for pretty. You wantchee, yes?"

Gill put down the toast, which was halfway to his mouth, and wagged an accusing finger at the serious face above him. "Tut, tut! That's not being a mother to me!"

"Wantchee mut-ter?" Ah Lau was puzzled, but only for a moment. Then he smiled pleasantly. "Can do."

"No!" Gill groaned, shaking his head. "I no wantchee mut-ter, grandmut-ter, baby girl, or anything else in the feminine line, you competent reprobate! Keep your nose strictly out of that department. I'll run it, see!"

Ah Lau regarded him with an unblinking look that was both equable and hostile. "My sav-vee! Lof pidgin belong Mas-tah pidgin."

Gill returned to his toast. Ah Lau went back to shooing flies, vigorously, unceasingly. By and by the whooshing rustle of the whisk slowed down and he said from somewhere behind Gill: "Two dol-lah too muchee!"

CHAPTER IV

CANTON,

September 1838

THE GIRL Mei-deh stood at the massive blackwood table in the Bamboo Pavilion and painted with full vigorous strokes. Her cliffs were cataclysmic blue masses and the gorges beneath them deep and black and primeval; her pines were vibrant with sap; her waterfalls rushing torrents; and now, with quick deft flicks of her fragile wrist, she made a sampan into a minor fury skimming the mist and fume of river rapids.

Not yet twenty, with clear direct beauty and a compact little body as tender and lovesome as a southern song, she painted in absorbed contentment—bending to the paper, making spidery strokes with a brush of sable hair; changing brushes and tilting an arm's length away to wash in gray haze with bristles from a wolf's throat. Then she closed her eyes in a dreamy smile to *feel* the scene again. She wasn't painting the groomed garden outside, nor a landscape from memory. Instead she was re-creating Nature to her own liking—multiplying its ecstasies and omnipotently omitting its nagging dreariness.

The Bamboo Pavilion where she painted was the same happy conceit—a summer fantasy materialized in stone and lustrous glaze. Set in a classical garden—suspended, you might say, from a skein of passageway raveling out this way and that from the harmoniously elegant houses of Gowqua, least of the five senior Hong merchants—there was nothing haphazard or half conceived about it. Its walls, inside and out, were upright lengths of bamboo —not the bamboo which grows in mud and rain, but porcelain replicas in tawny glaze. Its windows were trellises of the same satin stems, while the tender green of painted leaf tufts crisscrossed overhead into a forest maze.

Gowqua had built the place five years ago that his favorite daughter, Mei-deh, might paint her heart out in it and thus acquire a measure of detachment and even, perhaps, tranquillity. Both were desirable accomplishments for women in general, he felt, but for Mei-deh in particular he had the notion they'd be compensatory treasures she'd stand in need of all her days.

There was a clink of loose tiles and the sigh of silk from the passageway, but Mei-deh went on spiking needles on the branches of a pine tree with her brush and did not look up. That is, not until her father spoke, standing there at her elbow.

"You reveal your man's spirit, my daughter, in today's painting," he said softly, his appreciative eyes dwelling on the tide of cloud bank and the sweep of line. "And—as a man might—you've left adroit spaces so the beholder may fill them with his own visions. Yes, I find this stimulating. A fillip to the spirit, as terse as a good epigram."

Giving the paper a slow reluctant look, Mei-deh moved away from the board and dropped her brushes into the jade holder on the table, and then turned to the emaciated shadow of herself in man's clothing. "Whenever you speak of my 'man's spirit,' Father," she said with a loving, taunting smile, "it is usually because you're in a coaxing mood."

Gowqua rubbed his parchment cheek, looked his fill again of the painting, and turned to the girl with unblinking solemnity. "Your face and body are eye-consoling—must you spoil their effect by speaking what comes into your perceptive mind? Often I wonder whether to envy or pity the man who takes you to wife."

They laughed together. It was a familiar joke between them, for they were both aware that Mei-deh would do the *taking*—in her deceptively gentle way—once she made up her mind to marriage.

Mei-deh crossed to the vase-shaped archway, clapped her hands twice as a signal for tea, and then returned to the table and covered the inkstone and color pots. She walked as easily and upright as a farm woman on unbound feet, which, of course, was a strange disfigurement for the daughter of the fifth-richest merchant in Canton.

She had grown into this oddity because of the whim of her father's father, who had returned from his post in Peking the very day she was born. He'd been so full of stories of Manchu princesses strolling pink terraces in the Forbidden City on stylishly unbound feet; of how men, nevertheless, desired and quickened for the touch of them; and how this physical grotesquerie in no wise hindered the birth rate in that northern city. Whereupon—in the telling of these tales, and the memory, perhaps, of his own contributions to that birth rate—he had decreed that this first granddaughter of a new generation in the family should walk as Nature meant her to walk, and not in the exquisitely helpless way Cantonese fashion had designed for her.

Mei-deh's father had agreed, saying that if the girl was to have big feet it might be expedient for her to have a matching mind, and subsequently had set her still farther apart by ordering her into the classroom with her brothers and their tutors. So, at twenty, she neither talked nor walked as other women in her father's household, where wives and concubines teetered about seductively on "golden lily" stumps and twittered gossip the livelong day.

Gowqua crossed to the railing to run his fingers over its translucent glaze. "The Viceroy has received edicts from Peking which concern the foreign traders," he told her.

Mei-deh came to his side quickly. "Windy words? Or trouble-makers?" she wanted to know.

"Both," Gowqua said, his eyes roving the canopy of purple blossom covering the camel's-foot tree on the second terrace. But there was a quirk of triumph in the set of his mouth.

Seeing it, Mei-deh was disturbed.

"Peking continues to regard these foreigners with moles' eyes," her father told her, still not turning around. "The Throne denies their petition again to open other ports for trade. Instead Peking requires a preposterous . . . *birthday present,* it is called."

The new servingmaid E-ling came slapping into the pavilion on thunderous feet at that moment, rattling cups perilously and slopping tea in her ardent haste, until suddenly she caught Mei-deh's observant eyes on her. Then in a fever of anxiety she dropped two almond cakes—squashing one into crumbs on the tiles as she reached for it, flushed an inferior red, and would have burst into tears if Mei-deh hadn't taken the tray from her and said calmly: "No one in the household brings tea as fleetly as you, E-ling. In time your feet will learn quietness. Now, instead of cakes, bring small chow."

E-ling whirled and banged off like a bullock cart in a narrow alley, remembered herself next second, and walked with a ghostly tread. She was still a little dizzy with delight at being allowed in this house—she, the daughter of a bean-curd seller.

Gowqua wrinkled his nose in distaste. "Why do you bring that ox in from the paddies?" he asked.

"She is a treasure," Mei-deh said with a smile, "being both honest and without avarice. I avail myself of rarities."

Gowqua nodded in quick dismissal. He sat himself in a black-wood chair shaped for a man twice his girth and drummed an impatient knuckle on the marble-topped table beside him. He had things to talk about, many and momentous.

Mei-deh poured the amber brew slowly, her nostrils pinching pleasurably at the salty sniff of its chrysanthemum flavor, put the lids on the cups, and slid one across the table for her father. But she held her questions.

Gowqua ignored the tea, and instead sat sliding the jeweled fingernail guard off and on his little finger indecisively. "The Viceroy, the Customs Collector, and the mandarins, naturally, are tacking *their* birthday demands onto the Peking extortion, and expect us Hong merchants to convince the foreigners they should pay! But—the demands are preposterous! They'll precipitate trouble, now, at the onset of the buying season. We need a device. A 'little plan' to circumvent a crisis. Put your mind to it, my child, and work out one if you can. The Hong merchants gather here this afternoon to consider."

Mei-deh knew then what the real trouble was. "Here? Howqua

Second and Mowqua choose to meet here instead of in one or the other of *their* houses?" she asked a little tremulously.

Gowqua nodded slowly, looking full at his daughter now.

The disquiet on her face was evident. She let her breath out slowly. "It has come then. The beginning strategy—the first step sideways?"

Her father inhaled tea aroma slowly before he sucked in a noisy gulp, and then sat brooding for another interval before he gulped again.

"So . . . Howqua Second and Mowqua, the biggest of the big, desire that you become a bright light until, in time, your brilliance eclipses theirs. Then, gradually, they dwindle into such little candles no one notices when they go out."

Gowqua sucked tea.

Mei-deh recited softly from a text written upon her mind. "Twenty-five million dollars Howqua Second has amassed as Chief of Hong, and yet he cannot retire while they are his. Three times he has openly requested permission to retire from the Hong, and three times he has been refused. Now—he becomes devious."

Gowqua closed his eyes, neither agreeing nor disagreeing.

Words were not needed between these two, so deep was their love, so implicit their understanding. Sensing indecision in him now, Mei-deh felt a quiver of terror for the future. Her eyes grew big, and she said: "You will outmaneuver? You will refuse to be big? You will remain obscure—and *safe?*"

Gowqua pursed lips dubiously, but there was no answering while E-ling's thumping rush in the passageway filled their ears.

The moonfaced girl gasped and paused at the doorway, and then stepped into the room in conscious sedateness, as happy with herself as a wife three months' pregnant. She was carrying a plate of shrimp dumplings—the boiling water in the compartment under the dish gurgled and steamed with each step, yet she neither scalded herself nor the others as she put it down. Her composure lasted until she was out through the vase door again, then abandoned her; and she fled in rollicking exuberance.

With a bamboo splint Gowqua speared a walnut-sized dumpling, revolved it contemplatively under his nose, and said: "Should I strain to protect a paltry two million? Or perhaps . . . accumulate *my* twenty-five million as Chief of Hong and gamble on being able to maneuver to enjoy it?"

Mei-deh let the words hang in the air between them for a full minute before she repeated the ancient adage: " 'Become too high, and you'll be toppled. Become too low, and you'll be trampled.' "

Gowqua bit through dumpling skin into savory shrimp paste. "Of my fourteen grown children," he observed equably, "it is curious that only one has an affinity for the middle way."

Mei-deh didn't answer. Yet she wanted to save him the pain of thinking of her two squandering elder brothers, and of the utterly charming and graceful and improvident brood of half brothers and half sisters who were the concubines' children. So she led him back to the immediate threat, saying: "You have created a pose, most certainly, my parent, and with consummate art. In less than a handful of years you have established a cardboard man for outsiders—a mild, tepid, blunt-brained man who is interested only in the tea trade."

Gowqua smiled thinly—not out of annoyance, but because he wanted to voice the question he had obviously been debating within himself before he'd even come near the Pavilion. "Mightn't that cardboard exterior be effective for two years, say, as Chief of Hong?"

Mei-deh didn't jump up and go running around the room to beat her hands frantically against the lovely bars, as she felt the impulse to do. She sat very still and small, putting a whole dumpling into her mouth and chewing it slowly because it was a commonplace thing to do, but all the while staring ahead into the years. "No!" she said positively out of that contemplation. "The strategy of the one cannot be stretched to cover the other."

"I wonder."

Mei-deh's voice grew a tone more incisive, but there was no harangue in it as she said: "Few desire to be you now. In comparison . . . you are believed small, and therefore arouse only minor envy. No one suspects you of having made two million dollars in tea, because you have neither interfered nor competed with them for the larger fortune. But . . . Chief of Hong is biggest of all. Twenty-five million dollars big! Everyone desires to be you. Immediately you are exposed to envy, cupidity, malignant suspicion—and a cardboard man tears easily."

Gowqua passed a frail hand down over closed eyelids before he said: "Fate was a miser when it made you a daughter instead of a son. Let us walk in the garden—I welcome the gift of its serenity."

High old willows drooped over the upper terrace path, their ribbons of shade rippling and swaying like a moving stream over the mossy stone pavement. Gowqua and Mei-deh walked it so slowly, so nearly imperceptibly, that the fork-tailed drongos seemed to regard them as two more of the gaudy-flowered shrubs, and flittered around in joyous iridescent flight.

Gowqua's eyes cherished the imagery of contorted rocks, the lacquered green of wild gardenias, the smoldering red of croton clumps, and the tapering profile of a four-story pagoda. It was a relishing garden—more comforting than food to him. In a ferment of pleasure he told Mei-deh: "I have acquired the adjoining land beyond us there. My thought has been to plant it with a crop of tallow trees—but seeing the garden now on this soft beneficent morning, I am moved to let you transform it into more garden . . . with infinite vistas and knolls."

Mei-deh smiled wistfully, looking a circle of the willows and stones and gardenias, and shook her head. "Keep it for tallow trees. We have garden enough here for the eye to behold. Enlarging it twofold would make a world, you might say, which would dwarf the beholder."

The metallic rasp of cicadas strumming their desperate songs of love in the willows overhead was her only answer until Gowqua murmured: "A consistent woman!" He sighed, raising his eyebrows halfway between horror and resignation.

They turned together and looked out over the brown river below to the opposite shore, where the sweeping green of young rice washed against the high gray walls of Canton itself. The river was speckled with slow sampans and duckboats, with lounging river junks and waddling ferries.

Watching the creeping pace, Mei-deh's eyes narrowed impatiently, and in a sudden tantrum of exasperation she slapped her hand on the stone parapet. "*Slow* sails! *Slow* oars! We should be using fire and steam—as the foreigners do. It is three years since the *Jardine* came belching and snorting up *our* river—wind or no wind—and we haven't matched it with one of our own."

" 'They are not of ancient design, nor of Chinese invention,' Peking says, 'and therefore unfit to ply Chinese waters.' "

"Even when the Hong offered to buy one *with its own money?*" Gowqua nodded.

"Blind!" Mei-deh cried in soft anguish. "What match are we against these faster ships in trade? Or—if it should come—in war?"

Gowqua tapped his amethyst thumb ring against the balustrade and said: "The Throne doesn't see the future because IT is so mesmerized by the past. China——"

"The Throne isn't China!" Mei-deh interrupted passionately. "Those usurping Manchu leading us backward into bygone ages! Are we never to face the future for ourselves?"

"Individually, yes. But collectively—I torment myself wondering if we ever shall." Gowqua's tone was conversational, but there was no mistaking the intensity behind it. "We Cantonese, for instance, are hot and wordy. We rail and fume. But do we rebel openly against foreigners ruling in Peking? No! We never seem to have a likely leader—out of all our millions."

Mei-deh listened acutely, making no movement, for she knew her father drew his words from a deep well of bitterness.

"The truth is—we can't keep ourselves from being aggressive individualists long enough to agree on a leader. We allow ourselves to be prey to snooping suspicions . . . 'Do his pure motives cover a black intent? If not, why not?' we ask. 'What can I make out of his elevation?' 'Can I do *business* with his eighteenth cousin twice removed?' Meanwhile—Peking fears our revolutionary blood always, and continues to coerce us with a *northern* Viceroy, a *northern* Governor, *northern* delegations sent to survey us and render decisions on what we shall—but usually *shall not*—do."

Under the camel's-foot tree on the lower terrace near the landing stage several of the younger concubines tottered and squirmed provocatively on their small stumps, nibbling boiled duck gizzards and playing bean bag with their three plump babies, while the gardener's two small daughters romped in and out of the crotons beside the steps. When the concubines spotted the Elder One and Mei-deh at the upper terrace balustrade, they waved and chirped and laughed out greetings, and then, like pretty children, went on tottering and squirming and nibbling and playing.

A duckboat drifted close inshore, its stink and chatter filling the air, but the ducks skimming around it, intent on duck business, were like yellow petals sprinkled on the brown water; and no one in the idyllic garden seemed to mind the stench, or the noise.

"About those *birthday presents*——" Gowqua said, turning back to the path. "Does some 'little plan' occur to you which might delay a crisis?"

"If the Hong—as a body—suspended trade for one month," Mei-deh reasoned aloud, "wouldn't that create a counterproblem? It means no Customs collection, no revenue for the Throne. . . ."

"And no money for the Hong," Gowqua objected.

"The Hong must lose either way," Mei-deh reasoned. "They are caught, as usual, between two irreconcilables. As it is—they are faced with paying half this *present* out of their own cashboxes so as to soften the outrageous demands on the foreign traders. Or, alternatively, the Hong attempts to collect the full sum, and thereby provokes the foreigners into resisting forcibly with their war craft. Both options are more calamitous than—shall we say, *threatening* the mandarins with halted trade."

Gowqua's eyes glittered suddenly, and he nodded conspiratorially. "Yes, the device has merit. It permits our countrymen to save face. They can reconsider their own demands before they are made public. Yes, I shall propose it to our body this afternoon."

"What hour do they gather?"

"At the half point after four by the foreign clock," Gowqua told her. "You will sit behind the screen, as usual, that I may have the benefit of our two memories of what transpires, and of our two ingenuities to cope with eventualities."

Mei-deh nodded agreement. "I shall order our special small chow, sweetmeats, and four varieties of tea—if that pleases you," she was saying when a commotion below drew them to the balustrade.

A handsomely lacquered and ornate mandarin boat was moored at the landing stage while four men strained and jostled to carry a far from inanimate fifth over the gunwales and up the steps. The concubines squealed and cackled; the babies shrieked; while the cargo himself bawled abuse steadily until, on the top step, he thrashed himself loose. He stood there in bawdy dishevelment, flailing the air with aimless arms before he began to walk belligerently in a lurking circle towards the concubines.

It was Gai-sun—the elder son—returned from his nightly revels.

The father's low mutter came tonelessly: "So—my First-Born manages to leave his joy girls and reach home by eleven in the morning, carrying a considerable cargo of brandy."

The boatmen scrambled back aboard, pushed off, and headed away towards Canton. The concubines, incapable of running, or even dodging, out of harm's way, gathered themselves and their babies into a moaning huddle; and the gardener's two youngsters crouched down out of sight behind the nearest croton. At this point there was a halloo from farther along the second terrace, and a young man in a sky-blue silk gown came running along it and down the first flight of steps, waving his arms at the quarrelsome Gai-sun.

Relief welled up inside Mei-deh. It was Second Brother, the

blithely impetuous Gin-min, who would know how to laugh and beguile the fuddled incompetent into good humor—or, at least, into docility.

Things happened before Gin-min could reach his brother, however. Gai-sun lurched against the nearer croton in his weavings and let out an angry bellow which evidently terrified the gardener's younger, for she ducked out from the bush and made a dash for the stairs. In her blind panic, though, she ran within sweep of Gai-sun's arm, and he cuffed her aside as he would a troublesome cur. The force of the blow sent her sprawling through the air, yards beyond the riverbank, out, over, and into the eddying brown water.

The concubines screamed; the little sister keened in shuddering whimpers; the cicadas shrilled a torment of strident rasp. Mei-deh caught her breath in helpless horror, watching for some sign of the child, and then gasped again as she saw Gin-min's blue-gowned figure sprint onto the landing stage and jump. There was a horrible interval of thrashing and splashing until Gin-min was clambering out of the water carrying the vomiting child.

Then Gowqua spoke in corrosive contempt. "My Second Son is an imbecilic deviation from normal. Senseless! Irresponsible! He —a married man, the father of children—deliberately jumps into danger for nothing. Risks life to drag in a coolie whelp!"

As nauseated as though she'd been kicked in the stomach, Mei-deh watched the dirty bubbles squeeze from her brother's sky-blue gown. But she turned and smiled a minimizing smile at her father. "Gin-min is safely back!" she pleaded. "He's unharmed. Oh, you can depend he'll never commit such an act again."

"Rubbish! I can depend on nothing—except that he's utterly stupid! Stupid enough to set off firecrackers in the rain."

Gowqua had built his house to harmonize with Nature, and then had refurbished Nature until it harmonized with the house. Or rather, houses—for instead of one great mansion it was a series of imaginative and fanciful small ones grouped around a corner of the river. Their pink balconies jutted over the water at intervals on the outer side between the fluid green of willows and yellow bamboo; but on the inner side the radiating pavilions were laced together by an airy blue-roofed portico which zigzagged between them and surrounded, on its way, a small oval lake.

Balcony doors and lake doors were rolled back now in the Afternoon Room of Third Pavilion to catch any errant breeze, but the only air which stirred was whipped by twelve agitated fans—the most agitated being the thirty-stick one belonging to Manqua—the last to arrive. It was too big for his hands, but Manqua was a vain and stubborn man, and his tastes had noticeably enlarged—along with his fortunes—these past two seasons.

"The word was passed to me on the Bund as I got into my boat to come here," he told the others in his high-pitched vendor's voice. "The Viceroy does a second raid tonight."

"Two thousand jailed last night! Another two thousand—or even three—tonight! Where will it end?" The dandified Chinqua pivoted his head like a startled magpie.

"It has ended already," Mowqua blustered, his face bland and bloodless. "The news is out. Consequently no householder is fool enough to have opium about when soldiers come searching."

Chinqua licked his lips and snickered behind a sleeve of pond-green gauze. "That's reasonable. Yes, of course. A token raid—satisfying Peking that last night's haul netted the only offenders in Canton. Clever enough!" He closed his fan with a snap and fished in the fan-bag at his waist for the two polished walnut shells he carried these days. Drawing them forth, he began the discipline of his brush hand—slowly, ecclesiastically rolling the shells around and around in little clicking circles between the tips of effeminate fingers. Calligraphy was his latest dedication.

Temperate and unamazed, old Howqua Second sat in the chair of honor on the host's left. His thin enduring face and composed manner made him a presence in this group he had headed for more than eighteen years. He rapped the table twice with his fan. "It is *not* finished. Far from it!" he said with sovereign calm.

Adjusting the tips of skeletal fingers together and tapping them lightly, he continued: "The core of conflict remains. Both forces being goaded by equal determination—the Westerners to trade freely, Peking to resist anything new—whether it be science, ship-building, medicine, religion, or trade. No, the conflict of ideas is not ended. Searching houses for illicit opium, arresting puny smugglers and smokers are incidental skin pricks. There'll be others, deeper, more painful . . . until war itself is upon us."

A sibilant sigh sifted the length of the room, blowing the word opium, opium, opium about like a shuttlecock.

Howqua stopped it. "Are we tapeworms in a belly that we swallow fraudulently digested pap? Opium isn't causing war. Opium is the pious excuse Peking would like to hide behind while putting the blame on others." He gazed around the circle as though challenging contradiction.

But when the others took to fanning or toying with thumb rings, he continued: "The conflict we face *is a trade war* caused by one, and only one, misguided fact—Manchu fear of free asso-ciation with life as outsiders live it. We speak this bastard nonsense of pidgin—*business English*—because learning proper English is punishable by death. Leaving China, or traveling on a foreign ship—even the ninety miles to Macao—are equally hei-nous crimes. Why? Because Peking is beset with fear."

Fans switched and swished, cicadas shrilled a crescendo, and heaped petals in twenty bowls drenched the air with muzzy lan-guishing sweetness.

"We are caught between two destroying forces," he pronounced prophetically, "unless somehow, some way, we relax Manchu fears!"

He saw the conviction of war shake and torment each man in his individual capacity; and watching them, Howqua seemed to be taking mental inventory of one face and then the next of these security merchants designated by the Throne—for a thunder-

ing fee, naturally—to a post of singular and devastating monopoly
. . . twelve men who divided between them the excessive burden
of China's trade with the world beyond its boundaries.

Directly across the circle was Mowqua—the stately and unctious
buyer for the British. Sitting beside him was scholarly young
Lokqua Third, blinking owlishly in his nearsighted studious way,
a third-generation Hong merchant who had inherited his place
from a cautious father and cautious grandfather, but who was still
untried and unproven in practical affairs. Manqua came next—
loud and empty-voiced, his face the color of new bricks. Acquiring
varied choice possessions recently, and still adding to them
omnivorously, he had yet to acquire that most coveted one of
mellowness.

Farther along, in dove gray, Cumqua sat—Cumqua the good of
heart, who dealt only in silk, and was so fastidiously, so ardently
honest it infected every man he touched. Foreigners bought his
bales season after season without opening them for inspection; a
bankrupt English friend who left the colony with Cumqua's blank
order for funds confounded everyone, except Cumqua, when he
repaid fifty thousand dollars four years later from the other side
of the globe. Cumqua was a sermon in goodliness.

As for the silent Paqua and his catfish mustache—who knew
him, or what lay behind that ambiguous stare of his? Was it distilled wisdom? Or was it, thanks to some muscular affliction,
merely the rigid imitation? The shield he wore was perpetual
and unvaried, however, for Paqua never opened his lips to reveal
how little, or much, he understood.

In the other half of the circle from Mowqua's left was the
dilettante Chinqua in poison-green gauze, rolling incessant walnut shells and fidgeting obviously for the chance to roll his tongue
around the calligraphy dialect he'd adopted recently. Not that
he could posture before his neighbor, the shrewd and vigorous
Tsaiqua, who was a direct and cogent thinker, and hated fools.
As for the next man—hah, even the obtuse Chinqua would shy
away from that restless, flighty, haunted one. Tanqua was so

disastrously overextended on his foreign bills he was scarcely coherent.

There'd be audience enough in the next two flabby youths, who were Poonqua's recent heirs, Yai and Yu. They were full of secondhand emotions. They sat and walked and talked together as though they were twins, and yet hadn't a brain to share between them.

Howqua didn't turn his head at this point in the survey and deliberately contemplate the man sitting beside him. But it was on Gowqua that his inner eyes remained the longest—Gowqua, the soft-spoken classical gentleman at first view, and at second an eminently proficient trader who never lost a penny and knew exactly what each dollar would buy. Yet he was assiduously unaspiring, assiduously pent up. . . .

Howqua tallied the count to himself, dividing the roomful into votes. Eight unpredictables, eight with unstable reactions to the "little plan" he was about to propose. Only four amongst them staunch enough, with perspective enough, to pay cash out of pocket for so impersonal a thing as a universal goal.

Howqua had little stomach for the step he was taking. In his years of business he'd scrupulously, even timidly, avoided any interference in politics. He'd decided long ago that his adventure with Fate would be selling and buying for Americans. Their breezy, candid friendliness and forthright dealing had appealed to him as a novelty in the beginning, but through the years he'd grown partial to them, and they to him. And to his son, Howqua Third, who was ready to succeed him, he would pass on this mutual preference.

For eighteen years he'd stood security to the Throne for the integrity and behavior of crews of dozens of American ships which came upriver each season. He'd been broker for their cargoes of tea, amber, alum root, cinnabar, musk, hemp, indigo, orpiment, rosewood elbow chairs, kaolin, wallpaper, nankeen, xanthin, medicinal rhubarb, grasscloth, porcelain, cassia lignea, and beeswax; and in all those years he'd kept his nose out of politics. But

now—*now* was extremity. The great unwieldy Flowery Kingdom was heading towards self-destruction—chivied, jostled, and
shoved by Peking's colossal ignorance—he felt.

Without further preamble he said: "Three times this year we
have made frettings on paper to the Grand Censorate. But petitioning that body is like scattering fog with a fan. Our target
must be the Throne's ear itself. Immediately and continuously.
Minister Ho, who has recently returned to Peking, has that access. Minister Ho showed himself during his Canton visit to be
inclined towards invigorating newness. Cash and facts will increase his eloquence, perhaps. But the cash will need to be in
quantity, and fairly repetitive. Our facts are sound, colossally
simple, and cost nothing to demonstrate. Namely . . . *open wide
all Chinese ports so hinterland millions acquire a knowledge and
taste for foreign manufacturies! Thereafter opium cargoes will
vanish from trading ships!*"

Howqua's meager elbows were pumping up and down to the
sonorous roll of his voice; and in an excess of sweating he flung
his sleeves back to fan one arm dry, and then the other, while he
drilled on. "American and English ships bring opium to our shores
because it is the only incoming cargo Canton will buy today. No
one knows more truly than we security merchants—that opium is
the only cargo which sells and gives foreigners enough dollars to
purchase *our* silk, *our* tea leaf, *our* rhubarb, *our* porcelain. Let all
China *want* foreign manufactures, and from that happy moment
foreign ships will load themselves with paying cargoes. The problem solves itself mathematically—they'll no longer require, or
have space for, opium!"

Behind the carved cypress panel Mei-deh sat looking at the
cloistral calm of the lake where water lilies floated like pink and
blue rice bowls. But her eyes no longer roved aimlessly. They
were turned inward, seeing the stark premonition of war. She had
prepared herself for harangue, for tedious guile and wile, for interminable maneuvering, but not for the word *war*.

The scuff of slippers on marble preceded six servingmaids

with trays of candied grapes on sticks, crystallized melon, pear pasties, and red bananas. Gowqua ceremoniously went the rounds, addressing each guest with: "May this whet your juices!" Behind him another six maids removed fragile Kang-hsi cups of jasmine tea, gone stale these several minutes, to replace them with *blanc de Chine* transparent enough to show the robust red of souchong beneath their milky glaze.

Cumqua spoke first when the servingmaids had gone. "That which you so excellently said, I echo. Tell me how much you require, and I shall give gladly."

Lokqua Third nodded slowly, saying: "I feel my revered father, and my revered grandfather, would coincide. Therefore I shall give—even though I do not know Minister Ho, nor any of his relatives."

"Do any of us?" Manqua asked skeptically. "Or how capable he is at persuading?"

"What matter if a bird sings sweetly in the forest where no one hears it?" Tsaiqua asked crisply. "Minister Ho's asset is access to the Ear. I'll subscribe money."

"Money, money!" Tanqua's cry might have come from a cracked flute. He wrenched the ring of longevity from his thumb to rock it aimlessly in a sweaty palm, breathing all the while as though he'd run up a long hill. "Why spend *our* money? The Chinese fleet is powerful enough to sweep the waters clean."

Mowqua fingered his elegant court necklace with plump fingers, saying: "There's excessive talk of war. Who would fight over such a commonplace as smuggling? Bluster, yes—until a deal is made. But no actual blows."

This was reasoning that Chinqua comprehended. He pried his eyes from blissful contemplation of the calligraphy scroll on the opposite wall and said: "I eat that thinking."

So it went: a seesaw of opinions, with four advocating Howqua's "little plan," four arguing against it, and four who remained discreetly, non-committally, woodenly silent.

Behind the screen Mei-deh grew puzzled, and by degrees apprehensive, her fingers curling and uncurling in her lap like seaweed in a running tide. This nettling silence of her father's. Could he do other than favor Howqua's device? It was valid. It aimed at the core of trouble. It wasn't odiously devious. Then why? What scruples, what expectations were working on him? Her father—the being she knew best, and yet . . . She put a hand to her forehead and found she wasn't wiping hot sweat, but cold clammy dampness. It came to her then that these were not the tremors of restlessness, but the shaking that came from double-tongued doubts.

At that moment her father cleared his throat—deprecatingly, as the cardboard man always did—and spoke. With his first words reassurance flooded over her, and she realized he'd been saving words for a last-minute lever on the reluctant three.

"In T'ang times," Gowqua was saying gravely, "likewise in the days of the Ming—*Chinese houses both, remember*—interest and friendliness were extended to foreigners. Their priests, scholars, and traders were given the liberty of the kingdom, and the interchange of ideas was invigorating. There was no lofty aloofness, no galling restrictions, no war, no talk of war. My instinct is to return to the prosperously happy ways of our *Chinese* grandfathers."

The smacking of lips as each tasted relief might have been at a hundred-course banquet. The kinks and cramps of indecision were over. Who would be unfilial enough to ignore the explicit precepts of a grandfather?

Yai and Yu looked at each other, pursing their lips, shaking their heads, nodding to each other in unspoken communion, until finally Yai said to Gowqua: "Your wisdom is profound, sir. We ally ourselves to it with money."

He'd scarcely finished when Paqua waggled his mustache loquaciously and raised a left hand in his usual signal of assent. Mowqua conceded: "Try it, then."

Manqua muttered a grudging "Yes," and Chinqua, preening his sleeves as though he'd emerged from solitary grapple with a dragon, recited: "'A captive bird longs for the old woods, a fish in the tank for its familiar pool. Long have I been kept in a cage. But now . . . free at last . . . I have returned to Nature's ways,'" by which he meant yes.

Only Tanqua had not agreed, but no one seemed to notice, or care. Certainly he couldn't put his hands on cash enough to pay his share today; and the chances were he'd fail and in a month be going free passage to the frozen frontiers of Asia—where bankrupts were sent.

The servingmaids trouped in again with trays of goose-fat buns, crisp slices of lotus root, savory beans, pickled plovers' eggs, shrimp puffs, and dried beef strips. The second six, as deftly and solicitously, whisked up the half-tasted cups of souchong, and in their place set cherishing little bowls of Mohammedan blue steaming pungently with a chrysanthemum brew. There was the snap of fan-sticks being closed, the crunch of crusty mouthfuls, and the gusty sucking of tea.

Howqua spoke again. "We have taken the long step first. Before it produces results, a short one confronts us. If we submit to Peking's demand for a birthday present, the foreigners will be outraged. If we don't, Peking will be outraged. Which can we afford?"

A fog of talk swirled around the room, obscuring individual words in shrouding tones of dreary, flat, and tedious gloom, except for Tanqua's piccolo chant of "Money, money, money!"

Gowqua didn't say the thing he'd been waiting to say until the others had wearied themselves with futilities. Then he broached it, leading them step by step into the subtle plan Mei-deh had given him that morning. He neither hustled nor palavered, and yet his bare unadorned words summoned and animated them into shaping a workable stratagem.

Howqua wiped one hand with the other in genial satisfaction. "Our ally is surprise—not once, but twice!" he said. "First we surprise the mandarins with threat to suspend trade. We double their surprise and confusion by delegating a new spokesman—our mild, unassuming, but cogent colleague, Gowqua. They've explored every crevice of my brain and know it's adherence to Americans. Likewise Mowqua and his forged links with the English. But Gowqua . . . he is unassessed, unlabeled, unforeseen, and therefore a puzzle they do not master before he masters them."

The suddenness of the maneuver! Mei-deh pressed a hand to her lips to stop the startled gasp which almost escaped. Her father was trapped. What plausible thing could he say or do to extricate himself now before these others? But something . . . anything. Refuse! *Refuse!* she willed silently, closing her eyes in a spasm of concentration.

But Gowqua did not refuse. Clearly, precisely he said, "You are overly polite, Howqua, my old friend. You weigh me with potentialities I do not possess. However, I recognize the factor of surprise, and what it might accomplish in these straits. If it suits you to designate me as spokesman, I shall put what poor faculties I have towards accomplishing our purpose."

The clatter of lids being put on teacups, the slippery sigh of silk, and the stir of slippers on the marble floor told Mei-deh the Hong were gathering themselves for departure. That is, these sounds would have told her if her mind hadn't already darted hours and days ahead to work out eventualities. Some sickness, some incapacitating ailment—administered in his soup, of course —to confine him to bed, to give the semblance of feverish ramblings. . . .

She didn't hear Howqua chuckle softly and whisper to her father during the hubbub of departure: "Never for an instant do I overestimate your potentialities, Gowqua. Always I remember you have Mei-deh. Dress her in man's clothing, and she'll outnegotiate any set of mandarins!"

With the early sun on it that way, the water shone as brightly as a sheet of wrinkled tin, Admiral Kwan told himself, happy with his words, happy with the weather, happy with the day. He took another two turns across the war junk's high

overhanging poop deck, and then, shielding his round merry face
with a silk fan, he permitted himself another squint at the busy
Lintin Roads. The gray boxlike shapes of seven opium hulks were
strung across the open roadstead one after the other like barges on
a towline, and around these floating warehouses were the fast ebb
and flow of longboats moving like centipedes on their fifty oars.
Thrusting up behind was the solitary gray pinnacle of Lintin
itself.

However, the Admiral's genial little eyes didn't linger on these
everyday sights: he was intent on the narrow deep-decked English brig moored in the roads, and in the bustle going on aboard
it. Crewmen were swarming up and down its shrouds, squaring
yards, loosening tackles, and rigging the hammock nets . . . Obviously 'twould be weighing any minute now.

He turned to survey the ten Imperial junks moored off his starboard beam, and slowly his cherubic smile turned into a pout.
Would those turtles never get off? Whatever was keeping them
now? Heaven knows they were stowed to the gunwales with
tribute; and there was no snag about the Throne's opium, or
theirs—the chests had gone aboard discreetly enough before daylight.

Naturally, not being a cat, he had seen *nothing* in the dark;
and, naturally, the officers had come an hour ago to present him
with a pretty little box which just happened, curiously enough, to
be shaped like a money chest. They'd protested imperishable regard for him, and he'd protested imperishable regard for them.
They'd taken ceremonious leave of the flagship, and he'd accorded it with equal ceremony.

Formalities were completed—then why in the name of the
Five Fundamental Principles of Behavior couldn't the turtle dung
move north and allow him to avail himself of a delectable arrangement of coincidence . . . "No autumn report on your opium-
suppressing activities to read the Throne. May we expect it will
leave your brush soon?" the Grand Censorate had dared to prod

him in yesterday's dispatch. Hah, they'd have their report—concise, pithy, but utterly sensational. . . .

The Admiral sensed the presence of someone moving behind him, and he turned towards the sound. H'm, the new gunner, Tsao—neither coughing nor clearing his throat politely, as might be expected—fumbling in that odd way with the loading mechanism of that poop-deck jingal which hadn't been fired this year. The Admiral smiled his bland good-humored smile and, without seeming to be aware of anything but the poetic morning air, studied the man minutely.

No . . . he couldn't feel comfortable about the man's broad obstinate jaw, his impudent stare, nor his meddling ways. Incongruous for a gunner, certainly for a new one aboard the Navy's pride. Moreover, the fellow didn't eat enough garlic to have a decent odor about him. A fighting man who didn't eat garlic . . . h'm he'd bear watching. In the meantime—*deference to the unknown, Manual of War,* page five. . . .

"Getting to the forward gunports would be good," the Admiral hinted mildly, and turned back to watch the Imperial junks.

Ah, dear Buddha, they were upping anchor at last! The lead junk was actually gathering sternway, its big bamboo and matting sails rounding to the steady monsoon; and in gradual rotation the other nine were bracing their saffron sails to follow at intervals. When all ten were gliding in formation like migrating birds across blue space, Admiral Kwan gave the order.

Beautiful clamor began. It spilled out at the near gunport—not from the gun itself, but from the bunched firecrackers at the end of bamboo poles suspended from the port—then exploded at a second, and a third, until all fourteen gunports were belching hullabaloo and pandemonium. A dazzle of banners flashed out across the gunwales, pennants flew from the shrouds, and great long dragon bodies of painted silk unfurled on the three masts to whip and snap and whirl like living monsters.

The Admiral beamed cherubically, nodding his head, clasping his hands spasmodically. Rapturous—and conspicuously expensive! Could anyone say he'd stinted the send-off? Could anyone say he hadn't awakened sleeping gods for miles around to sanctify the voyage?

The northbound junks were well away on their third tack when the first officer began marshaling the seamen on the well deck. He ranged them in precise lines facing the poop-deck rail, made sure their shiny rattan shields were held chest-high, and bade them stare up at the Admiral in customary awe.

Joss sticks were lighted in the niches; a battle gong boomed. The Admiral stepped regally from his cabin, his face unutterably blank; and in the same heavenly catalepsy he advanced to the railing. He was dressed in full regalia. Hanks of red-dyed cow hair erupted from the center button of his rattan battle hat; a fire-spitting dragon in gold embroidery covered the breast of his purple jacket; and his mauve court sash spread tastefully from left shoulder to right waist. When he elevated the jade scepter of command in the classical salute—as he did at this moment—two lavender jade bracelets slid along the pale fat of his arm. Under the other arm he carried the *Manual of War*. He was formidable, breath-taking: every inch an admiral!

He lowered the scepter and laid it at the edge of the parapet for everyone to see, then settling the *Manual* on the ledge behind it, he peeled away the tome's satin wrappings, opened it to DRILL FOR BATTLE, and began reading aloud. His voice was oratorical, full of glissando and bravura, sliding up and down the tonal scale for page after page as fluidly as a reed flute. It held the men spellbound—that is, those who understood his Mandarin dialect. Those who didn't composed their faces, naturally, in the spellbound look.

The Admiral closed the book. His voice undulated to profundo depths. "I admonish you—who are about to enter the jaws of the Dragon—to recollect the fundamental, *the primary rule* of tactics, page one, third indentation . . . which is 'Draw in on an adversary *only* if you are absolutely sure you can demolish. Otherwise leave room for turns of fortune or for compromise. DO NOT

OFFEND!' I admonish you thus, for we are about to confront decision. We, the pride of his Celestial Navy, must mercilessly drive a foreign-devil ship from our waters!" He clenched his fist, then flung it open as though tossing away crushed nothingness.

There was a moment of dedicated silence while he surveyed the indomitable force of men under the red-and-white basket hats below him and watched a gust of breeze flatten blue shirts and short blue trousers against—no, not meager bones, agile nimble ones.

"But who knows," he asked the air before him in sweet reasonableness, "whether wind or tide be headstrong? Who knows whether Fate be peevish? So—I repeat from the *Manual of War*, page twenty, 'Of thirty-six alternatives for handling all possible human situations—flight is the safest!' "

He rewrapped the *Manual* in silk and signaled the first officer to issue the tot of tiger-bone tea.

Cups were passed along the lines, and the teaboy came running with the big white pot to splash each cup with a dollop of liquid courage. Today's tot wasn't Number One tiger-bone powder, the Admiral remembered. It was that lot of ordinary bone powder he'd been lucky enough to pick up at half the price of tiger-bone. But, brewed this way with a bit of opium mixed in, would any of them detect the difference?

With fine flourish he downed the first tot, slapped his chest heartily, and stood beaming while the seamen gulped theirs avidly. Next minute they broke ranks in a rush and, running to their stations like schoolboys, hauled in banners and pennants and silk dragons. By the time the last one came fluttering in, it was abundantly apparent that grins were becoming expansive, gestures wider and more heroic.

The English brig had upped anchor and, instead of the brown-ribbed skeleton of a ship she'd been a moment before, she had become a great white bird skimming the water as she turned on her keel, gathered way, and bore eastward down-bay to the China Sea. The Navy's pride was after her pell-mell, its brown matting sails tight-spread to the wind like a fish hawk swooping its prey.

Lintin fell away. The bustle of warehouses and fast-oared smuggling boats disappeared over the sea rim. The green hills of Sheang Chung on the right revolved astern on each larboard tack, and dead ahead the vaporous ridges of Lantao deepened into purple and filled the whole horizon. In all that immensity of water and land the brig and the war junk were like toy ships jerked by strings, for whether they were slanting on one tack or beating before the wind on the other, the six lengths' distance between them neither closed nor lengthened. When the brig shivered sail and made as though to tarry, the war junk was quick to tarry also. Yet when the brig clapped on topgallants and royals in a mighty rush, the war junk staggered forward under every inch it could crowd on until the gap between them became a relentless six lengths again.

Except for one crucial interval. Except for the unpredictable, horrifying moment when the brig came about abruptly and, instead of easting on a larboard slant, came thrashing for the war junk's bow.

Admiral Kwan blanched, and struck a hand to his forehead in astonishment. What had gone wrong? What were the unsophisticated cutthroats up to? They'd turn everything into a bees' nest in another minute with such dangerous, such ominous, such . . . ah, merciful Buddha!

The 32-pounder on the brig's fo'c'sle puffed smoke. A shot came hurtling at them, to scream through the rigging a bare ten feet above the war junk's upper deck. The Admiral shrieked, leaped sideways, his body plummeting forward to the deck, where his battle hat went rolling in wide circles.

"Decapitated!" the first officer wailed in horror as he threw himself down.

The brig stood on towards them, coming up fast, to spew the air with grapeshot from its 5-pounders. Like flies before a whisk, the men on the junk scattered, flattening out, hugging the deck, crawling into nooks and crannies.

That is, all but Tsao, the new gunner. He leaped over squirming bodies to reach the nearest larboard gunport. He dragged a gunner's mate up by the queue to help, and together they loaded the gun, ran it out its port into position, and fired a broadside charge at the brig passing them now at hundred-yard range. The ball arched out and down, splashing into the sea fifty yards short.

Tsao danced in queer anguish, and then grabbed up a sack of powder to break it open against the gunwale and ran a handful of powder-scattered sand through his fingers. He heaved the mess overboard, broke open another sack, and another, and pushed them away in the same helpless desperation. Then he scrambled forward to the next gunport and was loading that gun when he heard a "Cease firing!" command. It came from the poop deck, and sounded like the Admiral.

It *was* the Admiral, peering down through the stairwell bay—not even slightly decapitated, but very intact, and very emotional. "Cease firing! You adopted-son-of-a-eunuch!"

Tsao stared back at the Admiral with a crooked leer, snapped the breech shut, and primed the mechanism. There was a muffled belch; the ball dribbled out the muzzle, toppled, and fell vertically into the sea.

The Admiral's face turned an inferior shade of purple. He gasped asthmatically for breath as he raised himself on one elbow and shook a detaining hand at the grossly stubborn Tsao. "How many times do I have to tell you," he cried, "'A true hero never incurs present risk.' *Manual of War*, page ten, second indentation. It's a case for strategy. Let the enemy believe they've won. Let them believe we're dead and done. There'll be time enough to show them we aren't—later!"

The brig didn't loiter there, though, or slacken its fast swing. It circled off airily and wore away eastward again towards the China Sea. But before it could reach open water, there were the green and indigo Ladrone Islands to pass. By the time the brig was in those winding stretches the war junk was behind it again— the harassing six lengths widened now to twelve.

It was off the nearer Lemma that the Admiral spotted a conspiracy of circumstances he could hardly credit. He looked a second time—yes, Fate had made him her darling. He couldn't have bettered it if he'd mapped the occasion himself. There they were —downwind ahead, the ten Imperial tribute ships nearing open sea, while here inshore was a sizable fleet of junks loitering under easy sail. "H'm-m, *some* would be fisherfolk from nearby villages, but *some*—in all that number—were bound to be smugglers. What admiral could ask for a more propitious audience?

He took the gamble. He seized it, laughing and laughing, and gave the signal to clap on full sail.

His ship surged ahead, nearer, and yet nearer, the brig; and he stood waiting in suffocated concentration. The brig must respond, it must, it MUST! Were they sleeping? Were they drugged—dawdling there! He gasped mouthfuls of air, masticating it thoroughly in the hideous anxiety of three lifetimes.

Then suddenly he was laughing again uproariously, laughing as though he couldn't stop. For the brig's stunsails had been loosed and set flying now, alow and aloft. The last inch of canvas was being sheeted home. She was kicking her heels and making a dash for open water ahead. He'd gambled successfully. He'd won. She'd never spare time to turn back now. . . .

Flushed and genial, the Admiral indulged in a last look at the consummate readiness of crew and ship. Impeccable, peerless! Fourteen forward cannon loaded and run out their ports; brasses and jingals smartly manned; ten iron baskets, absolutely mammoth, heaped to the brim with giant firecrackers, and all in suspended readiness on bamboo poles jutting from the gunwales; row upon row of men poised, fiercely ready with cymbals and drums. Why, the aural impact would be colossal, stupendous, indescribable, echoing from hill to hill, reverberating downwind to the Imperial junks! With the high spirits of a twenty-year-old he bounded to the gong hanging from the mast and struck the shivering tattoo of battle signal.

Clamor washed over the water. Fourteen cannon spouted flame

as fourteen balls sped out levelly, thundering dead right, and dead left, for a full fifteen yards before they struck water. The trajectory of their splashes was enormous. Brasses and jingals rattled a fierce staccato as they too lashed the water into appalling geysers. The triggered crew went charging madly about the decks, bounding up one gangway and down the next, clashing cymbals, hammering gongs, beating drums, and screaming like souls in torment. Over and above this was the repeated clap of doom as one salvo after another of giant firecrackers rang out, prolonging and intensifying the roar and fury of battle until the Imperial junks had disappeared and the brig was only a white speck on the horizon.

No time to swab guns, clear decks of debris, and get ship-shape now, though. Not with the junk fleet scattering here and there into the island maze. Being single-stick craft, however, they couldn't get far; and with the spread of its three masts, the war junk was after them like a pelican chasing ducks.

The first three they overtook had big trolling nets wagging out behind, and obviously were fishing. But the fourth, hurrying past the spoon-shaped Bay of Crabs, was low in the water with cargo, and a likely prize.

Admiral Kwan swept around it in a tightening circle until he could be sure its deck cargo was pigs, not humans, and that the only guns it carried were jingals. But—thanks to the bombardment of sound back there—he had no need to lay a shot across its bows, for as he came up the crew struck sail and waited, hove to and sullen, for the next unkindness of Fate.

Grappling hooks were made fast, and a searching party went aboard. But the Admiral watched them disappear into the cabin and come out empty-handed. They ripped up deck boards and uncovered dried fish. They stabbed fat bags with spears, and rice grains trickled out into white pools. The Admiral's smile grew less lenient, but it was still a smile as he tapped the poop-deck rail with his twenty-stick fan.

Find something, you sons-of-mouses, he willed them silently.

Find something to compensate for a long day. Otherwise these blind passages will gobble up the remaining prizes. Three vanished already behind that first headland. Or was it the identical headland beyond? *Ai-yah,* he was weary. He turned to wipe his face in the hot towel the kitchen boy brought him.

It was then the triumphant shout went up, and he lifted his face from the towel to see the leader of the boarding party and a crewman come staggering out the forward hatch lugging a telltale chest between them. Another, and another, appeared as the men dived back in for more, until eleven were stacked there on the deck. Eleven! H'm-m, with the market above a thousand dollars for Patna, that was eleven thousand dollars less *squeeze,* of course, less reward for the crew.

The Admiral shouted to be heard above squealing pigs and beseeching junk crew. "Bring the smugglers and their contraband aboard! Fire the ship!" he ordered.

The bedlam grew unpleasant, and he crossed to the windward rail to compose his mind. Here it was, an hour to sunset, and nothing but small chow to eat all day—small wonder he was weary. What would he have for dinner? Barbecued fresh pork with sweet-and-sour sauce was a foregone conclusion. But why ignore geography? The Bay of Crabs was but a short row away. . . .

His thoughts were distracted by a bulbous whiteness in the green depths below, wavering there as opalescent and ethereal as the moon's shadow; and then as it rose to the surface, he saw it was one of the deep-sea jellyfish come in to spawn in the shallows. One of many, actually—for milky shapes were pulsing up all around now, their noxious tendrils undulating out behind as innocent-looking as dancers' veils. In a grim sort of fascination he watched them rise and sink and float up again, until suddenly an idea took hold and tugged at him. His lips grew moist, and he licked them twice in strange relish, laughing his merry, cheerful laugh.

The thud and clank of released grappling hooks and the gusty lick of flames on dry wood brought him back to things at hand.

In quick order he dispatched two men in the ship's sampan to row ashore and fetch a batch of crabs. He superintended the stowing of ten chests—top-grade Patna, thank Fortune—in his own cabin, and indulgently bestowed the eleventh on the crew as reward. He saw to it that his writing table was brought out into the salubrious breeze on the poop deck and his best inkstone prepared. By the time he was ready to view the prisoners huddled below in the deck well, the junk had dwindled to a brushstroke of smoke in a blue immensity.

Bah, riffraff! *Tangka,* by their talk—boat-people sentenced by Fate and the statute books to live their lives out on water-borne planks within sight of land, but never on it. Puny scarecrows— all ten of them. Not one of the lot with sinew enough to be worth his rice aboard this Son of Thunder.

He signaled the first officer to his side, but intoned clearly that all might hear the order. "By virtue of the mercy the Sublime One invests in me, I do not condemn these smuggling scoundrels to death by fire. Instead I consign them to their element—the sea from whence they came. Cast them into it—*on the windward side!*"

He heard gasps of horror go up from his crew, and from the prisoners, as they glimpsed the school of poisonous jellyfish below. With stoical calm he closed his ears and mind to them. He was about to withdraw from the scene when the incredulous stare on Tsao's face caught his eye. Who was this audacious upstart, anyhow? No ordinary gunner, certainly. Planted here undoubtedly . . . to tattle? To spy? To lay malevolent traps?

Admiral Kwan fought to master the convulsive emotion which gripped him suddenly. When he could trust his voice to be calm, he said: "Cast the traitorous Tsao overboard also. He disobeyed orders! He flagrantly interfered with strategy!"

He turned and strolled composedly to the shady haven of his writing table, sliding the two lavender jade bracelets from his brush arm. Then, with minute nicety, he selected a brush from the holder and warmed it slowly between moist red lips. It was sometime later—after the splashing and anguish of eleven doomed men was silenced—that he began to write. He chose his words carefully: he wanted them without the high-flown gloss and hyperbole of court talk. He wanted them plain and to the point as befitted a simple fighting man. He wrote:

We rejoice to report that Your Navy is ever triumphant and invincible. Its equal cannot be matched in any waters of this earth, nor in the Nether Springs beyond.

We have this day engaged in desperate conflict with what might the foreign-devil English could muster. Ignominiously they fled before us. But steadfastly we pursued to the outer reaches of our command, inflicting damage upon damage until they were forced to creep away, too broken and crushed ever to show themselves again in Chinese waters.

Having relentlessly driven off these curs, we then turned effort to capturing a despicable cargo junk flagrantly engaged in smuggling contraband opium. We burned the craft and eliminated the villainish crew summarily.

Thus: in one day we have rid Canton waters of all polluting influences, and return them pure and undefiled to the Face of Heaven.

Reverently receive this, and note the tenderness of our regard. We place our head beneath the Sublime One's foot. We breath and live only to serve.

His report was finished and sealed, ready for the express messenger who'd take it to Peking, when the Admiral heard the ship's sampan returning with the crabs. At that same moment there came drifting up from the kitchen the good smell of pig being fried in sesame-seed oil and garlic—ah, plenty of garlic!

'Twould go delectably with fresh crabs, soft and luscious and tangy with the flavor of their own pink fat. He summoned the first officer and, with his gentle assuaging smile, said: "Old One, we have spent the livelong day rendering service to the Throne. Now we have need to pander to interest in our health. We must force ourselves to eat in order that we may be strong enough to render still greater service another day."

He clapped hands for the kitchen boy to bring tea, pulled out a chair, and sat to the meal.

CHAPTER V

MACAO,

September 1838

MACAO BECAME a city of bells at intervals during the day. First the great bronze gongs in San Lorenzo's butter-colored towers led off with passionate calls to piety; next Santo Domingo's deep nagging boom started; and then the two cathedrals on opposite hills, the convents of Santa Clara and Saint Augustine, the colleges of Saint Joseph and San Paulo, along with the chapels of the five forts, joined their clinking and clanking to the metallic uproar. Conversation, and thought itself, hung suspended. Then gradually the throbbing tumult subsided bell by bell, and Macao lapsed back into somnolent quiet until, in another hour or so, the bells began again.

Overtaken by one of these parenthetical intervals, Gill stood before the Mannings' big teak gate and waited for the barrage of sound to fade enough for his puny knock to be heard. Young Stacey was with him, having stopped by Gill's house earlier that afternoon to lead him the roundabout way down successive streets of steps and through medieval *travessa* that burrowed between old stone houses.

As they waited Gill glanced curiously around at the neighboring houses, and was caught by the pink façade of a large one farther along. Something about its elongated tiers of windows and the bonbon curlicues framing them reminded him of an engraving he'd seen.

Glimmering memory sharpened into focus when Stacey exclaimed: "Suds! I nearly forgot to show you the local version of Sans Souci—the house-that-opium-built. Rumbullion, isn't it? Belongs to the Portugaler Pinto. Paid for it with one year's profit, they say."

Gill shook his head in silent wonder, and then turned and rattled the Mannings' knocker. A black gateman with a fez sliding off his knobbled head tugged the heavy panel open and bowed as reverently to them as though they were royalty. He led them across a small flagged courtyard and up a broad, covered stairway, where the moist green of hanging ferns and banked begonias was like a cooling poultice on the eyes after the glare of the street.

In the cavern of the hallway a servingman waited to take their sun helmets and walking sticks. Gill dropped cards in the silver salver already heaped with other cards, and waited while Stacey pawed apologetically and comically in one pocket and then the other for his card case. On the second go-around he pulled it forth triumphantly from the pocket he'd first searched. Grinning in resignation, he led the way through the first open door into the muted shadows of a large drawing-room.

Gill felt a throb of pleasure pulse through him as he saw Lael Manning rise and come towards them. She was dressed in another marvelously cool frock, a filmy something-or-other in mint green which made her skin even milkier, and set off her lovely halo of hair. Several ladies and gentlemen were chatting around the tea table, but Manning wasn't amongst them, Gill noted in a quick glance.

Lael said to Gill, with a smile which seemed wholly personal: "We hoped we'd be lucky enough to see you this afternoon." She greeted Stacey and turned back persuasively to Gill. "Please come and meet my friends before you go into Uncle Timothy's meeting."

Stacey had blundered into the drawing-room, Gill realized, instead of taking him directly to Manning's study. He would rather avoid a tea-table group, but he felt it was too late to back out now. "I shall be honored," he said quietly.

The first introduction was to Senhora Pinto, the lady of Sans Souci itself—a tadpole of a woman in puce-colored bombazine whose short body seemed all bosom and chins. She acknowledged him with a torpid, heavy-lidded smile and a nod of her splendidly beribboned cottage bonnet. Instinctively Gill searched her for ruffles, remembering the incredible laundry hampers he'd seen yesterday, and was disappointed to see none.

Standing beside her was a short thickset man in his late fifties with curly white hair that foamed like soap suds on his head. When Lael introduced him as "George Chinnery," Gill remembered the famous Irish portrait painter Tad had described in his letters as an incorrigible wit. Chinnery's pudgy hands were waggling in broad gestures, but he paused long enough to shake hands with Gill, peer at him over the top of spectacles which had slid to the tip of his long red nose; then, in the oblivious eagerness of a monologist, went on with his story.

The grizzled Englishman, Olyphant Thane, in the white twill suit was cheery, robust, friendly, his flushed face ample testimony he wasn't on his first glass of sherry. The other was Lieutenant Ian Lashmore, off the H.M.S. *Larne*, the 18-gun sloop at anchor in the roads. He was in his late twenties: tall, blond, finely drawn, and insolently languid. Gill wondered which irritated him more—this mannered droop or the fellow's excellently tailored yellow nankeen trousers and alpaca coat with a handsome neckerchief tucked so casually under the snug lapels.

It was certainly a varied group temperamentally, but Lael seemed at ease with each of them, and conveyed that sense to Gill as she said in her agreeable voice: "Mr. Thane, here, is a former official of the East India Company who, fortunately for us"—she paused with a teasing smile at the ruddy-faced Thane—"has traded England's icy blasts for the soft winds of Macao for his retirement."

"Soft winds be damned!" Thane scoffed. "It's the soft glances

of ladies which chain me here! Young man, you see before you
the Sultan of Macao. Part time, worse luck! I only assemble my
harem in winter, when husbands—*and would-be husbands*—are
up in Canton." He looked pointedly at the lieutenant on this last
designation, wheezed, and rubbed his hands together in simula-
tion of high glee. " 'Twon't be long now till I start polishing soft
phrases and innuendoes." He was obviously a favorite, and knew
it. But his courtly manner and jolly eyes robbed his performance
of swanking.

The lieutenant ignored the thrust. He fixed a monocle to his
eye and stared at Gill before he drawled: "Another *fan kwae*
swelling the ranks, eh?"

Gill smiled in uncertainty. "This makes the second time I hear
the expression. Perhaps you'll be kind enough to tell me its
meaning."

The lieutenant's answering smile was derisive. "I shall be delighted . . . *fan kwae* permits two interpretations. One is 'outer
barbarian'—outer in the sense of being the rankest kind of barbarian. The other is 'foreign devil.' Please take your choice."

Gill laughed, suspecting the fellow of pulling a newcomer's
leg. "You make it sound absolute."

"Not as absolute as the Chinese," the Englishman retorted with
curt emphasis. Then, relapsing into the languid mold, he transferred his attention completely to Lael.

Platters of hot scones and intricate pastries appeared in the
hands of two white-smocked servingmen. Senhora Pinto's por-
cine little eyes glittered greedily as she fluttered over her choice
with proscribed ladylike politeness. Finally she appealed to
Chinnery: "Do help me, dear Mr. C," she begged languishingly.
"Choose me the one you'd like best for yourself."

The Irishman drew himself up aghast. "My dear madame, you
put an intolerable burden on me. Even for my own mother I
couldn't be that self-sacrificing!" Whereupon he forked a piece of
plain sponge cake onto her plate and gave himself the largest and
most delectable confection on the platter.

The lieutenant's monocle dropped. Stacey snorted boyishly, and Thane wheezed: "Irish to the ultimate bite, by Christopher!" But Chinnery blandly ignored them all, chomped the last shred of coconut, licked his lips rapturously, and said: "Reminds me of the day in Lisboa when the Duke de Pombal . . ." and was off on another lively yarn.

Gill refused both food and tea. "If you'll excuse me," he said over the lieutenant's shoulder to Lael, "I'd best join your uncle now." He made his adieus to the circle, and Lael disengaged herself from the monopolizing lieutenant to walk to the doorway with Gill.

Crossing the room, Gill saw it was one of a pair—both elegantly proportioned and furnished: both with domed ceilings, crystal chandeliers, marble fireplaces, and parquetry floors strewn with silky Chinese rugs. A gallery half as wide enclosed them on three sides, its marble floor tiles banked magnificently with plumy ferns and potted frangipani. The outside walls seemed to be at least three feet thick, and Venetian blinds on the windows modulated the daytime glare to an aqueous green. It was a princely establishment, Gill realized, and quite obviously was run with a princely disregard for expense.

At the doorway Lael's eyes searched his face—perceptively, it seemed to Gill. "When you talk with Uncle Timothy," she told him softly, "remember he's neither enigmatic nor cynical. They are outward scales, you might say, he uses to hide his soft core. I suspect you could penetrate to that core—if you've a mind to."

How immensely attractive and forthright she was! How without pretense!

She must have seen the appreciation in his glance, but her remote little smile did not acknowledge it. She nodded good-by and turned back to her guests.

As Gill was shown into the handsomely paneled study, Manning greeted him from behind a desk littered with the trivia of a man who used it regularly and often. Manning merely pointed to a chair, neither rising nor offering Gill his hand, but continued with the business of fitting a sheaf of letters into a tin box. Finally he closed the lid, got up, and put the box on a cupboard shelf alongside more of the same tin boxes. Then he carefully closed the cupboard doors and bolted them.

"Defense against the destroyer—Mr. Cockroach and his overwhelming progeny," Manning offered in explanation, but not in apology. "They reduce documents to pulp in one season. Mildew does likewise to papers, and our minds, during the long summer."

Conversation continued at random for several minutes. Manning painstakingly examined the nib of a quill pen, then gave the same scrutiny to a paper knife, while Gill replied to several unrelated questions he put.

Abruptly he said: "You didn't mention yesterday that you'd sold Bennett Brothers."

So the news had come in the *Seraph's* mailbags, Gill thought.

"There were obvious reasons, sir," he said with no intention of sounding defensive. "One—news of Tad's death. Another—it didn't occur to me it affected anyone here. When I discovered it might—at Sur Manoel's house—it seemed neither the time nor the place to discuss it."

Manning took the penknife from a desk and began a slow deliberate sharpening of a quill point before he said: "You sold the business without Tad's knowledge?"

"Yes."

"Why?"

Gill felt his gorge rise. "You're hardly entitled to that explanation, sir," he said coldly. How to explain the heritage of Corwin Bennett to this stranger? The nausea of poverty? The fear that Tad was being made a cat's-paw by Russell and Company?

Manning regarded him levelly. "Tad's last letter could not have arrived in New York before your, er . . . precipitant departure. Therefore you are unaware that I had offered him a partnership to handle our tea business."

Gill was flabbergasted. The only thing he could think to say was: "Then Sur Manoel's hint of a merger was true?"

"It was not!" Manning tossed the pen on the desk, folded his hands, and looked fixedly at Gill. "His surmise, however, had elements of fact. I'll call your attention to my exact words—I did not say *merger*. I said . . . *your brother* was offered a partnership."

Gill understood now, overwhelmingly. "I see," he said between tight lips. "And what did Russell and Company propose to do with Bennett Brothers—and me?"

"Nothing whatever. Neither being within the province of Russell and Company. Your brother made it a condition of his acceptance, unfortunately, that you have the final word in his decision. I accentuate *unfortunately* because quite obviously you did not choose to accord him the same consideration when you sold the partnership without consulting him."

Gill didn't intend being lectured like a schoolboy by a stranger. "My reasons were sufficient and valid," he broke out wrathfully, and then subsided with a shrug, "but what difference now? Tad's gone, and I can't explain to him. Also, your deal with him is finished."

Manning shook his head. "*Not* finished." He peered through half-closed eyelids at Gill with a strange, almost baleful animosity in his dark eyes, as though something were going on behind them that the man resented. He flicked a hand in dismissal of the subject, saying: "There isn't time to go into it before the factors arrive. But if you will be good enough to remain after the meeting, I shall explain. I'd like to hazard one guess now, though . . . your motive in coming out East was to go into opium?"

Gill's chin went up defiantly. "Yes," he said.

Manning jumped up from his desk and paced the length of the room several times, tapping his right forefinger against his nose as though he were arguing something out with himself. Then he came to a halt and said with a sardonic smile: "One more fly in the web!"

In twill suits, as meticulously white and alike as uniforms, the factors arrived singly and in pairs—the majority British, but a fair number were Americans. The diversity between them was within each nationality itself—the keen, astute, resourceful-looking men scattered between windbags and obstinate pudding faces; but all shared the similarity of drawn, washed-out looks a hot climate puts on men.

Manning introduced Gill to Warren Delano and Russell Sturgis, two partners of Russell and Company who'd been Tad's friends. But neither they nor the others Gill met in the next few minutes offered him more than perfunctory attention or inquired his reason for being there. Evidently Manning's introduction was guarantee enough. He caught the word opium again and again in snatches of talk; and it seemed to him the general temper of the group was strained, and on edge.

Manning officiated as spokesman because the meeting was called at his house; and when the men had seated themselves, he riffled through a batch of documents he held in his hand and said: "Gentlemen, we have a hornets' nest in our hands—with the hornets still in residence." His voice was neither droll nor mocking, but grimly earnest. The other faces in the room were settling into the same mold.

"Our friend Gutzlaff is still translating the Emperor's edicts, and will bring them along directly he's finished," Manning said, detaching the topmost paper and waggling it for all to see. "This is the Viceroy's instructions for the approaching 1838–39 season. As usual, he neither addresses us as *foreign factors* nor as *foreign merchants,* but continues to dub us *'fan kwae.'* I shall use the exact translation as I read his message, that we shall remain mindful of the Viceroy's attitude." He cleared his throat and began to read in precise tones:

"His Celestial Majesty, Tao Kuang, Lord of the World, Ruler of Ten Thousand Nations, who in the highest degree sheds his benign influence with equal majesty upon the uni-

verse, is graciously inclined to receive tribute from outer barbarians who come from darkness to worship the light! Therefore I, Viceroy Tung Yu-shing, make known to such of you foreign devils assembled to receive these multiple benefactions that you may trade in Canton under the following conditions."

Indignant snorts came from several chairs, but obviously the majority were attempting to withhold comment until later. Gill felt a quickening of interest. The language of the manifesto sounded like a boastful boy. Manning continued reading:

"FIRSTLY—*All vessels of war are prohibited from entering the Pearl River beyond the Boca Tigris forts. Those acting as convoy for foreign-devil trading ships must anchor at sea outside until the merchantman sails.*

"SECONDLY—*Outer-barbarian ships arriving with merchandise must come directly to Whampoa Anchorage. They may not loiter outside the river, nor rove the outer bays at pleasure, and sell to the rascally natives any goods which is subject to duty, and so defraud His Celestial Majesty, Ruler of the Civilized World.*

"THIRDLY—*Outer-barbarian men are not permitted to bring their wives, or women, to Canton. Neither are they permitted guns, spears, or any arms.*

"FOURTHLY—*Outer barbarians are prohibited from rowing on the Pearl River in pleasure boats, as this nourishes pride, profligacy, and indolence. They will be allowed to take the air on the eighth, eighteenth, and twenty-eighth day of each moon, when they may issue from their abode and visit the flower gardens and joss house on Honan Island, across from Canton, provided they do not issue out in droves of more than ten. They must return before sundown, and cannot spend the night away from their segregated dwellings, nor collect together, nor carouse.*"

Manning paused to sip sparingly of a glassful of lime and barley water beside him, but his hand shook as though the control he exercised over his voice did not extend to his hands. The absorbed group before him was silent as he continued:

"FIFTHLY—*No outer barbarian is permitted to complain, or present petitions to me. Let him submit anything worthy of communication to his Hong merchant.*

"SIXTHLY—*Outer barbarians may not loan money, or extend credit, to Hong merchants and other Chinese.*

"SEVENTHLY—*All Chinese, under pain of death by a thousand tortures, are prohibited from teaching the Chinese language to foreign devils.*

"EIGHTHLY—*Outer barbarians must return to the barbaric country they call home after April first. Or they may go to Macao and wait until the Monarch of the Universe graciously declares Canton open for trade.*

"NINTHLY—*Outer barbarians may not ride in sedan chairs. Walking is good enough for their kind.*

"TENTHLY—*Chinese authorities will engage all servants for outer barbarians and decide the number needed.*

"*Oppose not these instructions! Tremble and heed them! Tremble mightily! Obey and remain! Disobey and depart!*

"That, gentlemen, concludes the Viceroy's instructions to us for this trading season," Manning said, folding the document.

There was a buzz of "Scoundrel!" "Debauched criminal!" "Shameful!" and "Galling!"

Gill sat back in his chair, knowing none of this affected him: that he wasn't going to Canton, thank God; that he'd chosen business to keep him here in Macao. But he was shocked that men of this caliber would consider doing business under such onerous conditions. Surely there must be—there had to be!—some other solution.

Launcelot Dent, Number One of the second-largest English firm, was the first to speak above the mutterings. "Usual balderdash we've received for ten years. Ignore it."

"Damned if I can ignore contempt!" the peppery Samuel Fearon said hotly.

Manning tapped a finger against his chin with peculiar impatience. "We have need to husband our indignation for the yearly touch from the Chinese Government. The Hong merchants have refused to present it, so the Viceroy himself sends it. I shall spare you the loquacious preamble, and only read the barefaced items themselves:

"Tribute to Emperor Tao Kuang .... $ 160,000.
Birthday present to Emperor .... $ 377,000.
Repairs, Yellow River .... $ 87,000.
Birthday present, Customs officer .... $ 60,000.
Birthday present, local officials .... $ 120,000.
Expenses, agent in Peking .... $ 61,000.
                                          _____
                                          $ 865,000.

It ends, genially, with 'The gods bless you with ten thousand sons.' "

"Preposterous!" exclaimed grizzled William Jardine, who'd come out as a ship's surgeon thirty-six years ago, and now was senior partner of the potent English house of Jardine Matheson. He jumped to his feet to rap the table with white-knuckled ferocity. "That's extortion!" His clicking Scottish consonants rattled like pebbles in a brook. "My company's share would run"—he did a rapid mental calculation—"around sixty thousand dollars, at least. *Agent in Peking*, bah! None of us has an agent in Peking!"

"Repair the Yellow River—two thousand miles away! Why?" Sturgis asked heatedly.

"Who says it needs repairing?" someone asked.

"That's beside the point," Jardine snapped, "the money's to *repair* the Viceroy's purse." He included the whole circle in his outraged look, and asked: "Shall we continue bending the knee to extortioners? It behooves us to take a stand."

"You advocate war?" Warren Delano asked in a stubborn voice.

"I advocate teaching the Chinese that international commerce is not despicable," Jardine answered resolutely. "What do you propose we do?"

Delano shrugged his shoulders urbanely. "I didn't come out for my health. I came out to earn a living the quickest possible way."

"We take them too seriously," Dent smiled tolerantly. "They're nothing but ignorant children. They haven't a notion what's going on in the world outside China."

"Diplomacy has failed." Fearon rocked his head dismally. "The Macartney and Amherst embassies couldn't even get into the Forbidden City because they refused to grovel on their faces and call the Emperor their liege lord."

"Gentlemen"—Manning's crisp voice cut through—"the issue is whether or not we continue trading here under increasingly preposterous conditions. If we decide we cannot—we have the alternative of either closing shop or recommending to our home governments that force be used. That brings us to the crux, as I see it . . . does any nation have the right to insist with gunpowder upon *liberty* to trade with another?"

Fearon jumped up, exclaiming: "Merchants here want trade with us! It's only corrupt officials who treat us like waterfront scum. I say use force—because it's the only master mandarins will *kowtow* to."

Innes, the fiery redheaded Irishman who'd defied all rules with his opium-running, was on his feet next, flushed and excited. "Force our way upriver with every gun we can lay hands on," he shouted. "Capture all five forts. Capture Whampoa Anchorage. Then use them as a negotiating lever, and the Chinese will soon come to terms."

"Agree! Get a commercial treaty!" half a dozen voices urged.

A pious-faced man named King stepped towards the middle of the room, as though disassociating himself from both groups of the British and Americans. "A commercial treaty to regulate opium sales?" he asked bitterly.

Not one voice, but an angry indistinguishable chorus answered him. The pudding-faced man sitting beside Gill—who hadn't opened his mouth yet—turned now and whispered solemnly to Gill: "Nonsense. Opium habit's no worse here than beer habit at home. Better for the stomach, actually. Cures summer complaint right off. Only thing for malaria!" And with that he relapsed into somnolence again.

Jardine's Scottish voice splintered through. "Understand this, King—the issue is free trade. We want ports opened to Western goods. Not under antiquated regulations, but under fair, reasonable, decent conditions. You, King, choose to make a boogey of opium, and have decided not to handle it. With the rest of us it's one more commodity to sell. We damn well wouldn't bring it here if the Chinese didn't scramble to buy it!"

King raised an admonishing hand, shaking it in Jardine's face. "What about moral principles?" he demanded.

The Scotsman's look was decimating. "Do ye dare to speak o' morals, mon . . . with the items of that 'repair bill' in your ears?"

An American Gill couldn't identify called out: "No, let's not speak of morals. Not as long as Parliament permits the Bengal government to support itself on the million pounds sterling it earns per annum from opium sales."

"Indeed, and do you have the statistical figures on what your good friend France makes each year from its brandy, absinthe, and wine sales?" Jardine wanted to know.

A door opened, and a short, squat man stepped into the room, bowing to them all. His large bald head, yellow skin, and the delicately painted fan he was using made him look Chinese, but when he spoke, it was in a thick, Germanic guttural: "Gut afdernoon, zentlemen."

Obviously welcoming the interruption, Manning said: "Thank you, Dr. Gutzlaff, for your work on these Peking edicts."

"You von't tank me vonce you read tem," Gutzlaff growled.

Manning glanced at the top paper, his lips compressing as he read the introductory lines. He motioned the Pomeranian pill doctor and Bible seller to a chair, and turned towards the others, silencing them with a gesture. His voice had an impassioned ring to it as he said: "The Emperor says no other ports besides Canton shall be opened to us." And he read the edict Tao Kuang had written when the fear of survival was on him that August day in the Summer Palace waiting for the cricket fights.

When Manning stopped, indignation exploded like a string of firecrackers around the room, crackling and flaring and sputtering as each pent-up man erupted into speech. The irate words were drenched with bitterness and frustration.

Talk: more edicts; talk; nothing agreed, nothing settled . . . English for an immediate show of arms; Americans saying opium's death knell was being sounded—better to give up carrying it now and preserve remnants of trade. No! Fight immediate intimidation and clarify the larger issue. . . .

Gill never knew what set him off—the inflammatory pitch of the room, the soggy heat, the impulse towards reason instead of being swept willy-nilly on this muddy current of emotionalism. But suddenly an idea struck him full force, and the next minute he was on his feet speaking above the disorder.

"Why not vacate Macao and Canton in a body? Why not set up shop on one of those uninhabited islands out there at the edge of the bay? In all those hundreds there's bound to be one that has a favorably protected harbor."

Surprise first, then a whispering murmur amongst the British. Stares from the Americans. His hands grew damp with effort, for he was not sure what else he was going to say. He only knew he felt afire with the desire to formulate this new idea.

"Select an all-year anchorage," he said, "so business goes on all year. Ships turn around faster. Probably chop four to eight days off, coming and going. Chinese merchants come to us—not five monopoly bigwigs appointed by the Emperor, but all Chinese merchants up and down the coast. We make our own laws and regulations. And . . . we're free to trade in opium, or not, as we see fit."

Gill caught Manning's eye, and saw an intent, interested look. But around him "Possibly" and "Might be the solution" were being outbuzzed by "Unfeasible!" and "Daydreaming!"

A Scottish voice spoke up. "How do you propose acquiring this mercantile utopia?"

Gill faced the speaker, the idea forming in his mind even as he spoke. "I'm told, sir, that Chinese are a practical people. Or should I say avaricious?" He couldn't help smiling at the quick grunt of assent which came from all sides. "If—as we apparently agree—they'll do anything for money, why not offer them a whacking price for one of those rocky islands out there which they consider worthless? It'd be cheaper than war—or paying exorbitant levies such as these 'repair bills.'"

He stopped, appalled suddenly at his brashness in spouting to older and more experienced men. His conviction peeled away from him. He bowed deferentially with a little gesture of apology and went to sit in an obscure chair against the wall.

But his words had touched off further harangue—a tug between pros and cons: between feasibility and utter impossibility. Hopefulness, as fast as it sprouted, was layered with pessimism; but always there was the corrosive animosity for the rogues in Peking.

Gill sat uncomfortably in one of the ornately carved study chairs, outwardly composed he hoped, but inwardly restless and baffled over what Manning meant to propose. He felt he didn't know his way with a man as substantial and important, and as enigmatic, as Manning. Besides, this was a devilishly heady place with heady standards . . . men talking straight-faced about sixty-thousand-dollar *presents* over and above their ordinary business expenses! High-placed English admirals getting social slaps in the face! One year's opium profits building a replica of Sans Souci!

Manning was really big—that Gill recognized now. But did

that mean the factor was highhanded also? Did it mean Manning had sized him up as a younger edition of the easygoing and chivalrous Tad? Was he supposed to be equally unrealistic about money? Forget his own affairs to help Russell and Company out of some pinch? "Damn it all," he said to himself, "I shan't be drawn back into the tea business. Not into that muffling net! I'll strike out in the thick of things, as I've always wanted to do."

Lord knows he didn't consider himself a swashbuckling soldier of fortune. Glamorous words, he'd decided, used to cover the indignity of poverty. Compensation for a jumping jack who hopped from one foot to the other, or ran faster and more breathlessly than the other wretches in his race. No, never mind wordy titles. Just let him get into this grab bag of Asia with both hands free.

Manning shoved the stack of edicts and translations to a corner of the desk and sat upon it, drumming his fingers on the mahogany top in a galloping tattoo as he gazed fixedly out the window. A farce of expressions chased across his grooved cheeks as the flames of the eight-branched candelabra threw a play of undulating shadows across his face. From somewhere beyond the window a zither quivered, incongruously soft and gentle and appealing.

Without turning his head Manning said distastefully: "Thomas, our tea expert, is now at the end of his tether. His wife suffers from an extreme of nostalgia. It doesn't seem to matter to her that the malady is utter nonsense, or that it's ruining her husband.

"She desires but one thing—to saturate herself in the actuality of New York . . . the Battery, Broadway, Wanamaker's. Her husband, poor wretch, prefers indulging her to watching it torture her here. He has declared himself irrevocably of the intention of pulling out—now, at onset of the tea-buying season."

Gill knew what was coming now. But he felt no tremor of excitement. He was quit of tea. Nothing could change that. *Nothing!*

Manning fixed Gill with tired eyes and said wearily: "To put

it bluntly—my situation is desperate unless you can see your way
to giving me your expert hand with tea in Canton this winter."

Chivalry being dragged in like a dead swan, Gill told himself
stormily, his sunburned face flushing with the anger he felt. The
presumption . . . bigwig flattering a nobody into postponing and
foregoing his own plans! Even selecting words calculated to make
him feel churlish when he refused.

The twitch of emotion on Gill's face evidently warned Manning, for he continued smoothly: "Actually, the deal can serve you
well. You develop substantial 'China legs' and learn business ins-
and-outs in this market for six months."

"Those six months being when opium either skyrockets or goes
bust," Gill reminded him curtly.

Manning pursed thin lips sardonically. "I prefer to state it—
six months during which you won't lose your shirt!" He snuffed
a guttering candle and went on urbanely. "Instead you add capital
through privilege tonnage—the usual seven tons' free shipping
we give for any purchases made on your own account."

"*Any* purchases but opium!" Gill said tautly, for they both
knew privilege tonnage was a homeward-voyage allotment, and
that opium was never a cargo for New York.

Manning frowned. "You can't be diverted from opium, then?"
he asked.

"I can't be diverted from opium." Gill repeated the words with
flat finality.

"Why?"

The question put Gill on the defensive again. He couldn't answer it without describing the hundred and one kicks in the stomach he'd had getting even this far. Not without groping for words
to explain his everlasting relief in being unhobbled. That Canton
sounded infinitely dreary—five months' incarceration: no women;
only men buying, buying omnivorously for the empty maw of
other men's ships and profits.

No, the obvious answer was the easiest; and he fended with it.
"Why is it human nature for a man to want quick returns? I can't

enlighten you. I only know the urge exists, and that it has me in tow."

Something in Manning's gnawed look penetrated Gill's defensive shell. Antagonism suddenly drained away from him, and his blue eyes softened in genuine sympathy. Impulsively he put his hand out and clasped Manning's. "Forgive me, sir. You've been excessively kind to me. If I could help you here in Macao, I'd gladly lend a hand. But going to Canton is quite impossible. I feel these next six months are decisive. They're apt to be the glorious opportunity I've waited for all my life!"

"Glorious opportunity to lose your shirt," Manning said with a foreboding headshake. "I've watched this situation firsthand for five years. I've learned to interpret flurries, I believe. My instinct tells me this is not another flurry. Peking is determined to maneuver us into complete cessation of opium trade."

"But cessation of opium smoking? Can that be halted overnight?" Gill argued.

"Peking *could*"—Manning passed a tired hand over tired eyes as he got to his feet and took to pacing the room again—"and *would* to maintain a calendar of yesterdays."

Gill looked his disbelief. "Are you telling me the central government of all China is ostrich enough to——?"

"The central government of all China is a frightened old man trying to keep his bottom on the throne." Manning cut in. "He hopes to cement it there with the rust of antiquity. His one doctrine is 'Look backward to dear, bygone customs!' We Westerners jar that doctrine. We topple it with new ideas and new ways. The richer we become, the bigger menace we present."

He flipped open the humidor, took out a cigar, snipped off the end, and bent to the candelabrum to light it. But before it caught, he snatched the thing from his lips in a spasm of impatience, crumpled it between his hands, and tossed the shreds into a basket. "Man, it's as plain as the nose on your face," he exclaimed. "The biggest stick Tao Kuang can shake at us—his only weapon —is taking away opium cargoes so we're forced to carry ninety-eight per cent bullion and two per cent merchandise on the outward voyage. Not that he gives a damn morally, but he hopes to put us out of business. Two hundred thousand Chinese may die because they can't get their daily smoke—but that's a bagatelle. Peking would willingly, and piously, pay that price to drive us from these shores."

Gill was impressed by the depth of Manning's feelings, but he was still unconvinced.

Manning halted abruptly and looked at Gill through slitted eyes. "Don't put money on opium now," he said bleakly. "They've a pocketful of devices to pry us loose, and they'll begin using them any day."

"But—Russell and Company are big dealers in opium," Gill protested.

"Russell and Company is a combine of twelve partners, sharing losses. Besides, every dollar we put in opium is protected by two in tea and silk. You're Gill Bennett, unattached, swimming in a tankful of sharks!"

CHAPTER VI

MACAO,

September 1838

EACH MORNING when Gill left the house, two coolies in livery and a glossy black sedan chair stood waiting beside the door. He'd waved it away two previous mornings, telling Ah Lau he preferred to walk, even in this heat. But here the thing was again today, drat the man's unblinking persistence! Why try to explain that the coolies' jogging trot gave him a seasick feeling, and that he got even more queasy at the thought of two men half his size carrying him up- and downhill while he had two adequately functioning legs of his own?

Impenitent and impassive, Ah Lau held out a bamboo umbrella covered with oil paper. With the same impassive firmness Gill refused it and dismissed the chair. The coolies didn't move, however, except to shift their gaze to Ah Lau as though for final instructions. In succinct gesture Ah Lau tilted his head while his eyes traveled the panorama of gray mist above, then he opened the umbrella and proffered it again.

Gill shook his head and strode off. It wasn't exactly raining now, and probably wouldn't for another hour. He'd have ample time to get to the graveyard on the opposite hill where the stonemasons were placing the headstone he'd ordered for Tad's grave. After that he was due to take eleven o'clock coffee with the Senhorita Zena d'Almada. He grimaced, remembering the stiff white card which had arrived last evening with "Please to attend on me and receive my distinguished apologies" scrawled on it in an embellishing hand.

However, a dozen strides under dripping roof gutters shook his determination, for several green stains were already spreading on his white sleeve. At this rate he'd be wearing a polka-dotted jacket by the time he reached the Senhorita's coffee table. He paused irresolutely, until he saw out of the corner of his eye that Ah Lau had anticipated even this. The chair coolies were quietly following ten paces behind. With a wry smile he shook a clenched fist at Ah Lau and climbed in. The coolies adjusted the hood and took up their shafts; but Gill, instead of relaxing back against the cushion, braced either elbow against the chair sides. At least he needn't be sick.

The lane zigzagged down past solid thick-walled houses, past latticed verandas and weed-strangled gardens. Now and again the maroon- and chocolate-colored shutters were ajar, and through the open casements there came the high sweet laughter of women, snatches of soft-voweled talk, the lonely shiver of a lute. At several of the oyster-shell windows dusky half-caste women leaned out to look full at him with big shining eyes and smile provocatively. He wondered if it were as simple a process as stopping the

chair and going upstairs. Or would there be sham formalities first
—introductions to duenna-like aunts and cousins?

Near San Lorenzo Plaza the lane was blocked by a wedge of
people staring at banners and uplifted images moving through
the plaza. He guessed it was probably another Papist procession.
They were incessant here, seemingly. He'd seen three in four
days.

He got out and motioned the bearers to meet him across the
plaza when they could get through. Edging forward between
straw raincoats, paper parasols and mantillas, he wriggled into the
front line as a dozen black-robed figures in the last throes of
sorrow dragged themselves by. There was no telling who, or what,
they were. Their faces were anonymous oblongs of black cloth;
their hands covered with black gloves; even their drums were
hung with crepe. Behind them another band of mourners reeled,
groaning even more piteously.

The wracking dirge of hand drums and the maudlin pitch of
sorrow were harrowing in broad daylight. Gill felt the skin of his
neck prickle with embarrassment; and he glanced around covertly at nearby faces, to find them bemused with a rapture that
made his indifference seem irreverent and profane.

He blinked in bewilderment, turning back to the procession.
Its mood had changed. Some twenty small girls, like dancers in a
ballet, came trouping in angel robes and tinsel wings. Their
lighted candles guttered and dripped wax at each step; their halos
wobbled; and their tarlatan skirts were streaked with rain, but
their pure little treble voices soared angelically in fluted and consecrated song.

Behind the small angels a heavy gilded platform, carried on
the shoulders of four men, came swaying and jolting, momentarily
in danger of dashing the men and itself onto the cobbles, only
to be righted miraculously at the last moment and teeter forward
again. One oblique plunge created a sizable gap. While the crowd
drew supplicating breaths, Gill ducked across to flower beds in
the center of the plaza.

By this time the platform was near enough for him to make out the life-sized image of a woman on a trundle bed. The rich brocade of a medieval skirt flowed out and over the platform in gorgeous disarray.

Pausing curiously as the muted chant of many lips greeted the image, Gill asked a Portuguese man beside him: "Who is that?"

The man's cheeks were streaked with tears. He gulped: "God's mama. She die. We sing whoobub for her." His eyes took on a fervid glitter, and he gazed balefully at Gill. "You insult God's mama crossing her cortege with hat on," he accused.

Nearby voices repeated the accusation in a snarling rustle.

"I'm indeed sorry," Gill gasped in instant apology. "I had no idea. I meant no disrespect." He snatched the offending hat from his head and, in an effort to demonstrate penitence, bowed low towards the image. To do it up brown, he turned, meaning to bow to the pious bystanders. But he saw they were advancing towards him, a knot of flushed half-caste Portuguese malevolently waving arms, walking sticks, and umbrellas.

His jaw dropped in utter amazement. These moody, murmuring, headstrong people! But the next minute he was moving: dodging around a palm tree; sprinting over cobbles towards a bunting barricade of several catchpenny street booths.

Behind them he was lost to view, but he could hear the pound of following feet, and angry shouts. In panic he ducked into the black tunnel of a doorway and flattened himself against the wall. The running feet drew nearer: came abreast; eight, nine, a dozen pair—and then, glory be!—went thrashing on. Their clatter was swallowed by drumbeats and chanting until there was no telling whether they'd gone, or where.

Gill mopped his steaming face, and he eased his laboring lungs as his mind darted from one stratagem to another. He couldn't think what to do. Outrun a mob in this clutter? Expect to take cover amongst Chinese raggle-taggle that came only to his shoulder? Then what? Throw himself on the mercy of this householder here, whoever he was? Ask for refuge? To be let out a back gate? But then where would he be?

Between questions there was growing awareness of a pervading odor in the hallway—it was sickish-sweet and cloying, like nothing he'd ever smelled before.

Suddenly, outside, a military band burst into shattering exuberance. There was the sound of singing, laughter, and a surge of handclapping. Gill crept cautiously to the edge of the doorway and looked out. The procession had ended: onlookers were breaking ranks, straggling after the band in carnival mood, or moving away to houses and shops. He could see nothing of the zealots who'd taken such umbrage at his innocent act. Evidently they too had dispersed and melted into everyday placidity again.

Glad to be rid of the odious sweetness, Gill left the shelter of the doorway. A Chinese barber had already set up shop on the cobbles and was busy with ear spoons digging wax from a customer's ears. Nearby a porcelain riveter squatted on a stool, whirling a hand drill in the halves of a broken plate. Neither they nor their customers even glanced at him as he passed.

He'd taken only three steps when a weight jostled against him. He spun around to find a skeleton-like Chinese collapsing in his arms. The fellow reeled on palsied legs, fingering Gill's arm with nerveless fingers, and murmured a singsong jargon. His breath, his silk jacket, everything about him, stank with the same hateful sweetness Gill had breathed in the doorway.

The man lifted a ravaged face and tried to focus clouded eyes on Gill. The pupils were pinpoints, searching, searching . . . Gill shuddered with a sudden uncontrollable retch as it came to him—the revolting odor was opium smoke, and this wretch was struggling out of its lethal dream.

At that moment two men in servants' dress came flying out the very doorway where Gill had been hiding and made a beeline for the tottering dreamer. Putting their shoulders under his arms, they half led, half carried him back into the house. So—this was the householder he had almost asked to harbor him, Gill thought.

Gripped by a dozen conflicting emotions, he turned towards the corner of the plaza where he saw his chair coolies were waiting. But even in the few paces it took to reach the spot he found himself surrounded by a band of urchins screeching for coppers. To get rid of them he tossed a handful of cash into the air. Before the flickering bits had even hit the pavement, though, the little scrawns were clawing and scratching and biting each other aside with animal ferocity.

Gill settled limply in the chair, glad of it now. As the coolies took the uphill lane leading to the cemetery, he fanned his flushed face with his hat and told himself that hunger and passion and the acts of God crowded mighty close in this green knoll of Macao.

The graveyard smelled of wet earth and decayed flowers, and mosquitoes swarmed from the urns brimming with rain water. The place was a green tangle of moss-grown stones, creepers, and wild gardenias, but Gill found a comforting majesty in the purple bougainvillaea growing up over a pine and fanning out the branches in regal canopy. It would be a perpetually verdant pall, he consoled himself, for a grave so far from home.

He found the coolies were waiting to set the marble marker into position, and he read the simple lines again to himself:

IN MEMORY OF
THADDEUS TYLER BENNETT
WHO DIED MACAO
2nd JUNE 1838
AGED 29

He'd tried to say more. He'd thought of . . . *Beloved brother* . . . of *honored, respected citizen,* and other verbal tributes. Yet when it came to writing them out on paper for the stonemasons yesterday, Tad had seemed to come between him and the paper; and in the end he'd written the simple bare words Tad might have chosen.

He nodded approval of the lettering, and he told them to finish the job. While the men lifted and tugged, he paced green aisles between other tombs and half-obliterated inscriptions to Scotsmen, Hollanders, English, and occasional Americans—many of them ships' officers—who lay in this spot of China, one of them since 1767.

Gill was struck by the tragic similarity binding these men and women and babies into melancholy fellowship—youthfulness. At nineteen, twenty, twenty-two, twenty-four years of age they'd been snuffed out, stone after stone testified, while the babies had not survived even that many months. It was mute proof, if any were needed, of a hard and grueling climate, and of cholera as regularly as the calendar wheeled into the heat of a seven-months summer.

Placing the stone on Tad's plot was soon finished. In a silent service of his own Gill offered the tribute he carried in his heart.

All Macao was having coffee with the Senhorita this morning, Gill found, when he reached the drawing-room, which, Macao fashion, was on the second floor of the house.

He hadn't bargained on a crowd. He'd taken it for granted from the wording on the invitation that he'd been asked to take coffee with the lady herself and, a duenna hovering in the shadows, perhaps another couple sipping discreetly, and just as discreetly taking themselves off in the shortest possible time. Their departure, he'd imagined, would be the Senhorita's signal for a vast rolling of black eyes and a torrent of overdone apologies.

Instead there were more than a hundred and fifty people here, and the Senhorita was as poised and gracious as a princess when she stepped towards him, seemingly out of one of the long cheval mirrors with which the place was lined, and offered her hand. The only recognition she gave to their previous encounter was to pucker full red lips provocatively and murmur: "Do you forgive?" A fleeting clasp of soft fingers seemed to add persuasion.

"Meet these loff-lee people," she said with throbbing enthusiasm, which made three moist and effusive Portuguese ladies seem very special. She led the way to another group, and another, reeling off names which, because they were foreign to him, sounded like the same one being repeated ad infinitum.

When she left him abruptly to greet another influx of callers, Gill couldn't help watching her move amongst the roomful. Her simple white muslin dress—edged here and there in the same yellow satin of the underdress—was light and airy amongst a preponderance of heavy maroons, and established a subtle sort of affinity with the elegant white-and-gold room. Her necklace—pearls alternating with gold filigree—was exquisitely simple, and exquisitely expensive.

Certainly a contrast to yesterday, Gill remarked to himself. Today she created an aroma of verve and charm, enhanced, no doubt, by the gilt luster of the room. Yet it was more than surroundings, he decided. It was something in her lively face with the springy black hair curling around it: in her voice, her gestures, the way she walked . . . something incalculable and, yes, exciting.

In the patio beyond two guitars and a violin were determinedly playing Italian airs, but they could only occasionally be heard above the magpie din of conversation. A ceiling punkah swayed regularly, rhythmically, endlessly, and hand fans fluttered genteelly. But nothing disguised the heat, nor the smell of Macassar hair oil; and the air was so laden with moisture Gill had the feeling that if he were to close his fingers on a handful of it water would trickle between his fingers as from a loaded sponge.

He suspected the guests were a mixture of Macao's elite and pseudo elite. The Governor was there with a gold-braided aide, and there were several English naval officers looking very spruce in their white uniforms. Less than a dozen factors of the British and American community had arrived, and still fewer of their ladies. The remainder were raven-haired, raven-eyed Portuguese —the descendants of land-hungry younger sons of Portuguese grandees come adventuring to Macao, the same as their German, French, and English counterparts a few centuries earlier had gone on the Crusades and grabbed land in Antioch, Sidon, and Acre.

The men had a proud, moody look that was without eagerness, without perseverance. The women, Gill guessed, loved love and the process of exciting it. Fashion, obviously, was an accomplice they trusted implicitly—for all wore identically ballooning sleeves which looked as though they'd been stuffed with pillows; and while no more than half had wound Bombay scarves into outlandish turbans atop their heads, the other half looked as though they yearned to. It gave the formal room a bizarre look—as though a convention of laundresses had assembled in the wrong hall.

At one point Gill became conscious of his own clothes. Not expecting a party, he'd worn makeshift white trousers and an odd jacket. With a roomful dressed to the nines, he decided he probably looked like a poor relation in hand-me-downs. But he was more conscious of the inner him—venturing into this glossy unfamiliar social precinct, without warning, without background training. What in suds name was there to banter about with strangers? What to do with the overwhelming number of hands he'd acquired?

He found he didn't have to do a thing. It was all surprisingly easy. If he stood still, someone was sure to speak to him—a gentleman, a lady, or maybe two—in the casual friendliness of exiles everywhere. "Is Macao to your liking?" "Do you bear with the climate?" they asked, and he answered what he really felt and thought. By and by he felt assured enough to move about more freely: to the gallery for coffee; to the collation table for another delectable confection of egg yolk and sugar, which was evidently a favorite Macanese sweet.

On his second trip he met the Senhora Pinto there, helping herself today, and bounteously. While she ate, the plump little tadpole seemed bent on telling him some interminable story in a ripe mixture of Portuguese and broken English, which turned out to be as unintelligible to him as her Portuguese. He nodded and smiled, agreeably he hoped, until he caught a startled look on her face, and hastily wiped the smile off. Whereupon she beckoned him to follow her and meet her husband, it turned out—a flaccid little man with a broad blunt nose and an ambiguous face. He was splendidly beruffled, though, at throat and wrists.

Pinto was in earnest conversation with three Portuguese men when the Senhora arrived to introduce Gill, and then bustled away. Pinto presented the others as the Senhors Barretto, Pereira-Marquess, and Pessanho; and they courteously switched to English to include the newcomer in their talk. It was about opium.

Gill couldn't believe his luck. Lesson Number One in opium! He concentrated all faculties on the job of listening and absorbing. The effort brought perspiration oozing from every pore, but fortunately, he told himself, his continual mopping of the brow wasn't a giveaway in today's humidity.

The names and trade terms confused him mightily, but he repeated each one inwardly, and filed it away carefully in his memory . . . Patna, top-grade, and Malwa, second-best: they were Bengal's two "black earth" products, called that, he supposed, because the balls looked as though they'd been rolled from mud. Bombay evidently produced an inferior "white skin"—the derivation of this name defeated him: likewise the "red skin" from Madras. Third-rate Turkish, he tabulated, used to adulterate better varieties, was collected in Smyrna, transshipped in New York, and—he couldn't help chuckling over the sequel—arrived out East so regularly on American clippers that Chinese buyers thought Turkey was a part of the United States.

The summer boom, it seemed, had boosted Patna to five hundred and eighty dollars a chest; and the price was expected to go even higher next month. Big houses and established independents were wading into the market with vast money rolls in an effort to tie up the Calcutta and Bombay new crop, consequently freezing out small dealers. India agents, scouting the countryside for additional supplies, were offering unheard-of premiums. Pinto and his colleagues related these happenings in high glee, chuckling over the march they'd stolen in a special joint buy of a whacking lot of Damaun in Goa, which they'd brought straight to Macao on Portuguese ships—meaning they'd escaped port taxes.

Gill's casual inquiry into these taxes met with lugubrious shaking of heads and doleful eye-rolling. Finally Barretto—making quite sure the Governor and his aide weren't within hearing distance—whispered that Macao had sunk to its present low state of prosperity, that it was no longer the thriving opium depot it once was, all because the Governor had chosen to put a levy of sixty-five dollars per chest on British and American transshipments. *He* said it was to bribe Chinese officials into turning their backs on harbor activity, Barretto hissed, but everybody knew whose pocket it was going into.

Gill shook his head over the irony—Portuguese greed had *driven* his own countrymen and the British to developing Lintin into an opium emporium. Chinese greed would *probably drive* them out of Canton to an island of their own. His idea wasn't pure fantasy, then. He hadn't been talking utter nonsense at Manning's the other day.

He kept thanking Providence that he happened to be right where he was at this minute. With the four biggest Portuguese operators in opium! What luck that he'd met the rotund little Senhora at the Mannings'! What absolutely sublime luck that she'd been annoyed? startled? bored? by his clumsiness at language divination and had fobbed him off on her husband! The blood-tingling—the staggering!—ins-and-outs of this game! The iron nerves it required. The stout heart . . . speculating thousands, maybe millions, on Peking's variable whim!

People and faces moving in perimeter meant nothing. If only— he hoped, he prayed—the quartet would remain intact a little longer, stimulating each other into talking shop! He noticed the bright-faced, indefatigable Zena, at two different intervals, come bowing and smiling into nearby groups. She hovered long enough to catch the trend of conversation in his group, he noted, but she didn't interrupt with social inanities—give her full marks. She listened without appearing to, and then went skimming off to bestow smiling hospitality elsewhere.

Gill was quick to prod with questions whenever the talk dwindled. He particularly wanted to know their opinion on the likelihood of Peking's clamping excessively restrictive measures on coastal shipping. Pessanho and Pereira-Marquess smiled, and shrugged shoulders in unconcern. Their dealing preference was second-quality Damaun, they said, and there'd always be buyers for it, one place or another.

It was the big plunger Barretto who gave Gill the most significant steer. The market was building to peak, he predicted, in a matter of weeks—four, perhaps five—pushed up by present restrictions. It would maintain, or collapse overnight, depending upon whether, and when, Peking relaxed. Barretto refused to guess that one. But Pinto smiled, his eyes twinkling wickedly: he had it on A-1 authority, from Jardine himself, that the Hong merchant Mowqua was confident Peking would legalize sales at the New Year's audience. Elevated eyebrows, polite reservation, malicious skepticism . . . was it genuine, or assumed? Gill wondered if a man in this trade dared confide even in himself.

The group broke up, each gentleman bowing and moving away in an opposite direction, and Gill bowing to each in return. But he didn't move from the spot. He stood stock-still, his head spinning with ideas . . . *peak market in four weeks, supply scarce, big money rolls.* . . . He had to get into it! He *had* to. But where to find more capital? He had the ten thousand he'd brought with him from the sale of Bennett Brothers. But that was measly! Chicken feed compared to the sums these operators were tossing in.

What did Sur Manoel mean to propose? Was there a glimmer of hope there? The little man's opium operations, Gill had gathered from remarks dropped by the quartet, had suddenly, phenomenally, increased. And this other interesting little morsel he'd picked up . . . their hostess wasn't all seductive graces; she had a remarkably sound head for business: she was actively taking a hand in the business she'd inherited, and already had her pretty fingers in several money-making local enterprises.

Gill looked up to see the lady herself approaching him.

"You are making friends, yes? My coffee is *muito bem*, yes?" she asked brightly.

Gill answered a convincing yes to both questions.

She smiled, but studied him shrewdly through veiling eyelashes a second before she said: "Please to remain after the other guests. I would talk."

"To convince me our first meeting was a mistake?" he teased, hiding his surprise.

She made a small face at him. "No. Another somesing." She said it coolly, without eye play or wile, and turned away to another group.

Gill noticed the drawing-room had emptied perceptibly, but that a considerable number still clustered about the collation table on the gallery. To kill time he made his way there again, thinking to get a cup of coffee—real coffee being a grand treat after the burnt-wheat variety he'd had aboard ship.

As he passed a settee he noticed the sole occupant was a plain, middle-aged Englishwoman with a formidable beak of a nose and bluebell eyes. He waited at the coffee table a couple of minutes until a fresh pot was brought, and, on sudden impulse, picked up a second cup and carried it to the beaked dowager.

"I was lucky enough to get a fresh brew. I thought you might relish it," he said affably.

"Never drink the filthy muck!" the lady said trenchantly, but without ill-humor.

Gill chuckled, unabashed. "In that case I'll drink both."

And he did, standing at ease beside her, forgetting her nose, and thinking only how incredibly blue her eyes were. He bowed as he finished the second cup. "You have done me a favor, ma'am," he said. "I'd only have had one, but for your disrelish."

"You're an intrepid young man," she observed. "Usually my nose frightens the male animal under forty."

Gill found himself laughing easily. "Perhaps they don't see your eyes in good light. When you decide to be in a rage—do you put on a blindfold?"

The dowager laughed. It was a short barking sound. "H'mph!" she commented, and swung around to look him over from head to foot with the rude stare of a horse trader. "You look alive," she said authoritatively. "About time—we need new blood here. The last lot were damned anemic. Not enough red blood in 'em to baste a pigeon!"

Gill chuckled.

"I can't abide a man without opinions—good or bad!" she announced. "What are yours?"

"Bad," Gill confessed readily.

The barking sound was louder this time. "I want to hear 'em. Not now. I've other calls to get through this morning. But—Saturday week. Come racing with us at eight. That means having breakfast aboard the longboat on the way to the course. I've a couple of fillies to make your eyes gleam. Four-legged fillies, that is!" She got up, agitating flounces and settling her bonnet as though they thoroughly irritated her.

Gill was quick with thanks for the invitation, and offered: "May I hand you to your chair?"

"If you'll just signal those drooping lilies in uniform at the other end of the gallery—they're my escort. Although what they'd protect me from, Heaven alone knows! At the moment they don't look fit enough to cope with a sneeze!" She strode towards the pair of young officers—whom Gill had chatted with earlier—turned midway, and in a peremptory bellow said: "Eight Saturday week," and bore off with flounces flying.

Gill watched her appreciatively, and turned to see Sur Manoel standing nearby, regarding him with dewy admiration.

"My dear, dear Bennett," the little man laughed softly, "you quite take my breath away. Landed only four days ago, without an introduction, without a sponsor. And here you are—taking coffee at the home of the toast of Macao! Your company at racing besought by Lady Prophet herself!"

Gill brushed the unearned awe aside. "It's Macao's courteous hospitality you must admire," he protested. "Not the lucky recipient."

Sur Manoel elevated furry eyebrows. "Lady Prophet is wife to Admiral Sir Garth Prophet, commander of the good Victoria's naval forces presently in these waters." He enunciated each syllable punctiliously. "Lady Prophet is not renowned in Macao for courtesy or hospitality."

He paused and fixed his dewy eyes on Gill intently. "I am indeed interested in what you so charmingly call your 'luck.' I anticipate our meeting at my house this afternoon—eagerly!" He spread his woman's hands, ducked his head, and went bouncing off.

The talk with Zena never materialized. As the guests thinned out, some six or eight Portuguese gentlemen determinedly remained—Sur Manoel was one, Pinto another, but without the Senhora. They were calling for a gaming table, and a round of écarté with the hostess before tiffin. Zena agreed with a sprightly smile. "We have an hour, yes. We play this instant." In her wonderfully flexible intonation she made it sound a fascinating prospect.

Next second she put her hands to her forehead in distracted apology and took several steps towards Gill. "But—I am forget that I would talk with Mr. Bennett." She spun around appealingly to the group. "I—I thought to persuade that he come with American guitar—call banjo, yes?—and teach me those so quaint slave songs New York sings now?" She was facing Gill now, hands clasped in mock entreaty.

Tepid exclamations of encouragement, together with several blank stares, came from the clustering bystanders. Gill could only murmur that he'd be honored.

She stepped slightly closer, cautioning him with a wink that only he could see. "Ah, *muito bem*. I do thank you, senhor. We have first lesson soon, yes? Tomorrow, yes? This hour? You agree? Ah, *muito bem.* I am happy. Good-by! Good-by!"

She spun around, half dancing, her heels clicking on the marble tiles as she waved to the others with both hands. "Come! Make promenade with me to the card room!" Then, breaking into an engulfing flow of Portuguese, she herded the gentlemen along the gallery and into what was evidently the card room at the far end. The impassive black shadow of a duenna went too, the fan in her hand wagging like a metronome.

Gill got his castor from a footman done up like a Rossini tenor, and went thoughtfully down the stairs and out into the noonday glare of a savage sun which had just emerged from the mists. He had plenty to think about . . . Why did the lady want to talk to him? The banjo lesson, obviously, being a red herring. Did she have any inkling of his meeting this afternoon with Sur Manoel? And what proposal, he wondered mightily, did that gentleman wish to make? Perhaps . . . perhaps by five o'clock he'd have a proposal of his own to make!

CHAPTER VII

MACAO,
September 1838

Sur Manoel sat propped behind his vast desk like a dandified puppet, except that his little pock-marked face was more animated, more spirited, more anxious to please. As though for punctuation as he talked, he nodded his head incessantly, ducking and shaking it in a dozen vivacious variations, but still his greased hair lay as slick on the small dome as though it had been painted there. At this moment, however, he sat very erect, very rigid, watching Gill's face across the desk with a devouring intensity.

But Gill looked baffled. "I couldn't have heard you right," he said. "It doesn't make sense—the Chinese only allow twenty-five ships of Portuguese registry into Macao each year. *Here*—a Portuguese colony?"

"How penetrating, to hit upon the crux!" Sur Manoel exclaimed, slapping the desk as though it were Gill's back. "Let me explain. That is, if you permit me to recount the merest crumb of history?"

"Certainly."

"Thank you. Ah, I forget myself . . . some tangerine brandy, perhaps? To offset the dryness of the subject? Of course, the very thing!" With a placating smile he squirmed up from the desk, opened a panel in the wall, and held out a cut-crystal decanter filled with liqueur as vividly tangerine as its name. "From Cintra," he said with smiling reverence. "From beautiful, beautiful Cintra!" He poured a glass for Gill and stood hovering for the verdict.

Gill put the glass to his lips. God-awful sweet, like drinking candy, he thought, and no brandy bite whatever. But with those moist pleading eyes on him, he forced a smack from his lips and said: "Real tangerine flavor, that." The tone seemed to come out flat, and to compensate for it he made a business of holding his glass so slanting rays of the afternoon sun changed it into a sparkling rainbow, and then overdid enthusiasm when he added: "The color's as striking as the taste!"

"Ah-h, you appreciate it? I'm immensely gratified." Sur Manoel danced back to his high chair. "Felicitously enough, I have this very week received a new shipment of it from Portugal. It is my pleasure to send you some. A case."

Gill was horrified. Was there no avoiding this man's tenacious generosity? He'd been so chary, arriving here, to keep his eyes from lighting on a single piece of bric-a-brac or possible gift. "No, I couldn't possibly accept it," he said.

The little man's eyes clouded. He shook his head despondently, holding a hand over his heart. "Senhor Bennett," he lisped forlornly, "is it your intention to be cruel?"

"No. Certainly not, but I . . ." Gill floundered in annoyance with himself for not thinking of the right words to side-step this second gift.

A smile broke through Sur Manoel's gloom. "Oh, I *am* relieved. You do reassure me. Then—it is finish. You accept. And now we speak no more of trivia. We speak history."

He cleared his throat and leaned across the desk as far as his truncated torso would stretch, to say sepulchrally: "Macao *is* Portuguese. It has been for nearly three centuries. By decree of a Ming Emperor. But since the Mings are no more, this Ch'ing dynasty—these *upstart Manchu horsemen* ignore the bargain. They demand paper proof of the Ming decree."

He paused, fished in his coat pocket, and drew forth an exquisitely fashioned ivory snuff bottle tinted in faded carmine and hyacinth, and sat fingering it gently in his incredibly delicate hand before he continued: "But *we—we* contrive to keep our documents out of their thieving hands. So the negotiations drag on— for generations. Meanwhile they demand rent money for the land this colony occupies. And they erect barriers to prevent our growing too important. This thing of the ships is one such barrier—twenty-five, and *only twenty-five,* ships of Portuguese registry may enter Macao in one year!"

No emotion showed in his doelike eyes, unless it was in the fixity with which he watched Gill. Then the lids closed down and he twisted the tourmaline stopper off the little bottle in his hands, fastidiously applied the snifter blade to one nostril, and then the other. He continued the ritual with sneezes and a flourish of silk handkerchief: stowed the ivory trinket in one pocket and the handkerchief in another, and leaned forward again.

"Do you see where we arrive?" he asked softly. "Do you see that the old names in the colony's shipping—Pinto, Barretto, Noronha—monopolize the registry because they were established long ago. Me, I am squeezed to acquire three places out of the twenty-five. *Three*—when I could use many!"

Gill's mind did gymnastics, but he couldn't make out where this talk was heading. He tried to keep the blankness he felt off his face, but because some comment seemed to be required, he asked: "You wish more?"

"Por Dios, I *must!*" Sur Manoel wasn't dolorous now. He squirmed and wriggled in an ecstasy of delight. "Six, eight . . . who knows how many I must have? My interests mushroom themselves. Now I get monopoly on all Filipino cigars sold in England and in America. I have a contract to build a lighthouse in Manila. Another to establish a bank there. A dozen, two dozen, other prospects. Here, there, elsewhere . . . IF I have ships!"

"How do you propose to acquire them?" Gill blinked, thinking of the inevitable *squeeze*, of bartered negotiations. But all the while wondering if the Portugaler would say piracy.

"*Through American registry!*" Sur Manoel pronounced precisely, and then leaned back as though he'd opened a jam jar.

Gill stared at him.

Sur Manoel nodded portentously. "Yes," he said in an augmented whisper, "by having an American partner who'd register the ships—as I buy them—under his country's flag."

Gill jerked forward abruptly. "Man alive! It can't be as simple as that! What about restrictions—laws? About the number of American ships allowed in Macao?"

Sur Manoel's eyes beamed. "There are no restrictions. No laws against it," he enunciated succinctly.

Gill's mind went racing, hurdling, leaping ahead. The Portugaler had let loose a dozen roseate phantoms which danced before him now like veiled houris, beckoning, enticing, dazzling. It was an incredible stroke of luck. And yet—not lunatic, nor erratically devious, but eminently logical. A practical commercial transaction. As simple as selling a pound of Dragon Well green over the counter. This customer would pay a price for ship's registry; he,

Gill, had ship's registry to sell at the market. All orderly, all immaculately legal, and no treading on anyone's toes! Why not?

"Exactly what would the partner receive in exchange?" Gill asked.

"A handsome suite of offices, prominently located, with his name and title on it," the penetrating whisper catalogued. "And, since he'd only have to lift his hand occasionally to sign registry documents, he'd have ample time to carry on his own affairs—*whatever* they might be."

"And what else?" Gill asked.

There was half a moment's silence, then the whisper asked: "You would expect more?"

"Yes."

"What?"

"In lieu of salary I should like a drawing account—call it a revolving credit—of, say, ten thousand dollars, interest-free, made available to me immediately we sign the articles of partnership," Gill said evenly, keeping all trace of inner excitement out of his voice. This was what he'd come to beg, to borrow at high interest, to raise somehow. Now he could ask it as a legitimate part of a deal.

"You are a hard bargainer, senhor," Sur Manoel said, but the whisper was neither augmented nor more strident.

"Not hard—*realistic*," Gill corrected. "You are in the market for an American partner. The commodity is extremely scarce. I can supply it. But a suite of offices, rent-free, is not adequate inducement."

Sur Manoel regarded him with soft, almost fraternal eyes. "Your decisions are as nimble as I suspected they might be." Then he got to his feet, bowed punctiliously, and said: "I agree."

Gill's first thought was that he should have asked for twenty thousand, it was so easy.

He slid forward to the edge of his chair, staring for a concentrated moment at this stranger, this foreigner, this alien ally he was about to espouse as partner. Then he asked: "You guarantee me your word there are no restrictions, no prohibitions whatever, on American registry?"

Sur Manoel's chest swelled prodigiously with the long breath he drew in, but his voice when it came out had none of this wind behind it. In his lisping miniature he said: "I guarantee."

Gill didn't ask himself what this guarantee was worth. He didn't ask a half dozen other hows and whys. He'd made his decision. He was ready. A boyish smile lit his face as he gathered his long legs under him to return Sur Manoel's bow in kind. "I salute you—with abundant hope for our joint success, partner," he said.

They clasped hands on the pledge. But when Gill drew his hand away, he was careful to sit down again in the chair, lest he tower above this proud little man during the time they would itemize the immediate course of their alliance.

Vaguely, in the middle of the night, Gill had been aware it was raining. He hadn't felt the warning switch of wind come whipping through the doors and set the tiny shell window-panes to rattling. It was the first big impudent drops of rain, bouncing on the tiles like dried beans in a tin pail, that roused him. In another minute the uproar had begun—the crescendo tattoo of a torrent hammering on roof and shutters. He had lain listening to its tumult until gradually the rain-rinsed air grew perceptibly cooler, so he could pull a sheet over his naked body and find it a comfort instead of muffling torment. By then the fury had moderated to a repetitious monotone of lulling sound, and he had relaxed into deep, refreshing sleep.

In the morning he walked directly from bed to gallery to look out over the new and still incredible universe he was inhabiting. Today, peering between the dripping arches, he found a new scene created. Rooftops and hills were flattened under a dense gray weight, with spires and domes so many props holding off oblivion. Like the squawk of destiny a flight of geese passed low overhead, coming out of nothingness and disappearing into more of the same, leaving only the memory of beautiful, unerring flight.

Gill looked his idling fill—while the green knobs of islands disappeared without a trace and banners of mist furled across anchored ships to shroud their toothpick masts and spars until they too lost substance and dissolved into etched lines floating on a gray void.

At breakfast Ah Lau put a slice of yellow papaya before him, and Gill found considerable relish in the melon-like fruit. But when he dipped his spoon into the boiled eggs he snorted with distaste. "Phew. They taste of herring!"

Ah Lau inclined his head in majestic gravity. "Suppose chickee have eat-ee fish, no can taste allee same cow," he observed.

Gill laughed. "I'm not asking for eggs that will pass for beef-steak," he said. "Just those from a landlubber chicken. Tell your friend the chicken man to feed his birds on corn or rice."

Ah Lau answered oracularly from behind closed eyelids. "My flen have catchee plentee chilo. Suppose pay rice to chickee, he chilo have plentee empty belly."

"That's a point," Gill admitted.

Ah Lau smiled cheerfully. But Gill's answering smile was wry and twisted, for he'd remembered the rack-boned starvelings here —the impotent hordes in every street and alley, dragging, hauling, lugging great burdens—animated only by the passion to exist.

Suddenly it came to him in a flood of unexpected revelation . . . *he'd never been poor!* He'd never known the scurvy, grinding emptiness of this kind of hunger. His shame of darned elbows and scuffed shoes was little and paltry. The cramped brick cottage and faded chairs had been opulence compared to these teeming, jostling, strident warrens. The realization pulsed through him, shaming and yet exhilarating, for he suddenly felt a surge of release from the burden he'd carried ever since he could remember.

He turned back to cold eggs, sopping them up, uncomplainingly now, with limp toast. As he put down the empty coffee

cup he remarked: "I still wish the chicken man would feed herring to his children instead of his chickens."

"Chilo no can eat-ee fish head. Chickee can," Ah Lau explained
with the placid patience of a kindergarten teacher.

Gill settled a chair in a protected spot on the gallery and opened
the latest issue of the *Chinese Repository*, the quarterly a group
of Protestant missionaries were putting out on a hand-set press
in Canton. He found the articles were local, but general—Chinese
history, Peking doings, travel descriptions, essays, discussions,
and current events: all written with a leisurely and liberal view-
point, but printed in such spider-track characters it was tiring to
read.

He laid it aside to pick up the more vigorous Canton *Register*,
the favorite newspaper of the free merchants, a weekly whose first
editor, ten years ago, had been a nephew of Washington Irving.
Opium prices were quoted in one column, side by side with the
news item that "ten independent opium smugglers had been
strangled by order of the Viceroy in his zealous clean-up campaign." Interesting . . . the Viceroy, he'd heard yesterday, was
an important dealer in the stuff, carrying it in his own fleet, which
flew his official flag, straight upriver to Canton's boom market
. . . a tailor advertised "Gentlemen's bespoken suits of heaviest
quality pongee silk $2." There was "Superior Sherry in butts and
hogsheads from the House of Duff, Gordon, $2–$12, and a few
cases of excellent Port Wine at $6 per dozen in cases of three
dozen each." And "The Society for Diffusion of Useful Knowledge" in Canton invited new members. . . .

He tossed the newspapers aside impatiently and took to pacing
tiles which shone like onyx after the rain, thrashing over a dozen
schemes which raced in and out of his mind.

Two hours later Gill—with his banjo as a precaution—climbed
into the inevitable sedan chair at his door and let the coolies take
him downhill towards Zena's house. But when the veiling mists
parted and a shaft of sunlight lacquered the banyan leaves in San
Lorenzo Plaza, he got out quickly, stretched his legs, and mo-

tioned the coolies to follow him. He felt eager, bouyant, excited.
He wanted to talk to Barretto, to Pinto as soon as ever he was
finished with this twiddling engagement with the Senhorita . . .
He'd cut it short: he'd make excuses, and get on to important
things.

He crossed the plaza, and was about to turn into the Calçada do
Bom Jesus when an ambling screen of baskets, lashed and stacked
every which way on a vendor's shoulder pole, blocked his way. Gill
skip-stepped to dodge around it, only to bump blindly into a
sprinting figure coming from the opposite direction. He felt something sharp and hard prod into his ribs, then fall heavily onto
his boot. It was a bundle wrapped in rags and raw-silk wadding.
The movement of his foot started it unwinding until the base
of a silver candelabrum showed through.

There was a choked cry, a flurried scramble, and a scooping
up of bundle. But when the furtive figure turned to dart off without even looking up, Gill put a hand out instinctively and caught
hold of a small thin arm.

"No! No!" a squirming vixen spat at him, trying to wrench
away from his grasp, kicking with both feet and flailing with
elbows, but all the while clutching the bundle tighter in locked
arms. In the scuffle her hat fell off.

It was Su-ling, the boat-girl.

The girl's eyes blazed at him in fury and panic. "Belong my!
Plen-tee belong my!" She gritted the words out between bared
lips, squirming frantically again. When she saw he had no intention of loosening his grasp, she bent swiftly and bit his hand.

Gill jerked away in pain, and she bounded off amongst the
laughing bystanders like a bouncing ball. Not to disappear from
sight, though. Some twenty yards beyond, separated from him by
a fence of staring humans, she stood poised for further flight while
she watched him sullenly.

Gill wrapped a handkerchief about his bleeding wrist. Had the
little wretch snatched this silver candlestick from some foreign
house to turn it into cash at the first pawnbroker's? He felt he

ought to do something. But what? There was no such thing as a policeman anywhere about. He couldn't go chasing the little savage all over Macao to find out how, or why, she had the bundle. Besides, he had other things to do.

He shrugged and continued on his way, turning some fifty yards beyond to look back and see whether or not Su-ling had retrieved her hat. She had. But, curiously enough, she was creeping along warily behind him, as though intent on seeing where he went. Twice, before he turned jutting corners in the twisting *calçada*, he glanced back, and thought he made her out behind, still following.

At Zena's the footman led him upstairs to a cool morning room above the patio, where the mother-of-pearl panes gave a soft undersea light. Zena caught his reflection in a mirror where she stood straightening gauzy-green flounces of a dress the color of new apples. She whirled around impulsively and came running across the parquetry floor on staccato heels to stop, stare at the banjo, and break into rollicking laughter.

Then she noticed the bloodstained handkerchief on his wrist and sobered instantly, to come plucking at his sleeve and examine the wound. "Someone harm you? You were attacked?" She was all sympathy.

Gill shook his head ruefully. "Got caught in a street scuffle, and someone bit my hand," he passed it off. "It isn't deep."

The Senhorita became practical at once, dispatching the footman for warm water, carbolic, and lint. When it came she bathed the blue indentations Su-ling's teeth had made, dressed the wound herself with quick purposeful fingers, and then got him a brandy.

Minutes later, sipping the excellent brandy, it wasn't her deft fingers he remembered. It was her nearness as she had bent over his wrist, and the frangipani sweetness drifting up from her hair. And it came over him how lunatic it was for him to sit here drinking brandy with this heady creature as a preliminary to talking high business with Barretto and Pinto.

But he went on sipping brandy and, over the rim of the glass, smiled at her. The duenna wasn't present; and, from the small glint in Zena's black-set eyes, he had a notion that supernumerary would not appear.

Yet the Senhorita seemed in no hurry to tell him whatever it was she'd had on her mind yesterday. She was attentive and cordial, though a little distrait as she toyed with her fan, watched several dragonflies darting about the patio, and ventured the hope that they weren't advance warning of a typhoon, as the Chinese thought them to be.

Gill told her he didn't know how many of them it took to make the forecast dependable, and repeated the rhyme Captain Macy had taught him about typhoons:

> *"June, too soon,*
> *July, stand by,*
> *August, look out you must,*
> *September, remember,*
> *October, all over."*

Smiling wistfully, and yet shuddering at the same time, she confessed: "Always I have fear of big wind—black fear. But enough, you and me . . . we talk happier things, yes?" she asked in her pleading way, and began chatting brightly, and at random, about the opera troupe arriving from South America next week; about the grand costume ball the Pintos were planning at Sans Souci; and then diffidently she suggested that since the banjo was there perhaps they should really have some music.

By this time Gill was nettled and impatient. Was this merely to be a social call? Had he misunderstood the signals? Did she actually have something to propose? Or had she changed her mind overnight? Being with her wasn't an ordeal—far from it! But not this morning, when he wanted to get along to Barretto, to Pinto, to one of the opium operators, and sound them out on the possibility of his buying his way into a deal with them.

He put his empty brandy glass down and begged off playing until the bandage on his hand wouldn't interfere. And, he mentioned casually, he must get along shortly to call upon Senhor Barretto.

Zena's glance became hesitant and dropped to the fan in her lap. "Senhor Barretto—he is *muito* big buyer, yes?" she observed. "Too big. . . ."

"Too big for what?" Gill asked.

Zena's small laugh was slightly flustered. "Ah, senhor, I think I am make little mistake yesterday. I am too quick—too with eagerness for talk to you. Today I am tell myself, 'No, Zena, no! Shame for make mistake.'"

"What mistake?" Gill prompted indulgently. He was only mildly interested in what all this was about. But, after all, he'd drunk her brandy, and would be coming back for another soon, he hoped.

"Yesterday I am busy hostess, yes?" she explained half apologetically. "Not so busy, *ola*, but I hear the Senhor asking opium questions. He is excite for opium buying, I say myself, and me I know where is little opium—so, quick, I want talk with you. But today"—she ducked an embarrassed face behind the open fan momentarily—"I am better sense. I . . ."

Gill leaned forward in rigid seriousness. "You know where some opium can be bought?" he asked.

Zena shook her curls in quick negation. "No, I have decide too difficult for me. Me—I am too coward."

"What grade?" Gill wouldn't be deflected.

"Patna."

"For delivery when?"

"Two days."

"What price?"

"One hundred chests—thirty thousand."

Gill drew breath as soberly as he could. He strove for reality as a shipwrecked seaman might stretch for hard sand beneath his feet. *One hundred percent profit in four, or five, days!* "Suppose you tell me more," he said flatly.

He held her glance with insistent eyes; and gradually hers lost their flustered look, to become coolly impersonal, shrewd even, and she leaned forward in her chair and scanned his face. For a disconnected moment she seemed to be appraising him intently. Gill had the feeling she was reaffirming some previous judgment she had made, for, with a conclusive nod of her head, she jumped abruptly to her feet and began to pace the room and talk in a low, tight voice.

"Me—I am not comfortable thinking on opium buying. I am unlike it. Business head I have, maybe, for buying silk—these crepes, brocades, pongees, I can see with my eyes. Dinner sets, screens, the same. For the buyer is there always. But opium, phut, it change up, change down, phut . . . and where is the buyer? Gone!"

Gill tried to gentle her with: "The risks are big. But so are the profits."

She halted to stare hard at him. "You have not the fear?"

Gill shrugged. "You haven't told me the deal yet."

In a catlike movement she caught up a spindly gilt chair, planting it squarely in front of him before he could guess her intention or rise to help. She didn't mean to woo him with her sultry nearness, though. There was neither guile nor wile in her as she sat tensely speaking to his mind.

"That is the wrong of it for me. That is why I say no . . . it does not make itself into a deal. It is single fact—*one hundred chests certified Patna selling for thirty thousand dollars.* Now—immediately. Or it vanish."

"Sold where?"

She glared at him balefully for a moment before she gritted out the words reluctantly: "At rendezvous two days away with Parsee vessel from Goa. Portuguese captain. Me, I discover through special Noronha Company papers. But—one hundred chests of opium are a big nothing without buyers. How, where are buyers to be found in the so blue sea? No, no, senhor—I have sleep well last night. I would sleep *muito bem* tonight, and every night. Me—I kiss opium with the big kiss good-by." She sprang to her feet tempestuously, to walk across the room, to whirl around, and come prowling back in gliding strides like a goaded cat.

Gill felt himself go dizzy and tremble over the sorcery in this opportunity. The cords twitched in his neck as he kept himself from letting loose an Indian war whoop. He'd thrashed through a dozen plans to approach Barretto for even the merest toehold, and here—here was a ladder practically to himself. A straight buy of thirty thousand, and a straight sale two days later for sixty thousand! It was mad. It was incredible. One of those freaks of crazy luck which sometimes happen to beginners.

Gill jumped to his feet to tell her out of his confidence: "Finding buyers isn't a problem. The waters of Chinchow Bay and Amoy are filled with them, I'm told. They cluster alongside before a ship's anchor is got down."

"Ship? You have one?" Zena demanded.

No, he didn't have a ship. He didn't even have thirty thousand dollars, Gill told himself in reckless impudence. But he had opportunity by the tail, and he didn't mean to let go yet.

Zena was pacing again, until she halted with an idea twisting her mobile face. She turned and came creeping to Gill's side to whisper: "A Noronha ship—maybe?"

"Of course!" Gill exulted, smacking one hand against the other. And now he laughed, loud and full and infectiously. "Zena, think . . . we stand to double our money in less than seven days!"

Zena's red tongue licked wet anticipatory lips. Then her eyes stormed. "*Our* money . . . no, no, *amigo,* not so fast! Maybe I loan Noronha ship, *maybe.* But money . . . that thirty thousand is *yours,* yes?"

Gill shook his head. "I don't possess thirty thousand. Twenty is all I've got—but how long do I have to raise the extra ten?"

"Four hours."

"Oh no. That's not enough time. . . ."

Zena shrugged despondent shoulders. "I do not make the time. A ship must leave here in four hours to meet Parsee ship at rendezvous two days from here," she explained, tapping her closed fan against the palm of one hand like the contrapuntal beat of a distant, but insistent, orchestra. "Rendezvous does not wait. No rendezvous, then no opium." And now her voice took on a throbbing organ note.

Gill didn't notice. He was far too consumed, too quickened with the urgency of the moment. This was his chance, his plunge into the market, to match brains with brains. And afterwards, with capital, he'd be drafting, planning, organizing a hundred purchases and a hundred sales—two, three hundred!—manipulating countless strings, each attached to a pot of gold. It didn't occur to him to feint, to side-step with polite flourish, or stall for time. The decision had to be made here and now. He'd tackle it willingly, with zest, with humble thanksgiving that charmed luck had found him. He strode towards the door. "I'll try! Maybe— on the guarantee of this deal—I can raise it in a hurry."

Zena came running to stay him with two hands on his arm. "Wait!" Her voice sounded a deeper chord, and she gazed up at him with surprised and wondering eyes. "You would risk all—all you own, and more too—on this *chance?*"

"Not chance—*certainty!*" he told her. "Everyone says the market will hold high for four, five, six weeks, at least. This buy will be sold in less than one week . . . finished, through!"

A slow smile seemed to come up from Zena's innermost being, to curve her red lips and light black fire in her eyes. "I am do it, then," she declared. "I am have courage also. To supply Noronha ship *Pombal* . . . and ten thousand."

"Hooray!" Gill shouted, and on sudden impulse he clasped her two hands in his and stooped to kiss one and then the other.

She disengaged herself hurriedly, to whirl away and throw her head back proudly. "Me—I have dreams too. Many dreams. I would have my ships carry more than other men's cargoes. I would buy and sell *my cargoes* by the shipload. Ivory, hemp, pearls, cigars, bolts of silk! Not common pongees. Bah, no! Elegant brocades—the most elegant! *My* ships with *my* cargoes supplying *my* warehouses—everywhere!" She threw her arms out as though embracing the universe.

Gill nodded in a happy daze, feeling unfamiliar chords in his being twanging in response to this unpredictable partner he'd suddenly acquired. She looked in that moment, to him, like one of the flaunting clipper figureheads come to life—superbly impelling and invulnerable. A passionate woman who—glory be! —had passionate convictions about what she wanted.

She smiled at him, and it was like wine pouring over him. The next minute he was gathering her into his arms and kissing her neck, her ear . . . "To seal the bargain, partner," he whispered. Then he found her mouth—as warm and eager as his own—and he had the feeling every blood vessel in his body was about to burst.

It was she who whimpered and pushed herself away, to stare up at him with a queer, almost frightened look and wring her hands indecisively.

But only for a minute. Then, as though shedding an unfamiliar garment which didn't belong to her, she twitched her shoulders . . . and was herself again—poised, certain, practical—telling him she must send a message out to the *Pombal*, that her boxes must be ready to go aboard in two hours. . . .

Gill filled his lungs with frangipani sweetness. He was dreaming, he told himself: none of this was true. His head was going in circles—from Zena? From brandy? From giddy mathematics? Or the combination of all three? He couldn't tell. Then her words began to filter through . . . He jerked around. *"Your* boxes? *You* intend going with me to the rendezvous?" he asked.

She drew back in astonishment. "Me—create scandal for my good name? Oh no, *amigo,* this cannot be if we live in Macao."

"But your boxes . . . the rendezvous?" He was confused.

She wagged a schoolteacher finger at him. "We have need of cool head, partner. Contemplate our situation . . . already I am arrange for sail on *Pombal* tonight for inspect my agents in Manila. Everybody knows—the Governor, my friends. Suppose I stay and give to you my ship for go? They ask questions, many questions, yes? Because *muito* mystery, *muito* gossip. No, for certain I must go! But"—she smiled conspiratorially—"they not know that since this little minute, partner *mia,* I divert for special rendezvous."

This development had never occurred to Gill. "You can't." He shook his head stubbornly. "It's a man's job. Buying, selling——"

Zena rocked her head from side to side, mimicking him fiercely. "*Si,* of a certainty, a man's job, buying, selling . . . a man not able for speaking Portuguese to rendezvous captain. What language you use with *Pombal* captain for selling that opium overside in Chinchow Bay?"

Gill saw the logic, but he didn't like it, and said so.

Zena stamped her foot tempestuously. "Please to have the brains! Consider, I ask you. Me—I change orders at sea; I give new ones, and it is '*Si, si,* Senhorita Boss-of-Noronha-Ships.' As for you—your answer is hard one . . . 'Mutiny!' " She snapped fingers in dismissal.

Then, darting across the room with an impish grin, she was at his side, palpitating, eager. "Come, we be practical *businessmen,* we two. We make the details—with heads! Not hearts!"

When Gill took himself downstairs a quarter of an hour later, he had written out a regulation purchase order in English for one hundred chests of Patna at thirty thousand dollars, had watched Zena's red lips as they puckered and unpuckered over the Portuguese translation she made, and signed both with her. He climbed into his waiting chair, and was on his way to get his share of the money bargain for this—this extraordinarily practical and exciting new partner he'd found on his sixth day in Asia.

CHAPTER VIII

PEKING, FORBIDDEN CITY,
October 1838

THE CUCKOOS were crying the fourth watch of night when the Face of Heaven brushed aside the sable rug that lay over his narrow knees and rose from the breakfast table. It had been a stoical sop—rice gruel, fried onion dough, and Dragon Well tea. Enough to appease the stomach during a pre-dawn audience, but not enough to dull the wits. Ah, sublime goal—acute government! Audiences before dawn, when men's minds were clear, flashing, perspicacious! Accomplishing the mission of empire lucidly. Accomplishing it with dispatch, sobriety, and virtue! The skin of his face shone yellow and dry: he looked ineffably dedicated.

There was a scuffle of knees on the rug, and the Sublime One turned to see the rose-purple blot of the Chief Eunuch's gown billowing on the floor.

"Your Celestial Splendor lights the new day!" the Chief Eunuch said devoutly, his head on the floor somewhere near his knees.

Tao Kuang signaled impatiently for the mound of stomachs to rise. "Cook's health today—how is it?" he asked anxiously. "Does he feel salubrious? Keen? Inventive? Amiable?"

The Chief Eunuch nodded portentously. "His mood promises well. It is undoubtedly a day to create culinary history."

The Sublimity palpitated happily. "A-a-ah!" he said, and ran an exploratory tongue around the circle of his mouth, thinking of today's traditional treat—the annual snake meal. Ah, the rich, delectable odor and taste . . . stewed with lean pork and shredded ham, garnished with white chrysanthemum petals and finely chopped lemon leaves. And that excellent hormonal tonic—snake bile in wine!

Audience bells throbbed out clear and pure on the silent night

—from Bell Tower beyond the innermost walls, and then nearer and nearer from the hive of pavilions and galleries in the Great Within. When their summons hushed, a vagrant breeze took it up again in elfin imitation, rippling amongst the little porcelain bells hanging on miles of eaves and tugging them into tinkling medley.

They were soon absorbed by other audience sounds—hinges groaned, doors slammed, sleeve dogs barked, feet padded, boots scuffed, doves quavered, torches crackled, chair bearers panted, and the high rolling rhythm of Peking talk hung on the air. "The Audience!" each sound proclaimed. "The Wondrous Presence!"

Tao Kuang recognized the increasing tempo of the sounds, took his cap of sea otter from the porcelain hat stand, and put it on. The eye of its peacock feather winked blue and iridescent an arm's length above his face, bobbing and bowing at each turn of his head like a mesmerized butterfly. His turquoise crepe gown hung heavy about his body, and the sea-otter hem hugged his yellow leggings, but still he drew on a purple silk jacket lined with sea otter. This Season of Cold Dew was finicky weather— its draughts had a way of chilling the stomach juices, congealing them, until even a four-course dinner became an ordeal. *Hi-yah*, what calamity!

Joining hands inside his sleeves, the Perfection strode through two succeeding chambers to the corridor door and sat himself in the gold-embroidered sedan chair. He suffered a sable rug to enclose his legs, drew his jacket tighter about his middle, and signaled the sixteen bearers to convey him to the Pavilion of Heavenly Purity.

In it ministers, officials, and mandarins knelt elbow to elbow facing north towards the august spot where the Presence would materialize. Behind them in the outer chambers three thousand court eunuchs kept vigil on their knees. And farther beyond, down marble steps and out into the bluestone courtyard, lesser mandarins and military were abased in ritual prostration. Each eye focused on the banners and screens enclosing the dais, for the first flutter of those Imperial banners would be the signal. Each head must go down, and none dare be tardy. It was not a thing of the mind or the will, but of eternal precedent.

The flutter came. There was a loud creak of silk as four thousand bodies bent, and heads touched the floor as one, rose in unison, and eight times more *kowtowed* deeply. A sibilance of "Unprecedented Serenity!" "Supreme Sovereign!" "August Sublimity!" sifted through the chamber like an autumn wind blowing through dry grass. The screens parted, the banners moved aside, and there on the glittering Dragon Throne sat a being as stiff and motionless and awesome as a thing of porcelain. Perfumed smoke from the bronze tripods might have been clouds on high come down to drift ethereally and mystically around It.

All thoughts, all minds, are on me! All wills are my will! Tao Kuang reassured himself conscientiously as he always did when he began an audience in this vast cavern. Also, the words had a way of reminding him to discipline his resolution, as well as his muscles, to the coming rigors of immobility. For no matter how carefully he held himself, he could feel the peacock feather above his hat flipping and wagging in silly irreverence. And today there was a stench of rancid candle tallow for his nostrils to contend with. Another ten thousand a month, he told himself wretchedly, to be dispensed to the Grand Chamberlain for more of that dratted sandalwood if this dais was to be endured during winter audiences.

With ultimate concentration, he pretended not to breathe for a full quarter of an hour. As the water clock dripped the minutes, he sat in magnificent state, silent, sacrosanct, inviolate, while four thousand others feasted their eyes, breathed the very air He breathed, and thus achieved the ritual of audience.

Before the Grand Censorate could start their frog chorus of futile denunciation, he inclined two fingers on his right hand, summoning the Grand Treasurer.

That jowled worthy inched forward on his knees to a precise spot before the dais, and performed the three-times-three head-knocking. The floor resounded with the force of each fervent bump, and he must surely have struck himself unconscious if it were not that mathematically—not by mere chance—he had gauged the exact distance to a hollow tile.

"There is one sun in the Heaven: one Emperor on earth!" the Grand Treasurer panted like a boar through his jowls.

Tao Kuang acknowledged the plain truth and spoke. His words, except for the Grand Treasurer and maybe one or two others, were like the chaffer of bamboo leaves in a glen. "It has come to Our ears that after night comes down in such poor uncivilized cities as London and New York, light is caused to shine upon their streets. Even in the darkest hour it is as though the sun were shining."

Swelling his chest with significant breath, he elevated his head slightly and stared into infinity—a tactful ruse to avoid seeing the money man's face just now—and decreed: "Let one million *taels* be drawn from Imperial coffers to light the four cities of Peking at night!"

The Grand Treasurer's jowls trembled as though seized by the fever shakes. *One million taels* when the coffer was already bare! Some "little plan" must be devised. Collect next year's taxes from the cloth merchants? Or maybe the wine sellers?

What might have been a word came out strangled and blurred. He controlled himself partially and quavered: "Bright Star of Good Omen! Our cities shall be splendid with light!" He made the head-knocking and inched backwards out of the room on his stomach.

Hi-yah, that should remove the Grand Censorate's mind—collectively and individually—from whatever it was they'd arranged to harangue him about today—subversive missionaries translating Bible tracts, using smuggler technique to get their contraband sermons into closed ports! God-worshipers reported gathering in Kwangsi—some such cramped nonsense he was powerless to check. Their minds needed a laxative, that's what! Look at them now! Tethered! Balked! Faces rigid, inanimate—or were they?

The Elder had lips open . . . was he belching? Or were words forming?

Hasten! Invoke ritual. Write two edicts. Introduce some alien subject. Alien? *Hi-yah!* Where was Minister Ho and his everlasting oratory about foreign ships in Canton? One question, and Ho would go like a water wheel.

A finger of the left hand summoned the Grand Chamberlain, who summoned Minister Ho.

Minister Ho was far too eager and elated and unmathematical to find the hollow tile. He groveled where he hoped it might be, and performed the knocking. An inferior thud came forth, infinitely fainter than the sudden thudding inside his head.

"Ten-Thousand-Year Master!"

The Throne recognized him, and spoke. "Balancing Heaven and earth as I do, complete virtue compels me to hear more of this amusing toy—this fire-wheel boat filled with hot water and fire which the red barbarians have lately brought to our Pearl River."

Ho beamed, clasped hands gleefully, and exploded into speech sent him by the Hong merchants. "O Sire, this unworthy menial will gladly tell. Millennial! These fire-and-water contraptions! They've set all tongues wagging in Canton. The commonality swarm riverbanks to watch it pass—belching smoke, rumbling and thrashing like twin dragons. Millennial! Walks the waters! No other words describe it. I swear! I vouch! Walks—wind or no wind. By light of day or darkness of night—straight up the river it marches. Never crossing left nor right. Never pausing for current, for tide. Millennial!"

Like a stranded fish, Ho gulped breath, and swam on, intent, ardent, smiling from ear to ear, mesmerized by his own oratory. "Walks with the webbed feet of a duck. Has the power of five thousand ducks. On its side, like a rosette on the ear of a bride, is a wheel with wooden paddles which rotate ceaselessly. How does it? A box of fire and a cauldron of vapor push it. Elements we possess. Only harness them to a wheel. To ten wheels. To a hundred—and we sweep the waters millennially."

Old Millennial's head was like a drum. Why in the name of all that was windy couldn't the insensitive old horse bone keep to the safe confines of description? Why exhort? Tao Kuang assumed a look of lofty aloofness as he devised a gag—one which would avoid the loquacious Grand Censorate, though.

"Sweep the waters!" Ho repeated the entrancing words, sweeping the air with both hands.

"We accomplish that without gimcracks," Tao Kuang observed, twirling the archer's ring on his right thumb. "Last moon our intrepid Admiral drove countless barbarian ships from Canton forever."

"Admiral Kwan's stomach is capacious with valor," Ho paused long enough to affirm. Then he rushed on heedlessly: "But, Sire, this vapor boat is incredibly swift. It outdistances anything with sails. Walking the straight path it does, it is at Canton and back in Macao before a junk even reaches Canton. Could we not utilize such speed in the Pearl River? The Yangtze? The great Yellow One? We'd have millennial advantage over the red-pates."

Pelting out questions in an audience! It was un-Chinese. It transgressed. Consorting with barbarians—merely looking at them —had tainted his mental vision.

Ho smiled in idiotic cheerfulness. "Let China fashion millennial fireboxes for its own glorious use!"

Tao Kuang flicked his head waspishly. "China, in its pristine grandeur, would have invented these paltry gimcracks long ago had they been worth inventing." He shook his head in petulant dismissal and summoned the President of the Civil Offices. He might as well get the penalties and demotions over with while he was in the mood. H'm-m, a short list. Well, let complete virtue prevail. Let justice be stern!

" 'Grandee of the Coral Button Kwei Yang-fu, for violating proscribed ceremony of office, demoted three ranks to Glass Button, posted as Magistrate on the Western Frontier. . . . Duke Chen, for consorting socially with reform-minded persons, removed from Grand Council, appointed Superintendent of Imperial Gardens. . . . Kwok Fu-yu, slandered by his friend, Han Yin-go, committed suicide on latter's doorstep. Therefore Han Yin-go guilty of murder. Thirty head blows with cane, perpetual exile from Peking. . . . Jen Pu-jen, bankrupt, has absconded. Entire Jen family thereby responsible for his debts. . . . Pan Ju-lin, a minor son of Pan Pak-lo, committed offense against his regiment of Yellow Bannermen. Son's decoration of Yellow Riding Jacket taken from him; father, responsible for minor son's dereliction, ordered to make payment of a hundred thousand *taels* to assuage mortification of Corps. . . . Eunuch Wa-ling, for speaking abusively to master, strangulation. . . . Linguist Tsu Ching-sze, for garbling Imperial edict, finger torture. . . .' "

Vermilion pencilstrokes authorizing the penalties made a continuous red smear by the time he'd finished. Tossing the list to the President of the Civil Offices, he said sadly: "Tell the culprits their indifference to the obligations of high station makes me sigh! Direct them to look up diligently to the Face of Heaven and regulate their conduct."

Through the window he could see the red mists of sunrise staining the sky. Merciful Providence, he'd managed to consume more than half the allotted time. Danger was past. There'd be no major diatribe from the Grand Censorate now. He drew easier breath and braced himself for the lesser tedium to come.

Meanwhile the Grand Treasurer had skimmed through outer galleries to where his sedan chair was waiting by the first bridge. He pulled his ermine-lined coat closer and got in. The usual swarms of court attendants, soothsayers, and astrologers were about, but looking neither right nor left, he sat with bowed head as he was carried alongside the purple-pink walls and through East Flowery Gate into the Imperial City, where he lived.

Inside his chambers he clapped twice; and before the echoes had flittered up into the acid-green beams of the ceiling, a body servant was at his side. "Summon the Military Governor!" he directed.

It would require time, for the Military Governor lived in the Tartar City beyond this Imperial one. Miles of stone flagging, innumerable waterways and moats, ponderous gates had to be covered, crossed, opened, and closed before that fierce and swaggering Manchu warrior would arrive.

Spasmodically then, with an animal's quick nervous tread, the Grand Treasurer paced his apartment, in and out and around its series of chambers and galleries. But time and again he came back, to stop there hypnotized, at the table where his little ticking watches were laid out in pairs like gems on jeweler's velvet. His eyes roved, fondly and doting, from the pearl-encrusted ones to those of sapphire enamel with fleur-de-lis underenamel, to ruby medallions, to blossoming roses in topaz, to diamond-sprinkled gold—oh, the enchanting, darling, exquisite two hundred of them, ticking away like a hive of bees!

In his mind he multiplied the length of the table, multiplied it again, and then measured the room itself for the reality of two additional tables full of the little beauties . . . remove that lacework partition of cypress and sandalwood, yes. Set the two gold spittoons over against the farther wall. Of a surety! An admirable arrangement. "Heaven is high. Who will know?" he asked himself in a hoarse whisper.

In the Hall of Heavenly Purity the Grand Censorate had nipped in and gained The Ear to say the nineteen-year-old English Queen, Victoria, desired sending Peking another embassy to discuss the thing called international trade. . . .

"The English maintain life on tea and rhubarb." The Elder alternated emphasis with soft sibilance. "Both are essential to their very life since they are unreasonably fond of milk and cream. This indulgence, as everyone knows, induces costiveness. Nothing but tea and rhubarb will clear their systems and restore their spirits. So . . . if we deprive them of these, then at once they will all fall ill. Turbulence and disorder will ensue in their realm."

Tao Kuang looked east and saw the fiery glow of morning. It was the hour for steaming *congee* with pickled carrot . . . or, perhaps, fried rice with morsels of ginger, washed down by mild autumn tea with its good back flavor. Oh . . . close this audience. Conclude it in Heaven's name.

He cleared his throat to say benignly: "I feel only cosmic pity for these English barbarians, but their embassy must be refused before it sets out. In so doing we are merely accomplishing the decree of Fate, for they must never hope to associate with us on terms of equality. Address a special mandate to this Victoria. . . .

"As for you, poor Queen, we fully recognize the spirit of reverent submission which animates you—but your embassies cause indecorous scenes and are merely a waste of time. The presents they bring are of no interest, or use. You would better be employed improving your knowledge. If you are loyal to Us, there is no need for appearances in Peking to prove that you are indeed Our vassal."

He raised the blue jade scepter and gave the signal. An orchestra of gongs, drums, and bells, accompanied by the slow solemn chant of three thousand eunuchs, filled the air as the Emperor descended the Dragon Throne and went behind the screen.

By this time the Military Governor had reached the Imperial City, and was admitted to the Grand Treasurer's apartment. He came flaunting into the room on legs shaped to fit a horse's belly, and the Grand Treasurer turned away from his soul's delight. The formalities they offered each other were meager, for a barrier of hate existed between them.

The Grand Treasurer announced: "Jewel of Heaven's Grace —long may he guide us!—has directed me to pay five hundred thousand *taels* that Peking will shine at night as though it were day. Let the streets be lighted!"

Relish glittered in the Military Governor's hawk eyes. "Hearing is obeying," he said with quick conviction. "I go with the speed of fire to do the Sublime bidding."

His words were only slightly exaggerated, for though he and his escort of Yellow Bannermen lashed their sturdy little Mongolian ponies to a lather, the way itself was devious with clogged gates, humped bridges, two-wheeled Peking carts, and strings of camels carrying coal. But when the Governor pulled up at his own red brick house, he dispatched two horsemen to the outermost Chinese city for the Chief Magistrate.

Two hundred petitioners waited in the Governor's courtyard, and another hundred milled and talked and dozed in the anterooms. Yet the Chief Magistrate, who was a tall weed of a man with a bilious face, was admitted to the inner sanctum immediately his chair bearers came panting to the steps.

The Military Governor began to speak at once. "Great are the wonders of China! His Sublime Serenity has granted two hundred and fifty thousand *taels* so Peking streets shall be lighted during hours of darkness. Their brilliance must exceed description!"

Belching twice, the Chief Magistrate marveled in awed tones: "A miracle to behold! Depend upon it—Peking shall blaze with light!" he promised, and withdrew without further words.

His sedan bearers were still drawing breath in agonized gasps, yet he ordered them back to the outermost city at the same pace they had brought him. Instead of returning to his own compound, though, he went to the *yamen* of the Chief of City Guards. In the inner office of that Chief he drew himself up to his utmost height, belched, and declared in rolling oratory: "The Son of Heaven—in His Sublime beneficence—has given one hundred and fifty thousand *taels* that all Peking may be radiant throughout the night. This shall be your responsibility henceforth." He withdrew.

The Chief of the City Guards plucked a sable-haired writing brush from the jade holder on his desk and began painting words on paper. His brush flowed in the "tendons-and-bone" school, with strength and elasticity in each stroke, and yet managed coveted charm and liveliness in the little hooks and dashes. When he finished, his eyes roved back over the text. Judiciously and critically he studied each ideograph as he read half aloud:

> HIS SERENE SUBLIMITY HAS DECREED THE STREETS
> OF PEKING SHALL BE LIGHTED FROM THE FIRST
> HOUR OF DARKNESS UNTIL THE NEXT DAY'S LIGHT.
> THEREFORE—LET THE HEAD OF EACH HOUSEHOLD
> HANG A SESAME-OIL LAMP FROM HIS DOORPOST THIS
> NIGHT. AN IMPERIAL ORDER!!! TREMBLE AND OBEY!!!

It was not the meaning he considered, but the symmetry of the fluted strokes. Twice he paused over connecting hooks . . . cramped perhaps? Not quite the epitome? With another brush as slight as a butterfly's antenna, he retouched them, rounding them subtly, and yet not detracting by a hairbreadth from their vitality.

"Ah-h-h," he sighed contentedly, and tossed the paper to an obsequious aide. "Post copies of this order before midday at principal gates, the markets, the wells, and temples," he commanded. Dipping the brush in water, washing it thoroughly, he shaped its sable hair into an exquisite point with delicate strokes.

Tao Kuang's chopsticks hovered like moths over the escort dishes of savory beans roasted in sesame oil, crisp grilled duck skin, and fried milk. Then the Lady Yi came from the antechamber and added to the happy quandary with bowls of plovers' eggs poached in mushroom broth, peppered herbs, and small buns filled with tender teal and shreds of reed bird.

"Hi-yah!" Tao Kuang breathed in muted ecstasy. "When they told me you had contrived a flowerpot kitchen here, I little thought you would achieve artistry."

The Lady Yi was quick to deny: "This unworthy menial is of small capacity." Then she laughed her fluting laugh. "But the marvel in your voice is an affecting melody."

She stood before him as slender as a lily, and as graceful, in a gown of lily color. Her hair, piled high above her high forehead, had neither jewelry nor ribbons twined in it, and shone as black as a crow's wing.

He smiled a connoisseur's slow relishing smile. "Your amiability is exquisite," he said. "Excelled only by your cooking." Motioning her to a place on the wide divan seat beside him, he placed a golden morsel of fried milk on his tongue and waited, trancelike, as its custard velvet dissolved into heavenly memory.

With small fluttering hands the Lady Yi slid a satin armrest across the cushion until it was under his left elbow, and he sighed in comfort. She caught up her glossy pearwood *pipa* and perched herself on the merest edge of the divan as discreetly distant from him as the seat would permit.

While he tasted, munched, and sucked through the tidbits, she plucked the four silk strings and hummed a soft questioning song. By and by she sang the words:

> *"The shuttling sun, the weaving moon,*
> *Inscribe the warp and weft of time,*
> *Determining our calendars—*
> *If life shall be a curse, or boon,*
> *If love shall speak in prose, or rhyme,*
> *Upon the pattern of our stars."**

She wondered that the tune held true. She wondered that the quavering throb didn't crack and betray tumult. Oh, exalted moment! Oh, moment of moments in this giddy, suffocating new world.

She was here, in the innermost core of Empire—the Forbidden City itself. Here, in an indescribably sumptuous, ineffably opulent pavilion where He had set her up magically and suddenly—with rose-madder walls about her, black-mirror doors, and ceilings of gilded and coffered beams. It gave her the feeling of climbing a cloudy ladder to Heaven—up through fogs of suspense, each foothold uncertain, each forward step obscured.

The numbing thing was . . . not once in these six weeks had

* Tseng Lai

she been summoned to the Dragon Phoenix Couch. Oh, ignominy! Oh, shame! Not once had the eunuchs brought her the swansdown rug for the fateful journey to the Hall of Vigorous Fertility.

Instead she remained a pampered prisoner in a purple-pink pavilion, adrift in a whirling void of intrigue—with eunuchs coming and going in whispering swarms, tittering concubine faces peeking at her from distant lattices when she walked her terrace. For company there had only been the gonglike throb of her own persecuted heart and the ache of hope.

She'd grasped at the comfort of practicality, plucking this little familiar chore and that to fit into her day. She'd wheedled rugs for marble tiles; brocades for cushions and curtains; embroidery floss for her needle; and, thanks to presents here and there, she'd turned a boxlike antechamber into a kitchen where she could chop and cut and brew the things she'd chopped and cut and brewed in her father's ancient, but impoverished, house.

Midway through a Pear Orchard song she spied frayed spots on the satin soles of His court boots. Fortune, another something for her hands to occupy themselves with! She continued the song, though, to its tremulous end, for it was a gentle ballad of yearning ardor, and matched her mood. Then she laid aside the *pipa* and went to fetch the unfortunate soup.

Destiny was askew. If only some intuition, some inkling, had been granted that His Brightness might visit her, unheralded, unannounced even, except for a sudden swarming of eunuchs at the doors. Today of all days, when she'd made the most ordinary of soups. There were fifty more intricate, enticing, succulent ones she could have made.

Trembling with mortification, she put a covered bowl of thin, translucent, off-white porcelain before him and stepped back, bending her head in humility.

Tao Kuang exclaimed in genial surprise. "Ah, ancient Moon-Pavilion porcelain!"

"It is so, Perfection. I coaxed it of the Chief Eunuch, knowing it to be a favorite with you. Some felicitous day, I dared hope, to serve you a concoction of my making in it. But, alas, *today* the eggshell"—she apologized with a pretty play on words—"is vastly superior to the poor egg." Slowly, slowly she removed the cover.

At the first whiff of savory steam Tao Kuang's head jerked forward and he stared at the nest of noodles floating in yellow broth. "What trick is this?" he demanded in a kind of awe.

"Only very poor and humble noodle soup I have made, Perfection. It humiliates me to offer such ordinary fare," Yi said earnestly, pointing with the porcelain spoon, yet not daring to serve him.

Tao Kuang snatched the spoon from her, stirred it deep through the noodles, and leaned to inhale the pungent onion aroma. "It promises well!" he exclaimed, scooping some into an individual bowl.

He tasted the broth once, twice, and a third time. With chopsticks he lifted three noodle strands and nibbled at them tentatively. Then he was pronging wads of noodles between smacking lips, swallowing the broth in gulps and holding his bowl for more. "The Heaven-kissing acme!" he laughed jubilantly.

"A nothing of a soup," Yi protested, eyebrows curving like willow leaves in bewilderment. She was ready to tell him such ordinary coolie soup could be bought at a thousand noodle counters, a thousand itinerant kitchens, anywhere in the outer cities. But something stayed her tongue.

Tao Kuang stiffened suddenly as though a scorpion had bitten him. "What special purse were you issued to contrive this?" he asked.

"None whatever, Perfection." Yi's fluting voice rose an octave in surprise. "Its cost is nothing—a few trivial pennies from my household purse."

Now it was Tao Kuang who was bewildered. He wagged his head like a door swinging in the breeze. "A few trivial pennies, *this* which transports me on wings of delight?"

Yi's eyelids closed as she savored gratitude for this curious respite. "Your slave is glad . . . I could not say it differently with a hundred mouths," she vowed.

His eyes devoured her as he leaned nearer and asked in jade tones: "Could you, perhaps, make it for me—*once each week for trivial pennies?*"

Yi laughed, showing aristocratically even little teeth. "I could make it twice, or three times, from my household purse, if you so desire."

"*I do so desire!*" Tao Kuang repeated the words buoyantly and held his bowl for more.

Bending closer, Yi ladled it for him. With her moth-white face so near his, and in the bounteousness of his feelings, he impulsively held a tidbit in his chopsticks to her mouth. He was titillated by the flush of pleasure which stained her face, and stayed her with a hand on her small wrist while he searched for another —a second-best piece, naturally—and fed it to her.

The dimples in her cheeks played hide-and-seek. He watched them admiringly for a moment, and said softly: "Such beguiling little wine hollows you have." Then with an intimate pressure of his thumb in the hollow of her hand, he released her.

She swayed away, dizzy with ardor, blind with hope, groping for her skeins of floss; for some task, any task, her hands could perform while she leashed inner tumult.

Minutes later she pointed to the frayed spots on his boots, and persuaded him to let her try what her needle could effect. She spread bright floss skeins across her lap and set to embroidering.

Dawdling through a fourth bowl, Tao Kuang looked across at the bright lily of her face, its elongated eyebrows arching now like distant mountains, and inquired: "What does my perfumed companion?"

She showed him five felicitous red bats she had embroidered in a way that each covered a frayed spot. He sighed, saying out of his thoughts: "Fate is a miser that I have met you so late. You possess classic virtues . . . you compose balanced poetry, and balanced dishes; you sing, and you darn; you are economical, and yet truthful. *And . . .* you are lovesome."

Blood rushed into Yi's face, and went singing through her ears.

"Come, another song before I continue to Green Hill and view the new dazzle of Peking's streets after nightfall," he coaxed. "Let it be a song of love whose words will linger with me until the moment when you yourself will whisper them in my ear."

Yi caught up her *pipa* to strum languorous chords before she sang:

> *"The arms of love are white and clinging;*
> *The voice of love was born to sing,*
> *The feet of love seem lilies, running;*
> *The words of love are never done.*
> *The eyes of love never need a lattice;*
> *The hands of love can open that;*
> *The heart of love is smooth, as mine is—*
> *The whole of love, my love, is thine."**

She stood for his going, her knees wet with perspiration. But he did not stride out in his usual stiff-legged stalk. He stepped softly to her and, as though she were a baby, smelled the fragrance of her flesh odor—the petaled seduction of her face, her slender neck, and small white ears.

Inhaling a third time, he spoke as softly to her as a man in a temple. "Absence from you for *one hour* will seem like three autumns."

"Ten thousand happiness!" Yi breathed, for it was the ultimate.

He turned away, and was gone.

She stood beating hands together, moaning softly. One hour, he'd said, *one hour!* She had need to act now, immediately, with the speed of fire.

She pulled the bell cord four times for Lan-fan, the lowliest of the eunuchs who served her. Someone must go. Not herself at this night hour. But . . . someone in this hive of hard-eyed stran-

* Peng Lia

gers to whom she could appeal. Would it be Lan-fan—the Chili
Province one recently come into palace service from Jade Emperor's Temple, the ancient, and ofttimes infamous, training
school for eunuchs? He'd given her a feeling several times that
he was friendly . . . the way he anticipated her wants; the two
times he'd saved her from committing blunders in court etiquette. . . .

When Lan-fan arrived, the Lady Yi was waiting with a purse
in her restless hands, but she studied him urgently in that isolated
moment . . . yes, patterned differently. Not the usual insipid tur-
nip face of a eunuch. Not the alternately groveling, smirking,
contemptuous manner. Young, above medium height, with a curious stalwart dignity of bearing. Quick, perceptive eyes in a long
almond face gave it a shrewd—or was it a striving, reaching,
ambitious look? Oh, what matter in this whirligig of time? She
must trust instinct, and instinct told her he could be an ally.

She crossed quickly to thrust the purse into his hands. "Go,
Lan-fan! Go quickly! With the speed of fire!" she implored, all the
impetus and fervor of her small being concentrated in her intention. "To the Red Temple of Immortal Chang who gives us children, and buy a blessed boy-image for me. Buy also a 'catch-baby
cord'—yellow, naturally—and bring them to me. Lan-fan"—she
pressed her hands together supplicatingly—"I need them before
the hour is out."

Lan-fan's eyes contracted in quick comprehending awareness,
and he nodded decisively. "You shall have them, Little Mistress.
I understand, and obey." He spun around, and was off: running
through antechambers, along galleries, and making courtyard pebbles skip with the quick spring of his feet.

Yi ran, too, around her apartment. Not in excitable helter-skelter, but with intention and purpose: gathering herself, good-luck
charms, talismans, oils, perfumes, for the transcendental encounter that awaited.

Meanwhile—Tao Kuang's ascent of Green Hill was the easy
ambling pace of palanquin bearers and lantern coolies mounting

a circular path through shrubs and stunted pine: through the azure green of malachite pebbles spread two hands deep over every inch of earth; and emerging finally at Green Pavilion at the apex.

Tonight Tao Kuang didn't even glance at the wondrous green of the pavilion tiles, nor at the wondrous white of the moon. This other dazzling wonder spread out below him . . . the dark core of The Forbidden City, surrounded by successive layers of light. First, the Imperial City. Beyond that, the Tartar City. And still beyond those two, the sprawling Chinese City . . . all a vast plain of luminous twinkling lights!

Tao Kuang chuckled exultantly. "We invincible Chinese! Can any other nation equal us?" He swiveled his body from west to south, and on around to east. Superb, splendorous, spectacular! A million *taels*—spectacular too! Was it too much? Had he overdone generosity? Probably should have tried less—say, half a million. . . .

He brushed lacerating doubts aside and climbed into his chair. He wanted the company of relishing thoughts. He wanted to think of the Lady Yi. O lustrous Fortune, could she, would she— he asked himself as his chair passed through the Gate of Spiritual Vigor—produce crabs, inimitable crabs with chrysanthemum-petal sauce, for tomorrow's full moon?

Yi was ready and waiting when they brought her the swans-down rug. Her prayers to Kwan-yin were made, and she held the blessed boy-image against her heart as they bundled her in the rug's voluptuous folds. Lan-fan was there too, lending a hand and lifting her onto the back of the great gross carrying-eunuch. But Lan-fan did not come beyond the doorway. He stood at the threshold, closing shutters and settling curtains as the procession crossed the courtyard under the bright watching moon of autumn.

There was one stop when they reached the Hall of Vigorous Fertility. It came after the jogging motion of stairs being climbed. Yi guessed they'd reached the Registry Chamber inside the pavilion where connubial records were kept. She felt herself being eased down onto a divan, but no move was made to unroll her. Next minute, through the muffling folds of swansdown, she could hear a eunuch giving her name and station. Then came the voice of a recorder repeating it, syllable by syllable, as he wrote new ideographs in the big book and entered the hour of arrival. As she was being lifted onto the back of the carrying-eunuch again, she could hear lewd whispers wagering the hour her departure would be added to the record.

After this, corridors seemed to stretch on endlessly, with interminable doors being opened and closed—until the last was reached. Yi knew it was sanctum, from the holy hush and ineffable scent of sandalwood, even before she felt herself being lowered slowly onto a nest of floor cushions.

She lay motionless, scarcely breathing, until she heard the swish of cloth soles retreating towards the door and the sound of wood against wood as the door itself was closed. Now . . . now . . . "O Hearer of Cries!" she supplicated Kwan-yin silently. "Let my body be fertile and harbor good seed."

Then she stirred, pushing her chrysalis aside by inches, and with it shed the skin of silk around her body until she emerged, small and naked, in a chamber of mauve shadows. The opalescent light of two porcelain lanterns showed her she had been deposited at the foot of a vast and enormous bed. The Dragon Phoenix Couch itself—*already inhabited.*

Her spirit fluttered and reeled, but she knew what she must do. In silent veneration she touched her head in dedication to the foot of the coveted couch, then slowly on her stomach she inched her way up to the pillow.

While Tao Kuang and Yi enjoyed the pleasures of the night, the three outer cities of Peking gradually darkened. In myriad lanes and alleyways the little oil lamps were being extinguished one by one as beggars crept from doorway to doorway, drinking the sesame oil from each lamp until, once more, the streets were tunnels of darkness.

Jade Snow leaned to her mirror: not looking at the face that was as beautiful and empty as a dream, nor at the blue-black mound of hair above it; but scrutinizing the skin itself, drawing away, tilting her head to the light, tilting from it. Was it sallow? Was a hint of yellow creeping in?

She shuddered, and clapped twice. A handmaid came running. Jade Snow turned on her in a blaze of coolie anger, screaming in a jay's voice: "You eyesore, you've been cheating on my daily pearl powder!"

The handmaid fell to her knees, fending two hands before her face to ward off blows. "Never, Imperial Mother!" she denied. "You've had the powder of two fine pearls each day. Not a grain less, I swear! Not even the dust of a grain less! Regard your face —it's the white of the moon. The white of hoarfrost, of——"

The wretched girl was lying, of course. Jade Snow cut her short. "Increase to four pearls daily. But show me the pearls. Then grind them before my eyes."

She waved the toad away with a flounce of her sleeve that was very like the Emperor's gesture of dismissal, and switched around to myriad jars and vials and flagons in her beauty box. The pygmy drawers danced at her snapping touch: clacking open, clacking shut in a devil's tattoo. Turtle dung—all! Frogwash! Astringent slops galore . . . patted, pinched, massaged on, but did that odious suspicion of sag in the mouth crevices disappear? Never! That new amethyst muck for the eyelids which had cost fifty silver big-rounds—may the vendor get fifty boils on his bottom!—did it erase shadows a sleepless night had rubbed on? Never!

In an offended swat she swept brushes, sponges, and jars tumbling onto the floor and jumped up to go coursing about the chamber like a minor typhoon—tossing gowns, skirts, jackets, slippers, scarves, furs, anything and everything, into the air in unleashed fury until she found a gown she fancied for today. Onion green it was, and adhering as smooth and tight across the swell of her breasts and the round of her hips as an onion's skin.

Choosing jewelry to go with the gown partially subdued the

tempest within her. The star sparkle, the moonbeam glow, the emerald shimmer gentled her; and as she fondled and caressed each cherished darling, a degree of confidence and security came back to her. She didn't choose her largest and showiest pieces—neither the pigeon-egg pearls nor the hundred-bead necklace of matched water jade that Heaven's Face had given her. Yet those she selected were ample to remind anyone that she was precious and Imperial.

Lastly she rubbed rouge into the palms of her hands and, holding them before her daintily to dry, went out into the Garden of Harmony and Longevity to wait for the Chief Eunuch. She wanted no third pair of ears eavesdropping on their talk. Besides, today's unhampered noonday sun spread a warm and comforting blanket over the closed garden; and the bloom of myriad chrysanthemums in beds and pots and urns there would contribute gentleness and tranquillity, she hoped.

Over the high wall, in the courtyard of the Rouging and Powdering Pavilion, Jade Snow could hear the steady din of soothsayers whirling Sticks-of-Fate in pewter cylinders as the daily fortunes were told. Mingling with it was the incessant dovecote twitter of young concubines, and the constant plop-plop-plopping of hoofs on stone pavement as other concubines came and went astride their white horses.

She looked around to find the feathered pretext she'd used to fetch the Chief Eunuch here. Requesting his presence was not enough these days. It took the gift of a bird. Not just any songster that flew on two wings—but unique, exotic, unheard-of rarities. For the Grand Eunuch had begun stocking a new aviary.

She found it across the garden on the wide well rim, where they'd put the golden lacquered cage she'd ordered; and she strolled nearer to examine the bird. It was boldly beautiful, about the size of a man's two hands, and watching her with an agate stare. Its body was the color of good red tea, with lustrous black and tawny markings. Its curious black topknot flicked open and shut like a fan, and its bill was as long and slender as an embroidery needle. A hoopoe—they called it—got from Arab traders in Singapore. But how would Ten Thousand Belly like it? Would it capture his fancy? Would he consider it a trophy?

Then she saw him step through the Moon Gate—a mulberry blot that came skimming along the zigzag path with a mincing half-run, half-walk. He passed the chrysanthemums without a glance—the cascades, the tree spirals, in bewitching brocades of color, were nothing to him. His eyes were on the fretwork cage he carried, and he was talking a steady conversational lingo to the drowsy nightingale inside. He skirted the rockery, the life-sized statues of the Eight Immortals, the pair of yellow ceramic Foo dogs, and stopped beside the cluster of granite mushrooms which he knew were garden seats.

His greeting was moderately courteous; and in leisurely fashion he inquired of her health, her son's health, the state of her household. Twice while she was answering these amenities he reached a hand into the cage to stroke the bird, to caress and caress it in repeated fast strokes, while the creases of his face settled into a look of beatific pleasure.

He commented upon the pavement of black-and-white pebble mosaic around the well. He spoke of the wild geese beating high overhead. He dwelt on the carnival of autumn the gingko trees provided as their turning leaves matched the yellow of roof tiles in this most imperial of cities. And he dilated on the piquant Autumn Classic being readied for tomorrow night's full moon.

Jade Snow raged within. Playing cat-and-mouse, h'm-m? Strewing the conversation with rude niceties as delaying tactics, h'm-m? Did that mean there was a shred of truth in the inconceivable rumor of some unknown concubine and a kitchen, of all things? When she could tolerate suspense no longer, she asked him, with a trilling little laugh, whatever the frivolous chitchat was about.

His placid countenance changed not a whit, but his voice was tender in admonition as he remarked: "An object costing one *lakh* of dollars can scarcely be described as 'frivolous.'"

Jade Snow exclaimed: "One *lakh* of dollars for a Minor Star!"

"No, for the kitchen of a Minor Star."

Jade Snow's butterfly eyebrows elevated disdainfully, and her full red lips curled sarcastically.

The Bulk read her expression and, like a turtle about to strike, pulled his neck inside the sable collar of his jacket. Then he struck: "Heaven's Grace commands that I spend one hundred thousand dollars to create a new kitchen in Western Pavilion for the Lady Yi . . . designated henceforth as Concubine-Consort."

Jade Snow gazed at him, her eyes like windows of an empty room. Astonishment and fear all but destroyed her, for she nearly raised hands in clenched rage to strike that suet face; she nearly opened her mouth to shriek black fury.

A temporizing interruption stayed her. Above the steady plop-plopping of horses' hoofs and sibilant conversational fripperies in the next courtyard, the high singsong of a discarded old concu-bine grated out patient instruction to a new one: ". . . you pound petals of balsam until they drip crimson. Mix with finely pow-dered alum. Apply paste to fingernails at night, cover well with bandages for once around the clock. Lo, you'll have nails a bril-liant, entrancing scarlet. . . ."

The interval gave Jade Snow time to settle her lips so they curled in a roguish, beguiling smile that showed her pretty baby teeth. In an innocent purr she confided: "I desire a summons to the Presence—preferably a 'swansdown' summons. How clever you are! Arranging it so my name-wand is selected tonight from the holder-of-concubine names beside His couch."

The Chief Eunuch surveyed her with voluminous serenity. "How extremely delicate you are—not to mention my fee for a 'swansdown' summons," he observed, letting the lids of his eyes close down and stay closed. "Possibly it has not reached your cloistered ears that I presently find myself unable to arrange such summons for a pittance less than fifty thousand dollars."

The baby teeth came together with a click, but the roguish smile only wavered slightly, until it grew more intense. "Of a certainty," she trilled. "How could you disarrange yourself for less?"

The hoopoe suddenly began a clucking burbling sort of chuckle. The Chief Eunuch's eyelids flew open, and he turned to regard the bird attentively. But, after a long moment, when these country sounds did not mature into pure sophisticated song, a sigh shuddered over the big frame and he turned back to Jade Snow. "In advance," he said.

The girl turned an inferior shade of red. "O Elder-born, O Uncle," she wheedled, "you shall have it—every penny of it. Only arrange my summons tonight, and tomorrow I pay."

"In advance."

Fringing eyelashes hid the venom gathering in her eyes. "But, Elder-born, affairs must be arranged . . . it is already midday. . . ."

He was on his feet and advancing towards her with unnatural alacrity. "You—favorite concubine for two years—*you* cannot put hand to a paltry fifty thousand dollars? A trifle . . . less than a trifle, amongst the gold filtering through your profligate fingers these two years! You vain *discard!*"

The impact of his words made her cringe momentarily, then she rallied and cried: "You'll hug my knees yet! Never forget— I know the location of five storage houses in the Tartar City filled with Imperial treasure. I know who holds the keys! Never forget —I bore an Emperor's son. I am an Imperial mother!"

The huge quivering mound of the Chief Eunuch bore down upon her. "Bah!" he spat. "You're nothing but a lusterless pebble!"

She squirmed back from the thing she saw in his eyes, hissing like a serpent as she crouched against the big bronze dragon by the well. But this symbol of fertile goodness didn't save her. He struck so fast air whistled through the fingers he clapped against her mouth, and with the other hand he heaved her child's body over the well rim and flung it down.

The choke of terror and the splash mounting from that black hole were absorbed by the noon crescendo of horses' hoofs and twittering, laughing, caroling concubines in the courtyard beyond. And all the while the hoopoe sang its chuckling song unceasingly.

CHAPTER IX

MACAO,
October 1838

MACAO'S CORDIALITY, Gill found, was like jumping into a tub of whipped cream—smooth, lavish, and smothering. The whirl of carnivals, balls, routs, operas, masquerades, picnics, concerts, dinners, and every other conceivable guise of sociability before the men went off to celibate exile in Canton was like nothing Gill had ever heard of, or even dreamed of, back in New York.

Day and night the calendars of the gentry were filled: even the non-gentry joined in the gala mood—strolling in dressy throngs, singing to zither music on their balconies, or massing before a mansion gate, eight or ten deep, to make a hilarious party out of watching invited guests go inside. He was both surprised and touched by the scores of invitations which the chit-coolies brought each day to his house. And in the devious course of answering these, or dropping cards on the senders, he discovered Macao was simply being itself—friendly, gracious, gently courteous. It was all so unlike the irritable hustling, the indifference, and suspicious skepticism a man met with in New York.

It was apparent to him that he wasn't being singled out for attention because he was Tad's brother, nor because of anything compelling or dashing about his own personality. For while he was trying to get his bearings, several other newcomers—a young English sawbones come to buy rhubarb, a Scottish shipbuilder, a Danish timberman, and a young Swiss hotelkeeper—stopped off at this same time in Macao, and he saw them accorded the same casual, tolerant, and undemanding friendliness. It was some special heritage out East, he told himself, some link, or tie, some instinctive bond, perhaps, between aliens in a very alien land. But whatever it was, he found it fortifying and appeasing to the spirit. It had a way of heartening a man, of tempering, and—yes—modifying him.

Take the first incredible dinner he went to at Lady Prophet's, for instance—dining off gold plate with forty at table, the punkahs swaying overhead, the lights of a hundred candles waving in unison while the mirroring crystal and silver multiplied them a thousandfold; and the fragrance of jasmine and gardenia floating in through the windows. Ah Lau had stood behind his chair, taking each plate and dish and wine decanter from a Prophet footman and placing it before him, and him only—even as the thirty-nine others at table were served exclusively by his, or her, Number One boy. The dishes they brought were green turtle soup, smoked salmon, plover eggs, fresh-water shrimps, mushrooms, whitebait, pheasant, suckling pig, chestnut soufflé, and as a final fillip, the tapers were extinguished and the table became a galaxy of blue light as puddings laden with burning brandy were passed.

Not that anyone required a performance after that one, Gill had told himself dazedly, yet the entire dinner party had moved along to see *The Rivals* put on by the English community, men dressing the parts of women, of course; and the irrepressible George Chinnery playing Mrs. Malaprop to the life.

Between acts Gill joined the flower of Macao in the foyer parade—passing and being passed in soft waves by Senhora Pinto squirming tadpole-like under mounds of purple brocade and a quart of amethysts; by the rotund Olyphant Thane with a waistcoat that matched his rosy nose; by Lady Prophet, regal in diamond tiara and a white satin cape, strolling with the stately and gracious Lael, who needed no tiara atop that crown of red hair; by Sur Manoel with a bathed, burnished, and foppish look which somehow didn't quite hide the animal cunning in his dark eyes. . . .

Salutations, greetings, curtsies, bows, much laughter, a pervading titillation which made one forget the stale hot air. Frangipani, sandalwood, cloying musk mingled with the fresher sweetness of mignonette, rose, lavender. And, foaming like spun sugar, Benares gauze wound into colossal turbans on the heads of the ladies. There was a dash and elegance about everyone, and stinging, intoxicating expectancy.

As Gill stood bowing and watching the parade, the incongruity of its lavishness flashed through his mind. Could this be a mercantile community existing precariously on bare sufferance of Chinese autocrats? Could these be colonists outrageously obstructed, persecuted, shoved . . . to the imminence of war?

The following night Gill was mingling with four hundred other bemused guests under the rainbow gleam of crystal chandeliers at the sumptuous masquerade Senhor and Senhora Pinto were giving upstairs and down in their Sans Souci—for the bedrooms had been stripped down to Savonnerie rugs and silk damask walls, the beds and bureaus removed, to make way for a hundred supper tables. The orchestra was sprightly and indefatigable, and the guests likewise, for they were still dancing the Parisian *galopade* at 5 A.M.—having changed sodden ruffles and shirts three times in the process, without apologies to the hostess for their not having been ironed in Goa!

Street fetes were indescribably elaborate. No amount of preparation seemed too much for the gay, mad crowd. They'd mask their houses with red cloth and palm fronds, and they'd tumble flower chains and tapestries from their upstairs windows until the street became a vast baronial banqueting hall. Incense puffed up from braziers, rose water was sprayed and tossed in all directions, while guitars and violins and zithers would sob out the haunting *fado* strains, and a woman's voice would sing an elemental lament for love.

After a while fireworks would go whooshing up into the indigo ceiling, often with feathered arrows attached to mark a money prize. Then the keyed-up hilarious throng would go pelting down some byway, or surge up a tier of cobbled steps, laughing, pawing, squealing over the descending arrow. And all evening long the forts on the five hills racketed with salvo after salvo.

Going to the races was a daylong excursion, whether it was up over the hill road by horseback—there being no carriages in the colony—or out around the green knob of Macao by boat. The latter was more congenial by far, for fifteen or eighteen could sit around on an airy matting-roofed deck while the oarsmen whipped the water with flashing oars until, in an hour or so, they beached on the race course itself. It lay flat as a tabletop where the isthmus joining Macao to the mainland narrowed to a slender neck of ocherous sand barely a hundred yards wide. Sitting on the commodious bamboo shelters built on piles higher than a man's head, and joined together by a continuous running veranda, they looked out on the blue water of the Canton Estuary on one side, and across the sand was yellow water trickling from West River by a hundred creeks.

"The stem of the lotus," the Chinese called this spot, and to prevent barbarian feet from straying across it into China they had built a barrier wall of stone and glass spikes across the sand more than two hundred years ago. The wall's fortress gates groaned open each morning to let farmers come jogging through with full wheelbarrows and carrying poles, and each sundown the gate groaned closed behind these returning farmers. But during the somnolent day foot soldiers sprawled every which way in its shade, horribly deformed beggars crept to vantage spots by it, and ambulatory blacksmiths, bakers, glass menders, and barbers set up the din of their trade. Except in those ecstatic, torment-crowded moments when a race was being run. Then they were on tiptoe—dancing, flailing, jostling, screeching, with the wondrous gamble of the horses.

It was a banging, thumping, pell-mell interlude for the factors too—some riding their own ponies hell-bent around the three-quarter-mile track: some watching, jumping-jack fashion, from their elevated seats along the lee of the track; and others whacking off to the paddock with a last-minute hope.

Race breakfasts were invariable—kippers, grilled kidneys, eggs, pancakes and molasses, served at ten so as to be out of the way by the eleven o'clock starting bell. Eight more races would be run off in the interval before three o'clock, whereupon a monumental curry appeared, followed by goolah—Malacca coconut pudding. The combination effectively glazed all eyes during at least two of the next four races. It was over at six—that is, the racing was, but there were toasts to be drunk to this and that winner before the lantern-hung boats started the procession back across the shimmering water.

Gill got to know, and like, the sturdy little Manchurian ponies they raced. Mettlesome, short-coupled little beasts, not more than twelve hands high, they were full of endurance and heart. He was too heavy to ride in a race, but frequently he wandered in and out of the stables, watching the *mafoos* groom them for the next event.

Once, on a sudden curious premonition, he'd stopped Lady Prophet from doping her—and everyone else's—favorite three-year-old just before the race. Not that that shrewd, salty, candid dowager had dreamed the lump of sugar she habitually gave her ponies before a race had been saturated this time with opium. Nor had Gill actually. It was something queer about the *mafoo*—the man's hooded look, or the straining tension of his curled fingers—that had pulled a warning trigger inside Gill's head, and he'd leaped forward to snatch the sugar practically out of the pony's mouth.

Naturally there'd been a fine hobble about the affair, and the *mafoo* had been banished from the course for all time. But it was Lady Prophet who'd looked at him squarely with those shrewd blue eyes of hers several days after the event and said: "I've respect for that intuition of yours. But I've a notion you don't always let it have the upper hand."

What did she mean? He asked himself the question several times. Was it that she didn't approve of the insipid, but tenacious, Sur Manoel as a partner? Or had his attentions to the bright and incalculable Zena reached a rumor stage?

Picnics on nearby Lappa Island, away from the rancid, musty, acid smell of Macao, were pure pleasure. As like as not there'd be a table set for twenty or twenty-four in one of the camphor groves beside a clear tumbling waterfall where they'd eat mountains of *arroz con mariscos*, the hearty Macanese version of rice with oysters, clams, and shrimps.

Gill would take his banjo along and play the quaint slave songs from Suwannee and Kentucky that had been the fad in New York when he'd left. Stacey had a homey, likable tenor, and it was good to hear it in the soft drowsy shade of the little Lappa glades, or echoing out over the moonlit water as they were rowed home. Soon it became a chorus, for Stacey taught the simple tunes to the other men in the group—William Hunter, Warren Delano, Russell Sturgis, Ian Lashmore, and Bruce Dyre, the two pink-and-white British naval officers who frequently came with them.

Lael was usually on these expeditions—her graceful, generous, refreshing self. Somehow, though, Gill became conscious of an element of reserve grown between them: some veil of indefinable aloofness, which the easy familiarity of these picnics did not dispel. There were times, suddenly, unexpectedly, looking at her—the white pillar of that lovely throat and the glinting fire in her marvelous hair—when he felt a quick stab of delight, a tug of urgency, which impelled him to rush to her and thrust all others aside, so he could clasp her hand, touch, be close to her.

Not that he ever actually did. Somehow the quizzically measuring look which came into her violet eyes these days when she looked at him had a checking effect. The other check was that damned effete Lashmore—always and forever at her elbow—debonair, attentive, and just a shade possessive!

Thus Macao revolved through its days—waiting for the trading season to begin in Canton.

Gill felt he had reached the absolute nadir of social futility the night he sat in a box at the gilt-and-plush little opera house to hear an operatic version of *Cinderella* done in Portuguese by Sur Manoel himself—Cinderella being a fat boy with saddle-tinted skin and a piercing falsetto. Except for an occasional oasis of *bem, mal, muito, faz favor,* and *adeus,* he was adrift in a desert of sibilant consonants blowing like a sirocco. But the white satin playbills, painted evocatively by Chinnery, were extravagant and delectable eye openers; and Sur Manoel was so touchingly grateful to Gill for having come and listened.

Long before the tardy tropical dawn one morning Gill pried himself from bed to sail to Lintin on a rousing beat-up between the *Seraph* and the British sloop *Alert.* The seamanship! The exhilaration . . . the pyramiding sails great sheets of light in the fresh and steady monsoon! The tattoo of blocks! The sea running like milk! The surging thrust of the low black hull as the New Bedford darling danced in a length ahead of the *Alert!*

For once Macy was happy as a ten-year-old, even though he was forced to celebrate the victory and receive his five-thousand-dollar purse in that "opium hell of Lintin," as he kept muttering under his breath. Dinner aboard the sumptuous roundhouse of the *Red Rover,* flagship of the twenty-three opium hulks stationed there, put him in a somewhat more amenable mood; or, at least, caused him to soft-pedal his muttering. By the time he'd finished his third glass of port and was out on deck dancing the quadrille with the Captain's wife under a bright moon that turned Lintin into an indigo pencil, he was entirely mellow—that is, for a New Englander.

As for what they saw of the opium trade next day—there was no sign of debauchery, no wantonness, no horror. Everything was spic and span—neat wooden boxes being unloaded in steady businesslike stream into four warehouses, and the same tidy boxes being carried out in orderly methodical streams from the nineteen other warehouses to waiting sloops and luggers and fifty-oared longboats.

It might just as well have been sugar, or tea, or spices, they agreed, as they were rowed ashore to climb the peak. Macy went along at Gill's insistence, for the party mustered ten and included the captain of the *Red Rover*, an English lady, Lael Manning, the inevitable Lashmore, and a Miss Coolidge, who'd only arrived from Salem.

The climb took them an hour and a half through camphor saplings, wild gardenias, and shell-tinted ginger. But when they got to the top, Gill was stunned to see twenty coolie attendants opening picnic hampers and wine bottles, and laying linen cloths on the grass! A ten-piece naval band from the *Red Rover,* encamped in the shade of nearby boulders, struck up a tune as the climbers hove in sight. After that the most grueling aspect was making a choice between veal pasty, galantine of duck, or charcoal-broiled chicken. Casually, as they ate, they debated whether the blue of the sky or the water was the more miraculous.

This was Macao life . . . the backwoods! The benighted geographical fag end he'd come to! Gill shook his head in wry amusement—and sent for the tailor to come and measure him for six more new suits.

In the beginning he'd gone to these parties reluctantly and with no impulse of gaiety in his heart, knowing he wasn't ready for them yet on account of Tad. But, gradually, he recognized them as opiates drugging his senses with bizarre fantasy. Pageants, masques—he, the gawking spectator, absorbing impressions and knowledge of the place—visually for the most part, but now and then through processes of selection and judgment. Then, too, he was meeting the community: he was becoming better acquainted with neighbors, with important business associates, with old-timers schooled in the China trade; and he was listening to their talk, digesting their experiences, that they might serve as the stones and mortar of his own foundation here.

At least, he told himself this as he set out for yet another gala evening. But often when he was alone on his hilltop, he admitted to himself that they were merely devices for marking time agreeably during the gnawing hiatus until the *Pombal* would come billowing into the roads again with the bright-eyed Zena and his multiplied dollars. Daily, at one place or another, he listened with a pang when people spoke of the Senhorita d'Almada's departure for Manila. With them he lamented her absence, and made it apparent he was counting the days until her pretty and lively face would be back to add to Macao's beguiling gaiety.

Yet each time he walked the beautiful green Praya amongst the modish blades and dallying couples, he carried with him the disturbing consciousness that back of these pink and blue and yellow bird-cage houses with flower-strangled gardens scarecrow thousands were living their insect lives: that gaunt skeletons groaned out the bitter rhythm of a toil song as they lifted and carried racking burdens which never earned enough rice to feed them and their shriveled babies; that warped, mutilated, rapacious women fought anywhere and everywhere and anyone over rubbish heaps for a mouthful of food; while, high above, kites wheeled ceaselessly in the sky dreeing the cry of doom.

It struck Gill as strange that in all the diverse gatherings he attended during these three weeks of waiting he had never once met a Chinese gentleman or a Chinese lady. It was as though they didn't exist: as though the vast swarming nation of Cathay was producing only two distinct breeds—miserable coolies and disdainful official rascals.

On his rambles about town, of course, he saw Chinese shopkeepers huddled together in their shop warrens—lantern makers inhabiting one street, silversmiths another, teak carvers, straw weavers, tailors, herbalists in still others. Also, Chinese carpenters, gardeners, stonemasons, shipwrights were busy everywhere doing the manual work which, he was told, the Portuguese detested and refused to touch hand to, even though the alternative was slow starvation.

Yet in neither British, American, nor Portuguese houses was he likely to meet, say, a Chinese scholar, a porcelain manufacturer with ten or twenty kilns turning out Canton Rose dinner services by the dozens, or an important tea planter specializing in that choicest and most pungent variety of black congou which has been flavored with the juice of ripe *lichi* fruit. He was curious about such men. He wanted to meet them: to visit with them in their houses and in his own, to know what they thought about, and did, and spoke. He told some of this to Stacey.

Stacey laughed. "Don't *begin* being balmy. There'll be plenty of opportunity to get that way later! Do you expect to do a heart-to-heart with a fellow in this farcial pidgin jargon? You'd be laughing in his face before you'd finish two sentences. *Pidgin* means *business*. So—*pidgin English*, then—is business English, whereby two aliens can buy or sell a hundred cases of tea at the best possible bargain. It's a mixture of phonetics, skeleton English, and a fair amount of Portuguese sprinkled in."

"Since I'm planning to live and do business here," Gill said, unfolding an idea that he hadn't been conscious of having five minutes ago, "why shouldn't I learn to speak proper Chinese? Why don't I hire someone to come each day and teach me?"

"Sleeping-dictionary variety?" Stacey grinned.

"No, not trollop's talk." Gill grimaced back.

"Well—that merely eliminates one kind from the remaining wide choice," Stacey went on in a half-serious manner. "Will you select Mandarin, which all court officials use? Or will you have one of the two southern tongues? Cantonese—or Hakka? You know the Hakkas—those workers we see everywhere around the waterfront, loading ships, sailing junks, wearing those crazy flopping lamp-shade hats. They're some different breed that comes from God knows where—bringing with them a completely different language."

He paused a moment to let the impact of what he was saying register with Gill, and then went on: "Remember, Cantonese won't get you a cup of tea if you're in Amoy—three hundred miles up coast from here. Amoy folk talk Amoy. You're up against the same conundrum if you go west of Canton into the Bohea tea country. Bang—it's another dialect. *Dialect* is not the word: these Chinese tongues are totally different languages."

Gill let Stacey run down, and said: "Since I want to deal with Chinese who live around here—Cantonese ought to do."

Stacey tilted his head the way he had of doing when he asked questions. "What makes you so all-fired certain a Chinese gentleman would deign to be on visiting terms with anyone so low on the social scale?" he chuckled. "Remember, in Chinese strata a merchant is bottom man. An outer-barbarian merchant . . . Great suds, lowest of the low! Social success under such handicap is precarious, isn't it?"

Gill laughed, and admitted it probably was. And while he sat turning the thing over, his mind reverted to this universal feeling of superiority in China: even the dogs seemed to have it. Evidences constantly showed through Ah Lau's mask of impassivity . . . odd, amusing little episodes they were, when considered singly. But with a kind of sandpaper irritation after frequent repetition.

Take the infinite pains the fellow took to groom him in niceties of Chinese ways—replacing American slippers, nightshirt, trousers, belts, lounging clothes, and even hats, with Chinese substitutes: bringing in Chinese dishes, Chinese wines, Chinese chopsticks—not to entertain, but because Chinese ways and dress and cooking were obviously superior.

Take the confounded lessons in tea . . . Three days of one variety, and then a new insinuating flavor of *lichi* juice, or a salty chrysanthemum-petal brew, or the pungent green called *Tit Kum Yum* would be introduced. Ah Lau, with monumental aplomb, would say solemnly: "How fashion Mas-tah Tad no catch'um plop-ah leaf? I plen-tee talkee how so. I very well savee first-chop leaf. But Mas-tah Tad, he no plop-ah savee. Too muchee catch'um coolie tea for belly wash."

Gill had succeeded in smiling these accusations off, knowing full well that Tad had always contended fancy teas weren't for American palates; and consequently had refused to stock them, even in small quantities. Being Tad, what he bought for American tables he'd feel bound to drink himself.

Yet now, sipping and savoring these new teas persistently thrust upon him—Lion Mountain black, smoky Lapsang souchong, amber jasmine, monkey-picked Fukien—so slight, so subtle, so flavorful, instead of acrid black brew that tasted like a hot awl unless it was laced with milk and sugar, Gill got the notion that Tad had guessed wrongly. He held out determinedly though, before ordering them for his own household, knowing full well that he was being made captive spectator to Ah Lau's unctious condescension.

He supposed the wily subterfuges and ruses which Ah Lau employed to keep from admitting even a small initial mistake were part and parcel of this superiority creed. There was the affair of the fresh eggs, for instance . . . those fat hens he'd seen in the market that morning, picking away at corn and grain! On the spur of the moment he'd bought four, complete with cage and rooster; and when they had been delivered to the garden, he'd announced proudly: "Now, by the Lord Harry, I shan't put up with any more herring-flavored curios! I'll have fresh ones every day!"

It had been a premature triumph evidently, for veiling lids had snapped down over Ah Lau's glittering eyes and the acknowledging bow had been a short, silent one. Moreover, day after day went by and Ah Lau reported stoically: "No have catchee egg."

Then, one breakfast, there had been the unmistakable cackle, so loud it couldn't be denied, and Gill had chuckled and dispatched Ah Lau to collect the egg at once. Ah Lau came back shaking his head. "Hen have talkee lie, Mas-tah. No have gottee egg." And for the next fortnight he had continued denial of any and all eggs; and then one by one the hens appeared, either in a fricassee, a stew, or a pasty, and Gill continued eating eggs the chicken man supplied, but with this difference—they were without taint of fish.

Another time Gill discovered, by chance, that the castor sugar stock had dipped excessively in two or three days since he'd purchased a new supply. "Missing? Missing?" Ah Lau had cried, indignantly striding to the nearest window and examining its latch. Then, making a grave and painstaking round of all windows and doors in the house, he'd come back, dismal, woebegone. "Bottom side doah no plop-ah shut. Have makee fix just now. Tomollo day sug-ah no belong missing!"

And it wasn't from then on. But coffee was, or flour, or lard, or spices. When inroads became too apparent, Gill went through the same farcial face-saving routine about safety.

The latest skirmish had been over a black puppy. One morning it had come over Gill that what he wanted was a dog to keep him company around the house, and he'd asked Ah Lau to be on the lookout for a young black one. An hour later a bumbling, clumsy, enormously beguiling puppy was dragged in. It was almost entirely white, with a few black patches. Gill had shaken his head firmly. "No, I said I wanted all black."

That same evening when Gill was smoking a pipe on the upper gallery, Ah Lau came leading a coal-black puppy on a ridiculously stout rope. The animal was a ringer for the pup Gill had seen earlier. It had the same build, the same muzzle, the same awkward legs and engaging friendliness. But it was incontestably black, every inch.

"Probably from the same litter," he'd told himself, and had paid the steep price its unseen owner demanded. Romping exuberantly in a rainstorm two days later, the puppy became a streaked and spotted gray where black dye had washed out—like a blond who'd changed her mind. The imperturbable Ah Lau's comment was: "Mas-tah no have talkee he wantchee bowwow *born* black."

It had been on a Friday—a fateful Friday—that Gill had been passing the Manning gate at the very moment when Manning's panting chair coolies drew up and a disquieted Manning stepped from the chair. "See here," he said in what was a rush for him, "something very untoward has evidently happened. I've not heard what it is yet. But they've called a special meeting of the Number Ones at the Senado immediately. I *must* be there. I've only rushed home to tell Lael I can't escort her to Chinnery's studio for her sitting—he's doing her portrait, you know. I wonder . . . could you do me the favor—that is, if you're not otherwise engaged—of escorting her there? Usually takes about an hour."

So it was that Gill was sitting in a comfortable chair across the studio from Chinnery's big easel. The artist had bustled about, twitching, smoothing, plucking at the folds of Lael's ice-blue gown until they suited. Meanwhile he'd kept up a running monologue on the glaring light, the weather, the new styles come out of Calcutta . . . but as he became more and more absorbed in his work, his talk lagged, and finally stopped.

Lael sat tranquilly immovable for what seemed an endless interval, and then broke out: "Oh, fah-doodle! Such solemn phizzes we have! Do let's have some talk to prove we're not statues! Mr. Bennett, pray oblige. Tell us about yourself . . . where you were born, what your first words were, where you went to school, your first heart affair—a ravishing brunette, no doubt—in fact, everything about yourself to date."

Gill was nettled. Why was she asking? Was it innuendo about Zena? Or, to relieve the tedium, was she saying the first thing which came into her head? He decided it was probably a combination of both, and begged off.

Chinnery bristled. "Come, come! You're the logical one to talk. Miss Manning here can't and keep that ladylike grin on her phizz. As for me—I need to give these blasted folds of the dress my full attention. You're elected. Begin!"

So, instead of being entertained by a merry-andrew of an artist, or left with his own thoughts, Gill found himself telling a lame version of his history in a lame way. He naturally skipped over details, listing the main points with the fewest possible words, and was recounting Bennett Brothers' small beginning when, suddenly, Chinnery stamped and threw down his brush.

"Holy murthering snakes, man! Must ye be a fuzz-buzz? Here ye've a Heaven-sent opportunity—the stage entirely to yourself to strut and be a somebody! And what do you do but wither our stomachs entirely with prosaic pap!"

"But—*my* life has been prosaic," Gill laughed.

"Then, damn it, make up one that isn't!" Chinnery blustered, snatching off his spectacles and pacing up and down theatrically. "Be an Othello! A Gulliver! A Sinbad! A Son-of-a-Somebody! For the love of God, man! Listen now . . ." He fixed a pious expression on his face and, with tremolo in his voice, said: "The very day I left my sainted mother's knee I . . ."

He was a born storyteller. He paced, he bowed, he clenched fists, he swept off imaginary hats, wrapped himself in imaginary cloaks, and drew imaginary swords. He lunged, he darted back, he skipped and capered on his short legs; he flung his hands about, panting, gasping for air . . . all the while recounting high drama.

When he paused, out of breath, Lael had broken pose and was gazing at him in a fond mixture of admiration and amusement. "Mr. C," she gasped, "did any of that really happen to you?"

Chinnery snorted, unabashed: "No, certainly not! Merely Lesson Number One for Lochinvar here in how to tell a tale to a susceptible young lady listener."

Lael looked levelly at the Irishman. "You've decided I'm susceptible, have you?" she asked coolly.

Chinnery darted a look at her over the top of his spectacles and changed the subject abruptly with an impatient exclamation. "There now—chaffering this way—the light's changed on that dratted skirt. It's all high lights. Come now, be a good girl and hold the pose while I see what I can make of it."

Some forty minutes later the silence of the studio was disrupted by a bang of the street door and running steps mounting the stairs. The door was thrust open without a knock, and Manning stood there—not his urbane and polished self, but perturbed and agitated, demanding even before he was in the room: "Where in thunder is Bennett? He can't have left!" Then, spotting Gill in the deep chair by the window, he exclaimed: "Thank Heaven, man, you're here!"

His voice was charged with emotion, his manner urgent and decisive. Ignoring Lael, who had risen and stepped down from the dais, and the staring Chinnery, he tossed his hat and walking stick on a chair and strode to Gill. "The coincidence of it!" he exclaimed tensely. "The utter miracle of coincidence—happening to meet you exactly when I did! Begging you to come up here in my stead! Such incredible luck! Only *I* know you're here. *They've* no idea where to search for you."

Gill stared, dumfounded.

Manning grasped Gill's elbow convulsively. "Merry Hell has broken loose for you, my friend, and the Portuguese gendarmes are out with a warrant for your arrest. We're one jump ahead! We've a squeaking chance—if only we can hide you till nightfall!"

It was lunatic! Gendarmes after *him!* "But who—Why——?" Gill stuttered.

"Come, step into the next room, and I'll break the details." Manning urged Gill out, talking steadily in low tense tones. "Shattering, I'm afraid. But not hopeless. I've a scheme. Quick, we've to put our heads together over it."

At the door he turned to the astonished artist, and to Lael, who took a step to follow them. "Stay here," he commanded. "There's one chance of saving his skin—I've got to know if he'll take it. If he does, we'll need your help later. Both of you. But now hold fast. If anyone should inquire for Mr. Bennett—you *don't know where he is,* understand?"

Chinnery pranced from toe to toe like a colt. "Oh, but you're abysmally wrong, my dear fellow! I know exactly where he is. He left here a half hour ago for a conference with the Bishop— the Number-One-Topside-Heaven-Pidgin Man." He waved his brush as though it were a saber. "After him, you Portu-gooses! After him—into the Bishop's palace!"

Gill turned dazedly along the corridor, and was about to step out the open door onto the gallery when Manning pulled him back. "No, not out there! Might be seen from a neighboring balcony. In here!" He motioned towards the cluttered salon; and when they'd both stepped in, he closed the door carefully.

Gill whirled around. "What in God's name is wrong? I've done nothing!"

Manning shook his head, his dark eyes curiously detached now, and yet curiously intense. "No, but that witch D'Almada has! Copiously! Abundantly! First off—she's an impostor! A sham! An actress adventuress who's been playing the part—consummately, I'd say—of the real heiress. Hoodwinked half the colony—that is, the male half—before she decamped with the boodle."

Gill felt walls crashing about him.

"It's fully confirmed, man. No question of doubt. A Noronha packet arrived this afternoon from Lisbon with the proper papers. Seems this hussy couched with the old man during his last days, so she learned enough of the gist of his affairs to perpetrate her hoax. Then she bribed the Captain of the *Pombal*, it seems, to bring her out East posthaste and linger until she was ready to go. What a pirate! Swooped up swag and ran for it!"

Pain was like corrosive acid eating into Gill.

"Got her hands on more than a hundred thousand here! How much did she milk you for?"

"Everything I own—twenty thousand dollars."

"Good lack!" Manning blew through his lips. "Well—you're in distinguished company . . . Pinto, Barretto, Pereira-Marquess, Sarmiento, Da Silva . . . all ponied up to her on one deal or another."

Gill groaned, beating his forehead with the heels of both hands. "I've been an utter fool! A credulous bumpkin. . . . But, good God, man, it was *my* money. They don't arrest a man for losing what's his own! Are they after Pinto and Barretto and . . . ?"

"No!" Manning shook his head emphatically. "The difference being—*you* signed a paper for her in Portuguese."

Gill nodded. "Yes, a purchase order buying one hundred casks of Patna."

"Not a *purchase* order, unfortunately," Manning corrected in clipped tones, "an order to Sur Manoel's Captain to deliver to bearer one hundred casks of Patna . . . signed by Sur Manoel's newly registered American partner."

Gill steadied himself against the mantelpiece, gasping, panting for breath, while his mind saw the ornamental little white-and-gold writing desk, the quill pen, the Portuguese translation Zena made, puckering and unpuckering her red lips, "partner *mia.* . . ." He turned starkly to Manning. "It's not true, sir. I wrote the purchase order myself, and signed what I took to be a bona fide translation. The Senhorita had cash to purchase——"

"She still has, that's the rub—*plus* one hundred casks of Patna belonging to Sur Manoel's company, of which you are a part. Or rather, *were* a part until a half hour ago, when Sur Manoel swore out a warrant for embezzlement."

"I haven't embezzled! I borrowed ten thousand, and I'm liable for it. I'll pay it back. I can explain. . . ."

"Explain," Manning said contemptuously. "Fah-doodle with what you explain. What can you prove—sitting in a Portuguese jail? Do you have funds to hire a lawyer? And an additional thousand or two for court fees and translators?"

Gill shook his head negatively. "Sur Manoel is a gentleman. He's extraordinarily kind and generous. He'll listen without arresting me."

"Wrong—on four counts," Manning snapped tersely. "He's not a gentleman. He's neither kind nor generous—beneath that humble veneer—unless it suits him. He won't listen to you right now. You didn't injure a slight thing like his honor. You've kicked him mortally in what he values above all things—his capacity for enterprise. You tricked him before he could trick you. That he can't forgive, because it's the one fundamental he recognizes."

The appalling enormity of the affair came tumbling in on Gill's consciousness. He floundered with thoughts, words . . .

then broke out desperately: "But, surely, someone will believe me! Allow me to atone. Settle it without going to jail?"

Manning's hand gripped Gill's shoulder. "If it isn't clear to you already—let me assure you that I believe you to be the victim of a very adroit schemer. I'm convinced you'll square things eventually —somehow, some way. But, believe my sincerity, that's not our immediate concern."

"What would you have me do?" Gill asked.

"The money—it's every cent you possess?"

"Except for eighty, maybe ninety, dollars I have in my purse."

"H'm-m, not enough for a Calcutta passage, even if a ship were leaving today."

"You'd have me run away?"

"I'd have you keep out of a Portuguese jail right now . . . until we get things squared by orderly process."

"India is a long way off for that."

"Exactly. But I wanted you to come to that conclusion yourself" —Manning's voice had resumed its usual dispassionate wintry tones—"before I conditioned with you. I have a proposal—*provided* we're able to keep you hidden until nightfall—that I hire a fast longboat to smuggle you out of the colony and up the back way to Canton."

In the agony of his mortification Gill could only stare bleakly at Manning, the muscles of his jaw so tightly contracted he couldn't swallow.

Manning continued: "You're beyond Portuguese jurisdiction there, but close enough to attempt clearing your name and making settlement when the time's right. Meanwhile for this season— until April, I mean—you buy tea for Russell and Company."

Gill's soul rebelled, but reason told him this was the only course left to him.

Manning nodded in unspoken agreement. "You're in a vise," he said, "but I would point out it's not of my making."

"No," Gill groaned, and the cry came from deep within him, "it's entirely my making. But the pressure's still there."

Manning didn't answer immediately. Then with a small lift of the shoulders he said: "Don't gnaw on remorse. You've bought yourself a portion of experience, that's all. Each of us does it, one way or another. Each paying a different price. Look upon six months in Canton as another portion you're acquiring—except you won't have to pay cash for it. You receive salary, maintain yourself decently, and stand to come out with both a clean name and a small plum in the way of privilege tonnage. That's preferable experience, surely, to mildewing in a Portuguese jail for a year or more whilst documents go to Lisbon, the court there decides the merit of your case, and the verdict comes the long voyage back."

Gill's mind worked in seesaw fashion as the enemies of memory warred within him . . . his scrimping past, urging ambitions, visions of a mercantile empire, antipathy to the tea business. But above all, his gullibility, his credulous acquiescence to the designs of this play actress, this . . . He shook himself free and looked squarely at Manning. Animosity went out of him, and again he sensed the bigness of the man behind the physical bigness of body. He jerked his head back and with a wry laugh said: "You see before you a tea buyer, sir."

The older man clasped Gill's hand firmly and replied: "Good fellow! I'm comfortable in my mind that uncommon good will come of it. Now—our problem is to conceal you till nightfall. Then get you down to the junk harbor and aboard a 'scrambling dragon' —fifty-oared—that'll take you up Broadway Passage to Whampoa Anchorage. Come, we'll talk it over with Lael and Chinnery. They'll help with ideas."

Hour after hour there was the steady whip of oars; the splashing, hissing, sucking sounds of water; the animal grunt of oarsmen; and the sustained thrust of the boat. It was neither lulling nor soothing to Gill, lying there with thronging thoughts on the matting-covered bench in the small main cabin.

He'd dozed off a time or two, only to jerk to awareness next minute—perspiring under the grease paint Chinnery had daubed on him and the coolie rags they'd decided upon as a disguise—to twist and turn, to stretch his legs and then hump them again. The cabin was high enough for him to stand in; and he'd prowled it twice, feeling his way in the darkness to the center table—for the lamp above it wasn't lighted—then groping on to the movable wall panel he'd been told to hide behind if another boat should come alongside, or if there were any commotion at the Customs check point.

Somewhere in the steady nightmare he'd got himself to the window and lifted its bamboo blind, to sit beside it for another eternity, relishing the rush of air on his body even though it was hot and damp. But after an interval he'd wearied of staring into the layers of darkness beyond, which seemed only a replica of the darkness in his mind, and he'd gone back to sprawling on the bench again.

About midnight they pulled into Heang-shan, the hot creek port some twenty miles above Macao, to have their Customs passes checked and countersigned. The din there was hideous even at that late hour. Men and sampans and abuse poured alongside in a steady stream, jumbled with hammers, roosters, gongs, pigs, fire-crackers, dogs, flutes, and drums. Standing with an eye against a shutter crack in the little cubbyhole behind the false panel, Gill watched the lurid glow pitch-pine torches cast on the lunatic scene.

He saw officers come aboard; and when feet pounded on the deck above, he went to crouch under rags in the farthermost dark corner. He heard hatch covers cannonade off and on, doors open-ing and banging shut, and voices yelling and shouting and shrill-ing steadily. But no one came near his dark hole; and when he felt the boat move forward again, he unwound cramped legs and crept to the peephole again, and watched as they passed through a barricade of war junks. Manning had evidently done a thor-ough job with the fast-boat Captain and Customs passes, he told himself as he opened the panel and stepped into the cabin again, glad that the hazard of the check point was behind.

It was perhaps two hours later that he felt the forward thrust of the boat begin to ease off and move in a slow glide. There was a swinging turn; another; and still another in smooth, silent water, with only a scattering of oars dipping almost soundlessly. He guessed they were threading one of the countless little creeks that veined the land—to rest the oarsmen, perhaps, or avoid pirates in the lonely light of dawn.

Gradually they stopped, as soundlessly as they'd come, to sway gently in an eddy of shallow water. When he lifted the blind, he saw they were moored to a stake driven in mud, a mantle of reeds hedging the boat so closely they seemed growing from the hull itself. Land sounds were all about—the deep-throated persistent croak of frogs, the metallic strumming of cicadas, and the high fluting rhapsody of a bulbul.

The papery shush-shush of the reeds and the gentle rock of the boat became cradling now, and Gill dropped off into the drugged sleep of exhaustion.

The next thing he knew, someone was nudging him. He sprang up and away, only to see it was a coolie with towels and a basin of water for him to wash off the disguising grime and grease paint, slathered on—was it only twelve hours ago?

Standing to wash, he was conscious the boat was out from the reeds and under full way again. The sun was up. Through the open blind he saw green shores, and a pagoda silhouetted against the porcelain blue of a clear morning sky. By and by they brought him a breakfast of tea, fried onion dough, rice gruel, and hard-boiled duck eggs.

Afterward from the window Gill watched an intricate patchquilt of islands and creeks run by . . . sweeping plains of rice flecked with unbelievable white birds; tawny, sun-drenched hills with hugging nutshell houses of thatch and stone; yellow cassia bloom cascading like silk; queer, white-barked tallow trees lining paddy dikes with a gnarl of crooked branches like old men raising their arms to Heaven; the soaring flash and flute of larks; the busy incessant flight of magpies in chattering thousands. . . .

The midday halt was made under the shade of a camphor clump, where drongos swooped in iridescent circles. The panting rowers flung themselves flat on the bank, resting comatose while a meal of fried shrimps, savory noodles, and sweet sesame cake was handed in to Gill. Yet he wasn't permitted out of the cabin even there.

Afternoon brought a pressing, overwhelming consciousness of man, for as they drew into the broad stretch at right angles to the main stream, there was never a void, never a foothold not taken over by man—by his grains, his orchards, his burial mounds, his ducks, his goats, and his brick-and-thatch houses.

The main stream itself teemed like a minnow pond—every kind of craft caught up in its boisterous turbulent swirl: tilted junks, gilded houseboats, fruit rafts, two-masted lorchas, duckwalks, sampans, anything and everything that would float, all converging tumultuously, it seemed, on the cove that was Whampoa Anchorage.

A small forest of clipper spars were moored there, and Gill scanned them with mixed emotions. He had successfully run the gamut of Portuguese authority: he was free, temporarily—to begin a new sentence! In another hour he'd be delivered to a Russell and Company clipper waiting at the Anchorage for the trading season to be officially opened. The following day a company cutter would convey him the intervening thirteen miles up Fiddler's Reach to their factors' house in Canton. To Canton! To six gagging, galling, miserable months of tea buying, he told himself bitterly.

CHAPTER X

CANTON,
October 1838

CANTON IS an old city and feels its age. The fables and traditions of ancientness, the repute and disrepute of many centuries have combined to make it one of the strangest trading ports in the world.

It has always had to do with ships and sailors. For since the beginning of things ships have been nosing into its yellow mud—come from hugging delta islands; come a thousand miles from vaporous Cloud Mountains in the west; or from deeply blue Eastern Seas, and southern islands beyond those seas—to trade: to barter cargo for raw silk, ginger and alum root, indigo, tea, melons, ramie cloth, lily-flower seeds, and xanthin.

Through the roll call of centuries the ships lengthened and deepened, coming from farther and farther shores until, ten centuries ago in golden T'ang days, Canton port was scattered with lanteen-rigged dhows of Arab and Persian and Indian merchants loading tea, wrought silk, lacquerware, and true porcelain for the *souks* of Baghdad. High-decked caravels and galleons and schooners began mooring there in the Middle Ages to take aboard the first sweet oranges Lisbon and Valencia were ever to see, the first sedan chairs for Paris, the first wallpaper, tea, azaleas, peonies, asters, primroses, chrysanthemums, tea roses, and apricot seeds for London.

By the time the nineteenth century rolled around, close to a million people had squeezed themselves, like seeds in a pomegranate, into a mile-square city bound tight by high gray walls. The port itself was a space some five hundred paces wide between the city wall and the river. Haphazard ranks of scaling, mottled, mildewed shops and warehouses stood every which way, with crooked lanes jig-sawing between. Surging in and out of these were coolies by the thousand, straining and groaning over bales from an incredible press of junks wedged against the stone embankment.

A city on water was farther along—mat-cabined sampans moored gunwale to gunwale in dense rows where waterfolk by the tens of thousands lived out enduring, vituperative, verminous lives: eating, loving, sleeping, begetting, and dying afloat a few planks. They dare not touch foot within the city, build themselves a mat lean-to ashore, consort, or marry with landsmen. The law of the empire forbade it.

Beyond this sampan city the thirteen brick-and-granite houses of the foreign factors stood in a solid row on low tidal mudflats. Handsome, white-limed, substantial, symmetrical, with a neat and tidy stone-paved promenade and small flower garden between them and the water's edge, they were a startling incongruity in the midst of the calico-patched waterfront. Their eastern boundary was a fetid creek—a sewer, really—running from the city wall; and the other two sides were hedged in by a pandemonium of squalid, ramshackle Chinese hovels and shops.

During his first weeks in Canton, Gill felt disgust, incredulity, and excitement. He told himself he would never get the hang of living in such a revolting, princely, exuberant, detestable and unpredictable place as this City of Rams, as the Chinese name implied . . . not literally, he was told, but in the zodiacal sense of the ram Aries—a vigorous leader always.

Russell and Company's compound was a range of four stone houses, built one behind the other, connected by intermediate courts and an arched passageway leading back from the big teak entrance door. The commercial area was on the ground floor, with offices for compradore, shroff, linguists, and Chinese clerks next to the countinghouse and granite treasury. There were assorted showrooms, and in the rear kitchens, servants' quarters, and storage rooms.

But up the broad main stairs it became a hotel, a club, an elegant and handsomely appointed mansion. Drawing-rooms, library, and a Chippendale dining-room were paneled in teak.

Chairs of Spanish leather were mixed with rattan and woven cane, the chandeliers were Waterford glass, and deep-piled Peking rugs as blue as summer twilight covered parquetry floors. Ten resident partners shared these living quarters, along with the two salaried employees, Philip Stacey and Gill.

A series of bedrooms with connecting verandas filled the upper floor—each a spacious, airy, comfortable haven—and were of sufficient number so each man could be alone. Each had his own manservant—a Cantonese which Peking forced the Hong merchants to hire—to do his room and look after his clothes. Belowstairs a staff of cooks and helpers kept the table laden with succulent and imaginative dishes.

Gill accommodated himself with surprising ease, he thought, to the princely style. He found it appeasing, but unsatisfying. There was no physical outlet: no exhilarating, or exhausting, way to work off the caged restlessness. No way to breathe deep and go striding forth until pulsing blood rinsed frustration and pettiness out of the body. They were allowed off the mud flat only three days a month, and they couldn't go rowing on the river at any time. The Edict said: "To row about in boats for mere pleasure, as well as riding about in sedan chairs, only nourishes pride and profligacy in outer barbarians, and is therefore forbidden."

Respondentia Walk had to do—three hundred meters long, a hundred wide between houses and river. At sunset they'd empty out of the thirteen agencies—pouring forth like boys out of school—to shuttle a thousand paces back and forth, in groups, and singly; trudging, sauntering, marching determinedly: seeking surcease, change, stimulation. They'd play one-old-cat, two-old-cat, rounders, quoits, and try handstands. Augustine Heard, the eccentric American independent trader, kept a pony, and regularly at five each evening rode it back and forth at breakneck pace.

Thinking it a wonderful joke, the Chinese watched. Soldiers standing guard at Old China Street, at Hog Alley, and at New China Lane—the three labyrinths leading back from the Walk into the native shops and houses—laughed hilariously over such unnecessary exercise. Shopkeepers, children, and the street riff-raff these soldiers were supposed to keep out looked on with good-natured contempt. One enterprising grogshop keeper, whose balconies overlooked the Walk, advertised the attraction with signs, and charged double price for the sunset-hour performance of the foreign devils.

Taking unnecessary exercise was a mystifying compulsion to the Chinese. One explanation they had was that foreigners, unskilled in using the abacus, were forced to tote up accounts by counting paces. Another pundit contradicted: "It's religious observance with them. They walk a 'thousand paces' to gain merit, in the hope they'll be re-created Chinese in the hereafter." Still another held forth the theory "So small are England and America, that if their traders and sailors all went back the land would overflow. They're compelled to keep a portion of population on ships away from home."

Gill laughed at these notions two or three days a week. But then there'd be the time when arrogant, blockheaded superiority would send him into a rankling inner rage. The day, for instance, he and three others were having a rousing game of one-old-cat, and the port magistrate—newly come from the north—arrived to discuss Customs fees with Manning. He'd halted his chair to gape at the players. After what seemed a horrified minute he turned to the Hong merchant Howqua and said: "Can you pretend such sweating ones are gentlemen? If they *must* play games, why don't they have coolies throw the ball, swing the stick, and run for them?" He'd ordered his chair, and his person, away from any such contaminating contact forthwith.

At times Gill's lonely restlessness was more than he could bear, and he'd go wandering up Old China Street, where a blazing, incandescent liveliness animated the thronging ruck of humans—stage-struck guards posturing like actors; barbers twanging giant tweezers with penetrating insistence; a leper wearing telltale hat and mat; hawkers trumpeting; vendors rattling wooden clackers; bargainers and buyers making wide gestures and shouting the harsh, strident Cantonese talk; load coolies—the *ku-li*, the 'eating-bitterness-people'—toiling antlike under unbelievable burdens . . .

Ivory shops hugging jade shops, silk and linen shops, umbrella shops; Physic Alley, Apothecaries' Lane, Mandarin Cap Street, Lantern Lane, Worn-out Clothes Lane, Little Furniture Alley, Big Furniture Alley—mazed lanes no wider than hallways— threading off at all angles. The acrid stench of drains; the acrid stench of humans; mutilation, starvation, tottering death every- where—and everywhere regarded with opaque eyes bare of pity. . . .

Gill could never get far on these rambles. In no time there'd be children and grownups jostling and pushing to get closer, nudging his elbows, stumbling over his boots, and hiccoughing with laugh- ter at every step and movement he made.

With the mob at his heels he'd head back towards Hog Alley, which opened onto the Walk. The reek of alcohol there was stronger than the reek of offal, but there was a string of grog- shops to be passed, along with the macabre whimsy of their signs— FIRST-CHOP RUM, HARD-A-PORT, LIQUID MYSTERY, NUMBER ONE CURIO BRANDY. This was the haunt of sailors on one-day leave from Whampoa—come to squander three months' sea pay in one day on the lethal intoxicants and aphrodisiacs these Hog Alley rascals concocted out of alcohol, tobacco juice, molasses, and arsenic.

Stacey hung about Gill, as lugubriously friendly as the streaked black puppy; and almost as clumsy in his advances and retreats. Gill was touched, and tried to interest himself in the younger man. But Stacey had started growing a mustache, so blond and soft it could barely be seen in anything but strong sunlight. He was forever working with it, smoothing the hairs with a reverent forefinger, and in the middle of a conversation he'd jump up and go to the mirror to study it. "Tell me honestly, Gill. I mean, please be quite frank," he'd say in pained anxiety, "do you think it will be long enough next week to cut?"

"Bound to be!" Gill would encourage. "It's a flourishing growth already."

"You mean it's *too long?*" Stacey would cry, rushing back to the mirror.

Or it would be . . . which wax to use on it. Beeswax had the right color, but mightn't it be too stiff? Macassar oil, blast it, wouldn't do for blond hair, supposed to turn it black. But, surely, there must be something . . . a cross between . . .

It didn't make stimulating companionship. So Gill would go wandering over to Marquick's Hotel at the far end of the Walk and play billiards, Russian fashion, or sit and chat in the upstairs coffee room with one or another of the ships' officers up from Whampoa. Or he'd go for a visit with the eccentric Welshman, Dr. Richard Cox, who kept a herd of goats in the garden plot of the Danish agency. Gill had learned to side-step the doctor's exploratory fist, for the medico had a way of doubling up his hand and, without warning, whacking at a man's stomach. If the victim doubled up, Dr. Cox launched into a lecture on the dangers of an unsound liver. If there was no flinching, the man—still the victim —was invited to a bountiful breakfast, mostly composed of goat's milk and cheese. Even watching this lively diagnosis, Gill found, was an occasional time-killer. No matter what he did, though, he had a feeling of being dried up, listless, without incentive— detached from the world of everyday men.

Then, one morning, emotion came crowding in upon him and he found himself, suddenly, very much attached to life and to the men around him.

He and Stacey were on their way to talk a tea deal with the venerable Howqua, whose town offices were in a high-walled *yamen* back on the thoroughfare behind the foreign agencies. As the two were crossing the Walk to go around by Old China Street, they found the entrance to it filled with a sizable procession moving towards them.

First came six guards in imitation tiger skins at a fast clip, brandishing whips and whipping people aside to clear the way.

Behind, at the same brisk walk, were eight retainers in the proscribed dress of servants, then a sedan chair and more retainers.
The strangest part was two strapping fellows carrying huge broad-
swords, a wretch tottering under heavy chains, and two men
lugging a cross. Six guards brought up the rear, and after them
the usual riffraff straggled.

What in thunder? Gill and Stacey asked each other a little
incredulously. The thing looked as though it might be an intended execution, but—that couldn't be. Not here! They watched
the procession cross the Walk and pull up before Russell and
Company's flagpole, where the Stars and Stripes whipped in a
fresh breeze.

The retainers set to, rushing about with cords and canvas which
soon materialized into a canopy. When they'd finished setting
it up, a magistrate—by his badge of office—stepped from the chair
and walked under the awning. He evidently gave orders for the
cross to be raised, for shovels appeared and digging commenced.

Gill caught his breath. "They wouldn't have the audacity to
attempt an execution here!" he declared.

Stacey stared back, his blue eyes wide with apprehension.

"But they can't! Not here—under the American flag!" Gill's
voice rose in anger. He moved forward, waving both hands, making signs for the diggers to halt.

Stacey laid a restraining hand on his arm. "Hold on! We need
linguists to translate. I'll fetch ours. Wait for me. Wait!" He
turned and sprinted towards their compound gate.

Gill didn't wait. He strode to the tent edge and, without a
bow or a salutation of any kind, shouted indignantly: "How
fashion this? No can do my side! *No can!* Savee?"

The magistrate fixed Gill with an insolent, unblinking stare.
Then he turned, unhurriedly, and seated himself on a chair the
retainers had unpacked. With the same insolent deliberateness
he poured himself a cup of tea, blew on it, sucked it up in several
noisy gulps, cleared his throat, spat, and looked into space. The
diggers went on digging.

Gill had the impulse to grab the rascal and shake him until he rattled. But he saw Manning come running out their doorway, followed by Delano, Cushing, Stacey, the compradore, and two linguists. Cries began going up from adjoining agencies, doors opened, and in another instant a score of factors were converging on the offensive tent.

Manning reached there first. Through his interpreter he demanded what the magistrate was doing on private property which the foreign traders had leased for their exclusive use.

The magistrate didn't move. With the same studied insolence he'd practiced on Gill he smoked a flutelike pipe a servant filled for him. He sat, as aloof and remote as an actor waiting his cue, while the other astonished factors gathered around. Then, laying aside his pipe, he composed his mouth and closed his eyelids the way a man does in talking to poor relations, and said he was merely carrying out orders. All land in the dominion, the Governor had ordained, was Throne land, and consequently could be used for the Throne's purposes. Its present purpose was to show foreign traders the sorry end of any wretch who smuggled opium.

Consternation hit the bristling factors like a bat flying into their red faces.

"We can't permit it!" The cry was torn from Gill. "We can't let them execute a man before our eyes because he's doing what we ourselves do!"

"No! Never!" The cry went up from others. "Stand fast!"

Precisely at this moment a boatload of English sailors pulled in at the embankment steps. They could hear the shouting, and came at a run to see what the excitement was about. What they learned in one minute was enough to set them off. The next, a Donnybrook had broken loose.

With a banshee whoop of "Clear the square!" the angry tars rushed pell-mell at the cross. They wrenched it loose from the ground with their hands. They whacked and beat at it until it was in splinters, and then with the splinters as clubs they threw themselves onto the magistrate's tent, snapping its cords, gashing its canopy, and scattering chairs, table, and teacups in all directions.

They were ready to turn on the magistrate himself if several factors hadn't intervened momentarily until that discomposed gentleman could scurry into his chair and be whisked away by bearers. The boisterous, bloodied sailors didn't care: they howled taunts and looked around to free the prisoner from his chains. But he was gone, they found, with disappearing guards and retainers and executioners.

This didn't end the affair, however. The straggling rabble of onlookers was still there—joined now by verminous thousands crowding, pushing, jostling into the Walk. Half were empty-faced youngsters, callous and doltish; and from this a mob was born.

There was a cry, answered by others. In a sudden flare of fury and hate these irresponsible thousands grabbed up stones, oars, bamboo staves, anything destructive they could lay hands on, and advanced on the little group of foreigners with animal snarls.

"Trample them! Tread over them! They're nothing but barbarians!" the mob chanted lustfully.

Before this malevolence the factors fell back, making for the nearest compound doors and barricading them. Gill and Stacey, with several young Britishers and sailors, thrashed out right and left with tent poles they'd snatched up to fend off the foremost.

"Let off! All of you!" Manning cried to the battling rear guard. "Get to your buildings and let the hoodlums cool off."

The British youngsters and sailors made a dash for their factory, and reached it, although they were pulling and carrying several wounded with them. Simultaneously Gill and Stacey managed to free themselves before the mob could close in. They skipped inside their own big teak door, and then leaned against it, panting and winded, as the giant bolt was thrust into its socket.

But the fury outside did not cool.

It swelled instead: mounting and mounting, to rabid pitch. Pebbles pelted at the door and cracked windows. Then cobbles replaced pebbles. Iron railing, torn from the flower garden, started a hacking tattoo on shutters. Swelling over this was a witless singsong of hate, and a baleful clap, clap, clap of hands which went on unceasingly.

Inside the compound there was the clink of silver as the shroff and his clerks frantically tossed dollars into boxes and trundled them into the granite vault. Storeroom doors banged shut. The bolts of cupboards thudded. Kitchen fires sizzled and steamed as they were doused. Bottles were smashed and glass shards heaped on the stones inside the gate in case the barefooted mob broke it down. Senior partners were upstairs and down, lugging ledgers and cargo manifests to the bedroom floor, hanging blankets over chandeliers, stowing celadon and ivory bric-a-brac in cupboards, and gathering up fire tongs, pokers, curtain rods, anything and everything that might serve as a weapon. They had neither firearms, cutlasses, nor pikes. Chinese regulations forbade foreigners such weapons.

Gill came running from the back passageway, to take the front stairs two at a time, hunting Manning. He diverted long enough to look out a front window, and saw what looked to be a battering-ram being improvised below in the square. It wasn't large, but was ugly enough. If the mob got it to working, the door wouldn't hold against it indefinitely.

Gill turned away, calling Manning's name until he located him. "I've just checked, sir," he reported. "There's not a soldier in sight. Even the guards have disappeared."

Manning smacked one hand against the other impotently. "I have close to a million dollars in the strong room. Howqua knows it. Why doesn't he send soldiers to clear the Walk?"

"We need to get to him. He may not know how serious the mob has suddenly become," Gill urged.

"Get through that filthy mob?" Manning cried.

"Not out that way," Gill explained quickly. "Over the roof. I've scouted our rear building. There's a way from it to reach the next-door roof. Beyond that is a low setback. An easy stretch and a jump will put me in the back lane. Then it's only a two-minute sprint to Howqua's."

Manning clutched Gill's shoulder in a convulsive grip. "What's the situation in the lane? Filled?" he demanded.

"Practically empty," Gill told him. "Before anyone can set up a shout, I'll be in Howqua's."

"Provided his gate's not bolted!"

Gill brushed the likelihood aside. "It'll be open, I'm sure. Everything's quiet in that direction. The trouble's all on our doorstep." He smiled confidently, beginning to move off. "Be back in jig time, sir—with soldiers."

"By George, I believe you will!" Manning exclaimed with an appreciative salute. "Good fellow!"

Gill was halfway up the staircase of the rear building when he heard following steps come pounding up after him. It was Stacey, red-faced, panting, but grinning impudently. "I've got a long stretch, too. Thought maybe I could help." He held up a length of rope and a cleat he'd salvaged somewhere.

"Right! Both counts!" Gill grinned back, and they ran on together.

Getting out onto the roof was easy; and provided they crouched forward and half walked on their hands, the parapet was high enough to shield them from any viewers in windows in the Chinese quarter. They managed to cross the next roof in the same crouching advance. But from there on they were in plain view of an *amah* hanging out clothes on an upper veranda, or of any other Chinese looking out an upper window. They secured the cleat and went down the rope hand over hand to the neighboring setback. Straddling the peaked ridgepole, they slid down smooth tiles to the eaves, and from there dropped straight into the lane.

The *amah* went on placidly stringing clothes on a pole, and either no one else happened to notice them or reconciled the eccentric proceeding with the other incomprehensible exercise foreigners were apt to indulge in. As for the lane, it was curiously somnolent. Cries of strife echoed no louder here than the usual discordant clamor of a Canton day. Several shopkeepers, sitting behind counters, torpidly eyed the two running figures, but raised no cries.

"It's closed!" Stacey gasped, pointing ahead to Howqua's big double-doored red gate.

"Blast and damn!" Gill groaned. "We'll have to find a way over it!" But when he pushed flat-handed against the small door panel set into one side of the gate, it miraculously swung open, and they stepped inside.

A gatekeeper came running with threatening arms upraised to stop them. But Gill brushed him aside with urgent gestures, shouting: "Howqua! Chop-chop!"

"*Fie-tee! Fie-tee!*" Stacey yelled his magic word.

But neither waited. They ran through the gatehouse, across the courtyard, and up into the main building.

Howqua had evidently heard them, for he came out his door towards them, his frail old face creased with concern, his tenuous fingers agitatedly shaking each other. "My chin-chin you werry fine day," he clacked off in an attempt at the amenities. Then, coming closer, he asked anxiously: "How fashion trub? Litty trub? Plen-tee trub?"

With the tocsin of hate still sounding in his ears, it seemed incongruous to Gill to use this baby talk to describe a raddled mob, but it was immediate communication, and wholly comprehensible. He assured the old gentleman it was "Plen-tee trub!" and asked for soldiers to disperse the mob at once.

Howqua closed parchment eyelids as though summoning strength for a decision, opened them almost instantaneously, and snapped out urgent orders for his messenger to speed—not to the Governor, but to the Viceroy himself—and obtain troops for the foreign traders.

Bowing with measured graciousness, Howqua led the way into his office, hovering frailly until they were seated, and then sank into his own chair with a long sigh.

After an interval, slowly, haltingly, pulling at his philosopher's wispy beard, he told them that, hearing of the attempted stran-

gling of some unknown opium smuggler in the Walk, he had
called for his chair and gone personally to the Governor's *yamen*
to beg, to *buy* even, a superseding order. He had been too late to
change the Governor's decree, as Fortune would have it, for only
minutes before, the Governor had finished his midmorning pipe,
and had already ascended into dreamer's paradise.

When the thin voice fell silent, there was cessation of time
in the room. And then a faint pulse smote the air, beating louder
and nearer. It was marching soldiers clanging gongs to warn of
fast approach, and thus strike terror to all hearts.

From that day inertia fell away from Gill. It was as
though, in the sudden emotional demands of the riot, he'd re-
gained identity. He could think vehemently and feel vehemently
again. With this came a mental acquisitiveness, a tugging curiosity
about the many-faceted life going on about him. He found he
wanted to inquire, explore, scrutinize, examine, investigate a variety of things. He even wanted to know more about tea leaf
itself.

He began to thumb through the old ledgers and cargo manifests for brand names; he talked with old China hands in other
factories. He pored over old files of *The Canton Register;* he read
diaries of sea captains, of tea buyers, and of missionaries who'd
been up and down the coast to plantations in Swatow, Foochow,
and Hangchow. The Reverend Charles Gutzlaff—the Pomeranian translator Gill had met at Manning's house his second day
in Macao—had written a variety of eyewitness accounts. Speaking
six Chinese dialects which he'd learned in Malacca, the unor-
thodox little missionary had been journeying up and down the
China coast the past six years on an opium clipper, impartially
selling Lee's Anti-bilious Pills, giving away translations of the
Bible, and acting as translator during opium deals. Also, there
were the quaint and amusing and definitive memoirs of a generation of tea buyers who'd trekked west into the weird canyons and

top-heavy mountains of Kwangsi Province to see the hand-rolled pearl tea, only to find it was done—by foot!

After a span Gill took himself to the town house of the Hong merchant Gowqua to talk tea. Gowqua, they told him, was a good leaf man. Not only were his deals absolutely sound, but he spoke better English. Moreover, he was an erudite gentleman with a nicely balanced reverence for, and knowledge of, the leaf he sold. Gill sent an advance letter asking for the meeting, but he was particular about the wording of his request. "Make it clear," he told the linguist writing the letter, "that I do not come as a trader to buy tea. I would come as a pupil to learn of the master."

When the answer arrived naming a day, Gill went alone. He wanted it that way to see whether—in his own fashion—he could hope to make friends with a Chinese man.

He was unprepared for the simple beauty of the room where Gowqua received him. Instead of incense there was the fresh cinnamon scent of cassia spraying from several large vases, making happy yellow splashes against ice-blue walls. The furniture was the mellow amber of Ming rosewood, superbly and forcefully simple. There was uncluttered space, and none of the usual overly-carved blackwood of Canton. Nor was there intricate scrollwork in the wall panels, except for the high twofold screen in one corner. Gill's mind registered a fluttering movement behind it as he sat down, but after an interval of no further motion he decided it had been a trick of reflected light flickering through the lovely fan-shaped window opposite the screen.

The compelling quality and dignity of the room, Gill felt immediately, was in the man Gowqua himself. Gill felt himself respond to it with a longer and deeper bow than he'd ordinarily make. When he straightened, it was to move slowly across the room, measuring pace and gestures to the unhurried precision of Gowqua's courtesy. He liked the feeling it gave him—well-being, a curious sort of harmony—and he thought how this little man could teach him much in courtliness, for in this moment he knew he had much to learn.

As he took the seat of honor given him, Gill recognized there was more than courtliness in this Chinese. He saw tolerance and intelligence in the keen eyes, humor and prankishness in the earnest smile, and something resilient and enduring in the incredibly fragile body.

They talked easily together . . . first it was about the weather, but not the usual inanities: not almanac fashion. Gowqua spoke affectionately of the blessed brown solitude which autumn brought, of affinity existing then between the elements and the human spirit . . . the cleansing rage of winds, soft tranquilizing mists, a plunging impulse the rains brought, and the soaring uplift found in infinite clouds. It set Gill to thinking. He'd never identified himself with the elements, and he liked the idea.

Their first tea was brought in celadon cups of crackleware as finely veined as the scales of a trout. Gowqua held his up, revolving it slowly and relishing it fondly. "My health-insurance cups," he told Gill with a puckish smile. At Gill's puzzled look Gowqua opened the hinges of his thumb ring and spilled a few grains of white powder into his tea. In seconds the inside glaze was changing to green to mauve to pink.

"Arsenic," Gowqua said, tapping the thumb ring significantly. "Even the merest pinch affects the color. At least, I shan't get a *bad* cup of tea in my own house."

Later, as they talked on, tea came in milky-white cups with lacework carving under the glaze that was so delicate Gill was moved to call it superhuman.

Gowqua smiled happily and said: "It is instinct, surely, which guides you to choose the word *superhuman*. For these Yung-lo eggshell have borne the familiar name of 'devil's work' upwards of three centuries."

After another interval, when a subtle near-colorless brew of steeped white peony petals appeared in cups of peachware, they left off the question and answer of porcelain, and began to talk of tea.

Gowqua's voice grew tender with reminiscence in telling Gill how he'd journeyed by junk to the clustering tea hills of Amoy as a youth, where the baby hands of little girls—being taught the sovereign lesson of patience—were set to plucking ceaselessly and gently at green hyson. He had climbed up Fukien peaks and down them, learning to distinguish flowering tea from its second cousin, the camellia. At Ningpo he'd gone inland to the poets' haven of Hangchow, tasting poetry with his ears, but with his tongue tasting cup after cup of long-green brewed with the wondrous waters of the Dragon Well itself.

"Tipping," "three-day flushes," "one-leaf pluck," "standard pluck," and "coarse pluck" were frequent on his tongue, along with "withering," "fermenting," and "tea sap," until, by the gentle imagery of words, tea ceased being one hundred and thirty-three pounds of black sawdust in a zinc-lined chest to Gill and became a brocade of vibrant green flung across valleys and wrinkled hills. It grew into a companion for contemplation, understanding, and vision.

The waning afternoon light reminded Gill how heedless he'd been of time. He jumped to his feet with boyish apology, and yet with a degree of mellowness still upon him. His smile was deeply content as he said: "I've given ample proof of my interest by staying far beyond the polite limits of a call. You have indeed been an indulgent teacher."

He hesitated, and then because the thought had grown more insistent within him these many minutes, he tried putting it into words. If this was to be a beginning of friendship, it would never thrive on a one-horse, one-rabbit basis. It must be compounded of mutual sensibilities, he reasoned.

Thoughtfully, groping for the right words, he said: "My head is bowed with the realization of how much we Americans could learn from you Chinese. But—I find I am able to raise it again proudly when I think of other things you could learn from us . . . if you but *would*."

Gowqua stepped very close to peer up intently at Gill with wary eyes, a curiously vulnerable look on his face. "One's acquaintances may fill the earth," he said, "but heart-interpreting friends are rare. Let me hear these things which we Chinese could learn?"

Gill nodded and said: "Chinese are heirs of great tradition. They have stored up the wisdom of ages, but it is not applied to living. A man named James Watt made a practical steam engine nearly seventy years ago, yet the Chinese do not have one." A kind of earnest pleading crept into his voice as he went on to tell about contrivances called locomotives: of how three thousand miles of railway tracks had already been laid in the United States so locomotives could carry passengers and freight an amazing eighteen miles an hour—eighteen miles!

He described power-whirled spinning machines; lucifer matches striking instantaneous light; Mr. McCormick's reaping machine; Mr. Colt's revolving pistol; paddle steamers running regular schedules up and down a dozen rivers; new screw propellers the Navy was testing; and free public schools established for every boy and girl in twenty states.

Finally Gill paused, drawing on the consciousness of pride, and yet keeping his voice temperate as he said: "Also—we Americans have two supreme heritages which China could well emulate . . . one—*civic consciousness of the rights of neighbors.* The other —*teamwork!*"

Gowqua's bright eyes never wavered until that moment. Then with a shuddering sigh he bent his head.

When Gill had closed the outer door, the girl Mei-deh stirred behind the screen and stepped slowly around it, as a sleepwalker might move in the tight confines of a hypnotic dream. Her father watched her; and when her eyes came to focus on him, he questioned her silently in the way they had with each other.

For answer she looked at him with soft wonder in her eyes and said: "*That one,* my parent, can never be called 'barbarian.' *That one* is ten thousand man!"

It was the ultimate in absurdity, Gill told himself for the fifteenth time.

Twelve men waiting three hours for one guest to arrive! And not here yet! No sign—except for those bumptious servitors who'd appeared an hour ago, who'd had the gall to come blustering into the drawing-room to order chairs put here, a table so, those doors closed. . . . The audacity! The effrontery! They'd been sent packing soon enough to the downstairs entryway and told to wait where they belonged. There they waited now, the surly brutes . . . meanwhile twelve amused and bored and nettled Americans waited interminably upstairs.

Gill jerked his furious gaze from the empty Walk and turned to stalk the length of two drawing-rooms into the vast dining-room and around its laden table. The best Irish damask! The silver service polished and gleaming! Muffins, tarts, blancmanges, galantines, pasties, jellies, jams, pickles galore! For what? A fiasco? To draw flies? Gill stalked back into the drawing-room again.

As he passed the whist table, Manning looked up from the hand he was playing with the partners Delano, Nye, and Coolidge to remark: "Lud, man, don't let it gravel you so! The fuzz-buzz uses us neglectfully, to be sure. But always recollect a Chinese would manage to be late for a tryst with Saint Peter—that is, if one of them ever had a tryst in the upper regions."

Gill grinned, shrugging shoulders as though it had ceased to matter to him, and took up post at the front window again.

But it *did* matter. He was directly responsible. He'd brought this ridiculous slight on the assembled company. For it was he who'd returned to the agency, so touched and moved by the genuinely sympathetic talk with Gowqua that right away he'd started advocating—yes, exhorting even—that they try a campaign of true cordiality and friendliness towards Chinese officials with whom they had dealings. A sort of opening wedge, he'd called it, which might evoke some response, some answering discernment and sympathy, and, in time, wear down this blasted artificial social barrier which always seemed to be between them now.

Take the new Controller-General of Canton Customs, he'd said—wishing now he could forget he'd ever uttered such dashed nonsense—who was a Manchu grandee of the Imperial clan itself in Peking. . . . Why not start off on a new foot with that functionary? His actual title was Hai Kwan Pu, so why not acquire the habit of pronouncing it Chinese fashion instead of the comically easy one of Hoppo some irreverent Britisher had invented years ago? Why not extend greetings, courtesies even, to this new official with whom they'd be having constant business for the next six months? Why not, for instance, start off by asking the old boy to a real American breakfast at eleven o'clock, say, since that was the hour these dignitaries liked eating their first important meal.

Gill ground his teeth together, remembering the load of optimism and enthusiasm he'd put into these arguments. It hadn't been too difficult persuading Manning and the other partners. They'd been skeptical, a bit dubious of any lasting improvement, but it was certainly worth a try, they agreed, especially since this new bucko seemed to want to direct affairs in the most minute, troublesome, petty, and contracted manner. Then, too, the *Hoppo*—no, no, the Hai Kwan Pu—had been so graciously prompt in demurring the honor. Of course, in proscribed Chinese etiquette, they'd been equally prompt urging him two times more; and upon the third invitation he'd professed to be so completely overwhelmed by their profound politeness that he couldn't bear to refuse.

They'd rehearsed the breakfast routine, decided who'd sit where at table; coached, coaxed, and threatened the cook; and cautioned each other repeatedly that his nibs was bound to be late—a good half hour, no doubt, Chinese having no reverence whatever for punctuality. Not one of them had thought he'd be three hours late!

Above the usual tumult of Hog Alley there came a sonorous clang of gongs and the high-pitched animal howls of heralds. The next minute a string of standard-bearers, soldiers, umbrella holders, footmen, and spirit chasers surrounding two sedan chairs came issuing from the alley. At a brisk running trot they crossed the Walk to the American agency's door.

Welcoming groups hastily deployed to stations—the younger men, William Hunter, James Wetmore, Gideon Nye, and Philip Stacey went to the front door; Gill was midway on the stairs with Robert Forbes, James Ryan, and Abiel Low; while on the landing above Manning stood with the senior partners Joseph Coolidge, Russell Sturgis, and Warren Delano.

With the curious feeling that he was reading it all in a book, Gill watched the scene below . . . His Excellency stepping slowly from the first chair; Howqua descending from the second with the same solemn ceremonial precision. Bowing with measured affability to Receiving Committee Number One, His Excellency leaned on a secretary's arm and turned to mount the stairs.

Gill got a good look at the Hai Kwan Pu now, the man who paid the Throne sixty thousand dollars a year for his job because it offered so many opportunities for reimbursement. He saw a poised and placid man, with a stub of black beard which lengthened his round face, but in no wise interfered with its serene blankness. The indigo robes he wore rustled richly, and the two phoenix emblems in scarlet embroidery on his chest and back stood out like placards. He wore a ruby hat-button of the first rank, and with it the coveted peacock-feather decoration.

Bowing his way upstairs and around the circle of senior partners, His Excellency looked at everything and everybody with a parrot's curiosity—seeing each face, seeing the clothes beneath these faces; seeing chairs, walls, portraits on them, and crystal chandeliers above. Smiling placidly at each chair and person, he leaned towards the secretary and murmured a question.

The secretary's voice was loud and harsh as he translated: "His Excellency expresses gracious interest in your country and asks about such a faraway land. He is told . . . it's a land of eternal darkness, that you have neither daylight nor a sun and moon."

Manning solemnly assured the secretary such amenities did indeed exist in America.

The secretary relayed this information, and His Excellency's eyebrows went up in prodigious surprise. He fingered his stub of beard in skeptical contemplation and asked yet another question.

The secretary translated: "His Excellency inquires whether you have any plants and flowers."

Manning assured him America was rich in plants and had multitudes of flowers.

When the reply was translated, the Controller-General cackled amiably in obvious disbelief. The secretary's eyes gleamed with the same strained disbelief, but his face remained impassively polite as he said: *"If* you possess plants and flowers, His Excellency observes, why is it, then, that your people make long voyages across seas to purchase ordinary plants such as tea leaf, alum root, rhubarb, hemp, and cassia buds?"

His Excellency had no mind to wait for another whopping invention, however. He signaled his retinue, leaned upon the secretary's arm, and walked into the dining-room. Ten stalwart Manchu guards sprang into a solid phalanx behind him.

Manning's eyebrows shot into peaks. He stared at the partners in amazement. They stared back in the same amazement. But there was no getting around six-foot guards with swords. Shoulder to shoulder the guards marched to the doorway. Five halted there, filling it. The other five stepped quickly to the table, gathering up chairs and moving them back against the wall—that is, all but one at the head of the table. With a gentle, charitable smile His Excellency sat himself in it.

Howqua had remained behind with the factors. He spoke softly now, his unctious voice filled with trouble, but coaxing, mollifying, assuasive. "Olo flen, my chin-chin you no makee trub! *Olo flen!*" he pleaded. "I talkee you welly good flen-pidgin—please you no makee trub this day. No belong my do. My how can likee? This man-ta-lee, he litty no plopper. He no savee what thing.

Suppose you makee trub this day, he plen-tee spoilum you ships bime-by."

"Does that dandiprat intend feasting whilst *we* play audience?" Warren Delano demanded *sotto voce*.

Russell Sturgis' lips twitched with laughter. "Whatever he intends, he has us in a box. He's our guest—at our explicit invitation, triple-compounded, remember?"

Manning drew breath between pinched nostrils. "Unfortunately that's so. We must see it through *his* way."

In another minute the secretary signaled and the guards moved from the doorway to join forces in a sort of barricading circle around the upper end of the table. The secretary made a second signal, indicating senior factors were expected to range themselves behind those servants. The remaining hosts stood in the doorway or around the lower end of the table.

A generous platter of scrambled eggs, hedged with grilled kidneys and bacon, was passed to His Excellency. With the look of a hungry crow he bent to peer at it. The secretary offered a pair of jade chopstocks. His Excellency took them, lifted a kidney to examine it clinically from all sides. With the same intent curiosity he stirred the egg concoction, sniffed it, but did not taste it. Then he sent the platter away with a suave wave of his jeweled left hand, wiped his chopstocks on the tablecloth, and sat benignly expectant until the next dish was uncovered before him.

It was fried chicken Maryland, with corn fritters and griddle cakes. The size of the portions engrossed him most. He turned a saucer-like griddle cake over in utter bewilderment. He nudged a chicken joint around the platter, and then a fritter, unable to grip or to lift either with the slender chopsticks. Sighing helplessly, he waved them back to the kitchen.

It was a big and bounteous breakfast. There were veal cutlets, ham steaks, scrapple, creamed chipped beef, Boston baked beans, apple pies, doughnuts, crumb cake, apple dumplings—all offered for his delectation, all inspected minutely, all dismissed without a taste. But always on the glistening round face was the gentle, forgiving smile of a martyr. Finally, with the conscious poise he believed infinite generations of gentlemen forebears had bequeathed him, he asked for a cup of tea.

When it arrived it was obviously manna from Heaven. He sucked it, smacked lips in fine rapture, sucked again, and set the cup in its saucer. Then he reached down under his skirt and took a rolled red document from the cuff of a morocco boot. This he handed to the secretary, who unrolled it in grave deliberation, cleared his throat, and read to the hosts. It was an exquisite speech of gratitude for an elegant, imaginative, delectable, luxurious, and utterly delicious meal.

The secretary rerolled the red document, handed it to the Controller-General, who returned it to his boot again and stood up to say something in a proclaiming tone of voice.

" 'I announce my departure!' " the secretary interpreted in the same proclaiming voice.

CHAPTER XI

CANTON,
November 1838

IT WAS in the yellow anchorage that it happened. Gill had gone down to Whampoa on the morning tide in the company's longboat—singing at the top of his voice as they ran past tawny brown hills and sedge-grass islands where francolin partridges whirred up and away, humming a love song as they passed Flowery Pagoda with each of its nine fluting stories as blue as the bright November sky, and then breaking into rollicking song again as they threaded through the thronging melee of Fiddler's Reach. He was meeting the *Seraph* to see his first tea buy aboard. But he wasn't singing on that account. He had another reason.

At Whampoa vivid orange and yellow blobs on the brown water, he found, were tangerine and banana rafts edging in and around the moored clippers like—like platters of Persephone! Gill chuckled at the high-flown phrase coming to his mind. Any other day he'd have said it was the bouyant morning air affecting him, or the beckoning countryside, and this incessant reading he'd been doing which was prompting such words. But not today.

Today the bounce and spring and glad release he felt could come from only one thing . . . the news Manning had told him at breakfast about the *Pombal.* It was back in Macao with dollars and opium intact. Not the proud caravel it had once been, but a limping cripple which had been mauled by ferocious wind.

The story—as Manning had got it—was that a typhoon had caught it off Chinchow Bay above Amoy, caught it while the Senhorita lingered to sell her opium cargo. That fatal once her blandishing pretense had come up against a relentless antagonist, and the impervious wind had sheered off the *Pombal's* rigging and splintered its masts, leaving it rudderless and barely afloat. Two days later the wallowing derelict had been sighted in the Formosa Channel by—and this was the uncanny, the crazy, cockeyed luck!—one of Sur Manoel's own ships, and forthwith towed back to Macao as salvage prize. Thus Sur Manoel repossessed his hundred casks of opium, every one of them, plus strongroom cash in excess of a hundred thousand dollars.

There was no Zena, though. In the end the wind and sea had claimed her. She'd been pinned under the canvas of a falling mast, and the next mountainous wave had carried her overboard.

Hearing she was dead didn't sadden Gill, for sorrow couldn't climb over the barrier of chagrin and mortification she'd built around him. Her death was retribution, he told himself—swifter and more cataclysmic than usual. It was a better ending, he couldn't help feeling, than the law caging that bright bundle of make-believe into a swindler's cell.

The *Pombal* actually back with opium and cash intact . . .
Gill thought he'd never known such a bounding sense of freedom.
A man suddenly inheriting a million dollars must feel the same—
soaring and expansive, foolish with laughter and song and hilarity. He himself, Gill Bennett, an actual millionaire, even
though he didn't have a red cent to his name. His twenty thousand in the *Pombal's* strong room automatically became Sur
Manoel's as salvage—yet it released Gill from further obligation,
so that now he didn't owe a single solitary penny to anyone. It
was release from the prison of his conscience.

The longboat pulled for the *Seraph's* ladder, nudging through
orange rafts and fending off a clutter of sampans filled with yelp-
ing, screeching, hooting washerwomen come out for the ship's
laundry—for the *Seraph* had only arrived at the anchorage. "My
washee! My washee!" they howled, waving singlets and drawers
as though they were flags.

As he climbed the ladder Gill heard big, barrel-chested Mathias Mission, the Salem man, cry out on a yard above: "There's
One-eye Mary! The heathen scalawag! Yip-pee Mary! Mary!"

A bouncing figure below waved three white shirts in one hand,
and with the other gestured up excitedly at Mission.

"Lord preserve us!" Mission roared. "Those be the three shirts
I forgot last voyage! She's had 'em for more'n a year. Iffen that
don't beat the devil for honesty. She's kept 'em for me. Good
girl, Mary! Belong Number One washee, you!" He bellowed with
laughter, and slapped skinny little Jonas Mews, who was reefing
with him.

The *Seraph's* bleached and tidy deck was as comfortably familiar as a well-loved home, Gill told himself happily, striding
towards the quarter-deck, where Macy waved vexedly at him. It
brought back memories of the long Pacific swell, the sense of
fitness and scope he'd discovered out in that blue immensity, and,
also, the frequent head-on clashes there'd been between his youth-
ful certainty and Macy's unbending, irascibly stubborn view-
point. Macy was a mixture of canker and bile, with vinegar in

his veins—came of eating baked beans for breakfast, no doubt—a composite of Bible and exasperation which deafened him to new ideas, Gill told himself.

Bounding up the quarter-deck steps, he saw Macy's long weather-beaten face was as truculent as ever. He stood waiting for Gill without smile or greeting. "Where are the barges, man?" he demanded. "When'll they be alongside?"

Gill couldn't hold back a laugh, and in a spirit of perversity larded his tones with excessive politeness as he inquired: "Why, how do you do, Captain Macy? I hope I find you your usual cheery self this fine and salubrious morning?"

A strangled sound came from Macy's throat. He raised his head to squint along his nose at Gill's face with eyes as gray and relentless as slate. "Pribbles and prabbles!" he barked, jerking around awkwardly and striding ten paces to the rail, only to pivot on his heel like a skittish animal pacing the length of a chain and come hippety-hopping back towards Gill.

Gill remembered this asylum and refuge of Macy's—inveterate pacing, back and forth, to and fro, in through doors and out again, all day long and into the night until he fell, dog-tired, into his bunk for an hour or two of sleep. Macy's pace was a constant barometer of mood, which itself was fairly constant—varying only in degree between petulance, pugnacity, and fury.

The Captain flicked a bony hand towards the crowded horizon. "I don't aim to load with that riffraff hugging my bow. Talk sense, man. When will the barges arrive? I must air the for'ard hold upwards an hour afore I stow fresh tea there."

Gill dropped his bantering and said: "They'll be alongside at one o'clock, Capt'n Macy. I passed them at Flowery Pagoda."

Macy muttered a modest oath. "H'm-m, hour after midday . . . these dratted washee-washee-women, and the fruit rafts, will have cleared off by then and won't be mucking around the cargo slings."

He turned to squint at Gill again, and gradually his vexed face unlocked into grudging affability. "Ye've had trouble, I hear.

Wull, comes to all of us, one time or t'other." He chuckled discordantly, "I'll waste no sympathy on ye now, though, because ye look more man for the jolt. Ye've shucked schoolboy eagerness for good sense, looks like. You're not the dandiprat I landed two months agone. Wull . . . no time to stand gabbling. Set yourself comfortable till the barges come. And welcome to chow with us when Cook's ready." He hurried off in a spastic hop.

Gill chuckled softly, touched by this perceptive, and unaccustomed, amiability. He knew within himself he'd come a long way on the road of understanding in two months. The chastening processes of self-reproach, penitence, and disappointment had given him an older and deeper look, for, luckily, he'd escaped bitterness and its corrosive marks. But it meant more than that . . . this jelling process into a new and stronger mold, he hoped.

He shouted hello to Mission and Mews up in the rigging and took himself forward to have a friendly word with Amasa Trow, the first mate. Along the way he paused to chat with the several Kennebec and Portland men who'd been friends ever since the blustering day in the South Atlantic when he'd struggled out of the miasma of seasickness to come on deck and pull his weight on the sails with them.

Today's nip in the northwest wind had made the sailors shuck summer ducks for regular Guernsey frocks. They sat about on deck, whittling whalebone and walrus ivory into pie crimpers, sail needles, and swifts for winding yarn. Gill found the same amusement now as he had back there on the slow Pacific swell watching big calloused hands finicking over precious scrimshaw work. He chaffed them for their girlish delicacy, and went on to poke his head into the galley and ask the pious cook—sure enough, he was stirring a spoon with one hand and holding a Bible in his other—what the chances were for molasses duff for dinner. Finally he sat down by the galley door and talked with Gedney Want, the sailmaker, while he patched a torn sail.

It was well after the midday meal, when the ninth or tenth

sling of tea chests was being heaved aboard, that the unpredictable accident happened. From the barge alongside, the sling had been hoisted up until it hung in position over the open hold, ready for the lowering signal. At that moment big Mission slipped somehow and lost his hold on the guide rope. The sudden release set the loaded sling flying.

It swung out, wide across one gunwale, and then—pendulum fashion—back across the other. As it careened beyond the larboard gunwale, a straining strand of mesh broke and dumped one chest. It turned end over end—one hundred and thirty-three pounds of it—to fall on a coolie in a sampan below with a ghastly smack . . . the *only* coolie in the *only* sampan on that side of the *Seraph*.

Gill saw it happen. Lounging on the larboard gunwale, he saw it from start to sickening finish. He was the lone witness. There were no other boats below, the neighboring clipper was too far, and there weren't any onlookers on deck anyway. As for the *Seraph's* crew, he happened to be the only man on the larboard gunwale at that precise moment. The others were either in the waist clinging to the heavy sling line or stowing chests below deck.

When the terrorized scream went up from the sampan, Macy came pounding forward. But by the time he reached Gill's side, there were only inert legs and arms spread-eagled on the sampan planks.

Macy stared bleakly, his face drained of color. "Bad! Mortal bad!" He shook his head, making a low keening sound. "I mistrusted that sling, and said so. But no . . . the bargeman was certain 'twas 'plen-tee, plen-tee strong.' Could be it's my fault—being as how I didn't *make* him supply another."

" 'Twasn't anyone's fault, Capt'n," Gill objected. " 'Twas an accident, pure and simple."

Macy shook his grizzled head. "These heathens'll be wanting blood for blood. That's their justice."

"I saw the thing from start to finish. I'll tell them," Gill insisted. "It was an accident. An act of God!"

"Act of God!" Macy repeated in a stricken voice, and stared at the far horizon with a strange foreboding look.

The mandarins demanded the sailor Mathias Mission be delivered to them for punishment. Immediately Russell and Company replied with a deposition explaining all details of the accident. A day later they repeated with a second petition; and then a third, when there was no answer, or even acknowledgment, to either.

The partners Hunter and Coolidge accompanied Gill and two linguists to the city gate to request an audience with the Controller-General of Customs so Gill might repeat his eyewitness account. Instead of being received they were mocked and jeered at by the detail of slovenly soldiers manning the gate, who refused even to listen to the foreigners' request. A street rabble gathered quickly around and started pelting them with mud and filth, until they were forced to retire. Next day, as they returned in a delegation twenty strong, the great gate was closed in their faces.

A week went by—Macy obdurate and inflexible, doggedly refusing to hand Mission over to any Chinese authorities. "It's not fitten. Mission weren't at fault, or careless," he maintained. "I'll pay recompense to the dead man's family, right enough. But there I stop! I'll give no sailor of mine into Chinese hands!"

The following day all loading was stopped by the mandarins. Their decree forbade coolies and bargemen, on pain of death, to transport cargo to Whampoa, put a single bale of silk or chest of tea aboard—not just Russell and Company ships or those flying the American flag—but all ships! Eighty-five British, Indian, Dutch, Spanish, Danish, and American merchantmen in process of loading first-crop tea.

The agents were stunned. Eighty-five ships and crews lying idle! The mandarins couldn't be serious, they assured each other. They'd never hold out. But they did . . . for a week. For ten days. For a fortnight. And now five more clippers joined the idle skeletons dawdling in Whampoa.

By that time the agents and Hong merchants were clamoring. They came to Manning's office singly and in pairs—Jardine, Innes, Bujorjee, Howqua, Mowqua, Chinqua, Jeebjeebhoy, Reeves, Daniel, Dent, Santiago, Viega, Bottlewalla, Fearon, Lindsey— each and all demanding that Macy be made to settle his difficulties forthwith and stop involving them in further extravagant delay.

On the fourteenth day, with ten incensed and infuriated men in his office smacking the desk with fists, scolding, cursing, thundering threats, Manning walked out and down the stairs to the tea storeroom. Not that he could put foot beyond the threshold, for it was full to overflowing with unmoved cargo. From the doorway he spoke to Gill, who—perched on a chest three tiers up— was checking inventory markings on another delivery.

"For God's sake, Bennett, take the fast boat instanter to Whampoa and fetch me that horse's ass of a Macy, along with Mission. Do you hear? I've tried to back him up, but I can't hold these factors off any longer. Remind Macy they've got rights too! Holding their ships idle costs ten thousand a day. From tomorrow on they threaten to hold me liable for the full amount!"

With the heel of his hand Manning wiped his forehead distractedly, and waited while Gill scrambled down from the chests and fell into step beside him. "Talk turkey to him, man. Pound some sense into that thick New England skull. He likes you; at least, he's civil to you, so maybe he'll listen. . . .

"Tell him I'm pledging my word we'll deliver Mission. Hell —all the Chinese will do is call a trial—the usual farce—listen to your eyewitness account, declare an accident, and fix a fine of five hundred dollars . . . top price for a dead coolie! They simply want to wrap themselves in legal righteousness, pocket the boodle, and *save face!* Then Mission's freed. And that's all there'll be to it."

When Gill climbed aboard the *Seraph* a couple of hours later, he repeated these words to the harried Macy. He reasoned, argued, exhorted, with a man all bone and bile, seemingly. He

repeated over and over again: "What are you afraid of? It was
an accident, pure and simple. I'm the only eyewitness who can
testify!" Sometimes he spoke face to face to the Nantucket man;
sometimes to a hippety-hopping back . . . pacing, pacing, pacing.

Macy rounded back from one prowl to say harshly: "Enough!
I agree to their blasted trial. But not for Mission. I'll go myself
in place of him."

Gill looked his utter astonishment.

"Ye needn't look at me like a poled ox!" Macy bristled. "I substitute for Mission, that's all. Who knows—mayhap the under-
lin' fault's mine, for I mistrusted that cargo sling, didn't I?
Besides—iffen it's as Manning and the others say, the mere formality of a trial, what difference who stands in the dock?"

The justice *yamen* was a pompous place of many
courtyards, vast chambers, and dirty unswept corridors. A pervading odor of decay came from mildewing plaster and dank crevices
between the stone pavement, which the cold sifting wind disturbed but did not dispel. In the courtroom itself the same cold
wind seeped through broken windowpanes stuffed haphazardly
with rags; and the chamber's musty, fusty smell mingled with the
stale fetid breath of humanity.

For the place was packed with clack-tongued people. Three
hundred—maybe more—raggle-taggle nondescripts along with af-
fluent townspeople stood crowded heterogeneously together in the
spectators' section. It was separated from the court—where seven
judges' chairs stood on a dais—by a latticework of tiles which was
ceiling-high and extended the full length of the chamber except
for two small corner enclosures partitioned partially by more
lattice.

In one of these corner enclosures some fifteen friends had been
herded, in lieu of family of the accused American—Manning,
Sturgis, Nye, Coolidge, and Gill, along with ten other American
agents and two linguists. Howqua and a troop of his own guards
had come with them, but the Hong merchant had been sum-

moned to the judges' chambers soon after they arrived. Taking two guards with him, he posted the remaining eight at the enclosure entrance, and along the lattice, to keep intruders out.

There were no benches, no stools, no seats of any kind. They stood, watching and waiting, for an hour through another trial preceding the American one. Gill fretted all that hour. Would all go well? Macy was a crusty martinet, but a fair and just man adhering to the principles of right and wrong, no matter what. That was the worry now . . . *what?*

Suddenly the big chamber was made hideous by banging gongs. The prisoner was unlocked from a wooden cage below the judges' dais and led out—a dazed, shambling figure moving in a trance.

Spectators shifted and streamed out, coughing and spitting. More came streaming in, scuffling feet on gritty stones, coughing and spitting with the same exuberance. Gill let his glance rove from face to face in that sea of baffling sameness . . . smooth skin without lines; opaque eyes without emotion; full lips in calm curves; but no differentiating signs, no tags of character which he knew and could recognize. Would he ever understand these people? he asked himself.

Another cataclysmic din of gongs sounded, and Macy was led in and locked in the prisoner's cage. But it wasn't a spry, quick-moving, erect Macy. This Macy came stumbling, head sagging sideways, his face a dopey mask.

Manning screamed, "The bastards! They've put opium in the food we sent him."

"Why?" Gill groaned in an agony of sudden apprehension, climbing a rung of the lattice so he could see over the heads of massed spectators.

"Chinese legal practice," Sturgis growled. "Stuns 'em. Keeps 'em from making outcry during trial."

"But—he has to testify, lucidly, in his own behalf!" Gill objected, the angry blood flushing his face. "How can he?" He felt an unreasoning impulse to shout the question at the court.

Sturgis humped angry shoulders. Manning turned to send a linguist at a run to fetch Howqua immediately.

A droning singsong began. One bailiff, a second, and then a third stood to read impressive red scrolls they unwound from one rod onto another as they scanned the text. Gill asked what it was, and the linguist told him: "Flowery preambles. Proclamations assuring the populace Chinese justice is ancient and pure."

The preambles continued a full quarter of an hour. Then the first bailiff rose and commenced reading from another scroll. The linguist whispered the charge against Captain Macy was now being stated.

It was neither short, concise, nor simple. It dragged on, in rising inflection and in looping undulation, enlarging and dilating until it seemed to assume the proportions of a historical epoch. The seven judges sat blinking, benignly impassive, hands folded over seven rotund paunches, all as flaccidly alike as though they'd been cut from the same bolt of gray silk.

The drone stopped. Crescendo wails burst through the doorway as three tottering women and five swarming youngsters were led in. They sobbed before the judges; they cried to highest Heaven; they beat heads in paroxysms of grief.

"Bereaved family of dead man," the linguist explained. "Eaten with sorrow."

The wailing family was led out, sobs ceasing abruptly at the doorway.

Gill was gripped by a sudden appalling thought. He turned to the linguist, saying: "There's no door from this enclosure to the court. I should be over at that doorway where the family went out, ready for call to testify. It'll take me ten minutes to get around. Quick, let's go!"

"We dare not." The linguist shook his head emphatically. "You're ordered to remain here until summoned."

"Damn queer," Gill muttered, turning to watch ten men in coolie blues file through the doorway he'd just indicated and take their places before the judges.

They spoke in succession, earnestly, piously, with conviction. When they weren't speaking, they were nodding their heads vigorously, corroborating, seemingly, what the other was telling.

The judges came to life now. They leaned forward in their chairs, asking questions or conferring busily with each other.

The Chief Judge dismissed the ten coolies with a signal and addressed the court in compelling tones. He stopped abruptly, and the awful clanging of gongs assaulted the air. The prisoner's cage was unlocked, and the unheeding Macy was hurried out. The judges rose and disappeared through a doorway behind their chairs.

"What's happening?" Gill wanted to know.

"All finish," the interpreter said.

"Finish? But—I haven't testified!" Gill's voice rose to a shout.

"Not necessary."

Manning cut in: "You mean he's acquitted?"

"Not necessary because ten men testify what they see," the interpreter explained.

"Impossible!" Gill cried. "There wasn't another human being down there when the accident occurred."

Again Manning's incisive voice cut in: "What have they testified?" he demanded.

"Testify American sailor threw chest upon coolie in anger."

"Perjurers! Liars!" Gill shouted, pushing his way towards the entrance. "Let me get to the judges. I'll tell them!"

"Too late," the interpreter said impassively. "Captain now without head."

"Make a rush for it!" several of the Americans yelled. They joined arms and shoved in a body, scattering spectators aside, moving towards the archway into the courtyard.

But when they reached it—there by the opposite wall was a strapping executioner wiping his broadsword. Below on the bloody block was Macy's headless body.

That afternoon barges dropped downstream again with cargoes of silk and tea and porcelain, and loading coolies clustered like beetles around clippers and schooners and caravels moored at the yellow anchorage of Whampoa.

CHAPTER XII

CANTON,
December 1838

MANNING GROANED. His wasted face twisted on the pillow, and his lusterless eyes roved across the ceiling towards the windows to stare out at the vast dead brownness of earth and trees and water. "Oh, God, why go on living? Why?" he babbled querulously in a voice thin with exhaustion. "No one can lick dengue."

Gill stirred in the chair beside the bed and reached out to touch the flaccid arm lying on the counterpane. "*You* can, sir," Gill said. He wasn't soothing a fevered incompetent. The respect and admiration and affection he'd now come to feel for this man was in each word he spoke. "You're better than yesterday. Much. Your fever has gone, and also the rash."

"Who cares? The hang-over's ahead. . . ." Manning's voice shuddered away in a sigh.

Gill had been warned about this. During the two-hour watches around the clock he and the partners had kept over Manning these three days, they'd explained dengue and its breakbone course. A sudden flaring fever which burned like a torch for thirty-six hours, snuffing out as suddenly as it started, to leave each and every bone, every muscle, every morsel of flesh feeling as though it had been flogged by a poleax.

Men didn't die of dengue, the partners agreed significantly. But they *did* die from gnawing debility which followed, from constant pinching ache and melancholy prostration which sapped what small will there was to live. Three bouts out here usually wrote *finis* on a man. This was Manning's third bout.

"I sympathize with the ache in your body, sir," Gill said. "But don't let it get into your mind."

A fretful tremolo came from the bed. "Mind? Haven't got any. Washed up . . . finished. Bones for the bone heap, that's all."

Gill leaned forward, trying to capture and compel the flickering gaze with his own eyes, and through them pour some measure of courage and vitality into the other. He wanted—if only he could—to transfer strength from his own body into this poor wracked skeleton. "You're the staunchest pillar we Americans have out here," he said, half pleading, half goading. "You rally us. You keep us headed on the right track. Every man of us depends upon you, sir, and needs you sorely."

The colorless lips pursed enough to emit a rude sound. "And more p-p-p—" Manning added, rattling his lips again in the same sound. All urbanity had drained away from him, until only a querulous consciousness of self remained—a sorry self dragging along the threshold of subconsciousness. Slowly the clouded eyes filmed with moisture, and a trickle of tears rolled down the chalky face. "My bloody eyes again," Manning sobbed, "watering like a hydrant."

Gill reached for the silk handkerchief on the pillow and held it to the glistening eyes. He wondered whether it was actually rheum he was wiping or if his declaration had penetrated sufficiently beyond the pain barrier to move the man himself. It might be a hopeful sign.

Could he pluck another heart cord momentarily? Could he hope to draw Manning's spirit away from the aching body and kindle it ever so slightly with the affairs of the agency? He tried.

He stood up, gesturing wide with both arms, and in an eager rush deliberately spoke about the thing nearest his heart and hope. "I'm having banging luck with the loading! Gowqua's giving me consistently punctual deliveries—taxes paid, documents complete without idiotic delay. I was so flabbergasted I hopped over to his *yamen* to thank him . . . and guess what? In that courtly way of his he told me he was pleased to practice this new-fangled thing I mentioned once—*teamwork!*"

Gill flushed with genuine pleasure in the recounting of this. He didn't expect Manning to care about the words. Only the tangible results could be heartening. Gill looked towards the bed for some flicker of interest, some encouraging sound. But all he got was a petulant thrash of legs under the covers.

He made himself go on. "The tally's—five hundred chests off this morning. That's three hundred ordinary: one hundred excellent Lapsang souchong; fifty best hyson and black congou. The other fifty's teacups and saucers . . ."

"Goddamn," came the moan from the bed, "isn't there anything besides bloody tea?"

Gill guffawed. "Aha, you're mimicking a fellow named Gill Bennett—as he was. Lud, I scarcely recognize myself now . . . up to the chin in tea, and liking it! This morning's shipment's my twentieth. And—I'm in the market for another twenty! It's so incredible I total the figures twice a day. They always come out the same. Five and a half million dollars in tea this year. *Five and a half million!*"

A wailing protest went up from the bed. "*Dollars* . . . I live amongst savages, corruption, injustice, pestilence, to sell filthy opium . . . for *dollars!*" Manning's wail fell to a whisper or rose huskily as his eddying stream of consciousness came aloud in words. ". . . I want to go home . . . sit in a rocking chair, and never see another yellow face. Let others go adventuring. Let them. I'm through . . . never be anything but a wreck . . . through at thirty-eight."

Gill looked on helplessly, knowing he should do something. Manning needed strength, he reasoned, to climb out of this mental morass. He stepped to the door, listening for a moment to the steady clink the shroff made counting silver dollars far below, and then he sent Manning's Cantonese boy to the kitchen for chicken jelly.

When it came, Gill carried the bowl to the bed. "Doctor's orders, sir," he coaxed, lifting the spoon. "Let me help you with it."

"No."

"Just two spoonfuls?"

"Go away. Too tired . . ."

At that moment the door was thrust open. A lithe youth wrapped in a long black opera cape and a black head scarf stepped inside quickly, and as quickly closed the door. Off came the opera cape and the head scarf.

"Uncle Tim!" the youth cried in a throbbing voice.

It was Lael—dressed from head to toe in man's clothing, her lovely hair cropped close to her head.

The effect on Manning was galvanic. He struggled onto trembling elbows, making glad sounds, laughing outright. "Lael, Lael, my darling girl!" he gasped.

Lael ran across the room to drop on knees beside the bed, kissing the wasted hands which clutched her firm white ones. "Oh, Uncle Tim—I couldn't bear it. I *had* to come, no matter what the Chinese laws are."

"Lael, Lael, you've cut your hair. Oh, my dear!" Manning's hand reached to the shorn head, touching and fondling it. His eyes clung to hers, straining in a sudden wistfulness of hope.

Lael saw it. With a quick intuitive smile she took her uncle's face between two hands and bent close, transfixing his every faculty with the serenity of her conviction. *"You shall recover, Uncle Tim,"* she willed. "I promise you—from this very moment forward you'll get better. Forget everything but that."

She drew back, arching her head provocatively as she said: "I knew you'd need a boss . . . to make you toe the mark. And since they say"—she included Gill in a defiant smile—"there's no one more determined than a redheaded woman I thought I was the one to come."

She jumped up and crossed to Gill's side. Even in man's clothes she was natural and comfortable and real, without affectation. She told him: "Lady Prophet sent you a message—it sounds as though you two had a secret understanding. Her exact words were 'Clasp his hands for me. Tell him my money's on him for this race IF he follows that intuition of his.' There . . . I leave it to you to decipher."

Gill chuckled fondly, hearing the indomitable and salty matron's dictatorial voice, seeing her incredibly blue eyes. He wasn't sure he grasped her meaning, but he was immeasurably pleased that she had thought enough of him to send it.

"I'll have to forego the 'clasping hands' part since you hang onto that bowl so preciously. Whatever is it?" Lael asked, stooping to peer in it.

Caught in the drama of Lael's sudden appearance and the emotion she'd generated in the sick man, Gill had been much too preoccupied to lay the chicken jelly aside. He grimaced apologetically. "My lame attempt to feed your uncle," he explained, turning to put the bowl on the table.

But Lael stopped him, sniffing at the contents. "Chicken jelly?" she queried. Gill nodded. "And Uncle Tim refused it?" she wanted to know. Again Gill nodded.

"I might have known." She tossed her head, taking the bowl from him and crossing back to the bed. "Lift him up for me," she directed over her shoulder to Gill, who braced a pillow behind Manning's shoulders and raised the sick man enough so he could swallow. "Open your mouth, Uncle Tim," Lael commanded quietly, but with inflexible authority. *"You are going to eat this."*

Manning's eyes flickered a moment, then obediently he opened his mouth and docilely swallowed each spoonful as she fed him. Between mouthfuls he asked: "Where did you get that God-awful rig?"

"From your clothes closet."

"Humph! Must have been something I was saving to give the missionaries. Who brought you here?"

"I brought myself," she told him equably, without concern. "I simply hired the same fast boat you hired three months ago for our friend, Mr. B here—and came scooting up the back passage-way as easy as *a b c*."

Gill remembered his own trip through that winding blackness, the hazardous din and hazardous silences of the stops, and found himself gazing at this girl with new eyes. Maybe not new, he corrected himself, maybe just more penetrating. He'd let himself forget—since that first meeting on the Praya—how lucid and fundamental and womanly she could be behind her very regal façade. Now he realized she was endowed with courage as well.

Manning had turned to look at the wreaths of mist rising like smoke from the river. "You undertook that distance . . . *alone* with Chinese boatmen . . ." he murmured incredulously.

"Stop gathering steam to spout like a stern uncle," she ordered imperiously, "and finish your chicken jelly."

Manning's gaze came back from the river mist to fasten on her face and cling there with submissive devotion. "You bully!" he cackled weakly.

The third day after Lael was secretly installed in the bedroom connecting with Manning's, fire broke out in the river quarter of the city. All afternoon sulphurous yellow smoke curled up from the spot, to unwind like a sash across the silken blue of the sky. It was dead calm that afternoon: no stir of breeze came to scatter the smoke, or fan the eating flames. Yet by sunset both persisted—ominously and implacably.

Darkness brought an ugly gamble. Contrary night winds had a way of puffing up suddenly, to blow across the delta like a bel-lows. Then what happened? Half the gimcrack city in flames? Thousands homeless? The blaze spilling over city walls onto the port area and its kindling pile of shanties and mat sheds?

The Hong warehouses there were jam-packed with cargoes. Russell and Company's last silk purchase was stored there, wait-ing for transfer to clippers at Whampoa—a million dollars' worth of bales and bolts stacked to the rafters.

Gill raced up to the roof for another look, not that it could have changed much since he was here a quarter of an hour ago, but because he couldn't bear sitting still in a chair while linguists twirled brush points and made verbal flourishes out of the quick, impassioned plea he'd just dictated to the Governor. Good God, it was so fundamental . . . "Open a firebreak!" he'd begged. "Level a space—blow it out with gunpowder—around the blaze. Now, immediately! Isolate the fire! It consumes itself without danger to the entire city. Allow us permission to work with your soldiers. We desire to aid and assist them with experience, good will, and sympathy."

The partners Delano and Forbes were stationed on the roof, telescopes trained on the slow crawl of two chopboats towards the port and Howqua's godown. They'd scrambled to hire these barges an hour ago, with double coolie crews on each, for immediate loading. At least they'd get a portion of the silk away, beyond the threat of sparks and looters, they said.

Gill joined them, to peer off into the yellow afterglow which gilded city walls and the minaret of an Arab mosque built in T'ang times in a brief moment of glory. He told them of the petition being written for him—with Manning's full approval—which he intended presenting immediately at the city gate. To give a proper deputation look Nye, Hunter, and Stacey were accompanying him, along with a linguist, naturally.

Delano shook his head skeptically. "Against custom," he objected. "According to tradition, you 'chase fire demons away vigorously, and thereafter resign yourself to Heaven's will.' "

"Gunpowder's vigorous," Gill argued.

Forbes agreed. "Try it," he urged. "We shouldn't overlook any possibility at this stage. The chopboats will remove what they can carry. Coolidge and Low are out tackling Howqua for more coolies. Wetmore and Sturgis are scouting more junks and sampans. You've got an entirely different notion. Sounds crazy, maybe . . . but if you *can* get them to act—you save the whole show!" He clapped Gill on the back encouragingly and returned to watching the port scene through his spyglass.

Gill walked the length of roof . . . mumbling half aloud: "Exorcising fire demons, Heaven's will," and thinking of a nation that had invented gunpowder, paper, porcelain, lacquer. . . . What mental inertia gripped it now? What subhuman inertia kept a Chief Magistrate, a Military Governor, mandarins, or soldiers themselves from lifting a hand to avert disaster? It was *their* city, *their* people, *their* neighbor! Toothpick balconies everywhere! Fretwork façades! Turrets, swaddling shutters, a forest of lacquered wood! The city was a stacked bonfire . . . waiting for the kiss of flame.

Voices mingled from rooftops along the Row—Austrian, British, Gujarati, and half a dozen others—as men muffled in overcoats stood in groups, gesturing argumentatively, training spyglasses on the port, chaffing river damp from their hands, relaying rumors: "Two thousand shops gutted already." . . . "The sampan fleet's moving to safer anchorage west of Honan Island." . . . "Not a coolie to be had at double, or treble, hire. . . ."

Swallows dipped and dived over the waterfront like angry thoughts. Beyond on roof platforms outlined against the column of smoke pillow-shaped figures moved in agitated jerks. And the air vibrated with a ceaseless high-pitched human jargon. Above this, above the continuous thrash of oars on the river, Gill caught a swelling throb of gongs and a discord of cymbals. "God in Heaven," he muttered to himself in a wave of suffocating frustration, "fire demons being fought with the weapon of noise!"

He swung back towards Delano and Forbes. "My petition should be ready. I'm off," he called. But instead his feet stayed rooted.

A stir of air brushed his cheek. Then a second. In that same instant the others felt the prefatory puffs. The havoc they fetched was apparent next moment, for the smoke pillar glowed luminously with new red life.

Gill smacked a determined fist against a cupped palm. "I've

got to succeed now. I've *got* to. It's our only hope!" He turned and ran for the stairway.

"Godspeed!" Forbes called after him. Delano's "Amen!" was as fervent.

On his way Gill detoured for the minute it took to rush to the sickroom and say he was headed for Petition Gate.

Manning raised a hand in quick salute. "I'm setting store by your resourcefulness. God bless, fellow!"

Gill took it as a benediction, and turned impulsively to grip Lael's hand, steadying her; steadying himself, he found, with the touch. "Remember," he instructed her carefully, "there's not a particle of danger to the Row itself. It's too far away, and anyway, sparks won't affect these stones and stucco and tiles. But——"

He stepped closer, loving the clear trust he saw in her violet eyes. "But—*if* the situation should change in any way . . . I'll either get back to you or send a messenger. Depend upon it!"

"I haven't a shred of worry. You'll settle it. I know you will," she smiled staunchly, sending him off in a glow.

The four Americans and Wah Kung, the bright, eager linguist who had become Gill's favorite, hurried out the gate minutes later. Half running, half trotting, they crossed the Walk, cut back through Hog Alley to the main thoroughfare, which led to Petition Gate. Usually it was a twenty-minute walk. In today's fast jog they made it in ten.

Petition Gate was on the opposite corner of town from the fire, and in the hyacinth twilight there was no sign of it here. No commotion, and no panicking refugees, hobbled the everyday melee of wheelbarrows, pigs, load coolies, and pedestrians coming and going through its brick tunnel. Beyond the walls a fire warden was beating a sepulchral drum in rhythmic recitative to a running song he made of his news. ". . . across the city, it is . . . far away, distant, very far away. . . ." he told the populace.

The Gate itself was a three-story pile of curling eaves and peeling red lacquer. It was at least a hundred feet thick at the base, with sets of mammoth doors at either end of the central passageway and a wicket for guards midway between. A single guard, who looked more cowkeeper than soldier in a miserable sheepskin jacket, stood duty—that is, he sat lounging on a three-legged stool with his back against the wicket. A rattan whip lay across his lap, and a rusty sword leaned against the nearby wall.

He grinned expectantly as the Americans came hurrying across the entrance square towards the wicket and called something into the adjacent room. Four other slovenly guards came sauntering out—fastening trousers, pulling jackets on, and wiping sleeves across running noses. They were obviously Cantonese, and no part of the spick-and-span military aristocracy of Manchu Bannermen quartered five to six thousand strong in the city.

"Don't eat time with formalities," Gill instructed Wah Kung brusquely. "Tell them briefly—we carry Number One emergency communication to the Governor. Kindly escort us to his *yamen* immediately."

Wah Kung launched into singing Cantonese.

The guards gazed stolidly at each other and shook their heads. "They say only officer can do," Wah Kung translated.

"Fetch one!" Gill directed.

Again the guards shook their heads mulishly.

"Officer on duty eating supper." Wah Kung pursed regretful lips.

Hunter cried out: "God in Heaven, we're here to stop a disastrous fire!"

"We're trying to save the city!" Nye urged in unison.

Wah Kung smiled in stoical calm. "They say fire not their pidgin. They not fire chasers."

Gill pulled two strings of cash from his overcoat pocket. "Use these instead of words."

Two of the guards laughed hilariously and snatched the cash, agreeing to fetch the officer. But their feet moved with less alacrity than their hands had a moment before.

"*Fie-tee! Fie-tee!*" Stacey shrilled.

The two ambling guards mimicked him in jocose amiability. But, sure enough, they quickened pace.

It was ten full unnerving minutes before the officer arrived —a dull, blunt-faced man, picking his teeth with a bamboo splinter and running an exploratory tongue around them. He listened obtusely to Wah Kung's impassioned harangue, then shook his head negatively.

Wah Kung shrugged in cheerful resignation. "Officer a turtle. Doesn't enjoy sufficient rank to permit you pass inside. He ask superior."

"Where is superior?" Gill wanted to know.

"Come after half hour."

Gill slapped hand to forehead. Delay, obstruction, hindrance . . . perpetually! He snatched at a compromise. "All right —tell him to take our petition to the Governor—now! Immediately! With lightning speed! We'll wait here for the Governor's summons."

Again Gill used the laxative of money. Clinking two dollars enticingly, he handed the letter to Wah Kung, who handed it to the officer, who stood dubiously staring at the envelope, spelling out its full honorific designation as though fitting each intricate brushstroke with some hazy mental symbol of the word. Then with the same negative headshake he handed the letter back to Wah Kung.

Wah Kung cocked his head on one side like a bright bird, not mocking the wriggling worm exactly, but wonderfully diverted by its struggles, as he explained: "Officer a turtle. Says cannot take august Governor letter from man so modest."

"Modest!" Gill's voice rose explosively. "What in Hell does he mean?"

"No title, sir. You name Governor by full titles . . ." Wah Kung read resoundingly from the envelope, " 'Exalted Administrator, Patrolling Soother of Canton, Super Attendant of Kwangtung Province, Imperial Censor, Judge of Universal Examiners.'

See . . . very full indeed! Officer asks you please name your American titles."

Gill saw red. Of all the twiddling fumadiddles at a time like this! Then, abruptly, he laughed. "Oh-ho, this turtle of an officer wants titles, does he? That's easy. Come along, Wah Kung. Just borrow brush and inkstone in that shop there across the square and start writing for me. . . ."

A minute later, with Nye, Hunter, and Stacey crowding close around him, Gill dictated in clarion tones: "This petition respectfully submitted by me, Gill Bennett, Archduke of Brooklyn, Shah of Flushing, Prince of Pawtucket, Caliph of Concord, and Soother-in-Chief of Bowling Green . . ."

"And," Stacey magnified, "Rajah of the Catskill Mountains!" He counted fingers, muttering *sotto voce:* "There—one title up on His Patrolling Nibs."

When the letter was handed to the officer again, he read the titles with irritating slowness, but obviously with growing respect. He tarried, however, eying Gill's purse deferentially as another Carolus IV dollar was counted into his hands. Putting each of the three he'd received between his teeth in turn, he bit it judiciously, and satisfied himself it wasn't lead. Then calling an order to the guard, he turned away into the city with purposeful strides.

There was no telling what was happening over in the vicinity of the fire. The Gate's spreading eaves blotted out the darkening sky; and although the wind had freshened into gusty puffs, it blew slantwise towards the river, carrying any burden of smoke and sparks in an opposite direction. In such gusts, however, it was foolish to suppose fire wouldn't burn as long as there was anything left to burn, and that the sparkling seeds it transplanted wouldn't blossom.

They couldn't bear putting futility into words, so no one calculated whether it would take five or five-and-twenty minutes before the officer would bring the summons. While the guards lighted giant lanterns in the passageway, the Americans joined step in anxious partnership to pace the length of the monumental

Gate, reversed, and completed the circuit. They tramped the square—escorted, hemmed in, followed apishly by ragtag rowdies.

They brought the antic procession to a halt when a string of eight or more wheelbarrows came trundling out of the city, piled high with bedding, babies, teakettles and stump-footed women. *"Fo tsoi! Fo tsoi!"* they wailed of the calamity of fire. As these homeless ones disappeared down an alley, a band of demon chasers came cruising along the city side of the Gate, chanting, whirling fly whisks, and lashing empty air with willow switches. The leering curiosity of the mimicking rowdies never shifted, never deviated, from the performing barbarian clowns, however.

After an eternity the officer came sauntering under the portal, plainly disdainful and arrogant now. He flung the letter on the ground at Gill's feet, unopened; chewed out an insolent jumble, half spit, half words; and flung an arm up to summon the guards. Before the baffled Wah Kung could decipher the ugly words and translate them, four guards had run to shut the big door on the city side of the tunnel, and had rammed rusty bolts into rusty sockets.

"What is it? What's wrong?" Gill cried out.

Wah Kung trembled unhappily, stumbling over words: "Sir, I beg pardon. The Governor's secretary refuses, sir, to present the letter. He sends word . . . not written on Number One quality paper!"

The four Americans could only stare utter disbelief at the woebegone Wah Kung. The stupifying words might have been narcotics paralyzing their vocal cords.

Suddenly behind them unearthly cries smote the air. They spun around to see five bawling guards advancing on them, whirling rattan whips overhead and cracking them with pistol-shot ferocity. There was no arguing with rattan whips. Gesturing helplessly, unable even to hear each other in the uproar, the five petitioners backed step by step out the passageway until they were beyond the portal. This was what the guards had wanted evidently. In a swoop they slammed the giant door shut, and with a clunk of finality dropped the heavy bolt into place.

A flood of fury blinded Gill momentarily. Then he was clawing at his face with both hands, wiping the hateful blur away, and crying to Wah Kung: "Get back to the factory and tell them our petition failed! We're going to the port to save the warehouse." He turned and ran in a sustained rush, leading the way, sobbing aloud with each step: "The swine! The swine! The swine!"

The port was a glare of scarlet fire. Its reflection hung in the sky like an incandescent dome, mottling the black glass of the river's surface, and daubing men and houses and ground with demonic red. Tinsel sparks showered on panting forms running every which way, and the cry of "Fo tsoi! Fo tsoi!" was a steady tattoo of calamity.

Howqua's godown had become a maelstrom of snarling coolies staggering a treadmill path across the mud embankment, up straddling planks to a hold, and back again for another grievous load. Half the partners were here—Low, Forbes, Sturgis, Coolidge, and Wetmore—funneling the moving chain of coolies, holding tally baskets, receipting sampan loads, directing, straining, dispatching. Gill took one look at the partially emptied warehouse and waved his team on. "We'd contribute zero there," he panted over his shoulder. "We'd best tackle the mess out back."

Sparks showered in crimson rain now with each eddy of the fitful wind—not onto immediate sheds and shanties against Howqua's walls, but amongst another jungle of sheds and shanties five hundred yards to the right. Wet sacks beating embers, beating wisps of smoke, beating daggers of flame, was a constant slapping thud as each householder defended his reed-and-matting contraption. If even one stopped beating . . . if the wind veered in odious caprice . . .

"These shacks must come down. We've got to level every one!" Gill screamed as though in the madness of necessity he meant to rush on them himself and start demolishing right and left. But instead, from that moment on through the hateful night, his fury seemed to concentrate in his brain and direct him in a magnificent frenzy of sanity.

First off he dispatched Hunter and Nye to Forbes in the warehouse for strings of cash—brass coins so paltry it took twenty-four to equal one American penny. But there was nothing paltry about the miracle of strength these strings bought from hovel owners.

They goaded men and women and children into slashing ropes which tied bamboo uprights to matting walls, into wrapping miserable debris into rolls and stowing them behind a boundary of Gill's making. They co-ordinated arms into hustling water from the river in a bucket brigade that hadn't a bucket in it, but was teakettles, crocks, and stewpans sluicing the pitiful rolls as fast as they were stacked.

When the wind quartered straight upon this spot and dropped a red curtain of sparks, the glowing bits fell upon empty ground —a swathe cut fifty yards wide and circling back from the river, crescentwise, around Howqua's three bare walls. When they fell on sodden sticks and string and straw coveted for tomorrow's shelter, the sparks snuffed into black nothingness.

But inside city walls the red glutton fed on until fifty thousand homeless wandered alleys and lanes, searching a poor inch of shelter, or collapsing in shuddering heaps, fully resigned to "Heaven's will."

At one point in the early evening a Chinese magistrate sat in his sedan chair before Russell and Company's gate—come to protest the agency's abominable discipline in permitting four juniors to create an incident at Petition Gate an hour ago in an audacious attempt to address the Governor.

The magistrate's retinue pounded the panels and shouted for attention. Nobody in the big compound gave it. Everyone was out: either at the fire, running with messages about it, or watching its deadly progress from the roof. There were only Lael and her uncle alone in the upstairs sickroom. Manning's Cantonese servant had gone downstairs to fetch broth from the back kitchen, where cooks were stoking dinner fires, rattling pans, and chopping an eternal tattoo.

The magistrate's guards pounded louder. One happened to try the door latch: it opened without hindrance, and they rushed in pell-mell. The chair bearers listened outside for sounds of strife, but hearing only the uncontested hullabaloo of their own men, they followed with the magistrate.

Imperative shouts echoing up the stairwell began to reach Lael in the sickroom. She thought instantly of Gill's promise to send a messenger if things got worse. She went running to the half-lit stairs and down through the shadows to the drawing-room landing, forgetting she was only half disguised—that, though her uncle's trousers covered her legs, the blouse above and the tucked jacket around her shoulders were unmistakably feminine. She caught sight of the magistrate mounting the main staircase, with uniformed retinue strung out behind him, in the same moment he looked up and saw her in the dimness above.

His lordly mask cracked with sudden perplexity, and his nearsighted eyes grew round and white as he stared up. But only momentarily. Then, with ineffable hauteur he closed his eyes on what remained baffling to him, raised a rolled parchment in his hand, and imperiously summoned the freak to his side.

Lael couldn't move. A sudden horrid weight of misgivings and indecision clutched her feet.

At that precise instant the sedate compradore and Wah Kung, on their way down from the roof, came hurrying along the lower passage. They stopped stock-still, too stunned at the sight of a mystical half-male, half-female figure wavering on the stairs to *kowtow* to a recognizable dignitary.

The tableau lasted one harrowing minute. Then the compradore, recoiling as though he'd sat on an ants' nest, composed himself and bent in reassuringly punctilious bows. But not Wah Kung. His pert bright eyes glowed with the frolic of this drama, and he went sprinting up the stairs to wave his arms in a melodrama of exorcism and chant at Lael in English: "Go away! Vanish! Vanish—you ghost of a half-foreign-devil female!"

Lael turned and wavered upstairs into the shadows.

Wah Kung spun around with swaggering flourish, crowing to those below in Chinese: "It was a ghost! A spirit who vanishes! Disappears! Becomes nothing!"

CHAPTER XIII

CANTON,
December 1838

WAH KUNG's prank failed. The nearsighted magistrate might have been persuaded the figure he'd glimpsed on the stairs was a transient chimera, but his retinue insisted the being —whatever its sex—was real enough. Household servants verified the rest.

The following day twenty soldiers had come to the Walk and hung a board on Russell and Company's gate, with an edict attached. The edict ordered the foreign-devil female to quite Canton immediately, otherwise fresh food would be denied foreign factories.

Howqua had thought gentle procrastination would be sufficient, especially with only five days to go until Christmas. His "little plan" for saving everybody's face was: "Suppose you talkee Missy can do truly after tomollow day. Bime-by three day Missy no ready, you talkee nother time two day truly can do. That belong mandarin fashion."

"Mandarin fashion," evidently, was not a code permitted foreigners, for the very next day, with no palaver, debate, or bargaining, the edict was clapped on full force.

Two hundred soldiers came bustling into the Walk. In an uproar of crackling whips and war hoots they'd waved wooden swords and lunged about with enormous pikes. Neither weapons had slashed at anything except air, but the ferocious posturing seemed to be enough to terrorize cooks and houseboys. They'd fled in fullmouthed panic, wailing like overgrown banshees that they were sure to be slaughtered if they remained.

During this uproar the soldiers barred the way of all vendors, and farmers come with pheasants, pigs, deermeat, vegetables, and fruit were turned away. Sampans loaded with shrimps and lobster and garrupa and fat crabs drifted up and down in midstream; and amongst them were quacking duckboats with eggs and plucked ducks, but each time any of these approached the landing steps they were bambooed.

It became a siege of wills, not stomachs.

In the Russell compound they kept all word of the affair from Manning. First off the conscientious and kindhearted Number One *taipan*, William Jardine—whom the Chinese had nick-named "The Iron-headed Old Rat"—came for a sickroom visit; and then hurried back to tell his Scottish and English colleagues how Manning's spirit had revived in these five days Lael had been nursing him, and that there was a good chance he'd pull through even this third bout of dengue.

Then the Parsees and the Spaniards and the Germans began stopping by to drop cards of encouragement, to give Lael a packet of rock candy, some dried plums, or a canister of coffee beans; and also to talk with Sturgis and Delano about the situation. They'd ride the emergency together, they pledged—at least until after Christmas—in the conviction that these additional days might see Manning through the danger zone, and sufficiently bolstered to continue his recovery without Lael's influence.

All along the Row they rolled up their sleeves and turned to the job of tending fires, roasting capons, boiling eggs until they were as hard as grapeshot, sweeping and dusting, waiting table, washing dishes, polishing silver, making beds, and emptying chamber pots. "The Housemaids' Brigade," they dubbed them-

selves; and to ward off housemaid's knee they were careful to
issue a special tot of rum with afternoon tea.

They met in the Walk at night to exchange recipes and experiences, and to abuse Tao Kuang and all his ministers. They
ran back and forth between the thirteen agencies, cheerfully lugging sacks, carrying crocks, sharing with each other what stores
they had of rice, millet, and potatoes. The Danes donated
chopped bits of salt pork to flavor cereals, the Spaniards saffron,
and the Germans dried herbs. The Americans evolved a gummy
mess of flour, molasses, and currants, christened it with a high-
falutin' name, and presented a batch of it to each household. The
Scotsmen followed with haggis, and the English with cheese. As
the hungry gaps grew wider, they took to toasting each other, and
Manning always, with frequent draughts of sherry and port.

Dr. Cox provided goat's milk twice a day for Manning, and
stood over him until he'd drunk every drop. The Parsee merchants
had managed to smuggle a fresh chicken and six eggs over for
Manning after dark the evening before. But to do it, everyone
knew, the Parsees themselves went without. Usually their rich
skin color set them above—and consequently apart—in Chinese
eyes from any of their restrictions and wrangles with barbarian
whites. But on this particular occasion it had only earned them
permission to do piecemeal buying—a meager minimum to feed
themselves, and not enough to share with others.

Yet the wonderment of Christmas was amongst them: good
will and fellowship and generosity were manifested a dozen ways.
There was a glad silvery glory in the carols they sang; their stories
were mellow and fraternal; and the wreaths and garlands and
bells they cut and pasted out of silver tea paper were blithe and
lively and gay. There was ample rejoicing and thanksgiving.
Only cupboards were bare.

At noon on the twenty-fourth Sturgis suddenly conceived the
notion of throwing the house open that evening to all friends,
which, of course, was everyone on the Row, and the five senior
Hong merchants as well. "Good lack!" Sturgis had exclaimed.

"What duffers we are! The only house on the Row with a lady, and we haven't offered to share her on Christmas Eve! We'll dance . . . do the Virginia reel, the Sir Roger de Coverley. That's the ticket. The younglings can draw lots to see who will play ladies to even up the quadrilles. And just to do it up brown for our favorite Hong merchants, let's send the Chinese rigmarole of three successive invitations in one packet!"

A little before seven that evening Gill let himself out the front gate. He wasn't running away from the evening's festivities, but before they began he wanted to catch a breath of fresh air. Skirting four Chinese soldiers posted at the landing steps, he fell into stride along the riverbank. Here, near shore, the water ran empty and black, with only the faint ghost of a moon silvering it in midstream. Beyond, a spattering of lights marked the Honan Island shore.

He had done two lengths of the Walk and was turning at the Creek end when he glimpsed the ornate silhouette of a mandarin boat putting in towards the landing steps. He heard the guards there holler challenges at it, but still the boat came on silently, and without a light of any kind showing on it. Gill told himself it couldn't be one of their Chinese guests arriving by water. A Hong merchant would have lanterns galore, and his lusty oarsmen would be outbawling each other to announce his full rank.

The guards converged with bamboo poles raised; and as the black prow came nosing in, they hammered at it until it ducked out and away. But no sound came from it, nor did it disappear. Instead it wavered forward against the current for a hundred, two hundred, yards; and then came sidling shoreward again as silent as a black hearse. The soldiers had never taken their eyes from it, and they went pelting now—all four—along the bank to the spot where it would touch.

With their first blows, a spurt of flame trickled across the forward deck and a blinding phosphorescent red glared in its cabin. With appalling suddenness rockets went whizzing up from where a lacquered canopy should have been—red, white, blue, green—

to burst into myriad stars. Sparks dazzled out in golden cataracts; pin wheels circled like comets. There was a crazy shus-s-sh and sizzle, and the whole boat belched into flame.

A splashing sound came as the two oarsmen plunged overboard. But they didn't jump on the landward side. Instead they bobbed out, farther away from shore, floundering clumsily in what seemed to be a tangle of roped gourds as the sweeping current gathered them downstream into the night. No poles were flung to them; no cries guided them shorewards. The soldiers seemed incapable of stirring or speaking, so spellbound were they with the red aurora of destruction spread before them.

They stared, oblivious to a sampan which darted into the dark landing. Nor did they see two crouching figures emerge from it and creep up through the gate, and run across the Walk to the oval garden plot, where they hid bundles they carried under low bushes, and then went flitting back to the sampan.

But from where Gill stood, concealed by shadows, he could see them plainly silhouetted against the fire—two small barefooted figures of women in coolie rags. They stooped for what seemed to be more sacks, and came back up the steps again.

In that instant the conviction flashed into his mind that this was deliverance—that these sacks, glory be, held food for the beleaguered colony! The mandarin boat itself—he almost laughed aloud—laden with its mesmerizing fire, had deliberately been sent ahead as a diversionary tactic to draw the soldiers away from the vital sampan. It was a "little plan"—daring, costly! Who—*who* could this wonderful friend be? This devious and impish strategist?

Gill held his breath, cautioning himself against making a sound, against any alarming movement. Silently, then, he glided out from the shadows until he knew the reflection of the fire was lighting his face—not to intercept the running women, but to let them see him and know he was there.

The nearer one spotted him immediately, and with an indrawn gasp stopped a yard away to stare at him. Next second she was laughing a soft contented little chuckle, crept closer, and thrust the two sacks into his arms.

Gill felt round rolling balls—dozens of them—under the sacking, and he caught the pungent fragrance of—oranges! "Who are you?" he whispered.

The girl shook her head, beckoning him quickly towards the garden plot. With rapid, telling gestures she showed where to reach over railings and stow the sacks underneath bushes. She took his hand in her small sinewy one, to run it over those other hidden sacks until he felt the fish and chickens and vegetables in them. Then she jumped to her feet, and with a swift, sidelong glance was estimating the fire's continued thrall.

In that second Gill saw coolie rags pinned together by thorns, and he saw a sweet beguiling face that—under smeared dirt—in no way matched coolie rags. He remembered her hand had been without calluses.

Then she was nodding towards the landing stones and motioning him to follow. How much more did she have? he wondered. Or was this the last sack?

In the dark he found he couldn't make out the second and somewhat stockier woman, who was below in the sampan now and handing up a heaving sack. But he saw the girl beside him stagger under its unwieldy weight, and he reached out quickly to shift it into his arms. Before he had it securely, there was a sound above and a soldier suddenly appeared at the gate.

The man came leaping down the steps at them with bamboo pole raised. The girl was nearer, and he aimed the pole to bring it crashing down on her head. In that breathless second Gill snatched her aside and butted the soldier's arm with his head to deflect the downward thrust. It was then the sack in Gill's arms gave a convulsive lurch. He felt a living thing escaping, and involuntarily his hands tightened on what they could find to hold.

There was a spectral flash of white, a hiss, and a huge goose surged out of the sack—to fly straight at the soldier's face. It hung there, beating powerful wings and hissing diabolically, as Gill clung to its feet. The soldier wheeled once in terror, and then with a surrendering moan tumbled backwards into the water.

Still gripping the flapping goose, Gill turned to meet a second, and a third, soldier. But no one came. No one called or seemed to notice the disappearance of the first.

That engagingly contented chuckle came from Gill's side. For a second he felt the girl's body pressed close against his and her eyes strained up to him in eloquent talk. But it was only for a quick pulsating second.

"Who are you? Tell me," he whispered.

She stepped back, making a soft confiding little murmur, and he caught the word "Friend."

She was speaking English!

Before Gill could put a hand out to detain her, or speak even, she was scrambling into the sampan and pushing it out from shore with the boat hook. The current caught them in its headlong race and bore them away into the black nothingness of the night.

The big drawing-rooms had never been so crowded, nor so gay. They were all gathered there smoking cheroots, drinking punch, eating dried *lichi* nuts, prancing through the Sir Roger de Coverley, fiddling, singing, or watching—two hundred and eighty contrasting, dissimilar, contradictory, and distinctive men.

They were even more incongruous in the clothes they wore— eleven Parsees in long white gowns and shiny cloven-hoofed hats; twenty Calcutta men in silk jodhpurs and looped turbans; two Arabs in Damascus *caftans* wrapped in flowing burnooses of camel's hair; five Chinese in lustrous satins and embroidered jackets lined with mink; and more than two hundred Scotsmen, Englishmen, Germans, Danes, Austrians, Dutchmen, and Americans in more than two hundred variations of blue serge, black broadcloth, neck ribbons, and moth balls. Yet they were completely, overwhelmingly unified in the bouyancy of good spirits. No one spoke of the cargoes which had gone up in smoke five days ago, of the poor opium market, or the higher price of raw silk.

Manning sat propped in cushions in a big chair by the fireplace, wrapped in cashmere shawls, his feet up on an ottoman. They had carried him down for an hour of the fun, that he might receive the homage and congratulations of everyone, hoping both would be good medicine for him. Obviously they were. His eyes were fully alive again as he looked from face to face in bright inquiry, and were quite without their former derisive mockery.

Between dances Lael took up post beside him, catching her breath, allowing a host of partners to fan her, hold her chair, hand her punch, pay her outrageous compliments, and she laughing over it all in a sort of incandescent gaiety.

When she'd heard invitations were going out, she'd immediately commandeered white silk from the storeroom, and basted and pinned it together into a wondrously simple thing with the flow and fold of Athena's robe. The bandeau she'd braided out of the silk floss and silver tea paper to cover the ends of her short hair added to the shining goddess look. Gill thought he'd never seen her more beautiful, and more unattainable.

He stood watching her from behind the velvet portieres of the big doorway. He and Stacey were waiting to do the Negro minstrel act of slave songs which they'd been practicing with the banjo all afternoon. They'd got themselves up in outsize clothes and blackened their faces. It was the second time they'd rubbed burned cork on that evening. The first was shortly before the twisted pine torches at the gate were due to be lighted for the party and they'd ducked out into the Walk to carry the food sacks into the Russell compound.

Not far from Manning's chair a bulky Howqua sat, bundled in at least ten layers of clothing and holding a live quail in his frail fleshless hands to keep them warm. When four violins—being played by Austrian, German, and American factors—tuned up again and sawed discordantly as they tightened strings in preparation for another dance, Lael stepped to Howqua and inquired:

"Elder-born, our musicians would be joyed to play your choice. Do you have preference for something dreamy? 'Träumerei,' for instance? Or perhaps a quick step such as 'Yankee Doodle'?"

Howqua inclined his head in benign thanks, the fingers of one hand dancing on the chair arm in pleasurable anticipation. "My chin-chin werry much," he smiled up at her eagerly. "My likee so fashion. This music belong Number One chop."

Lael's smile never faltered. With admirable poise she sent word to the violinists to continue their tuning up for another five minutes. She stood beside Howqua, nodding appreciatively when he nodded appreciatively and raising eyebrows panegyrically over discords which satisfied him most. When the violinists stopped, she acknowledged Howqua's gratitude and turned back to the dance partners claiming her.

William Jardine led her off for the Viennese waltz he'd requested, remarking audibly that since he was leaving next month for England he deserved this parting favor from one of the fairest ornaments of creation. This persiflage from the man who wouldn't have a second chair in his office so as to keep people from loitering and gossiping there!

Gowqua, sitting next to Howqua, had missed none of this. His bright eyes followed Lael with a parrot-like curiosity as she danced, swiveled to the old codgers around the room who preened and straightened neckerchiefs as she passed, and took in the young ones holding themselves in leash only while the music played, but obviously ready to swarm about her the minute it stopped. He cleared his throat politely behind his hand and, leaning out beyond Howqua to address Manning, said: "If I should be lucky enough to live as a man in the next world, I would hope to be a Chinese. But—in case I am born female, may I be an American woman!"

It was after Gill and Stacey had sung "Barbara Allan," "Old Dan Tucker," and "Bound for the Promised Land" that they changed clothes, scrubbed cork soot from their faces, and began passing mandarin oranges, divided into quarters so each would have a taste. Because the Hong merchants were present, they'd agreed, it would be oranges tonight, but in the morning there'd be a grand division of the other food sacks, with each household receiving its portion. To stop the astonished chorus of exclamations they'd concocted a glib answer: "Been in our storeroom all week. Just saving them for a Christmas surprise!"

Gill would have enjoyed telling about their elusive little "friend," about that slim willow wand of a girl who chuckled so beguilingly and mesmermized soldiers with firecrackers. But he dare not, not with the five senior Hong merchants listening.

When he'd finished passing the oranges, Gill went to the stair landing outside the drawing-room to stand his empty tray against the wall. As he turned to go back, he saw that Gowqua had followed him there. In lustrous dove-gray satin the Chinese stood balancing his section of mandarin orange on a pedestal he made of his jeweled fingers.

"I find this *symbol* too precious to eat," Gowqua told him. "I can only admire it—and the spirit which shares a very little with many."

Gill sensed the man was probing for information, and laughed easily. "Call it Christmas spirit, Gowqua. It prompts us to do unpredictable things."

"I believe it does," Gowqua said quietly, twisting the orange in his fingers so the waxen shred of skin holding several sections together was uppermost. He examined it thoughtfully. "I am acquainted with this particular variety. It is called 'Twelfth-Moon Yellow,' and is not for sale hereabouts. You see, it is only grown in one spot . . . a certain orchard over on Honam Island, across the river."

Gill felt his muscles tighten; he seemed to be listening with every pore. "Yes," he prompted, "and its owner is . . . ?"

Gowqua smiled the same gentle smile, his eyes traveling up the paneled wall, but looking far beyond it. "We Chinese have an interesting observation on life, Mr. Bennett, which you may not have heard. It is . . . 'Fish dwell in deep waters, but can be taken on a hook. Eagles nest on the side of Heaven, yet can be reached with an arrow. But the heart of a woman, at a foot's distance, cannot be known.'" He left Gill standing there and went back to his chair beside Howqua.

Across the room Samuel Fearon picked up his pearwood lute and ran his fingers lovingly across the seven strings, plucking at them in evanescent minor melody. As conversation quieted, the melody swelled, and he was playing in the slow soft Southern style. First he sang a coolie song of loneliness:

> *"A crow on a far-off bough*
> *outlined against falling snow,*
> *Is a picture matching*
> *the echo in my desolate heart."*

By and by the Cantonese words were a tremulous lament for love; and as Fearon's voice lifted high and hung in haunting waver, there was no memory amongst the others in the room of a peppery and eccentric little English factor in rusty broadcloth who'd spent five years of evening study to learn Cantonese. It wasn't even a man singing. It was a heart crying aloud for love.

> *"The moon at Heaven's verge is like a sickle hook,*
> *Its shimmer floats on the long river and,*
> *nothing loath, flows down the stream,*
> *Tinging my thoughts with love—*
> *The willow which melts souls in sorrow*
> *plucks darkly at my garment.*
> *O Willow, since thus thou canst evoke passion,*
> *how canst thou suffer love to delay?*
> *Evening clouds and vernal trees: the moon at*
> *Heaven's verge . . .*
> *My eyes strain for the sight of love."*

The Chinese words meant nothing to Gill, but the emotion in them strained at cords within him. He stepped to the doorway, impelled with the desire to find Lael, and found her a few feet away, coming to look for him. The sight of the heart-shaped face gave him a quick sense of comfort and pleasure. But there was a quickening too, a surge of hot impulse he couldn't keep out of his eyes as he gazed into hers. The violet ones were steadfast in return. But then he saw her lips purse wistfully, and he knew something was disturbing her.

He stepped quickly to her side. "What is it, Lael? Tell me!"

Still she looked at him for another tender wishful moment, and her head drooped. "Uncle Tim's ordering the *Angola* to leave Whampoa tomorrow with me aboard," she said.

"Leave?" He groped amongst his emotions. "No, Lael. No! I——" He didn't know what he was trying to say.

She shook her head. "There's nothing we can do," she said, as though recognizing some need within the two of them to delay the parting. "Uncle Tim knows about the siege now."

"How?"

"The Hong merchant Gowqua has just told him."

"Gowqua!" Gill was astonished.

She nodded. "Yes, the one in dove gray—who is far from being a dove, I suspect. He came to our party tonight, it seems, with an extra-special 'safe conduct' pass for me, all made out by the Viceroy himself. It takes me downriver in princess style—'*for the good of the greatest number*' is the way Gowqua puts it."

Gill told himself it was inevitable. They could only hope to delay her going a day or two more, with Manning so on the mend now. Besides, he asked himself in a clattering panic, what was this wash of susceptibility he was floundering in like some moon-struck sophomore? What was it? Prolonged Christmas? A diet of sherry and port and claret on an empty stomach? All work and celibate Canton? Propinquity—precious propinquity—with a good and beautiful girl so above him, so far above him! Him . . . of all persons! Without definite prospects. Without money. Without a job even in another four months!

In an excess of torment he groaned aloud.

Lael's eyes probed his. "Do you want to tell me?" she asked.

Gill jerked around to look off into the drawing-room . . . at the carol singers by the fireplace, at the burlesque gentility of men choosing other men for dance partners, anywhere but into Lael's eyes. When he'd stifled the gnawing words within him, he said, brusquely to convince himself: "No. I've nothing whatever to tell."

Was that a hurt gasp from Lael?

What words might have tumbled from his lips in another breath, he'd never know. For at that moment the milling dancers spied Lael there on the landing and came trouping out boisterously to bear her off.

CHAPTER XIV

PEKING,

New Year's Day, 1839

THE DRUMS of morning struck, but by the time their summons reached the pavilion beside the Altar of Heaven the matted cypress boughs of the forest there had strangled the rolling reverberations, sifting and sieving them, until they shrank to puny quavers. Tao Kuang was yearning for the signal, though, no matter how faint it came. For an eternity of seventy-two hours he'd been anticipating its release. He lifted the last dipper of purification water and trickled it over his flinching skin.

There, finished—the final austerity in three days and nights of absolute austerity. Ritually he was prepared to address the Supernal Powers at today's dawn, and personally he was overwhelmingly ready to shift the problem of Canton's punishing futilities from his mind to the superintendence of Heaven.

"*Ai-yah!*" he exclaimed, toweling himself briskly and wondering if it actually was morning drums sounding. Or was it his abused stomach thundering protest? This co-mingling of flesh and water in the Season of Small Snow, in solitude . . . this fasting and praying and fasting, in solitude . . . this unalterable ritual for conference fixed by infinite precedent . . . which monkey of a Ming had started it, anyway?

The candles of walrus fat guttered in the draft he made wrapping himself in successive layers of white silk padded with floss. Then he stooped and carefully pulled on white fur boots. The final enveloping cocoon of white fox skins lined with winter ermine lent comforting warmth, and he smoothed its solacing fur with appreciative fingers. Yes indeed, a thoroughly absolving symbol of immaculate purity—and practical as well. He'd designed it for today's chilblains.

Obligations in this austere cell were completed. He was ready. Overwhelmingly purged, cleansed, shriven—inside and out—he could quit the Hall of Annual Abstinence, leave it securely behind him for another twelve moons. That is, unless those beastly and degraded foreign devils became infuriated to the state of war. . . .

No, he calmed himself, walking to the waiting chair, let some comfortable middle road be found. Avoid provoking them calamitously, he counseled himself as the eight bearers carried him across a courtyard to the ringed altar of altars standing supremely open to the sky.

In solemn concentration he mounted triple terraces of white marble, and on the upper dais knelt before the great axial block which marked the center of the universe. Above him altar candles bloomed like red flowers and a caul of incense smoke came drifting about him, until he could have been mistaken for the spirit of some white fox kneeling in a dark and misty garden.

Then he spoke in the high-pitched ritual voice.

"I address the Trinity . . . Heaven! Earth! Ancestors! I make the nine knockings, three—and three—and three—to each," he intoned, bowing towards marble pavement, but merely denting a silk cushion with his forehead nine times.

More candles bloomed on the spherical flat altar. Moon lanterns rose around it to bathe the yellow earth sprinkled on its white surface with celestial radiance. Across the center a dead bullock lay with evergreen branches covering the body so only head and tail were showing. Tao Kuang rose from his knees to carry offerings to the altar—vessels of rice and wine as the symbols of life; ten pair of foodsticks in thanksgiving for the past year's mercies; gold paper flowers in tribute; incense in veneration—and placed them beside the bullock.

He returned to kneel again, and drink the Wine, and eat the Food of Felicity. When he spoke this time, he included the Spirit of Fire and the Spirit of Water in his salutations. *"Wu-hu,* oh, alas! In the watches of each night I mourn inconsolably for our Black-haired-Race-of-a-Hundred-Surnames!" he told them. "I cannot sleep, nor eat with appetite. I am grief-stricken, and shake with anxiety. Our world of imperfect people is afflicted by extraordinary ills, and we are bowed beneath calamity. My self-abasement knows no limit."

He cleared his throat, and his voice ascended the tonal scale: *"Wu-hu,* oh, alas, only by adherence to honored precedent do I hope to achieve absolute validity. O Supreme Tribunal, guide my course with untamed Western Ocean devils, who are costive with conceit and unreason, whose words are rough, whose minds are confused. Prostrate, I implore Imperial Heaven to pardon my ignorance and guide me entirely henceforth."

He cupped hands supplicatingly. "Give ear, Imperial Heaven! Instruct me with signs—that reason and intelligence may continue the pivotal cult of my reign. *Wu-hu,* oh, alas!"

He continued apostrophe and report until the yellow dawn— making nine times nine knockings and assuring the Supreme Tribunal he would follow its guidance. Whereupon he rose, his mind a blissful blank. He had complied with precedent. He had wiped the slate. Whatever occurred now, it would be Heaven's will.

Walking to one of the four cardinal stairways, he raised an uncovered left hand to learn the daybreak direction of today's telltale wind. In that first moment he took it to be from a south-easterly angle—the forecast of epidemics and sickness. But no . . . he was facing the yellow rub of daylight, and the wind puffed full in his face.

"*Wu-hu,* oh, alas!" he moaned. "The wind of sorrow rises! The wind of war!"

With fire speed the sign had come! Did that mean war was already amongst them? That it was upon them? Why hadn't the court astrologers and horoscopers foreseen it?

Irresolutely he stood on the topmost step and gazed about him . . . upon the singing grandeur of snow-white marble wrought in multiple design of nine—the concentric circles of triple terraces, each outlined by three hundred and sixty balusters, and connected one with the other by stairways of nine steps. He turned left—and there was the circular Temple of Heaven rising in triple tiers towards a sapphire crown of three diminishing circles of roof. Before him, radiating from the altar like spokes from an axle, were alleys of black cypress stretching in infinite purple perspective beyond . . . beyond. . . .

He shook his head in weary perplexity. These ancient riches yielded no answer, unless it was the testimony of beauty far too precious to be polluted by alien eyes.

Hours later, with twitching fingers, Tao Kuang jiggled the complicated gold-wire puzzle some nincompoop had given him for New Year's, and then in exasperated defeat threw it on the floor. Another flicking futility added to the day's account.

The noon drums sounded, telling him the time had arrived for his present-bestowing audience. A smile of quiet malice lifted his pouting lips as he remembered the sophisticated rebuke he was about to administer to Old Millennial before all six Boards of Ministers . . . designing it had required certain ingenuity because, of course, there'd never been another like it, and it had to be made to specification. He chortled outright, cracking his

knuckle joints . . . done, completed now. A materialized salutation, you might call it, to a windbag incessantly prattling about
foreign-devil inventions. . . .

He adjusted his ceremonial sable hat with its peacock feather
frolicking high above, and stepped out jauntily, his new sapphire
court skirt rustling proudly and sounding every bit as costly as it
was.

In the second anteroom an indiscriminate stone-gray shape rose
up suddenly from the rug and caught at the lustrous hem. Tao
Kuang looked down in startled surprise and saw Minister Kan's
frog-bitten face looking up beseechingly. What puking triviality
was this? He bestowed a disparaging look, and wondered why
in thunder the old crow wasn't waiting in audience with the other
ministers, where he belonged.

Kan snatched off his velvet hat in contrition. "O Emblem of
Righteousness, I transgress! I approach you unbidden. The calamitous present goads me," he begged, grinding and clacking his
teeth in mincing terseness. "Sell the follies of last year, I beseech
you! Sell them that today's commencement may start clean. Banish pernicious foreign mud from our palaces. YOU, our Emblem!
Banish it here, and our Black-haired-Race will copy."

"What nasal bleatings are these?" the Emblem demanded indignantly. Did Old Bitter-Tooth have to exhort today? Today,
with wracking decision still to be made on whether or not to make
the Special Imperial Commissioner appointment! How to coerce
three hundred foreign devils into abandoning opium, let alone
curb three thousand domestic eunuchs inside these Flowery Gates
. . . it would create rebellion, anarchy, dissolution—the wells
would flow red!

"O Emblem, your eldest son by the concubine of our Yehonala
clan became a guest of Heaven an hour ago," Kan told him.
"Already his two brothers by that mother are quarreling over the
division of opium he left behind."

The Emblem closed his eyes, trying to recall the youth's exact
features from amongst his nine sons and eleven daughters, for he

was reminded now that he hadn't seen this particular lad in six—or was it eight?—months. Ah yes, the sickly one . . . with neither aptitude nor taste for pulling a bow, for hunting, or even for riding. No, this death was less than a bleeding pain, he told himself. The youth had chosen a comfortable way.

Kan's sepulchral voice brought the father back to the present. "Calamities bind us like shrouds! A shaking of the earth is reported in the very birthplace of our dynasty—in our Tung-pei homeland between the Long White Mountains and the Amur River."

Tao Kuang looked with white eyes at the bone-meager face of this croaking Manchu crow. "Opium doesn't shake the earth," he snapped.

"Its evil angers the Dragon who *does* shake the earth," Kan mouthed fearfully, and poured forth a tocsin of exhortation and prediction—"for the welfare of the dynasty, for the welfare of the Old-One-Hundred-Surnames"—all the while, between nervous fingers, he kneaded that new sapphire hem as though it were a lump of dough.

The Emblem interrupted by shaking his sleeve in instant dismissal. When he saw this ignored, he reached down and twitched the lustrous satin from those crumpling hands, demanding: "Lend me light!", which meant "by removing yourself," and stalked out of the room.

"I transgress! I transgress!" Kan cried after the Emblem in supplication. But when no ameliorating contradiction came from the Lips to redeem him, the old man shuddered to his feet, and with corpse eyes went groping homewards to make his only possible and final apology by drinking a cup of poisoned tea.

The swarming Court of Astrologers, as the Emblem passed it, was a blue blur of sandalwood smoke. He heard the fast rattle of divination sticks in pewter cylinders, the whirl of horoscope wheels, the slapping shuffle of zodiac tiles. But above the din he caught snatches of portent—dismal, oppressive, heart-squeezing, drat them . . . "ill-omened gray herons flying west at noon . . . planets in atrocious aspect . . . intercalary month . . . candles guttering inauspiciously . . . ill-starred handles breaking, breaking, breaking" . . . It was unsettling, unnerving.

Yet when he stepped onto the audience dais before the "hatpin and tassel" clan of ministers, the weight lessened temporarily. For right off the Chief Eunuch came to kneel and proffer the customary gold Fate plate with its six dice. The Emblem scooped the omens up, shook them between two cupped hands, and cast them on the plate.

O lustrous Fortune, each turned a different number!

The Emblem beamed happily, so the ministers knew even before he told them that the omen for the coming year was good luck. Backing away quickly, the Chief Eunuch removed the plate before any ferreting eyes would see that each dice bore only one number.

In an aura of pleasure the Emblem conferred six sable coats on the six Ministers of the Council itself. He conferred twenty jade scepters on lesser ministers . . . *ai-yah,* he told himself, the glut of these futile *ju-i* still left from grandfather Ch'ien Lung's reign, even though he himself had been doling them out at New Year's regularly now for nineteen years!

On the ten most scholarly ministers the Emblem bestowed volumes of verse by that most conscientious of poem writers—the same august Ch'ien Lung. Giving these books really rallied his spirits—in still handsome brocade binding, they'd been uncovered from a dusty corner of one Imperial storehouse a week ago during the inventory-taking that practical head of the incomparable Lady Yi had thought up. Refreshing, exhilarating almost . . . ten useless books disposed of! And yet a scholarly present for the scholarly!

Now, *lastly* . . . the climax. Minister Ho's present standing there on the centermost table—a shapeless silk-wrapped bundle nearly two hands high.

Ho regarded the package with the calculating look of a hungry crow. "Millennial!" he murmured. "Absolutely millennial!"

The Emblem motioned Ho to open it before everyone.

"O Your Brightness! O Lord of the Universe!" Ho protested exuberantly as his fingers untied the cords. Silk and wadding slid away, and the porcelain statue of a dog appeared. But it wasn't a Pekingese. Nor a sleeve dog. Nor the classical lion-dog of tradition. It was a yellow cur of a dog sitting on its haunches begging . . . a foreign dog!

"Oh my heart and liver!" Ho exclaimed, unable to pry eyes from the dog. Staring . . . staring . . . he broke into that country laugh of his, until it snagged, suddenly, on a sob.

The Emblem cleared the place by summoning Lin Tse-hsu—the Fukienese terrorist! The bold and uncompromising reformer!

Moments later the inner door swung on dowel pins and the black-mustached, black-bearded Lin walked quietly into the room, bowing his head over clasped hands, since this was not formal audience. It was, by his count, the nineteenth he'd had in a fortnight, repeating and repeating identical arguments, identical persuasions.

This was Lin Tse-hsu, Peking's shrewdist economist: Peking's most vigorous analyst; the man who'd traveled to Nanking, Hankow, and Chungking recently to consult merchants, and come back and address three forceful petitions to the Throne detailing the steady impoverishment of China through the drain of bullion to buy opium. His gown today was the somber color of ripe plums, but richly lustrous and richly embroidered. Above medium height, prosperously fat, with a pleasant, vivacious expression on his thoughtful face, his appearance in no way matched his reputation for reckless violence.

In Peking's current officialdom Lin was that rarity—a man of the land: the son of a day laborer who, in his time, had become owner of a small porcelain manufactory in which he'd begun his labors. Lin's own eminence had been achieved in the heartwarming classical pattern—aristocracy through a learned mind. At twenty-six he had passed the Third Degree in national examinations, and thereafter his combination of ability, charm, and rigorous zeal had boosted him upwards rapidly to the office of Imperial Censor. A year ago, at fifty-three, he'd been made Governor-General of the two "Hus"—Hunan and Hupeh.

Lin's twelve months' jurisdiction of those northern provinces had labeled him even more of a rarity, for he'd applied himself with implacable honesty and Confucian idealism to the self-appointed task of eradicating both gambling houses and opium smoking. He'd succeeded in both, abruptly and completely, but with certain deficits appearing in population rosters, which, rumor added—or perhaps multiplied—to a grim total.

The Emblem clasped hands over his middle to steady misgivings beginning to seesaw within him again. He gazed curiously for a moment at this resolute and talented man whom he *might* entrust with supreme authority. In two hundred years the Ch'ing dynasty had conferred such authority only three times. And now, in extremity, should he make it four? *Kinchae . . . Special Imperial Commissioner*—outranking Governor-General, outranking Viceroy: with power to search their offices and households at will. Kinchae, exalted substitute of the Throne itself. . . .

The Emblem saw Lin's keen penetrating eyes were watching him—reading his thoughts, no doubt. He spoke comfortably, without ceremonial intonation. "My five viscera are cramped with anxiety. Yet I believe you go to the very root of our opium plague. Your plan deals directly with red-pate importation. I am convinced we must restrict them . . ."

Lin nodded emphatically.

" . . . *but not unbearably.*"

The bright watching eyes narrowed.

"Cantonese are already overly independent," the Emblem argued aloud, convincing himself anew with words Lin had said ten audiences ago. "The most independent of our people! The least loyal! Let English and American devils install themselves firmly in that city, they'll incite Cantonese hotheads to further rebellion. They threaten peace, and must be humbled."

"As plain as water," Lin agreed in a remarkably clear and strong voice, a good steadying voice.

The Emblem took a vase in his hands, a vase as delicate and white as hoarfrost, to stand stroking it aimlessly as he asked: "But which strategy? Which to choose? Deprive them of tea and rhubarb upon which their very lives depend? Or would that drive them insane with constipation?"

"Compassion is wasted on them," Lin said decisively.

The Emblem nodded. "I agree. I remember my august grandfather Ch'ien Lung felt pity for them, and permitted several Jesuit priests to visit his court. In magnanimous charity he offered to take one of the Pope's nieces as a concubine. Imagine, if you can, the Pope never replied. Tck, tck—they're without cultural ambitions, even."

"They'll understand severity," Lin promised.

Lapsing back into indecision, the Emblem sighed: "Unless it should infuriate them. Not measuring to any known standard is their difficulty. Koreans, Japanese, Loochooians, Annamese, Tibetans have readily appreciated Chinese culture. They've adopted our etiquette, our religion, our philosophy, our art—but not redpates. No! Steadfastly I make soothings on paper to them, addressing generous edicts. But to no avail whatever." He seemed to be reassuring himself of adequate forbearance.

Lin disagreed. "I would remind you, Sire, that it is easier to catch a tiger in the mountains than to move the world with speech."

The Emblem regarded him in silence a moment, and then began his querulous enumeration again: "They rove north as far as Tsingtao, running into bays, trading, taking soundings, selling opium at night. I endeavor to convince these ungovernables that OUR laws restrict them to Canton port, where their welfare can be safely guarded. I endeavor to convince them. But, alas, they remained unconvinced."

"Convince them with clubs," Lin urged dynamically, leaning forward, his eyes sparkling, his face alive with dedication.

He infected the Emblem, but only momentarily. "Isn't that the crux? Do they have stronger clubs than we?" he wanted to know.

"Never!" Lin stormed. "Their vessels of war are monstrous heavy, taking water to a depth of tens of feet. Capable enough on outer seas where they break waves and sail before strong winds. But—we defeat them utterly with strategy. We avoid the sea. We lure them into harbors and rivers. Their vessels become unwieldy. We have total advantage."

As Lin spoke, his voice, his face, and his gestures gradually underwent change, increasing in forcefulness and vigor. Not that he'd ever seen a foreign ship of war. But he'd read naval reports and talked with admirals. Now, as he repeated the logical-sounding words, enthusiasm took hold of him, flashing from his eyes and rolling sonorously from his tongue, until he was victim of his own oratory.

"Suppose their soldiers come ashore—what then?" the Emblem demanded.

Lin snorted lively contempt. "We annihilate them! We confuse and terrorize. We coerce them ignominiously in the merest twinkling!" Excitement still fanned his voice, and now the birthmark on his nose began swelling and turning black.

Before his shaking hands might drop it, the Emblem returned the white vase to its stand, and wiped moisture beads from his upper lip. "You say . . . 'We shall seize all opium stock.' But how? How take chests from the hulks at Lintin? From coastal vessels? These barbarians are too rebellious. They'll rise up crying tears of blood."

"Tears are my daily meat and drink," Lin said, not boasting, only stating incontrovertible fact.

"But—what merit to empty a pool of water *if* a fresh supply drains back into it in six months?" It was everlasting catechism. He'd asked it a dozen times already.

Lin gave the same steady answer he'd always given. "We force them to sign indemnity bonds calling for strangulation if they ever bring another chest of opium to China."

"They'll refuse."

"Then we cancel trading privileges. They can't enter the Pearl River. The Hong merchants can't supply them."

The Emblem's head ached grievously. His mouth was dry with forming words. Suddenly it came to him he'd promised himself a look at the Dragon Dance over on the ice of North Lake . . . skaters crouched under a green body wriggling drunkenly about the ice, with big flickering tongue darting in and out of a livid mouth, breathing gusts of flame and smoke. It was excruciatingly droll always—so gay, so carefree. Bright kites galore sailing the sky, shuttlecocks flashing, multicolored wine jars and embroidered sedan chairs everywhere. . . . Ah—there'd still be time to get there and enjoy the comedy before dressing for the deadly ordeal of the State Banquet given by the Board of Rites. Besides, here was a strong willing man! A man ready and eager to hoist the outer-barbarian conundrum onto his able shoulders.

The Emblem turned to Lin. "Kinchae!" he pronounced impressively. "Leave for Canton at once. Go with the speed of flame! Let Heaven and Fate have their way!"

In the faded yellow light of noonday sixty-four eunuchs followed the Chief Eunuch in procession to Western Pavilion bearing the Emblem's present for Honorable Concubine-Consort Yi. Each of the sixty-four laid the five folio-sized manuscripts he carried on the peach-colored rugs of Peach Anteroom until three hundred and twenty volumes grew from the floor in bewildering stacks.

The Lady Yi stood watching the strange parade with round eyes, not comprehending its meaning: only knowing that sack of suet, the Chief Eunuch, was there in her pavilion. What trick was he perpetrating now? Had he guessed her intention? Had he moved against her before she could topple him? She felt a buzzing in her ears, and tasted the acid of fear in her mouth.

"Western Pavilion *Empress!*" the Chief Eunuch addressed her in elaborate artificiality. "I convey that most tantalizing of presents—the collated wisdom of a talented cook. These are memoranda of Low Man-kee himself."

Laughter rippled from Yi's unclamped lips, as though from a schoolgirl. Low Man-kee—the master, the tutor, the authority of China's legion of sublime chefs! Of course! These three hundred and twenty volumes were his *Hints on Cookery.* They had become hers now, *hers!* The Emblem of Righteousness had put them in her hands.

She stepped to the nearest stack to run a small caressing hand across the topmost cover as though it were a flower. She opened pages, fingering through them, beguiled by fluted brushstrokes, transported by tinted drawings of subtle ingredients, and of the supreme final concoction itself.

The Chief Eunuch was talking—thanking her with gemmed words for the pair of doves she'd presented him for today's present. He had the Phoenix-head White, the Toad-eyed Gray, the Magpie Flower, he said, and the Iron-Ox, the Jade-Wing, the Flowery Neck, the Purple Sauce, but not such rarities as she'd given, these Dagger-breasted ones.

His tongue interrupted itself to lick moist lips as he lingeringly recalled the soft beauty of those exquisite white breasts with only the single spot of ruby feathers in the center. Wiping an excess of dampness from his face, the Chief Eunuch uttered a profusion of conversational platitudes—facilely, verbosely, with consummate courtesy—until he quite convinced himself he'd indicated unswerving homage, devotion, and fidelity to this ascendant star.

Yi heard his words, knowing they were empty as drums, but let neither the realization nor the words themselves interfere with her quest amongst the book pillars to scan pages here and pages there with high pleasure.

After an interval the Chief Eunuch bowed himself out, and in the corridor he sang under his breath:

> *"May common wind blow on her,*
> *Bring fever to her body, ulcers to her lips,*
> *And shake her apart with coughing!"*

But in the Peach Anteroom, Yi couldn't hear him; and read on, stirring only when she turned a page, so absorbed that the dripping of the palace clock was like a distant brook.

She had no need to busy herself about the pavilion. She had chopped and cut and stuffed dumplings yesterday so she would not cut luck today. She had seen two days' water drawn from her pavilion well and its top sealed so its guardian spirits could go visiting on this commencement of the holiday moon. She had hung the finest scrolls she possessed on her walls and lined the corridors with the jewel fruit of dwarfed *chin-chü* and pearl-cherry trees. Her own apartment bloomed with bowls of Water Fairy lily, with flowering quince, pink camellias, and the lemon called Buddha's Fingers. She had only to prepare her body—*and her mind*—for this evening's visit of His Brightness.

Later that afternoon, when she'd returned to her inner apartment, the young eunuch Lan-fan arrived carrying a velvet sash box under one arm. He crossed the room quickly and set the box upon the blackwood dress chest against one wall, rattling its dangling brass bolt to show it was securely locked, and then turned to hand the key blade for it to Yi.

"The pearl cape?" she asked in awe.

Lan-fan nodded. "Yes, Little Mistress."

"And its guardian? We are safe until . . ."

"The guardian will not speak for two days," Lan-fan told her positively. "To cure the itch I purposely administered to him three nights ago, I have now given him a bowl of nerve-deadening broth—the same nerve killer we Dedicated Ones drink before castration. I have reason to know its efficacy."

Yi nodded thoughtfully, turned the key blade in her hands a moment, and then flipped it open to its full length and slid it into the groove of the lock. She lifted the lid—standing as still as water to stare at the magic thing inside.

Lan-fan took up a moon-white horn lantern and raised it above their heads to add its glow to the milky luster of threaded pearls, sewed row after solid row into an elbow-length cape—not seed pearls, not grain pearls, but nacreous orbs as large as peas. Dozens, and more dozens, were as large as canary eggs.

"Three thousand, five hundred pearls——" Yi said in a queer choked voice.

"—pilfered from the good Ch'ien Lung"—Lan-fan took up where her voice failed, as though reciting a remembered text—"by his Chief Minister. Restored to the Throne by Ch'ien Lung's son. In this generation pilfered yet again by——"

Yi interrupted by banging the lid down, snapping the lock shut, and hiding the key blade inside the neck of her gown. She was mortally uneasy. She was frightened. She had the feeling of riding a headlong current, a pushing, panicking element. To quiet herself she sat in a straight-backed audience chair and assumed the rigid formal pose. "You have completed sale of five thousand objects in hardstone, carnelian, and agate?" she inquired.

"Yes, Little Mistress."

"And their total is . . . ?"

"One quarter million dollars, Little Mistress," Lan-fan told her.

Her deep bright eyes grew brighter, and she held out her hand. "The receipt?"

From the velvet sack on his wrist Lan-fan took a paper and gave it to her.

Yi examined it, and each of four seals in each corner, then crossed the room to her desk and laid the paper with others in a top drawer. From a lower drawer she took an itemized list of many pages and handed it to Lan-fan. "You will now sell, as clandestinely as previously, these two thousand items of rose quartz and lapis lazuli," she directed incisively. "It is a lesser consignment, since there's bound to be less buying money in this interval immediately after New Year's. Remember, though, no lowering of price, even if it requires an additional half-moon to dispose of the list."

Lan-fan bowed. "I hear and obey," he said.

Yi turned back the empty enveloping cuff of her sleeves as though girding herself for an encounter. "Now," she said, "tell me today's facts, and *their proof*."

Lan-fan dealt out words. He had memorized the bleak realities he had to tell; and he ticked them off now, succinctly, without gestures, without tonal embellishment, without fuddling pauses.

Yi heard him through, interrupting only twice to repeat after him the digits he quoted. When he finished, she nodded and said solemnly: "I have them catalogued in my mind now . . . I hope and pray," she added in sudden pensive wistfulness, looking at Lan-fan now. For, at this stage, he was the very structure of her existence.

As she looked, her mind registered again the stalwart quality in him: the reasoning intellect behind those alert eyes. Also, essential calmness. There was none of the frustrated restlessness: none of the biting, caressing fidgets; none of the hostility and sloth and viciousness that complete castration evoked in the other eunuchs. Was it because she had given him man's work to do in this purple dovecot of domesticity? Was it because he'd set himself the goal of freedom—of the mind?

She didn't give gold or a jeweled ornament now. Instead, out of the urge of her feelings, she told him of the verity bringing such abundant hope. "Your star is tied to my star, Lan-fan. For now I bear the Sublime One's child within me. Add your daily entreaties to mine that it be a ten-thousand-happiness son."

"*Ai-yah! Ai-yah!*" Lan-fan exclaimed, sinking to his knees and making the formal *kowtow*. He snatched the hem of her skirt, pressing it to his forehead a dozen times, and then kissed it. "Imperial Mother-to-Be!" he whispered in devout hope. He gazed up at her for a full moment, a gamut of expressions crossing his face. But the one that remained longest, and was still there as he bowed himself out, was reverence.

Before she went to anoint and tint and perfume her body, Yi lit fresh incense on the rosewood altar table and knelt before it, clapping hands to attract Kwan-yin's attention. "O Hearer of Cries, grant HIM mellowness after the trial of the one-hundred-course State Banquet! Grant me opportunity to accomplish my desire!" she begged aloud. She clapped hands again, repeating the supplication, and stayed kneeling for another interval as she tested the temperature of the floor tiles with her hand. Then she was on her feet, ringing the bell and dispatching an immediate command for more coal in the subterranean firebox which puffed hot air through the conduits under these floor tiles. Mellowness, after all, was a consequence of well-being.

The curfew drum sounded its four beats when the bearers put the Imperial chair down at Western Pavilion. The Emblem belched as he stepped out, and belched again as he came stalking into Yi's apartment on those narrow rider's legs of his. He paused appreciatively at the warmth of the room and its lily fragrance before he stepped closer to Yi to breathe in the languishing aroma of her cheeks, her neck, her hair. "How does my perfumed companion?" he asked, stepping back to comfort himself with the look of her.

She stood, as tapered as a brushstroke, in a gown the color of morning stars. The strand of waxen lemon buds twined through the knot of coiled hair on her neck was her only ornament, except for that small oval face the color of sugar and those new-moon eyebrows over deep bright eyes.

"Supremely happy," she smiled at him from her heart, "now that Unapproachable Perfection has come to me."

He shed his sable coat by lowering his arms and walking out of it: unbuttoned the stiff board of a ceremonial gown until it dropped away from a loose underrobe of Imperial yellow. With a deep shuddering belch he slumped onto the cushioned divan.

Yi plucked the kettle from the brazier and poured boiling water over tea leaves already mixed with a stomach settler, and, on her knees, served him a bowl. "This will ease your Worshipful Complaint," she promised earnestly.

He drew the comforting warmth into his lungs, and then sucked it in small swallows. Yi watched his face, trying to read its signs. Was he too weary with today's incessant ritual? Was that sag a holdover of the unpredictable moodiness that had shaken him these weeks?

He returned the bowl to its jade saucer, and Yi filled it again. He let its jasmine aroma dissipate in steam while he picked two *lichi* from the dish at his elbow, but instead of crumbling their papery shells between his fingers, he rolled the nuts from one hand to another vexedly. "I ponder, and search, and probe . . . did I caution the Kinchae sufficiently?" he murmured aloud in colorless monotone. "'Don't tread with too firm a foot,' I said. Severity, yes . . . but only to a degree. To that certain discreet boundary. H'm-m?" He looked questioningly at the sandalwood panels, at the mother-of-pearl windowpanes, at the thick altar candles of walrus fat, until his glance came to rest on Yi kneeling there beside him.

She swallowed twice. What was this communion with himself? Invitation to her—Merciful Heaven, the opportunity Kwan-yin was granting so soon? With soft diffidence she asked: "Is this domestic person correct in assuming My Lord speaks thusly because he wishes my ignorant counsel?"

Tao Kuang sensed a quality of sympathy and comfort in the voice, and instinctively responded. "These plaguing red-pates in Canton—they cramp my head, my heart, and my belly excessively!" he sighed.

Yi handed up another bowl of cleansing jasmine brew to him. When he gave it back empty, her adoring eyes milked further words from him. "A differing breed," he told her perplexedly. "They don't resign themselves to Fate. They fight it."

Yi nodded. "Yes, I'm told that '*endure, endure,* and *endure*' is not their creed."

"Because of that," Tao Kuang hastened to explain, "I believe the Kinchae should proceed tentatively . . . Increase severity, yes, certainly. Here, maybe there. But not too much, not . . ." His voice trailed off uncertainly.

Yi smoothed the cuffs of one sleeve, and then the other, and said: "May this unconsidered item bring to your memory the saying that 'a bird cannot roost on two branches.'"

He stared at his restless hands, winking nervous eyes.

"May I trouble you further with my inordinate chatter?" she asked. When he gave consent with his eyes, she said: "It comes to my ears that, of one thousand soldiers the Governor sent to garrison forts below Canton, two hundred were sent back totally unfit because of the opium habit."

She barely paused, and she scarcely drew breath; but she smiled bravely: *"Your Kinchae* is proved a zealot; proved honest. Both are innovations in Canton. *Your Kinchae* must divide himself— soothing foreign merchants with honesty, controlling corrupt mandarins with zealous rigor."

While she talked, Tao Kuang's face lapsed and changed. Now it brightened. He caught at the hope she offered. "Yes, that's what the Kinchae will do. I see it now." It was a relief, a burden off his mind.

For the duration of his smile Yi rose and hurried to the desk, taking two small rolls of gold tissue from the top drawer. She laid them on a satin cushion, then ran to the divan, where she knelt and held the cushion towards his hands, indicating the nearer roll. "Tomorrow's poem for the court," she said. "May it please you."

He unrolled a paper dimmed with the shadows of plum blossoms and read the poem on snowflakes she had written for him. "As light and gentle as the falling flakes themselves, your words," he said.

She shook her head in denial. *"Your words,"* she said. "You speak through me. Seeing you, breathing your aroma, makes me feel poems. Otherwise I would spoil paper."

He rerolled the letter poem in its silken cover and returned it to the cushion. "And this?" he asked, fingering the second roll.

"My New Year's present to you," Yi told him happily. "Nothing I can give equals my regard. So, instead, I give the fruit of that regard."

Diverted, Tao Kuang picked up the second small roll, and in elephantine playfulness unwound its glistening tissue. "Eh? Whatever is it?" he asked, peering at an officially stamped receipt. "'Silver *sycee*,'" he read aloud, "'to the value of two hundred and fifty thousand Carolus dollars deposited this mid-moon in Imperial Treasury.'" He laughed indulgently. "Ah, you bestow elves' money for household accounts this coming year?"

Yi shook her head solemnly, without flicker of smile. "Not elves' money, Your Brightness. Honest silver of the realm . . . obtained from selling five thousand agate, carnelian, and hardstone objects from Imperial Storehouse Number Three. They have lain untouched—judging from Gobi dust upon them—since K'ang-hsi's time."

Tao Kuang stared incredulously. "It's real—the silver? It's actual? From selling rubbish?"

Yi became buoyant with frivolity now, her eyes sparkling, her dimples deepening. "They were monsters!" she giggled. "Excruciatingly bad art."

Tao Kuang's hilarity roared out. He quivered with satisfaction, slapping one hand with the other. He elevated stringy eyebrows. "Oh, oh! Twenty Imperial warehouses—and you've tapped only one!" he gasped, and was off on another seizure of mirth.

Yi stiffened abruptly. Merciful Kwan-yin . . . was this the time? Should she choose silence? Or leap into the unpredictable? The Bag-of-Grease-and-Grain had sung high opera today *to her face*. But tomorrow what? The day after? And she—with this life growing under her heart?

It beat wildly now, that heart, as she plunged. She told of fires —mysterious and simultaneous fires—destroying warehouses Five to Ten the very day she'd completed inventory of Four. She told of blatant intrigue: of wooden cannons, straw soldiers propped on defense walls, adulterated gunpowder; of bloodshed and crop damage in Shensi and Kansu; of plots hatched by secret societies called the White Lily, the Red Eyebrows, the Yellow Turban, the Triad, the Association of Elder Brothers; of libraries languishing throughout the realm; of rice riots, and plague, and taxes collected thirty years in advance.

Tao Kuang's face grew remote, and in one terrible moment he looked at her with stranger's eyes.

Her only defense was that brave smile, and the clear white of her intention shining through. "I would have your fragrance pervade one hundred generations," she told him. "I wear no jewels. I possess no golden ornaments. I do not covet them. Your regard is ornament enough. So, my heart asks . . . 'What name do you desire to leave in history?'"

He spoke at last, and it was between a groan and a sob. "You have proof of these treasons? These wooden guns and adulterated gunpowder?"

"Absolute."

"Who?"

"The lover of birds—who idolizes feathered beauties while he himself has the disposition of a hungry crow!" she told him in a voice heavy with contempt.

Tao Kuang called an oath. "That turtle egg!" Then he multiplied it in a short angry voice that ran up the scale. "I shall decree banishment. Immediate banishment to Chili," he stormed.

Yi tended incense at the altar table, straightening sticks, blowing embers, smoothing ash piles, so she would not speak too quickly. "Chili abounds with eunuchs, and with castration surgeons who live by creating eunuchs. If Turtle Egg returns there, will it not forecast merely a change in pilfering devices? His acquisitiveness remains. He is a gully of desire which never fills."

Tao Kuang regarded her fixedly. "You would sever him *from* his acquisitiveness?" he queried, concentrating on her reply.

For answer Yi beckoned him to the velvet sash box on the

blackwood clothes chest and unlocked it. When she judged the blood of amazement had stopped pounding his ears, she gave him a paper with the addresses of five *personal* treasure houses scattered in the Imperial and Tartar cities where the Chief Eunuch kept his pilfered hoard. The pearl cape had been found in one of these.

"Now I, too, have a fierce longing to see his head separated from his body," Tao Kuang said, stroking his face with both hands. "But no, that is too easy a death. I shall send the golden cord itself to him."

Yi bowed her head in agreement, seeing with her mind's eye the exquisite sixteenth-century box of Peking gold lacquer holding a noose of yellow cord which would go to the Chief Eunuch at dawn—the silken invitation to suicide because he was no longer acceptable to his Emperor.

"The cape of pearls——" Tao Kuang said, thinking to pull himself and Yi away from the picture of death.

"—should be cut row by row," Yi suggested quickly, believing she was speaking his mind. "It contains far and away too much temptation. Retain a handful—two handfuls, perhaps—of the rare canary-egg pearls, but sell the other three thousand?"

Tao Kuang tossed his head in an anguish of indecision. "In all the wide universe," he argued with himself, "there can be no duplicate of it! So richly rare! No, we'll wait—wait . . . for the course of events. If it should be war, then, perhaps, maybe . . ."

Yi bowed her head submissively to his indecision. "It goes to Imperial Treasure House Number One in the morning after *new locks and new guardian are installed.*"

He heard the emphasis, and felt a wash of comfort flood over him. He smiled a kind of acknowledging gratitude at her. But midway in the smile appreciation warmed, and quickened into yearning relish. "With candlelight shining in your eyes," he told her softly, "they are silver seas."

At his shoulder she murmured like a contented dove.

"Come," he urged, still more softly, "I would see myself in

the mirror of those eyes . . . as we climb a ladder of clouds." His hand crept inside her sleeve, sliding up skin as smooth as an egg, to lead her towards the inner room.

" 'With cinnamon boat and orchid oars we'll pierce the moon-beams—ascending a stream of heavenly light . . .' " Yi sang in little humming quavers, her body sidling close to his, her eager steps matching his.

CHAPTER XV

CANTON,
March 1839

CANDLES BURNED a restless red in the giant ceiling lanterns, lending a guttering vitality to the blood-red dragon bodies coiled around a dozen pillars; and hundreds of tiny horn panes in the incessant windows around the room gave back the same ruddy gleam, for the day beyond was still a gray phantom. Red was Lin Tse-hsu's color. It was brisk and ardent. It nettled, goaded, stimulated.

Lin bounced to his feet now from the audience chair, glaring at Howqua Second and Mowqua. "They matched skills, these Pale-Bristles, in foot races, rat hunting, and flagstaff climbing *yesterday!*" he exclaimed apoplectically. "They mocked my third opium decree with levity?"

"No, Kinchae," Howqua Second and Mowqua denied simultaneously in abject seriousness, their faces a foxy red in the lantern light.

"Western Ocean men are born with nervousness of the rump," Mowqua soothed in standard unction. "It doesn't permit sitting still in contemplation."

"Games are their device to eat time during suspension of trade for opium negotiations," Howqua confirmed. "You demand opium stocks and indemnity bonds. They counter with the offer of one thousand and thirty-seven chests—valued at seven hundred and fifty thousand dollars at today's market."

"Which I reject . . . with utter contempt." Lin's excited face contorted demonically. "Shall I accept less than one twentieth of their stock when I have said *all* . . . *all* . . . *all* . . . ? Do they consider my words air?"

Never, never, the two Hong merchants vowed. Foreign traders had been warned—emphatically, conclusively—the Kinchae was not a big wind.

"I didn't journey Cantonwards to juggle words," Lin stormed, his eyes flashing red fire, his sonorous consonants smacking the dragon pillars and hissing back like serpent sounds. "I've come to accomplish. Sixteen days—and the record remains blank. I have issued three decrees in that time. Instead of being obeyed as bolts from Heaven, what happens . . . rat hunts, foot races, flagstaff climbing! Bah!"

Howqua's papery voice fluttered between the lanterns, assuring the Kinchae foreign traders had been told a firm new broom swept here now. In the retelling Howqua dilated on the inflexible quality of this extraordinary Imperial Broom who disassociated himself from all born-in-cheap-wombs officials, from all guilty mandarins, by setting up both office and residence in Collegiate Hall of Examinations. Paying actual rent for it! Paying the entire keep for himself and retinue from his own purse, *of all miracles!* Not from the commonality's taxes! Not from *squeeze* as . . . as . . .

Lin wasn't listening. He turned, scuffing shoes against a bulge in the matting laid over the brick floor, and stamped on the bulge, grinding it under his shoes as he barked to the secretary who sat at a desk, inkstone rubbed and brush poised: "A decree—Two thousand soldiers will occupy Respondentia Walk day and night. Another thousand will fill 13 Hong Street and the alleys behind the foreign compounds. A double cordon of rafts and junks will blockade the river side. All servants and clerks must depart. All food and water are denied. All communications with Whampoa and Macao are severed.' Now"—he spun around excitedly towards the two men braced upright on their chairs by the ramrod of habit —"will these wolves and jackals hunt rats? Or will they submit opium?"

The faces of the two listeners cramped with woe. Howqua clasped skeletal hands under his chin, bowing his head, and pleaded: "O Kinchae, these be neither vermin nor tigers."

"Bah!" Lin flung back, dancing in tiptoe rage. "I would see them driven screaming from the land! I would see them die, vomiting blood!" He whirled away to dictate a second furious edict, which canceled trading privileges *forever through the ages* unless opium stocks were submitted in two days, and ended with: ". . . your escape is as impractical as a man trying to bite his own navel!"

The two listeners sat immobile, wooden, under the bludgeon of these decrees. But Howqua pleaded again. "Will you not meet with them? Talk with them? Learn for yourself the stamp of men they are?"

Lin's face lit with a rapturous smile. "Yes, I will meet with them." He beamed. "Fetch me 'Iron-headed Old Rat.' I'm told he controls more than nine thousand chests."

Mowqua—chief trader for this largest of British agencies—answered by shaking his head. "William Jardine left two moons ago for England to retire. His partner James Matheson—using the Danish flag and serving as Danish consul—now heads the firm."

"Then bring me Devious-Devil-with-Two-Nationalities! Bring me No-tail Dent. They control two thirds of stocks between them."

Mowqua picked words as carefully as though they were stepping stones fording a torrent. "The partner Matheson, and the bald-headed Dent," he said, "most assiduously covet that miracle of incarnate awe. . . ."

"I smell the fried-rat odor of an IF. Speak out directly," Lin screamed.

"*If* the *Kinchae,* in his beneficence, will guarantee safe return after the meeting," Mowqua finished.

There was nothing scholarly and bland, nothing thoughtful and hidden about Lin's face at this moment. He turned away with an oath to stride out of the room, calling over his shoulder to the secretary: "Prepare the lanterns. My guests depart at once."

The adjoining room Lin Tse-hsu let himself into was small and dark, a closet of a room lit only by altar candles. Four hooded men knelt before the altar, awaiting him.

He gave a mystic sign. The men rose, faceless, anonymous, to raise both arms in double vow with him before the altar. "Death! Death! Death! To foreign dogs who infest our Kwangtung countryside!" they swore in scalding hate coming from their very marrow. "Catch! Cage! Exterminate foreign swine! Peel skin from their bodies, and make it into rugs for our Black-haired-Race-of-a-Hundred-Surnames!"

They pledged again, until they were hoarse with hate. Then Lin gave each a letter of instruction, together with *sycee* in bags. "Rally more to our secret cause," he charged. "Spread amongst soldiery in downriver forts; amongst estuary sailors, repeating to them the prophecy of 1635, 'Our tranquillity will be threatened, our daily life subject to men who will come with long beards, aquiline noses, and pale eyes like unto cats' eyes.' Remember—my price is two hundred dollars for each live white foreigner, one hundred for dead ones."

An hour later when Lin crossed an upper terrace portico and paused to look out, the sky was the clean and washed and promising blue of March. Yes, yes, he reminded himself, the calendar called for such a day on the beginning of this Cycle-of-Insects-Emerging. Beyond the brown bronze of the river he saw vibrant green of young rice spattered with yellow fields of rape-flower and mustard rippling in the breeze like watered silk. As tender as a T'ang painting, he told himself, cherishing the image, and thinking to carry it with him all that long day.

But when he reached the petrified beauties in his rockery of unhewn stone, they stole mind from body, and he entered a parenthesis of reverent wonder as he stepped slowly along a mosaic pavement of black and white pebbles in geometrical designs.

Ah, the strength, the grandeur of grooved *Ling buk,* he inhaled blissfully. Its poetic slant! How superlatively imaginative—those gray-black wrinkles on the underside! He closed his eyes dreamily . . . the satisfaction, the relish, of bronzy wax stone, as smooth and warm as a woman's skin. And when he was surfeited with its charms, there was the pristine simplicity of *Tai hu* stone to turn to—hanging there in a petrified slab by a thong from its holder. He stooped to study its bleached whiteness again, and took a small stone hammer from the padded satin bag at his waist. Tap, tap, tap, his hammer went on the *Tai hu* slab until it chimed as sweet and lonely as a mountain bell. He tapped on, listening acutely to its silvery minstrelsy. Ah-h-h, such purity of tone, divine purity, unequaled by any of fifty other stone chimes. . . .

In the tender warmth of the sun he came in snail-like progression to the granite drums he used as seats and sat himself on one to contemplate the peach-blossom stone of *Ya fa* as he held it under water, and watched the opal red come beauteously alive. Could he ever, ever tire of it?

Turning the *Ya fa* this way and that under water, he mused aloud: "How can this foreign race remain so stolid, so dull? Their taste is abominable in everything, even art. The household fripperies they buy are sleazy coolie embroideries, crowded wallpapers, overly decorated dinnerware, Canton lacquer, the poorest variety. They evince no instinct for pure art, for Han bronzes, Wei and T'ang sculpture, Sung celadon . . . they never evidence a comprehension of austere and visionary art—as we Chinese do."

Gowqua's own apartment was simple, the inner abode of a conservative and prudent man. Fretwork and carving, mirrors and mother-of-pearl inlay, marble columns, lacy sandalwood panels and the other monstrosities of fashion he'd consigned to the Flowery Halls of his home, where visitors came to see, be impressed, and thus entertained.

Here, where Gowqua lived with thoughts and books, plaster walls were fog gray, cypress partitions and beams a warm, hand-rubbed chestnut, and cutting away the whole outer wall was a moon window looking far across a corner of river onto rice plains backed by grape-colored mountains. The window scene gave Gowqua perpetual appeasement as each succeeding miracle of the seasons performed its painted cycle before him. Two other landscapes hung on the side walls—both small scrolls Mei-deh had done of chasms and torrents and wondrous hazy heights.

Minutes before, Mei-deh had sought her father out, pressed by the urgency of news the boatman had brought from Canton. Sitting there on the window ledge, with rippling young willows behind her, she was a blithe, vivid, frivolous creature of spring in peach-bloom silk. But her small face was not blithe: her moth eyebrows were tightened into a frown, and her words were far from frivolous.

"This Lin Tse-hsu must be told! Reasoned with! Shown——" she cried, outrage and tears whipping her voice. "'He's a frog in a well who has never seen the ocean.'"

Gowqua nodded in tacit agreement.

"I grant he's not a table-companion minister." Mei-deh tried to control herself. "He's a zealous worker. Yet, apparently, a man composed of good and bad qualities in equal proportion. His goodness is bright, white honesty: loyalty to the Throne and to China. But his badness—obviously it is ignorance and multiplied blindness. He begins his campaign with the outworn credo of a century ago—'Awe with abuse, then soothe with small gifts.' He cannot apply such generalities to this century. Nor to these foreigners."

Gowqua pursed lips, but words that were upon them remained unspoken.

"He rushes at things with rash menace," Mei-deh criticized, miserable with the conviction of what she was saying, "instead of approaching with expediency."

"What expediency?"

Mei-deh scrutinized his dear, familiar, secret face a moment before she replied: "The inevitable doctrine of *giving and taking simultaneously*. These foreigners crave to sell wares in our vast hinterland. *Give* them this privilege, and *take* indemnity bonds guaranteeing no further traffic in opium."

A small smile dug at one corner of Gowqua's mouth. "You evidently consider it expedient to nullify any need for Hong merchants."

Mei-deh chuckled, acknowledging the thrust, and in a voice as light as gauze she probed: "Would you care?"

Gowqua smiled full at her, willing to share this secret now. "No," he admitted. "I have now resigned myself to being 'one snail who doesn't reach the winning post.'" He let breath out slowly. His eyes dimmed with faraway vision, and then brightened. "Besides, the co-Hong's days are numbered," he said succinctly. "It's an outmoded trading device, and therefore needless."

"Have you told Lin Tse-hsu?" Mei-deh asked quickly.

Gowqua shook his head in the merest fraction of negation. "Lin Tse-hsu has not asked me," he told her.

"He should be told—he *must* . . . a thing so crucial," Mei-deh insisted. "Yours is an honest voice he'd listen to." In quick, deft words she detailed a plan of expediency: she assembled facts; she marshaled devastating proof of the Chinese Navy's inability to wage war with modern craft. She urged and begged and exhorted her father into being the man to temper Lin's reckless despotism.

Gowqua heard her out, his hands motionless in his lap, his eyes roving the horizon. When she stopped, he shook his head in firm refusal. "No, I shall not meddle," he said. "With all our national culture and erudition, we Chinese have yet to achieve protection of personal rights. My indifference has survival value for my entire family."

Mei-deh knew her cause was lost.

Gowqua went on: "A clash was inevitable. I have observed Lin

Tse-hsu closely. He arrived intoxicated with success—with an inherited, secondhand contempt both for Cantonese and for foreigners. Having made his name a terror to the locals, he is now a man who 'raises two hands above his head and thinks he touches the sky.' "

In mute agreement Mei-deh nodded, knowing instinctively her father had not finished talking.

Gowqua smoothed the skin of one emaciated hand with the other, saying: "Talk will not move Lin Tse-hsu at this stage. Conflict of *his* will against *foreign* will is the necessary teacher. He is the kind who must develop respect for them as antagonists before he can respect their morals, or their brains."

"War comes then, to our river, our very doorstep . . . because of ignorance, bluff, and childish misunderstanding?" she asked incredulously.

Gowqua nodded stoically. "As usual. War is never the act of an astute man. It is the consequence of vanity . . . and the other word for vanity is ignorance."

With that insane bedlam of drums and gongs and shouts generated by massed soldiers in the Walk outside, Gill had to strain to catch words being said inside in this conference of heroic indignation. It was farcial and tragic in the same breath. Pell-mell courage, corrosive contempt, itching greed, florid elocution. . . .

Captain Elliot, for instance—who'd summoned them to the British Hall an hour ago: Captain Charles Elliot, nephew of the first Earl Minto, as everyone quickly added—a baffled, harassed, rhetorical, crusading gallant, whom British merchants called a vacillating fool because in three years as Her Majesty's Superintendent of Trade he'd never decided how far to close his eyes on drug traffic.

Yet at first news of Lin's tempest Elliot had quitted his 18-gun sloop, which was protecting thirty merchant vessels of Macao, to come dashing in two buckety-buckety days upriver in a ship's gig

—armed only with identity papers, and rowed by four steadfast sailors—to do his best to shield British lives and property.

As Lin's blockade was being clapped on, he'd landed—a tall, gaunt figure in blue-and-gold uniform—to exhort the merchants dramatically: "Be calm! Be firm! God's gracious mercy will save us!" in a high nervous voice that was anything but calm.

Gill looked around the room. The finger of Fate was apparent on each face, and the feeling of war hung as oppressively as a thunderstorm in the air.

"We're trapped!" tall Lauris MacMinnies said despondently for the third time. He dealt in wallpapers, but commissions on opium sales were double his other income. "No choice but surrender!"

"We daren't!" It was fiery Innes shouting, the volatile red-headed opium-runner with "smug" boats up a hundred creeks this very minute. "Crawl under Chinese thumbs like vermin? Never! We'll fight!"

"Not me," scripture-quoting Tom Ilberry rose to declare piously. "I stand guarantee for consigned cotton goods to the value of half a million pounds sterling. I could suffer great damage— as would my supplying merchants in Manchester, Leeds, Liverpool, and Bristol. I'll surrender a—ahem, a *trifling* opium stock instead."

"Thereby pullin' the rug from under larger dealers who've loaned you comfortable shade during the sunny seasons," bald-headed Launcelot Dent rumbled with deceptive bonhommie, his ruddy cheeks bouncing in the folds of a bottle-green neckerchief as he spoke. "I've nigh on seven thousand chests at hand . . . and I scarcely intend tossin' upwards of four million dollars into the laps of these quaint, utterly charmin', corrupt, and inferior Chinee because you change your mind today about dealin' in opium."

"Hear! Hear!" several voices exploded. But many more were glumly silent.

"Besides, the new decree smells to me of play actin'—another seven-day law made so's copyists will have something pretty to write in the big books. Seven days . . . then it's completely for-got." Dent chuckled indulgently, looking around with large confi-dent blue eyes. "Suppose I accept this rooster fella's invitation for a chat and forget about a safe-conduct guarantee? He'd never harm *me*. Probably wants an audience for some fancy bluster. Hah! Well—I'll jolly him along with presents . . . there's a dozen pair of Nottin'ham lace curtains come by last packet I'll donate. Two to one I strike a bargain with the bantam!"

"He'd hold you for hostage! No, I can't permit you to be scape-goat for the entire community." Elliot's voice shook the draperies, but his fingers plucked constantly at one front button and his long unmatched face was grooved with fatigue. "No, by God's gracious mercy, we'll stand united in the face of calamity," he vowed, "even though we are defenseless without a single sloop here."

"But we can summon plenty more!" Innes hurrahed. "Does a tuppenny commissioner-cum-admiral think to frighten the victors of Trafalgar?"

A scattered cheer greeted this, and lobbed off into brooding silence.

Gill avoided asking himself what he really felt about this sud-den passionate embroilment, or what he thought the outcome might do to his life. Certainly his sympathies were divided at the moment: both sides seemed eminently right in their way, and both were being confoundedly human about it. But right now the solution didn't appear to be a personal aching thing to him, and he wasn't sure he was ready to hear his own answer. Not yet, not until . . . later, probably, when he got to the point of making the decision where his future lay out here.

This beautiful enameled month of March meant he was about to become disconnected, footloose again—or nearly so. Another fortnight, and he'd be going downriver with seven tons of privilege cargo aboard a Russell clipper—fourteen thousand pounds of good hill leaf for which he'd plunk out every cent of salary when the time came. He'd sell the lot in New York; and then ponder, cast around, be pushed headlong, most likely, into another fateful choice—whether to return at *twenty-eight* as a hired hand buying tea or come out as an amateur *adventurer* with the skimpiest of nest eggs. He felt no indecision about wanting to return.

But was he actually cut out for the role of *adventurer?* It was an elastic word, having good or shady implication, depending upon success. Whenever he thought of the word these days, his mind reverted to James Matheson, and he jerked around now to gaze at the tall dominating *taipan* with light gray eyes and thin lips who'd returned from London several weeks ago to head the largest, the most influential and respected agency in Canton.

Gill knew Matheson's story by heart, and hated him intimately for having been so successful at so young an age and by so many subterfuges . . . The son of a Scottish baronet, Matheson had come out East from Edinburgh University at twenty—*at twenty,* Gill underscored it to himself, rubbing salt in the raw nerve of envy—to start a partnership which had dissolved, switched, merged, and liquidated a dozen times until Matheson emerged the galloping pace setter of coastal opium smuggling. In twenty-two intervening years he'd used the Spanish flag, Danish, German, Dutch, or any other that was handy, to shield multiplying cargoes which his swift new clipper fleet was carrying to Lintin, or to a dozen rendezvous spots upcoast.

As Gill studied this man of many talents, he saw Matheson come to a sudden decision, and heard him say: "It means war!"

A gust of sound blew through the big room. Everyone turned to stare. What Matheson had to say was significant always. But here and now it could mean stability or bankruptcy.

"For decades we factors," Matheson began, including each in his open, friendly glance, "have fumed over China's restrictive trading policy—enduring it because we realized it stemmed from their marvelous degree of imbecility and avarice. But today, no! *They push us too far* with conceit and obstinacy."

A staccato of voices agreed.

Matheson's voice rapped on: "Detention of British subjects, seizure of British property, is *casus belli*. The inevitable next step is war with China."

Gill felt Manning stir in the chair beside him—an entirely restored and capable Manning—and get to his feet. His firm voice cut through hubbub. "As an American—I cannot agree," he said.

Gill felt a quick irresistible sense of rightness flood over him—he didn't know why, and he didn't have time to ask himself.

Matheson blinked at Manning in consternation. "You mean—you would refuse to join the British in common action against this coercive Canton system?"

"Our government requires us to submit peaceably to the laws of any country where we choose to trade," Manning explained with quiet authority. "Consequently, in today's extremity, my partners and I consider ourselves bound to deliver up our opium stocks."

"But, my dear Manning"—Matheson was obviously aghast—"you can't mean you'll sign an indemnity bond agreeing to *trial for life in a Chinese court* if a single ship consigned to your care should ever carry opium to China!"

"The prospect is not infatuating," Manning said mordantly, "but I mean to sign."

At this moment a clank of heavy chains sounded against the door panels as they were flung open, and Howqua Second and Mowqua walked in. The assembled merchants stared incredulously at these two familiars—with felons' chains around their necks and hanging the length of dirtied robes, hand-cuffing wrists and hobbling ankles; chains so heavily linked the frail Howqua could scarcely support himself. Buttons of rank were cut off; embroidered emblems of office ripped from gowns. They were miserable, frightened, old men—and they held the stricken, straining attention of every man there.

Then they were babbling and moaning over Lin's demonical rage, over his inordinate conviction that Hong merchants were encouraging foreigners to resist, over these final afflictions and indignities he'd heaped on them before ordering strangulation *unless*—and here Howqua and Mowqua shuddered in wrenching entreaty—*unless* in final appeal they persuaded the merchants to obey Lin. "Immediately! Chop-chop! On the instant! With fire speed!" they beseeched above the clangor of chains.

Elliot jerked his head back to stare at the ceiling in sudden decision, exclaiming: "By God's gracious mercy, I shall settle this affair now!"

He strode resolutely to the desk, and drew paper and pen towards him. "I shall call the roll by companies," he told them. "As I do, please give me close approximation of opium stocks you possess at Lintin, or at other points in China waters. I believe I have hit upon the only workable solution for the British merchants. Dent . . . you said seven thousand chests. In what proportion?"

"Three thousand top-grade Patna. Four thousand Malwa," Dent reported.

"Next—Jardine, Matheson?"

"Three thousand Patna, six thousand two hundred and fifty-odd Malwa," Matheson replied.

Elliot continued through the roster until he had reached a total of more than twenty thousand and two hundred chests. He made rapid calculations on paper, frowned a moment at the figures, and said: "Gentlemen, I believe this to be a disastrous crisis in which British lives and property *must* be protected. I stand ready to extend the Crown's guarantee of reimbursement *at today's market price* for a total of twenty thousand two hundred and eighty-three chests to be delivered to Commissioner Lin."

There was a sharp chorus of surprise. The British merchants gaped at each other. The promise was incredible. *Twelve million dollars in hand instead of losing everything!*

His eyes aglow, Matheson hurried to clasp Elliot's hand in a genial pumping handshake. "Magnificent! A very statesmanlike action!" he applauded. "It's a bridge across calamity—a calamity augmented, certainly, by the decision of our Yankee colleagues."

"I would remind you, Mr. M," Manning said tartly, "that I am surrendering stock worth more than a million dollars, and that we Yankees have no Queen to guarantee our loss."

Elliot rapped for quiet. "If you agree, gentlemen——"

There was an instantaneous clamor of "Ayes" from the British.

"—I shall convey the Crown's guarantee on paper. Our two most pitiable friends here can take it to the Commissioner."

"What about indemnity bonds?" several voices demanded.

"Held in abeyance until I receive definite instructions from London," Elliot replied. A cheer went up. He completed his guarantee to Lin and handed it to the bedraggled Mowqua. Then, in formal courtliness, he stood bowing to the two Hong merchants as they went tottering out in clanging unison.

"The end of Canton trade," Samuel Fearon said, brooding wistfully. "Business can never be safe for us here, now that they've won. They'll *squeeze* us . . . and *squeeze* us. . . ."

"Precisely," Matheson agreed. "We must consider that this action marks the end of an old system—and the necessity for choosing a new one."

Gill was on his feet next minute, his face shining with sudden revelation. "An island depot, as I suggested six months ago in Macao, to avoid the monopolistic grip of Hong merchants and Peking's levies! It's not a dream any more—it's a necessity!" he said exultantly. "We get one—set up our own trade emporium on it, sell to anyone who comes, and administer justice *our* way!"

He glanced around quickly. He saw partial interest, hope, prejudice, scorn, and pudding-faced unconcern. But amongst the faces he noted Matheson's, and that the gray eyes scrutinized him intently.

"You voice *our* conviction," Matheson corrected in wintry politeness before he turned to Dent. "I believe it a natural solution. Personally, I favor the island of Lantao. But before he left for England, Will Jardine recommended the colony move—lock, stock, and barrel—to Formosa. His idea was that we maintain ourselves there with the combined gunboats of England and the United States."

Heedless of what Dent was on the point of saying, Gill groped for words. "No, my idea is quite different," he tried to explain. "Not a big island—and not maintained by guns. I mean a small compact island which we'd purchase on a safe, and honorable, and permanent, basis. The smaller it is, the more barren, the easier 'twould be to acquire. And—the cheaper the price."

He broke into rollicking laughter, infecting others about him with his shining enthusiasm. "We'll set up warehouses—department stores, really, filled with all sorts and kinds of merchandise. The island becomes international—a free port where anyone can buy and sell! We don't require a big one for this."

He couldn't stop. He *had* to go on. "What we do require is—an all-year harbor. If Nature isn't kind enough to provide it—then by Christopher, and George, and all the other saints!—what's to prevent our helping Nature out? Tumble granite into likely mud flats for a breakwater. Scoop out the mud . . ." Gill panted with eagerness, dripping at every pore with excitement over the certainty of this vision. For with it had come the glimmer of an ultimate idea—without shape or form or substance yet—of what he could do with his life from now onward.

April

With all the wives and concubines and babies and *amahs* strewn along the river terraces of Gowqua's garden in their bright spring gowns, they were like ravels of colored serpentine winding through the crowding green. Babies tossed bean bags and shuttlecocks, wives teetered enticingly on golden lily stumps, concubines chirped in the mellow fluting tones of a covey of laughing thrushes, and the girl-minstrel roamed—through the camellia grove's pink haze, in and out of rock grottoes streaked mauve with wild violets—whimsically plucking her four-stringed *pipa* and singing high haunting songs that spread the honey of love.

Yet, despite the topsy-turvy straggling, they were united in proud purpose. They were here to honor Gai-sun—to wave, and scream good luck, and flutter a rainbow of banners at *their* Gai-sun. Any minute now his flotilla would appear at the bend, to sweep by majestically and continue on its gala way to Whampoa to officially wish "good wind and good water" to ten American and ten British clippers standing ready to weigh this very day.

Of all the sons of all the Hong merchants it was Gai-sun—Gowqua's eldest; Gowqua's heir; since Gowqua, as everyone knew, had not interceded for the foreigners in any measure—whom Commissioner Lin had chosen as his exclusive emissary to make formal presentation of his gift tea. Lin's special advance messenger had already gone ahead asking—begging—the foreign ships to delay departure another hour for this measure of his regard, as he put it.

For Lin, in a settled air of expansive good humor, had suddenly begun ordering caddies by the hundred, made of Canton lacquer and filled with ten pounds of Canton leaf, as his personal reward to each and every foreign sailor who had aided in transferring opium stocks these past weeks to Chuenpee . . . "To teach them the beauty of obedience," Lin had explained it. Moreover, the apparently mellowed despot had stressed that these individual gift caddies were his personal present. They were not a part of the bulk of indemnity tea China guaranteed to pay foreign firms eventually, at some unspecified date, in the ratio of three caddies of leaf for one of surrendered opium.

Mei-deh hadn't gone down to the river terrace with the others. She waited above in the octagonal pavilion, which she'd appropriated yesterday for a witchery of orchid plants newly arrived from Manila. They were birthday felicitations from her father—a treasure she tended now with concentrated love. Gowqua remained with her, sitting on a garden stool of hawthorn porcelain, enjoying the way she managed to blow a veil of mist around the butterfly blooms with a laundry-sprinkling contraption she'd commandeered from one of the wash *amahs*.

Through latticed windows Mei-deh kept watchful eyes on the river's constant promenade. But meanwhile her fingers were busy discovering the texture of bladed leaves, the unearthly blue of a spotted swamp-orchid, and the resilient tiptoe liveliness of a spray of mountain-whites which danced like midget moths.

A deep soughing breath of sound came from beyond the willows, from beyond the clumps of tasseled bamboo, swelling stentoriously above the song of *dayal* birds in the high camphors. The family rushed pell-mell to the balustrades, and saw a big two-decked ferry swing around the corner. But a different ferry from any they'd ever set eyes on before. This miraculous one had a giant paddle wheel on one side which went sloshing round and round through the brown foam . . . a wheel turned by thirty coolies stepping on a treadmill.

The babies squealed with delight. The *amahs* and concubines and wives trilled full-voiced wonder. Farmers working fields of horse-beans and golden sesame across the river lined the bank in amazement. Shouts of alarm and anger went up from rafts and sampans near the marvel's foaming wake. But Mei-deh only stood scowling in cold contempt, her ears filled with the sobbing toil-song of thirty panting coolies.

She mimicked caustically: " 'Match foreign boatbuilding? It's easy! Be progressive? It's easy!' Matching progressiveness, eh, using coolie power instead of steam! Using the man crop instead of acquiring the knowledge of tomorrow!"

The side-wheeler churned out of sight; and as the sound of its going sifted into nothingness, there was only the soaring song of skylarks, and the whine of golden orioles foretelling rain.

Gowqua's gray lips twitched stoically, and a cramp of woe settled on his face as he said: "The Emperor K'ang-hsi warned the nation in 1717, 'There is cause for apprehension lest in the centuries to come China may be endangered by collision with nations of Western sea barbarians.'" Gowqua shook his head in enduring resignation. "I believe that time has come. I believe we shall have that collision soon—and that we shall discover their sea power superior to ours."

Mei-deh nodded in abiding frustration, but her eyes were following the mauve pattern of wild violets growing between the paving stones, the wet tightly rolled buds of fern fronds, and, on the terrace below, the scarlet-fringed glory of a flamboyant tree. The girl-minstrel's song came floating up—a coolie fret of spring:

"*I planted beans at the foot of Southern Hill,*
  Grasses grew so the bean sprouts are sparse,
Early I rise to pluck the weeds, and till the field,
  Then lifting my eyes, I gaze long at Southern Hill,
Where the flying birds circle back and forth in pairs.
  At night I return, carrying on my back the moon and the hoe,
The road is narrow and the bushes thick and tall,
  So dewdrops dampen my clothing.
In these things there lies a deep meaning,
  Yet when I wish to express it, I forget the words."

A pulse of drums and a trill of flutes came loud and clear now. It was Gai-sun, for certain. There was another rush for the balustrades as thirty-two family and eighty servants jostled into line, laughing, calling, shouting, waving banners in a frenzy of excitement. The head coolie waited for the precise second that Gai-sun's prow appeared before he touched lighted punk to a ribbon of five hundred firecrackers suspended from the highest camphor, and obstreperous uproar blared forth.

Gai-sun's ceremonial barge—shining like the sun itself in the morning's bright gilding light—led the procession of ten tea barges which fanned out behind. There was crescendo of drums and firecrackers as another, and yet another, ribbon was lighted to scare jealousy, and all taint of it, from the air. Gai-sun stood waving at them from the forward deck, bowing respectfully towards the upper terrace, where he suspected his father to be.

Gowqua acknowledged the tribute with precise formality, murmuring a prayer, as he always did whenever this First-Born was involved.

Mei-deh spoke suddenly, asking: "Did leaf for this gift tea come from your godowns?"

Gowqua shook his head. "No, I supply a large share of indemnity tea later, but this lot is a special purchase Lin made himself. He even had it packed by special men in his own *yamen.* I'm told he canceled the usual two hundred per cent export tax on tea leaf—so as to make this wholly a gift to the foreign sailors."

In the lambent sun of that blue-eyed morning Mei-deh shivered and shook. "For all this gifting . . . I fear that Lin Tse-hsu," she muttered. "I believe him to be 'a man with ten thousand mouths, but without vestige of one heart.' "

Chuenpee is a green nubbin of small crags and gentle valleys where the Pearl River rushes from the Tiger's Throat to spill its burden of yellow silt into Great Bay. On this April day a soft scent of golden sesame lay on the air, but mingling with it occasionally was the voluptuous reek of fried shrimp and pork dumplings. Azure-winged magpies flashed and streaked; there was the green and yellow flitter of siskins; the unceasing tonk-tonk-tonk of water birds singing monotonously of love.

Within the vast bamboo stockade built around a central creek no one looked, or thought, or listened to the birds. Only one thing mattered; only one thing happened—a toiling blue chain of coolies pouring black poppy juice into clay trenches, walking a trodden path to fetch other chests for emptying, and still others by the hundreds. The goal was eleven thousand.

Seven million dollars' worth of baneful juice being cast into trenches—openly, conspicuously, unmistakably—with an avid audience watching and authenticating destruction in subsequent stages. "This day"—Lin Tse-hsu's clarion voice rolled out from his platform seat in jovial pride—"marks actual beginning of China's Reformation."

The hillside around was streaked with the indigo uniforms of cavalry archers and the scarlet and white of foot soldiers. The bamboo viewing pavilion was gala with color—roofed in yellow, strung with purple banners, and laced with red-and-white bunting. The floor was covered with Peking rugs, and scores of tables were set for eight. In a nearby pavilion musicians sawed two-stringed violins, trilled reed flutes, and beat cymbals in shattering disharmony, while the cooks out back concocted ecstasies of aroma with their frying and boiling and barbecuing.

Lin Tse-hsu sat at one table, the Viceroy nearby at another with his ladies, the Governor beyond with his, and so on down to the ninth layer of the Kwangtung provincial government. But the strangest, the most incongruous, in this assemblage of paradise silks and jewels was a dun-colored trio at a far table—William King, merchant, in rusty black frock coat, Mrs. King in faded puce bombazine, and Captain Benson in brown alpaca. King and his wife were here at Lin's express invitation because King was the only head of firm who, for conscience's sake, had never dealt in opium. Captain Benson had brought them to Chuenpee in his ship.

Lin had received them genially and jovially, clasping his own hands and speaking to them through an interpreter with smiling vivacity. He asked quick questions about clipper designs, about guns, trying not to laugh at the poor movable gun carriages and swivel cannon contraptions they described. Nor did he believe their ridiculous story about these new clippers making it to Calcutta in eighteen days when everyone knew it took eight weeks, even with a favoring wind. Nevertheless, he continued solicitous about their having a front-row table, cushions for their chairs, and double portions of everything the cooks had to offer. Thereafter —he ignored them completely, and the other officials copied him.

Alone, the three foreigners sat staring now, inarticulate and mum, uncomfortable and yet compelled by the grotesque flourish of destruction going on before them. Directly below the pavilion a parallel of trenches extended a full hundred and fifty feet—not hastily shoveled ditches, but broad and stone-paved, supported with timbers seven feet deep, and half flooded with creek water. Planks bridged them at intervals, and from these the coolie chain continuously poured black muck into the water below. Other men with giant paddles stirred the brew. Brine was added after an interval; and last of all unslaked lime dumped in to make a boil-

ing, bubbling broth—a scalding furnace of disintegration—until
the plug was pulled at the end of that particular trench and its
evil mess drained into the bay, where the ebbing tide carried it
away.

Lin Tse-hsu sat stroking his philosopher's beard with delicately
arched fingers. There was nothing stern and fanatical about him
today. He looked young and refreshed. He couldn't resist an occasional bland smile to the Viceroy and to the Governor—both
near to swooning at this spectacle of so many pipefuls going to
waste. But Lin watched the bubbling, boiling broth with deep
content.

So . . . the barbarians had rung like gongs these weeks with
their wagers over how many millions in confiscated opium Lin
himself would manage to divert into his own pockets. The born-
in-cheap-wombs! The turtle dung! They'd learn a lesson in honesty today. And their teacher would be Mr. Mealymouth King
and Mrs. Drab Jay—why else invite the breed?

Suddenly Lin pouched his lips in puffing rage. What was that
jellyfish spawn down there doing with a hand coming out of
pocket? Rubbing opium muck on denim? An ounce, two ounces,
sticking to his palm . . . Lin screamed a strangled command.

Two overseers converged on the man, snatching at his hand
and the telltale black glaze in his pockets. Then the giant executioner was there, swinging a double-edged sword.

The momentum of the coolie chain slowed when the head
bumped onto the ground and rolled away, and then the trudge
began again. In the viewing pavilion the Chinese women were
as round-eyed and impassive as baby girls. There was no moan,
no mutter, no sound at all amongst them—save the gasping scream
from that jay of a foreign-devil female.

Lin's eyes wandered beyond the stockade, where he watched a
cinnamon bittern take clumsy flight from its nest in the reeds.
Then by slow degrees his eyes traveled on across dipping hummocks of buttercups and wild roses to Chuenpee's guardian fort
over on the river shore. The first of five stalwarts defending the

vital defile of the Throat, it was China's greatest fortress, the outer defense of Canton itself, and eighteen million dollars had been spent on it.

He traced the proud outline of the ramparts with appreciative eyes. Those mammoth stone blocks. Those impregnable walls. That magnificent battery of cannon—imbedded so solidly, so immovably at permanent range into the masonry of each loophole. Ah, Heaven, their blast would be utterly devastating.

Beyond the mossy ramparts Lin now made out the moving spars of a foreign clipper, and another behind it. He nodded genially; that would be the lead van of ships he'd released—ten British and ten American—carrying his gift tea aboard. His fine eyes twinkled with fun, and he chuckled softly. Such beautifully lacquered caddies! Such special leaf. . . .

As the procession passed, he kept tally. Already three pyramids of white sail were out in the bay. And those others behind were dropping down fast with a favoring wind. Excellent, excellent, they'd be out and away from land, well away from China's shores when it happened. "Good wind, good water!" he wished the stately spars.

The twentieth clipper had passed Chuenpee, and was billowing down the great broad bay with all canvas out, when one of Lin's men came with a message. Softly, for Lin's ears only, the man whispered his words, and then repeated them a second time before Lin could fully comprehend the tidings. . . .

Gai-sun was dead—Gai-sun, and all those others aboard his official barge, save two half-dead rowers.

The barge Captain, it seemed, had pilfered one caddy of the gift tea to brew a jolly round for guests and crew. One by one they'd fallen in agony, until the shining red barge became a hearse by the time it nosed amongst the Western Ocean ships at Whampoa.

As for the barbarians, the messenger related, they'd taken one look at those cyanide-reddened corpses and straightaway had tossed a couple of caddies of the "gift tea" into the river, and then had watched dead fish come floating to the surface. That had been the end of those ten gala and festooned barges! Furious British and American sailors had swarmed over them, tearing down the bunting and pitching every caddy overboard until the river ran red with tea and dead fish.

CHAPTER XVI

CANTON,

May 1839

IT WAS a magic day. The shadowless blue sky, the yellow sun, the patterned green of the land, all had enameled clarity about them that was more than things the eyes saw. It became a wildly tingling thing of the spirit.

It gilded him, covering him with the shining armor of buoyancy, Gill felt as he ran across the plank onto the ferry and raced the hilarious multitude for a place on the upper deck. In boisterous victory he flung himself into a spot on the forward rail where he could watch the incessant parade of the river as they crossed, and he turned to wave commiseratingly at Stacey and the other ten of their outing group who seemed equally intent on getting themselves amidships to watch the incredible coolie treadmill which turned the giant paddle wheel.

Today was their first of freedom—the first absolute, full, carefree day—after six weeks of confinement to the factories. Forty-two days of overeating, overdrinking, overconfabulating—discussing, reasoning, guessing, without even meager exercise.

Well, they'd burst bonds today, all right—exploding, catapulting, you might say, onto the Walk which Lin's battalions had vacated last evening after the last opium chest had been delivered.

From where he stood on deck, Gill couldn't look back on the Walk now, but he laughed aloud remembering the convulsion of activity which had been going on there since daybreak . . . milling promenaders; leap-frog and rounders players; the placard CANTON REGATTA CLUB being tacked on the ex-soldier mat shed at the landing, and a dozen debonair crews in boaters and fancy yachting costumes launching two new four-oared gigs and a couple of London wherries for what they airily called the regatta drill.

But, with gilding sun on his body, Gill had felt an urge to get across to the green enchantment of Honam Island—to walk and revel in that lush green tangle of grass and trees and bird song on the last day before he left Canton. Stacey had felt the same impulse, and had rounded up seven other Americans and two linguists to conform with regulations for visiting the Fa-tee Gardens on Honam.

There was noise, noise everywhere, generated by Canton's perspiring thousands. It pressed from all sides, from the city, from the waterfront, the river, from here on the ferry—an over-all, overwhelming babel of voices in high-pitched, excited jabber which set up a palpitating urgency . . .

Each man wore cut and color of gown the law proscribed for him—barbers twanging tweezers as large as tuning forks to herald their services came thrusting sampans between upcountry craft and waddling houseboats; fortunetellers, whirling cylinders of Fate, edged out quacking duckboats and food rafts. A reed pipe bleated behind Gill as a man put trained mice through a routine; the *basso profundo* gutterals came from a band of jugglers performing double-jointed tricks in and out of a mammoth jar; and strident bickering came from two weird hags plucking live crabs from a basket and tying them on strings. At the point where Gill thought his eardrums would surely burst, he caught sight of a man stretched on deck, with head propped on the porcelain pillow the South Chinese use, sleeping blissfully.

The ferry churned through a line of immense coasting junks which carried cargoes to Celebes, Borneo, and Java. On the shore ahead Gill made out the two gingerbread forts—appropriately called follies, since they looked more like summer residences than fortifications. Beyond on the left was the proud lift of Guitar Pagoda; and below it he saw long tiers of smaller junks—probably the famous salt junks, he told himself, which belonged to the wealthy salt-monopoly merchants.

"Merchant . . . *merchant!*" He tried the word aloud twice. No one in the babbling press around him would pay the slightest heed; and anyway, with that impervious armor of buoyancy he was wearing today, he didn't care whether they did . . .

Yes, sir, *Gill Bennett, Merchant!* That's what it was now. He was in business—business for himself starting tomorrow morning. He had a ship. He had a whacking good cargo. He had a very feasible project—*and the cash to finance it!* He slapped his hand on the rail and laughed aloud in the exaltation of reality. Not dreaming. Not imagining. Not hoping. But actuality. It gave him a magnificent feeling of security.

The ferry swung into the Honam landing; and once the headlong surge for shore had expended itself, Gill and his companions straggled after, being careful not to be caught in the equally headlong surge of oncoming passengers. And so they passed, elbow to elbow almost, a procession of prisoners being carried aboard, each cage tagged with a name and a crime. It was a revolting spectacle.

But the sight became a gray smudge on the memory. It had no place in the vibrating brilliance of today's sunlight. The willow-hung road they took was filled with incident and constant variety. Men were strolling in cloth-soled shoes, carrying butterflies in delicate porcelain cages or eating from split-bamboo baskets of cherry fruit; whole families rode complacently in wheelbarrows; water-chestnut vendors sat in the shade spearing crisp white spheres on bamboo skewers and talking to men who smoked long bamboo pipes of reeking tobacco; a leper, wearing his peculiar telltale hat and shoulder mat, stood watching an itinerant performer throw a trident in the air, judge its fall, and then stand under so the gleaming prongs barely grazed his body as it plunged earthwards.

There was the winking flitter of gold in field flowers and butterfly wings and orioles. There was the tinkle of harps and lutes in a succession of teahouses along the riverbank, where women in gauzes, lustrines, sarsenets, and senshaws were as fragile and gaudy as butterflies.

They reached the maze of shops and lanes on the turning to Fa-tee Gardens when a bride's procession cut Gill off from the others walking ahead of him. It was not the bejeweled and calcimined little bride herself, but the lengthy parade of her gifts to mother-in-law and father-in-law, along with her trousseau, going to the groom's house. Provided these were acceptable, she'd follow after a modest interval, in a scarlet cage of a sedan chair for the ceremony.

Gill was forced to jump back into a shop doorway to avoid being hit by running load coolies whose yokes were stacked high with baskets of red-, green-, and blue-dyed chickens. After them came trussed pigs in harlequin splotches of magenta, gilt, and silver. Then the furniture followed—lacquered chests, beauty boxes, tables, stools galore, and one of the high Nanking beds which Cantonese women are so proud to own.

In this interval the others disappeared into one of the little lanes, which, to Gill's eyes, were almost identical. He was sure he knew the one they'd taken, and he set out at a run, expecting to overtake them around the next turning. But there was another turning, and another, and still no Stacey, no sauntering group. Gill turned and cut back to reach the junction spot again. But he couldn't find it.

Instead he found himself in open country, with fields on one side and a high stone wall on the other. Between occasional crevices in the ornamental tilework of the wall he could see the contorted branches of tallow trees in an orchard sloping down to the river. Evidently the orchard joined some sort of garden, because, on rising ground ahead, he could see the eaves of a pavilion and parts of a small pagoda. There were dwarfed trees also, trimmed to sampan, elephant, fan, and basket shapes, as in Fa-tee. Probably Fa-tee all the time, he told himself. He'd simply reached the goal by another path.

He saw farmers working off in the fields, but on the lane itself he met no one—except for azure-winged magpies crisscrossing ahead of him like mocking street urchins. Occasionally ruddy skylarks shot up from the grass like plumed arrows. Gill longed to do the same—skim up and soar and whistle and sing at the top of his lungs.

He reached a breech in the wall—made deliberately, he could see, for hauling in the hundred or more mature tallow trees so recently planted the earth was scarcely dry. The missing stones and tiles from the wall were stacked, ready to go back into place; but there were neither masons nor their tools about the wall or the orchard now.

Gill stepped through the breech and cut across under the waxen blush of young tallow leaves, kicking at moss clods and grass clumps, but all the while staring ahead at an incredible orchid canopy of blossoms spreading across a tree on one of the lower galleries of the big garden. He breathed headily, feeling the rare intoxication of the day.

He found himself walking on a mauve and magenta carpet of fallen petals, with dragonflies and bees darting by in the dappled light. Farther along the gallery he could see the blaze of a flame tree; and he was conscious of a marvelous awareness of Nature as he turned to climb a flight of mossy steps to the uppermost terrace—a breathless urging of all his senses, a zest for the smells and sounds and imagery and dream shapes around him.

He walked softly, but not warily, sauntering in a kind of enchantment until he rounded a knob of earth and came upon a small pavilion of glazed tiles as green as camellia leaves in the rain. There was the delicate tracery of mother-of-pearl inlay in the cypress window trellises, and an inverted lotus canopy made a small porch. A trickling waterfall in a nearby rock grotto surrounded the spot with a cool splashing sound.

As he stepped from behind a shielding bush, a thrush that had been pouring forth its mellow song jerked to a stop in mid-note, and the startled bird whistled a sudden fright call as raucous as a jay's. The contrast tickled Gill, and he laughed aloud.

Next minute running footsteps sounded inside the pavilion, and a girl appeared on the lotus-petal porch, the fingers of her left hand bristling with slender paintbrushes. She was dressed in a filmy billow of apricot-colored gauze shot with gold thread which sent out beams as she moved, and a single plait of hair the color of night hung over her shoulder. It was bound with the red cord of an unmarried girl. Her lips parted to show teeth as small and white as a baby's, and she smiled a quick and recognizing smile.

Gill thought her face was every flower he'd seen today, or had ever thought of. He was wholly caught by the pale oval face, the glossy blackness of hair and eyes, and the sweetness, the wooing femininity, of her small body. In the dappled sunshine and green shadow she seemed to symbolize the unattainable loveliness he'd dreamed would be Cathay, the grace and elegance of illusion. In a sudden pang of heart hurt he closed his eyes, half expecting her to vanish, to dissolve, mirage-like, into pulsating atmosphere.

But when he opened them, she was there. Emotion drifted to him and away . . . much as perfume from the jasmine and gardenia and pagoda-flower came drifting on the soft air, eddying on and away. . . .

A smile shook the girl's lips, and her soft round eyes caressed him with intense awareness. Gill felt a familiar something about her. He couldn't think what, or why . . . as though he'd been near her before somewhere, seen her in some hazy unformed memory, like a half-remembered fragment of dream. He didn't know—he couldn't think where. . . .

In the wonder of this moment he walked towards where she

stood under the lotus-flower canopy; and now he saw that the room inside the pavilion contained a large easel set up near a window.

"Your painting?" he queried, motioning with his hand towards the easel. "May I see it?" But he didn't step up on the threshold stone until she smiled permission.

There was no word from her, though, as she led him into the octagonal room. It was two rooms, really, being divided across the center by an airy teak partition with doors in it. The second room had a divan and two low tables in it, but in the nearer one there was only the easel, and paint pots on a table beside it.

Gill stopped before the painting. It was a soft, washed thing of muted color—a gorge swallowing a torrent, a solitary pine stricken in years, an ocean of lotus bending in the breeze, and behind these a glory of mists and crags. The rhythm of her brushstrokes added exaltation to his mood, and in a surge of delight and awe he took the small hand which had created the mood in his two—thinking, somehow, to express his pleasure.

But as he looked down at those apricot-colored cheeks, flushed now with blood pulsing through them . . . she became a peony swaying; a plum blossom, pure and sweet. She was jasmine and gardenia and pink-lipped ginger. It came to him that seduction was equally there in the air between them.

For a second he tried to fathom her thoughts—as she stood there so close to him, so silently, so smilingly acquiescent. But in the next crowding second he felt he couldn't hope to bridge the chasm of speech and thought stretching between them. He could only recognize the drumming of his senses, the impelling demand of his desire. . . .

She answered the cry of his heart by drawing still nearer, to raise her free hand and stroke his cheek with questing, searching fingers, all the while gazing at him in soft-eyed wonder. She smelled as sweet as a baby.

He whispered to her, and it was as though she knew the words he was saying. Yet she gave no spoken answer, except for a sweet breathless little moaning sound.

He turned, leading her towards the divan in the other room. She went unresistingly. Yet, with a woman's priestly precision, she twisted a hand behind her as they passed through the partition and, with a fragile wrist that was not fragile, closed the carved teak door.

Far-off bird songs came to them on the breezes of love, and the easy fragrance of frangipani and gardenia was as lovely as a dream. Gill had the feeling that after years of muddled pursuit he'd found a fragilely sweet today. He followed the reason of his senses, and loved Mei-deh.

CHAPTER XVII

GREAT BAY,
May 1839

GILL SPAT the small seeds of a *Nor mai-chih* into the running brown foam of the river as he peeled pebbled strawberry-colored skin from another *lichi* and sucked mouthfuls of elysian juice. It seemed as though he'd never get enough of this strange and wonderful fruit which was Canton's own.

Besides, eating—*gorging*—on them now kept him occupied. They kept him from bounding about the ship like a schoolboy—opening caddies, peering into storerooms, asking a dozen primer questions a minute. He'd had one marvelous week aboard her in the stewpan of Whampoa, but that hadn't been long enough to become really acquainted—what with getting his first cargo aboard, installing Ah Lau as compradore, going through the farce of Customs measurements, and paying far from farcial fees.

They'd pulled out of Whampoa at daybreak today; and all morning they'd passed tranquil orchards of *lichi* and pear, which alternated with the deeper green of lemon and orange trees, and with rimming hills and mountains shimmering in the heat haze. But now jumbled granite narrowed the river and a hot breath was pushing them pell-mell through the defile of the Throat.

Gill watched the rock walls draw close, so close on either side the aromatic scent wild thyme gives off with the sun on it was like opening a herb jar, and the blush of new leaves on massive camphors seemed near enough to pick.

Close-hauled, they swung and slewed with the current in a breathless skimming surge that had Gill running to one rail and then the other in prayer and astonishment. As they drew abeam of Chuenpee, he grabbed a handful of *lichi* and hung out over the larboard rail to have a long look at the spot Lin Tse-hsu had made famous six weeks before.

He made out the grim details of a sizable stockade on rising ground where fifteen million dollars' worth of opium had been destroyed. But now, incongruously, the hills above it bloomed with serene bouquets of pink and white hawthorn trees streaked with the flash of kingfisher wings. Except for the barren trenches gouging red earth Chuenpee was as green and lovely as the lush countryside upriver. Each promontory, each meadow they'd passed, was an engrossing new book to him today, but one he'd learn by heart, he told himself, in the months and years ahead.

Through spyglasses he studied the two guardian forts— Chuenpee and Ty-cock-tow—on opposite shores. Expensive, awe-inspiring edifices, but no longer military instruments, he decided. They were mossy sixteenth-century affairs, with cannon fixed immovably in each socket of the ramparts so they could be fired only point-blank, and never take true aim. Always providing—Gill shook his head at the likelihood—the target hadn't been frightened into limbo by sight of those ferocious and ravening tiger heads painted on each wooden gunport.

He couldn't help wondering why Peking had spent nothing on modernizing these greatest fortifications in all China. Why, *why*—in three centuries—had successive generals continued to as-

sume so ineptly that Chuenpee's targets would always be calculated ones without strategy enough to hug the shore, to cut in
close and thumb noses at the impotent guns above?

The clipper swung in closer. Something about the solid immobility of the rows of tents alongside the fortress caught Gill's
eye, and he agitated the adjustment ring on the glass to be sure
of what he saw. There was no ripple of canvas in the breeze;
there were no opening flaps. The tents weren't tents. They were
pyramids of earth painted to resemble tents!

And the soldiers manning the ramparts . . . Gill focused the
glass on them at this close range. Inert, inanimate, the bodies
leaned in suspended catalepsy against each embrasure of the parapet like straw soldiers. That's what they were! Gill slapped his
hand on the rail in sudden conviction—uniforms stuffed with
straw! This was the imitation war of juveniles! Counterfeit tents,
straw soldiers, tigers' heads! To fool what age, what kind of
enemy?

The clipper rounded out into the wide water of the bay and
bore away eastward for its rendezvous with Captain Elliot's merchant fleet waiting off the place called Kowloon—Town of Nine
Dragons—on the mainland. Gill hoped the name was auspicious.
He'd be delivering his first cargo there tomorrow—a cargo worth
seven thousand dollars in commission to him.

The crew, in white ducks and straw hats tilted at jaunty angles, sang at their tasks, glad to be moving after the long prison
of Whampoa. Captain Jarvis called an order in Nantucket twang;
and there was a scurry of bare feet and tarpaulins on the white
decks, a hubbub of grunts and shouts from the bowsprit and along
the waist of the ship, a firm settling of straw hats as all nineteen
hands fell to running out the stunsails.

Gill watched the job, squinting fore and aft, and liked what he
saw. The crew was a rugged sun-stained lot of Kennebec and
Portland men, with only a couple of Italians mixed in. They were
seasoned veterans, and—because discipline and rations were fair
—they went at their tasks cheerfully, as well as competently.

Gill moved to the deckhouse, seeking its shade. Already this had become a favorite spot, for he could stretch out full length on the deck and, as the ship rose and fell, watch the water running alongside. Above him the great sails bowed out, filled with steady wind; and here and there, still clinging to the rigging, were squares of red joss paper. The scuppers were littered with the torn bits of firecrackers which Ah Lau had insisted on setting off at the moment of departure to propitiate the entire river-and-stream pantheon of gods, and so win their approval of this new venture.

Lying there, gazing upwards at the rakish masts, Gill thought how he loved this ship—this *Dolphin*—which benign Fate had thrust into his hands so abruptly, so miraculously, and with such snug practicality.

His mind roved back over the sequence of events—Matheson, and twelve other Scottish and English factors, refusing to sign indemnity bonds; Lin Tse-hsu in monumental rage expelling them from Canton and canceling all future trading privileges there; his own brain storm—to act as agent for ousted traders by conveying their legitimate cargoes between Canton and *some* island loading station in the outer bay, where their company ships might come freely. Naturally it had to be legitimate goods, such as tea, silk, tin, cotton, Birmingham manufactures and the like, since he'd been amongst those who'd gone bond never to touch opium cargo.

That momentous day he'd been able to hand Gowqua ten contracts with Matheson, Dent, Fearon, and others, appointing him agent, and agreeing to the going rate of two per cent per month commission, plus seven dollars a ton for a steady all-season shuttle of cargo. Then, *then*—that banging day of days when Gowqua, against the collateral of those ten substantial contracts, had loaned him initial working capital, including enough for the immediate purchase of the *Dolphin* itself! Not on a partnership basis. Oh no, his sole possession! *His, Gill Bennett's, own trading company!*

"I'm grasping the cloud," he remembered saying, falling into

Chinese metaphor as he did whenever talking with Gowqua, "but it's loaded with silver this time, I hope."

And Gowqua had agreed—both that Gill's agency business was a sound supply of unprecedented demand and that Gill's dream of establishing an island emporium for future trading was the only way out of the present Canton impasse.

Lying there on his back, Gill raised one knee and poked a finger in the hole he'd worn in his duck breeches during the busy, fagging week in Whampoa. He chuckled softly, still thinking of the honest, candid, and unfathomable Gowqua . . . a staunch, shrewd, poetic man; a good friend, a very good friend, within scrupulous limits, for always there was that curious dividing line in the room between them.

Ah, that was a specific example. During all their talks, their lengthy, wordy explorations of self and tea and thoughts and business, invariably they'd been at the office *yamen* Gowqua maintained behind the foreign factories. Never once had Gill been invited to Gowqua's real home on Honam Island. Never had it been suggested that he meet Gowqua's sons, Gowqua's official wife, or any of his children.

Queer, though, their last meeting. Gill had an idea it had held a revelation of sorts, if only he himself had sense to read whatever it was . . . the small patriarch stroking a parchment cheek and specifying he wished repayment abroad, asking Gill to make future contractual deposits at either a London or a New York bank in the name of—and this was the real quirk—a single heir: a daughter with the name of Mei-deh.

And take that last morsel of business advice Gowqua had offered . . . "You Americans are overly generous sometimes. But, remember, don't confuse emotion with business in China. Always remember in dealing with us Chinese—*we are never grateful*. We have contempt for openhanded kindness. Or for anyone who gives when it is not absolutely necessary. If we give, we want something back."

Gill had said right out: "You're giving me this money—what is it you want back?"

Gowqua's lips had twitched twice with tugging wistfulness. But his eyes gazed bleakly at Gill as he said: "You use an erroneous verb. *Give* is incorrect. I *loan* you this money because of the interest profit it will pay my daughter. You see, you will be working for *her* in the years ahead."

Gill's body swung with the rhythm of the ship. How marvelous it was, he told himself, this looseness of muscles and spirit, this sense of fitness and ease, as though he'd discovered his arms and legs again. Here, in sprawling contentment, with a sure focus ahead, he was most surely himself. How different life would be now. He was deeply, surely certain that opportunity which he had the ability to grasp lay here for him in this new business evolved from the present emergency; that he would be a part of setting up a good and honorable trading post where the world would come to buy the practical beauties which Chinese imagination evolved.

He sat up suddenly, clasping strong brown hands around his knees. Something had reminded him—contentment, perhaps, or the unutterable beauty of white sails arching against celestial blue—of that one exquisite interlude of love. He'd left Canton next morning for Whampoa, and he'd not gone back to find out who she was.

It had been a wrench, a queer torment. But reason had told him he'd best sever, at one cut, all threads binding him to fantasy, to pure and wild and delirious fantasy. It remained a treasured memory—not wholly entombed yet in a deep emotional crypt within him.

The *Dolphin* moored that night in a strangely quiet and subdued Lintin Roads. So quiet, and so subdued, that when Gill was rowed back to his ship after dinner aboard the ex-hulk *Phoenix* he carried with him an agreement of sale for that floating warehouse. He'd purchased it for the whacking bargain of eight thousand dollars—cash upon delivery at one, as yet unspecified, island in Great Bay.

With the steady northeast monsoon blowing, they couldn't risk squeaking through Capsimoon Pass to reach Kowloon. They had to go the long way around Lantao Island, into a bay that was not a bay, but a tugging stretch of crosscurrents and racing eddies between an infinity of islands which rose in green and indigo and vaporous purple ridges into a continent of hills where the sea twisted and channeled as though it were a lazy river.

The Portuguese had a short name for the islands—the Ladrones, they called them, the *Robbers*. The Chinese called them Old Ten Thousand Hills, and admitted there was probably a robber for every hill. Even allowing for fluent exaggeration, it still left a sizable number of villages which lived by varying degrees of piracy. Passing through the Ladrones was a calculated risk, even as typhoons, the Strait of Magellan, and the doldrums were risks.

As the *Dolphin* rounded the southern tip of the great sprawling island of Lantao and came into the Ladrones, Gill took his place forward on the peak, straining and searching for any sign of danger. He had confidence in the *Dolphin;* he had confidence in Captain Pickin Jarvis of Nantucket, who came from the same excellent and capable mold as Macy; and he thanked Providence that he hadn't skimped on crew, that he'd taken them over on a good fair contract, plus bonus—these seamen who'd been willing to throw in their lot with him on a two-year contract.

The *Dolphin* turned, close-hauled, into a winding stretch between green walls; and with the studding sails and upper sheets furled, she rounded a high headland on her larboard beam. As the bay opened to view, they discovered a two-masted schooner in it. Gill identified the long low hull and junk rig immediately. It wasn't true schooner, but a lorcha—a bastard sloop born in China waters, half Chinese, half Portuguese, and manned as often as not by men with ancestry as crossed as its own lines.

The thing was—the lorcha wasn't moored. Its canvas billowed tautly, and it came sweeping up fast towards them. As Gill and Captain Jarvis stared at it, a cry went up from the strange craft —a cry that was high, fierce, primitive, and exultant.

The *Dolphin's* men ran to the rails, or swarmed up the shrouds for a better look.

"Pirates!" the barrel-chested Amasa Dewing's voice roared to those below. Others picked up the cry forward as they came tumbling out the fo'c'sle and the deckhouse. "Chips" flung his hammer aside and ran for the arms chest, and the sailmaker was in such a swivet to stow his needle he jabbed it in his hand instead, and left a trail of blood to panic those still scrambling out on deck.

There was a milling and seesawing of men and mates running every which way—Gill amongst them—as they shook off the grip of surprise and mustered to stations. Captain Jarvis clawed past mizzenmast stays to the larboard rail to scan the raiders with telescope.

The lorcha stood straight on for the *Dolphin's* bow, thrashing through a chop of cross-water, her yellow sails tight-braced. Gill saw the raider must take the wind abeam until she was clear of a froth of rocks off her larboard. Once beyond, though, she'd have room to come about hard on the larboard tack; and with her speed she'd be alongside them in minutes, ready to broach them broadside. Obviously that was the lorcha's intention. Obviously it had all been plotted out beforehand, with the aid of lookouts posted above in the hills to signal the clipper's course.

Gill measured the channel ahead with his eyes, the granite cliffs on both sides, the frisky wind; and then glanced back at the open water behind. He could stay, and let the pirates have the punishing broadside of his five 18-pounders. Or he could run for open water, take a chance on Jarvis outsailing them, to bring the *Dolphin* through untouched.

Gill took the chance, and signaled Jarvis.

The Captain understood immediately. "Hard alee!" he ordered the helmsman. And to the crew he shouted: "Slack loo'ard braces! Brace up to windward! We're running for it, men!"

A cheer ran round the *Dolphin*. The sailors recognized the maneuver instantly, and knew it for a skillful dodge. Instead of risking the bottled channel ahead they'd claw off for more generous sea room. It would bring the pirates into their wake, and the clipper spread more canvas than the lorcha.

The *Dolphin* swung hard on her course, and a flaw of wind staggered her before she lay on the full starboard tack. Then she filled away and surged forward, sensitive and responsive to each spoke of the wheel and each yard of canvas.

"Lay aloft, men, and unfurl t'gallants!" Jarvis cried.

In a jiffy all hands, and even the cook, were scrambling up the shrouds and out onto the yards, pawing their way over each other in the urgency to crack on more canvas. With topgallants set, Jarvis called for royals, and even skysail, pressing them on as he dared.

On deck the three mates were here, there, everywhere, lending hands, untangling ropes, and kicking tackle aside. There was the tattoo of blocks, the screaming strain of canvas running out and slapping taut, the hiss of rushing wind and water; but no sound came from the men now. As they fisted the sails together, the Kennebec and Portland men were grimly silent, grimly intent on the gamble they were engaged in.

Gill's sense of smell, hearing, and perception seemed to sharpen. He lived a decade in the minutes to come. He knew the clipper couldn't kick her heels and start running yet. She had to fetch up short of an island ahead, make a sheer slant on the larboard tack, and be ready to pick her way through a narrow gap between two smaller islands before she'd reach wide water.

He hung over the rail, his head swiveling between the land barrier ahead and the ominous lorcha behind. He heard gasps: quick, noisy gusts of breath; and it was minutes before he realized they were coming from his own throat. The heart thumps, the wrenching ache were his . . . he gulped mouthfuls of air. He lifted the cutlass in his hand and swung it up in a swift, practicing slice. And then, in a loud, laughing exuberance he'd never felt before, he carved the air in a second and third mighty whoosh. It wasn't empty-headed exhilaration. The *Dolphin* and its cargo were his body now, his life. It was *himself*.

The clipper skimmed the water like her sporting namesake, cleaving cleanly, curving, darting, frolicking almost, as she drew ahead, while the lorcha threshed doggedly behind. Twice the lorchamen shortened tack. Twice they tried cutting the *Dolphin* off before she reached the two gatelike islands. But each time Jarvis came about and circled out as easily as though he were steering a mackerel smack. And each time the lorcha's clumsier hulk refused to obey and brought up, lurching and wallowing without making way.

Once the *Dolphin* was opposite the opening, she came about with the wind dead aft and Jarvis could put on the extra spurt they'd all been waiting for. "Run out booms," he cried triumphantly. "Out stunsails! Set flyin'—alow and aloft!" And he turned to shake a fist at the pirates. "We'll show you—you braying heathens!"

The men on the yards sheeted home, and the *Dolphin* fairly leaped ahead under the cloud of sail, the deck drumming with the beat of wind in the rigging.

Suddenly Dewing bellowed from the foremast yard: "Chow-chow water ahead!" and flung an arm towards the narrow passage.

Gill saw it now—contrary currents sweeping around two land masses, ebbing tides, and concentrated wind, all meeting to kick up an unholy stew. The sea sloshed around like suds in a pail. Eddies pulled one way; currents raced another; whirlpools dug pits, and tossed up peaks. Every meter, every span of the surface spewed, frothed, curled, or spun. It was a hideous narrow mile.

Gill and Jarvis looked at it bleakly, and then at each other. But neither spoke; neither grimaced, or flicked a hand to change commands. They knew the planks under them were good American oak and elm. Timbers and rig had been built for any sea, even the murderous one below the Horn. They ought to hold, then, in this wrack ahead, especially with freshening wind dead astern.

The *Dolphin* plunged in—to buck and shudder and yaw at each vicious grip of warring currents. Young Patch and the black-maned Peletti, with muscles like hams, hung on the wheel to hold her to course. The sea ran like milk along her sides, frothing away to mingle with spume sloshing against granite shores.

It was a sickening, crazy spell while calamity rushed at Gill pell-mell from land and sea and rocks. Behind him the two steersmen held the wheel, now and then groaning out praying words. Dewing's booming voice was quiet for once, and the sharp-eyed little Mews beside him, and Mathers, and one-eyed Bedloe, clutched the jackstay in nauseated silence.

These were scarred and toughened men, so scarred and toughened by the sea that they knew each new duel with it for a ruthless and elemental crisis. Jarvis' pinched face strained forward in the same silent concentration. It was as though, all together, they were merging their determination with the *Dolphin's* and *willing* her through.

She made it. She kicked through the unholy lather and came flinging out into clear roomy water, where she circled, free as you please.

"That's my darlin'!" Gill screamed. "Now—show us you can outstrip anything that sails these waters!" He pounded the monkey rail; he slapped Jarvis' shoulders; he raced across deck to see where the lorcha was now.

She had refused the passage. She was hove to, watching them.

Dewing led the crowing shout that burst forth. "Blast and shrivel 'em!" he roared, loosening a hairy arm from the jackstay to thumb his nose. But—one foot slipped off the foot lines and he slewed sideways against the yard, half clinging, half dangling in space, the wind tearing to dislodge him as though he were a scrap of paper. There was a horror-stricken moment, then he righted himself, and straightway raised fist again in the same rowdy contempt.

Mews and Mathers, who'd screamed out and plucked frantically at the air to catch him when he slipped, now laughed uproariously at the antic.

"Hurrah! Hurrah!" those below shouted in quick release, and went on in high pride, stomping feet and slapping each other hilariously; joking, making catcalls, as though the whole encounter had been an event in some mismanaged regatta.

Even the cook—a pious man who prodded salt beef in the boiler with a tormentor in one hand and a Bible in the other, and complained constantly about blasphemy—ducked into the galley, and a minute later came running out on deck again, beating a basting spoon on a kettle as he promised treacle duff for dinner.

But Gill—Gill went to the taffrail and vomited.

As the ship held northward in each swiveling tack, islands swung left and then right, until it was they which seemed to revolve giddily while the *Dolphin* remained a stationary speck in an immensity of shining blue. By afternoon the islands were closer together, the ridges higher and deeper. They'd reach Kowloon by sundown, Jarvis estimated.

Perhaps an hour before that time Gill picked himself up from the deck where he'd been lying and went to sit in the shade the mizzen spread over quarter-deck stairs. Propping his back against the monkey-rail post, he leaned elbows on knees. In the bow he could see Dewing and Mews coiling ropes. Along the waist the 5-pounders were being rolled back into position, breeched, and secured. And now Gedney Want, the sailmaker, spread a torn sail by the galley door and set to patching it as he harangued the cook about the future.

But, restless, Gill started prowling again.

He rounded the foredeck, to stop abruptly and stare at the peak rising out of the sea dead ahead. A fantastic bastion of a peak—lofty, remote, profoundly majestic, rising higher, and higher, in crenelated ridges. It was soft green; and then, as a covey of small clouds skimmed over it, the emerald sheen changed momentarily to mauve, to purple, and went green again, for all the world like a mountain of shot silk changing shape and substance with each puff of air.

Gill walked on to ask Jarvis what the colossus was.

"A worthless bulge called Hong Kong." Jarvis said it carelessly. "Nobody lives on the place 'cepting ragtag and bob-tailed fisherfolk. Nobody wants to. And when Chinese won't live on a bit o' land, you can lay your bottom dollar it's genuine worthless."

Gill said nothing, staring at the peak ahead.

Jarvis went on: "Doesn't amount to a row o' pins. No fields, no level ground for crops, nothing to make a man a living. You'll see it yourself. Kowloon's behind it—only a mile away."

The hot night pressed in. After the evening meal was finished and the *Dolphin* bedded down for the night, Gill sat on the quarter-deck steps, staring thoughtfully at the blue peak before him. Densely solid rock, yet it had a chimerical appearance —an indigo blot suspended between silvered water and a starstrung sky. It made him feel immeasurably far from everything he knew, although the steady whittling sound from the galley was probably Chips busy with his hands as he and the cook sat talking. Forward that would be Peletti singing "O Napoli" as he kept larboard watch. Off behind there would be the lights of some thirty British merchant vessels waiting for the cargo he'd brought. But from where he sat now there were no other lights, no other ships; nothing save the *Dolphin* riding the mystic blue. Ridges and knolls and crags rimmed the place like a fluted bowl. Presiding over all was the ineffable peak called Hong Kong.

A chair scraped in the Captain's quarters; and there were footsteps as Jarvis, stripped bare to his skinny waist, came out fanning himself. Gill roused from the steps and followed Jarvis onto the foredeck, unbuttoning his wet shirt and pulling it off as he went.

"That water's probably as cool as it looks." Gill leaned out over the rail and brushed perspiration from his eyes.

Jarvis shook his head in denial. "You daren't risk it at night hereabouts. There's sharks this time o' year—and sometimes the stinging spawn of jellyfish as well."

"Very tempting, though." Gill surrendered the idea reluctantly.

"Aye," Jarvis said. "The place is tempting, seductive, and useless."

"*Useless!* How can you say that? An enclosed tideway with two entrances? A ship could get in and out of here in any kind of wind—all year long."

"True," Jarvis agreed. "I've sheltered here in typhoons. It's the island itself that's useless."

Gill was silent, considering, calculating, repeating a formula of caution . . . yet there it all was, spread out—a magnificent sweep of deep water; an amply protected harbor, landlocked, you might say, except for those two entrances at either end; no farm land; no population to dispossess; just a barren pile of granite. Had he happened onto his loading depot the very first night? Could this beauty be it? *Could* it?

"Who does Hong Kong belong to?" he asked.

Jarvis shrugged negligently. "Anyone who wants it, is my guess. Neither Peking nor Canton considers it worth a row o' pins. Even the smugglers can't hide in it on account o' the harbor itself being too wide. As for the miserable Hong Kong men themselves—well, there they come, the poor wretched lot of 'em." He pointed off left.

Gill turned, and saw a procession of flaming torches gliding supernaturally across the water like disembodied fire, since the boats beneath them were swallowed by the night. A thumping sound came pulsing across the water. It might have been from a drum, except that the beat was too thin and flat.

"That's oars they're pounding on thwarts. Lures fish, *they think*," Jarvis laughed, obviously having no truck with such rubbish himself. "It's not as though they fished for anything civilized.

It's *grayling* they're after . . . measly little smidgens o' skin and bone and guts."

By and by Gill pivoted slowly on his heel until he'd completed a full surveying circle. As he turned he said: "Deep water, and wide. Steam packets could lie here. . . ."

Jarvis' hand banged on the rail. "Steam packets! I hope I never live to see the day," he scoffed.

"Belching freaks burning pitch-pine logs! Any idiot'ud know they'd need a forest to get across the Pacific, so where could you stow the cargo? 'Travel on heavy dew,' *they said*. But Cape Horn waves weren't dew. One of them down its ugly funnel, and it'ud blow to smithereens entirely! Fads, pure and simple. A novel way to go upriver from New Orleans to St. Louis. Or New York to Albany. But—lunatic talk to speak of crossing the Pacific regularly on paddle wheels. . . ."

Jarvis' tirade stopped, and he breathed like a man running uphill—a tired man who'd run the same hill before. Gill stopped listening after the first sentence and let the old sailor run out of breath.

Minutes later Jarvis muttered, half apologetically, half defiantly: "I'm a sailing man, born and bred, and'll die one!" He turned away, then halted long enough to say: "I'll sail this here *Dolphin* for you in and out of these islands. I'll skin her upriver, fair wind and foul—anyplace, any time ye've a mind to go, Mr. Bennett—and right gladly. But don't ask me to tolerate steam packets. . . . Me, I'm turning in now."

Gill wished his Captain good night. But when he himself moved, it was to go into the prow to feed eyes and spirit on the blue beauty of the night. The fishing-boat torches were islands of orange light, drifting near and floating off into blue void like spectral illusions, except for the occasional reality of that thudding beat of wood upon wood which carried to him on currents of hot air.

In that isolated interval Gill felt that he was walking hand in hand with Vision this night—but with common sense looking over

his shoulder. Whatever fumbling Fate did with his life out here
—wherever luck carried him this year, next year, and all his remaining years—he knew that Hong Kong would be an exalted
conviction with him the rest of his days.

CHAPTER XVIII

MACAO,
June 1839

SUDDEN SLUICING rain rinsed the hot June air, and
succeeded in muffling the clamor of bells and cannon which had
been dingdonging and booming all morning to celebrate another
fete day.

Lael watched the downpour spread a veil of water across the
gallery windows, and turned to Lady Prophet in dismay. "You've
called for your chair, I know, but you'll be drenched. Pray sit
again with me until the shower lessens. Let me get you tea? Barley water?"

"Certainly not!" Lady Prophet's blue eyes were bright with
outrage. "Quite enough water outside without slopping more into
my insides. Give me a brandy, pet. It'll ward off non-existent
chills—and, perhaps, the devils of nostalgia. I'm actually sorry to
go, you know. Macao's a hellhole, of course—but an engaging
one!"

Lael's easy, full-throated laugh was always good to hear. She
dispatched the Number One boy for the brandy decanter, and
then shook her head in pensive denial. "Not nearly so engaging
without you," she assured the older woman, meaning what she
said.

"Nonsense! Another freak who tells the truth is bound to happen along," the dowager scoffed, pawing away a ribbon which
dangled from her cottage bonnet onto one cheek.

Lael shook her head again. Crossing to Lady Prophet's side, she reached for one of that lady's lean leathery hands and pressed it between her two white ones. "I can't replace a friend, ever," she said in simple earnestness, "for you have been true friend, and my only confidante. I'll be lost—without you."

"Tosh, pet." Lady Prophet tossed her head in embarrassment like a neighing horse, but she clasped Lael's shoulders for a second in a hearty, encircling arm. "I'd gather you up and take you with me to Calcutta if I believed that. But I don't—not for a second. Besides, you've to be here when *your man* comes for you!"

"But suppose he never does?" Lael asked tremulously. "Suppose he becomes too absorbed with this new venture . . . to have time for me?"

"It's exactly when he'll want—*and need*—you. You, specifically, Lael Manning." Lady Prophet was emphatic. "The fella's got a dream by the tail—but he's not one to like soaring helter-skelter. Essentially he's reaching for solid ground, because that's the pattern he's cut on. One of these days, pell-mell, he'll be wanting *your* special grade of council, *your* grade of comfort, *your* grade of womanliness. And you've to be here to give it him when he asks."

Lael's eyes misted with tender wishfulness. "Oh, I do hope . . . Ever since that night at Delmonico's in New York when he took time to encourage and bolster the spirits of a gawky girl at her first dinner party, I've yearned for him."

"Call a spade a spade, pet," the older woman coaxed.

Lael smiled, lifting her head in proud admission: "Ever since that night I've loved him with my whole heart."

"Bravo, pet!" the eagle-nosed dowager applauded. There was nothing incongruous about her knowing nod as she said: "It's good to love wholeheartedly and recognize it. Better still to find a man worth the anguish."

The Number One boy returned silently, on cloth-soled slippers, from the dining-room carrying a decanter and glasses on a tray. Lady Prophet barely waited for him to fill hers before she scooped up the glass and raised it eye level. "Salute, my bonny, to the absolute, irrefutable, and positive fact of a wedding!" She drained the contents at one gulp, and without cough or grimace held the glass for another filling.

Breathing in gusty relish, she was about to raise the second glassful to her lips when the parquetry floor in the drawing-room gave off its crackle and squeak warning that someone was crossing it towards the gallery.

Both women turned towards the interrupting sound, and saw a bizarre, medieval figure step through the archway. He stopped there, to stare at them through the eyeholes of a flowing satin hood which enveloped his whole head. He was carrying a lighted taper in one hand, and wore a loose surplice gown of cerulean blue satin which ended at his knees. Below were white trousers streaked and spotted with mud.

They both recognized the garb. It was today's saint-day costume for the procession due to reach the steps of Sao Paulo Cathedral at noon. But who was this intruder? Why had he forced his way here?

"*Hi-yah!*" the Number One boy exclaimed, rustling warily towards the eccentric figure.

The stranger broke into panting, heaving gasps. With an expiring breath he blew out his candle, and then stood swaying and quivering in a paroxysm of—*whatever emotion was it?*

Next second, making an effort at control, the man reached up and yanked his hood aside. It was Gill, exploding with laughter. "I wanted to surprise you both—but not that much!" he cried.

Lady Prophet let out a whoop of laughter. "Damned if Providence ever backed me up so promptly," she trumpeted to Lael.

By now Lael was laughing too—in a mixture of surprise and happiness. "Gill!" she exclaimed. "What are you doing in that lunatic costume?"

"Always respect religious fervor in others, young lady," Gill said, mimicking scandalized disapproval. Then, looking down at himself, he chuckled: "Zany, isn't it? I borrowed it in an alley—

somewhat unceremoniously, I'm afraid—from such a devout little man a half hour ago. Only disguise I could think of to get me through the streets unmolested. I'm still technically under arrest here. I——"

Lael interrupted him with a small sign and turned to the Number One boy, who was enjoying the spectacle—but pretending not to—and waved her hand in dismissal. But then, looking questioningly at the dripping surplice Gill wore, she motioned for the decanter tray to be left with them on a small table. She poured a glass for Gill and took it to him, saying: "This is to ward off chills and fever, *and*—to wish Lady Prophet *bon voyage*."

Gill whirled around, astonished. "What's this?" he demanded as though it were a personal affront. "I thought Admiral Prophet was returning to the China station any day!"

"So did I!" the lady told him. "But the Admiralty in its infinite wisdom"—her sanctimonious inflection was dulcet with sarcasm—"sees fit to keep him based at Calcutta. I refuse to remain a grass widow indefinitely, so I'm off to join him."

Gill's mind filled with the image of the firm and decisive and astute Admiral, and of how differently he might have handled the Canton imbroglio if only he'd been left on station here last spring.

Lady Prophet seemed to discern his thoughts, for she said: "My husband is an inveterate question-asker—thank God! Possibly his incessant *whys* bothered those who had to dig up answers."

Gill nodded in quick understanding. "So—history turns on how——"

"—on how the dithering Elliot chooses to interpret Lord Palmerston's vague and ambiguous orders for handling the China impasse," Lady Prophet interrupted succinctly. "Poor man, at present he pleases no one—that is, except Messieurs Jardine and Matheson."

She rustled her flounces, subduing two balky ones with majestic bats of her hand, and observed: "The downpour's finished—thereby robbing me of further excuse for lingering." Her intensely blue eyes softened abruptly in a dazzling smile of affection. "God bless, my dears! I'm joyed to see my two favorites together"—she rested a cheek against Lael's, and then clasped Gill's hand with both of hers—"even though you've taken to wearing pinafores!" Her barking laugh followed her out.

The gallery grew smaller with her going, closing in, closer, closer, on the two of them. Lael broke the spell of Gill's engulfing glance with: "You're sopping-wet——"

"Very rude downpour five minutes ago," he told her contritely. "Broke up a banging good parade, luckily enough, almost at your doorstep so I could dodge out of line without being conspicuous."

"You must get into dry clothes. I'll fetch Uncle Tim's——"

"No!" Gill said firmly, grabbing her hand impetuously and pulling her towards the seclusion of the begonia grotto at the farther end of the gallery. "Wet or dry—clothes are non-essentials. I need to talk to you—*now and fast!*" he told her urgently.

She smiled eagerly. "I want to hear!"

The provocative timbre of her voice plucked cords within him, as it always did. Lord—two words with her and he felt on easy terms again, as though there'd been no intervening six months since they'd said that unfinished good-by in Canton on Christmas Eve.

A tremor of feeling gripped them simultaneously, and they halted, to stand and read each other's face with deeply inquiring eyes.

In a sudden irresistible sense of peace Gill murmured: "Oh, Lael, it's so satisfying to be with you!"

Her violet eyes shone back at him with good humor, tenderness, and hope.

Then, in sudden alarm, he caught at her hand again. "Hurry, Lael, hurry! I've a lifetime to tell you—and only bare minutes for the telling before I've got to streak back to the inner harbor."

Behind shielding shelves of begonias he sat her at a little table faced with Cintra tiles and drew the opposite chair out for himself. The shell windowpanes shed a yellowish undersea light on them, which played luminous tricks with the fabulous tawny color of her dress. How could he have forgotten that lovely stem of neck? The extraordinary whiteness of her heart-shaped face? How could he have?

He felt such flooding pleasure in being near her again, such peace—smelling her perfume, relishing her abundant simplicity, even the way her body pressed against the table as she leaned towards him—that for the moment he didn't care what she said, if only he could sit there and enjoy her.

Then, next minute, he was pouring out words—"Oh, Lael, I've come to tell you . . . something has happened to me in a rush. I can't explain exactly—but suddenly I'm different. I'm not waiting around for circumstances to shove and force me. I can see ahead. My feet are set on solid ground, and I'm walking the right path. All the flounderings, chance encounters, uncertainty, and groping I've done all my life are done with. They're suddenly cleared away. I know now what I want to do—what I want to be. It's a complete reversal. Instead of being intrigued, being lured, down pretty and deceptive bypaths I've got my feet on the right one for me. Not a straight and narrow and dull one, but wonderfully bright and shining and *good* . . . and I want—I want you to walk it with me, sweet."

Lael's eyes misted, and her hand groped towards him.

Gill stooped, kissing it; and then her forehead, in devout pledge. And next breath he was telling her of the *Dolphin*, his agency project, his Hong Kong vision—and he cared very much what she'd say. He cared intensely, acutely.

Her cheeks flushed in quick response, and her eyes widened. "How wonderful! Gill, you'll invade China with ideas instead of guns," she breathed, nodding her head in rapid emphasis of each word. "You're pioneering unheard-of things in Asia—freedom, honesty, equality! It's magnificent!"

Leaning forward in rapt concentration, she thought out loud . . . new merchandise would generate new ideas, she said, and that was the push and pull of history itself. As she talked, the

split-bamboo blind behind her tapped a steady rap, rap, rap
against the wooden window frame. Without interrupting her talk
she jumped up and quickly anchored the two lower corners on
nails, and dropped back into her chair again, saying the course
of history had always followed this pattern, and always would;
that the exchange of merchandise and ideas were the core of
civilization. This rubbing, this friction of differing ideas, evolved
morals and intelligence and judgment. This Hong Kong depot,
then, which he dreamed of setting up, would be another, a newer
meeting place of ideas. . . .

Deep within himself Gill knew her response wasn't superficial,
nor prompted by affection. It was the gauge of Lael's own vitality
and curiosity in living. He'd never heard her express these adult
thoughts before. But—he asked himself in all fairness—had he
ever encouraged or triggered them before? And would he, until
now, have been one to listen entirely if she had?

It came to him suddenly . . . *here is a pioneering mind! Here
is a pioneer woman!* Not the physical, tending-campfire, driving-
Conestoga-wagon-into-darkest-Kentucky woman. But one in
spirit, mind, courage, vision, and steadfastness.

The pulse of feeling grew between them as they talked of his
future. It wasn't the pull of desire, or excitement, or poetic fancy.
And yet it was all three—with tenderness, respect, admiration,
and companionship stirred in. The realization of it was like a
clean song out of the sea to Gill.

A clock striking brought him to his feet. "Whew! I've got to
push. Stacey and Ah Lau are down in the inner harbor loading
clothes, necessary furniture, and themselves on sampans we're
running around to the *Dolphin* in the roads so we can ferry the
stuff across to Hong Kong. I need them to set up housekeeping
aboard our new floating warehouse."

Lael had a sudden thought. "I have just the thing for you," she
said, and disappeared into the drawing-room, to return a minute
later carrying a delicately tinted ivory statue. "My housewarming
gift," she announced bouyantly. "I couldn't resist buying this small

ivory yesterday—now I know why. It's Chou-lao, the God of Longevity. See—he's holding the peach of happiness in each hand. 'Rub them with a finger every morning,' the curio dealer told me, 'and you'll receive "utmost plenty." ' " She wrapped the statue in a piece of silk and thrust it into Gill's hands.

Gill was pleased. "Mascot for a merchant prince," he proclaimed solemnly, and then, looking down at his gaudy satins, broke into rollicking laughter. "Certainly dressed for the part, too. Never mind, I'll take care next trip of the rigmarole of petitioning the Senado to rescind their warrant . . . *next trip,* three weeks from now, barring typhoon. Oh, Lael, Lael." He reached out and took her into his arms, holding her softly against him, then kissing her cheek once, twice, three times.

She smiled at him in comforting permanence.

Gill spotted the five Portuguese loiterers, ostensibly sheltering under an opposite portico, the minute he stepped outside the Mannings' high-paneled gate. He saw one swarthy nudge the next and nod his head as though in identifying signal. Whereupon all five began moving towards Gill.

They'd barely taken three steps when a swift little figure came darting down the lane, to brush against Gill, and—before he realized what was happening—snatch the silk-wrapped little statue from his hand, and then sprint on full tilt around the shielding corner of the next wall.

With a bound Gill followed. He heard startled cries from the Portuguese band behind him, together with the ominous clatter of their pursuing shoes on cobbles; and he forced himself into a faster run. Ahead the scurrying, barefooted figure turned enough to see Gill was behind, and immediately ducked left. Gill followed, gaining, until the culprit dodged right, then left again, through a honeycomb of alleys—all bewildering, all multitudinously identical.

Gill couldn't make out whether it was a boy or a girl he was pursuing. Nor had he any idea where he was—on the way to the inner harbor, he hoped. But his one immediate thought was to overtake this confoundedly agile and pantalooned reprobate ahead before he, or she, melted into complete anonymity. Luckily the spitting rain had cleared this warren of its usual thousands.

After the fifth or sixth turn Gill realized the Portuguese were no longer trailing him—at least, not in a body. But—had they taken some short cut? Were they waiting in the next lane for him to run into their inconspicuous arms? And he, instantly recognizable in this gaudy sore-thumb outfit!

He pounded on after the thief, cursing a nation of robbers with each panting breath. Lael's mascot—*their* symbol of happiness and plenty together! And he'd let it be snatched from him, like a booby, five minutes after she'd bestowed it!

He mopped sweat and rain from his streaming face with the skirt of the surplice—and in that second lost his quarry. Disappeared, gone, lost! Not a being in sight!

He stopped stock-still. Somewhere, he told himself, between this spot and the next bisecting little lane the fox had taken cover. Gone to ground in one of these hovel entranceways. There were four. He tiptoed forward, reconnoitering one blank wooden door, and then the next. Both were bolted on the inside, he found when he pushed against them.

He crept on, passing the third when the closed door swung open, a hand reached out and pulled him inside a passageway. He lunged to grapple with the unknown foe, and saw . . . Su-ling, the boat-girl, doubled up with silent laughter.

Limply she handed him his silk-wrapped bundle and braced her convulsive body against the wall to enjoy the excruciating spectacle of his astonishment.

"Su-ling! You devil! Whatever possessed . . . ?" Gill fairly shouted.

Su-ling's face went rigid with fear. She put a quick restraining hand over his mouth, while she listened acutely to street sounds. Hearing nothing alarming, she slid to the door, opening it a slow imperceptible half inch to peer out until she satisfied herself no threat was waiting there.

Next minute she was grinning; and in lively pantomime, aided by an occasionally whispered word, made him understand that Ah Lau had sent her to fetch him. Her graphic gestures, pieced together with a few guesses, gave Gill an idea of what had happened at the inner harbor while he'd been away seeing Lael.

Three of his sampans had finished loading, and were already out around the point on their way to the *Dolphin* when Portuguese gendarmes, he gathered, had discovered the furniture belonged to him—a fugitive. This had happened about the time the final piece went aboard the one remaining sampan, which happened to be Su-ling's. In their peremptory way the gendarmes had ordered everything ashore again until proper court papers were processed to sanction the removal.

At this point Ah Lau, putting on a beautiful act of humility, hoaxed them into permitting the sampan to shift nearby to dryer ground for unloading. Once it had cast off, though, he'd maneuvered around a clutter of concealing junks and quickly moved out to join the thronging melee in the channel leading to the outer harbor.

En route, however, Su-ling had been transferred to an incoming sampan, with instructions to find Gill, lead him secretly to the Praya, and thence out to the *Dolphin* in the quickest possible time. Snatching the apparently precious little bundle he carried, it turned out, had been her own emergency device to arouse him into instant action which would remove them both from the neighborhood, and thus elude the Portuguese bailiffs she'd found waiting outside the Manning gate when she arrived there.

Su-ling didn't wait for approval or thanks. Signaling him to wait there, she slid along the passageway into the courtyard beyond and disappeared. Gill heard a baby crying nearby, and the undulating singsong of voices through the walls on either side. He braced himself for the inevitable moment when someone would come flinging through from the courtyard, or open the street door, and discover him in horrible hullabaloo. But when a rustling shape materialized from the shadows, it was Su-ling, carrying coolie rags and straw raincoats.

Gill shed his sorry satins, thinking to retain the white duck trousers he'd kept on under them. But Su-ling wouldn't have it. Shaking her head in vehement contradiction, she indicated the blue denims would be too short unless he stripped. Then, while he did, she stood by in matter-of-fact silence, handing him pantaloons and jacket, both plentifully patched and soiled, gave him a hand in fastening the straw-layered mantle around his shoulders, and helped him to tie the small bundle of his statue inside his pantaloon belt.

He reached out both hands, rubbing them on the dusty, soot-covered wall, and smeared the grime on his face. Su-ling nodded pert approval and showed him how to wedge the prongs of an enveloping basket-hat down over his ears.

They shuffled out the door, a miserable, drudging pair of pole carriers heading towards the Praya for a workload. It was noon, but a gray noon of gloom and smothering mist. The unfortunates who were out in it walked with heads bent, and with half-shuttered eyes.

Brown foam slewed and ran from the oars as Su-ling's covered sampan wobbled away from the Praya embankment; there was the distant growl of thunder, and the ghostly melancholy of unseen gulls crying bale and woe in the mist. Nature seemed to have set a Cimmerian scene for mischief and villainy.

But nothing happened. No one chased or accosted them. No meddling sampans came nosing their way or sought to divert them from their course.

Once, above the lipping sound of water, Su-ling shipped her oar and came to say: "You wantchee my go Hong Kong? You wantchee my makee lof pidgin allee time you? Yes?"

Gill slid the basket-hat back from his face and looked at her as a tired uncle might gaze at a fractiously persistent child. "No, Su-ling. *No wantchee!*" he told her with enduring patience.

She threw her head back, laughing uproariously. "Whassa mattah you? No can savee my Number One good, my no good! Must wantchee one time try!"

He doubled one fist, and with a melodramatic scowl shook it slowly in her face. She roared again in cheery good humor, and went springing back to pick up her oar.

The *Dolphin* was ready to weigh when he reached the ladder and climbed up on deck. At sight of him in coolie blues Stacey and Ah Lau sent up hurrahs of thanksgiving and came running to grasp at his arms, his shoulders, in happy relief. But before he started his story, he got ten silver dollars from Ah Lau, tied them in the coolie jacket, and lowered the bundle in the ship's basket down to Su-ling.

The girl pounced on the bundle like a terrier, pawing it open and clinking the dollars excitedly from one hand to the other. Her feet did a dance of high glee on the bouncing deck, and with a lewd wink she shouted up to Gill: "My plen-tee savee! My *double* Number One good! Yes, yes. Bime-by my come Hong Kong! Bime-by!"

CHAPTER XIX

PEKING,
July 1839

CENTRAL LAKE wasn't a lake; it was a pink plain of lotus blossoms quivering in a nuzzling breeze. The spire of White Dagoba over on North Lake wasn't tapered bronze, but a boding finger pointing at celestial blue. And in the magic sun glare of noon even the yellow-tiled roofs of the Forbidden City became a glittering infinity of beaten gold.

It was Heaven-kissing beauty to Yi's tender eyes. It was uplifting and soaring. It gave her the feeling of wings; it aroused the exaltation of prayer. Or was this because she was already aroused?

In meditative curiosity she glanced along the crowded terrace of the Pavilion of Purple Effulgence—this hall dedicated to the empire's military prowess—where the court was gathered in full luster for annual review of the Eight Banners. There were swaggering dukes, princelings with girl-eager looks, the Grand Secretary, the six Presidents of the Council, the Ministers of the Board of Rites, lovesome Manchu princesses wearing provocative patches of vermilion in the center of their lower lips, assiduous courtiers in colored sashes of rank, the Imperial bodyguard in leopard-tail uniforms, and the usual covey of Minor Stars pivoting pretty concubine heads from side to side to see who was being most admired.

Yi could detect no spiritual, no Heaven-kissing impulses amongst those many winsome and arrogant and sleek and suet faces. Dignified sham, yes; elaborate artificiality, and the dewdrop joy of complete frivolity, she told herself with the same inward ache she'd been aware of these weeks and months; and she sighed for the thing that could never be here.

The yearning ache did not reach her face, however. She was careful to keep it irresponsibly blank. So, leaning on the marble parapet in a froth of hyacinth gauze, she smiled placidly at the Imperial Flower sitting on the dais at his special table. She conferred the same calm, invulnerable smile on the hovering dozens near him. And because Concubine-Consort Yi had given birth a few weeks ago to a stalwart son, each of those within the compass of her glance refunded her smile twofold. It was only the new Chief Eunuch, Lan-fan, who didn't smile. Covertly he studied her every expression, her every gesture today.

A piercing and primeval cry came from the parade ground, simultaneously with the rushing pound of hoofs. Another breakneck charge of the empire's military elite—this time a thousand mounted archers of the Bordered Red Banner—demonstrating the uncanny skill which had jerked Mings from the Dragon Throne and kept an intractable and perverse mixture of Mongolian nations subjected for a hundred and ninety-five years since then.

Exuberant, madcap, audacious—these riders of the steppes seethed by, rank upon rank, standing high in stirrups, waving bows and arrows aloft and belling like wolves. Skimming to the far boundary of the parade ground, they wheeled swiftly and came careening back on their short-legged and shaggy little Mongolian ponies. It was wildly stirring—evoking open grassland, campfires, black-felt tents, and a thousand years of tradition amongst these Peking-tamed brethren.

Before the golden dust had settled, they galloped back in bands of twenty, to go spinning about the field in individual feats of horsemanship like bright-colored tops at carnival time. Their physiques were superb: their co-ordination and timing fantastic.

Riding full tilt, they snatched scarves from the ground with their teeth; they tiptoed, they danced, they held poses standing on the saddle seat itself; they crouched unseen in the off stirrup, then reared suddenly and vaulted across to the other; they even swung down and under the pony's belly to cling there, upside down, like animated burrs. At the same reckless clip they festooned targets with arrows shot from the same improbable positions.

Yet when they whirled off the field, there were no wild hallooing cheers, no jubilant shouts from the reviewing stand. Neither bustle nor commotion ruffled the sedate and self-conscious composure there. Their Chinese manners were only skin-deep, these Manchus of the sixth generation, but they obeyed the dictates of adopted culture now.

There was a glow in agate eyes, though; and embroidered chests heaved. There were sighs, and tremulous breathing. Memories of bygone hunts fluttered the cobweb linen the Imperial Flower wore. His pulse quickened—remembering stripling days spent coursing the Chili wilds with that hard-riding grandfather, Ch'ien Lung, who hadn't taken yet to poem writing—until he was popping one sugared lotus seed after another into his mouth, never counting them, never considering the consequences. "Ah, the fragrance of antiquity lasts forever!" he seemed to discover happily.

Yi's eyes flicked dubiously over the bowl, though, and its diminishing contents. She thought how, for these months, she'd managed to keep all manner of aphrodisiacs from the Imperial meals, particularly lotus seed.

But did it matter now? Now that she'd brought forth a Great Happiness instead of a Small Happiness? Now that she'd decided to. . . . Need she concern herself with what passed those gray lips? Or what stirred those tired passions? Especially during this month of the Lotus Moon, when everyone fed copiously on them? When choked moats and choked streams and interminable tubs of them everywhere vaunted potency?

Lan-fan—in the sober dignity of gold-threaded gauze—came bustling to the dais to refill the Imperial sweetmeat bowl, and Yi felt the clutch of habit. Momentarily she wavered, and then managed control. Lan-fan would have thought out each act he performed today, she told herself, each infinitesimal sequence, each breath, even, that he drew. If Lan-fan were deliberately kindling Imperial desire this day, then he would have laid plans for the quenching of it in due time . . . *in due time!* Oh, Great One Above, Yi made silent entreaty, let the glass of time run swiftly today!

She composed her face and turned her gaze from the terrace . . . towards young willow branches swaying slenderly in the breeze like the sleeves of a dancing girl; towards the green flutter of elfin fan leaves in giant gingko trees. . . .

The field filled with spanking squadrons of foot soldiers carrying bamboo shields on one arm and staves in the other. They came hurrying in short urgent steps, to wheel right abruptly at a single drumbeat and accelerate into a half run. It was delusive and misleading, a foxy feint; for in another minute two beats sounded and, in a synchronized flash, they whirled in reverse to dash left in an encircling swoop.

It was the five-rap signal, though, that brought the spectators to rapturous attention. Barely had the fifth beat begun than each soldier was crouched small behind his shield. Using it as a rocker, he flipped himself forward and over in a complete somersault. Then, leaping erect in the posture of attack, he shrilled a high, unnerving, curdling cry. It was the famous "intimidating somersault" maneuver which Sung warriors used seven hundred years ago in achieving notable victory over Tartar tribesmen. And now the Manchus had adopted it for their own.

In an interval the acrobatic troops were replaced by several hundred spearmen and foot archers, who advanced carrying scaling ladders and dragging siege catapults. Ah-h-h, sighing pride mounted to humming acclaim in the reviewing stand, and from spectators along both shores of the lake. Ah-h-h, the spectacular ones! The old invincibles! With their stone-toothed catapults they'd breech any wall built by man, most assuredly. They'd hurl defenders from the breech with those ingenious slingshot bows that tossed iron balls from cups with incredible accuracy! Hearken to the sound they made in the air! The shrill whine of death! Ah-h-h!

The Imperial Flower beamed. "Matchless thews of empire!" he informed the hatpin-and-tassel clan around him. And they were sibilantly vehement in absolute accord.

"When I think how formidable we are—with one million eight hundred thousand of these stalwarts——" the Imperial Flower exhorted complacently.

Yi shook her head ever so slightly, thinking how a week ago, or even two days ago, she might have uttered such words as: "Formidably paper-strong!" But today—her spirit was bound and tied. Today she was a cooing dove.

". . . I laugh at the threat of nations who call themselves modern!" The Imperial Flower threw back his head and showed how he laughed. "They're frogs in a well who've never seen the ocean. Provinces calling themselves empires! That's what! Those Spanish, Ottoman, and Austrian people I hear about. Those others—

those English, Russian Mogul, and French people. Their galls will shrink to rat size were they ever to encounter this mobile fortress of ours. This magnificent buttress of genuine empire! The very fact that our civilization has persisted for more than five milleniums is a triumph of both our art and the propriety of our manners!" His eyes made a circuit, collecting lavish approval. Only the Lady Yi did not turn her head nor take her eyes from the swaying willow wands.

The spearmen on the field deployed into ten running circles as the men gathered speed in approaching and hurling spears into fixed cylinders. Round after round of dazzling accuracy and incredible stamina was run, until all but ten contestants were eliminated; and now the spearplay became a breathless gamble amongst the princelings and courtiers, among princesses and Minor Stars, amongst any who could raise five fingers to make a bet.

Out in the field the cylinders were replaced by long-necked, narrow-mouthed vases; and the circling rounds began again, punctuated by mewing gasps and hoarse whispers from the wagering spectators. On and on they rotated, until the winner stood dizzy and anguished for breath. He had only to collapse into a glossy and sumptuous green palanquin which eight bearers rushed out to his side, for it was his prize. However, by that time no eyes were even on him. They were concerned only with giving or receiving promises to pay.

But . . . not the Lady Yi. Not the new Chief Eunuch, whom, everybody knew, she had persuaded the Imperial Flower to appoint several months ago. They both had the reputation of being quaintly abstemious, quaintly ascetic almost, in such second-nature affairs as gambling. Capriciously contrary, the court tittered, to deny one of the fundamental laws of human nature! It could only mean—eyes and mouths and hearts of the court whispered—they two were maneuvering for larger stakes. Cumshaw is cumshaw, after all. If one doesn't acquire "gold sand" by obvious device, then one is acquiring it by a more devious one, it stands to reason.

The noon banquet got under way with sober pomp. It was more summer picnic, though, than real banquet—served outdoors this way on the terrace, and with less than forty courses. But it was gala; hoped-for, anticipated these months because it brought traditional dishes of the Lotus Moon.

And there was the bewitching butterfly look of the terrace itself: the flutter and flirt of incessant color—precious beauties in clouds of apricot and peach and onion-green gauze; poised courtiers parading masculinity as they clinked jade bracelets and flashed jeweled thumb rings and belt buckles, each wearing a cone-shaped hat of bamboo filament which terminated in an exciting tuft of hair taken from the belly of red oxen. And fans everywhere. Thirty-stick marvels—of feathers, carved peachwood, Foochow lacquer. A fan-bag dangling from each man's belt; a round fan palpitating in each lady's hand, and gently pervading the air with verbena and rose and frangipani, according to the contents of the waggling little sachet tied to each handle.

Servingmen came swarming with fried frogs' legs, roasted quail wrapped in lotus leaves, creamed clover, and jellied duck soup. Then they were back with fresh turtle, delectably stewed bears' paws, iced bitter-prune soup, and fried milk Tai-liang style. There was the melting richness of green pea wine and mountain mutton, silvery-stone fungus and mushrooms from Szechuan, and amber golden-coin chicken.

The crisp, the tender, the smooth, and the soft succeeded one another until silver serving dishes crowded thirty to a table by the time the sherbert called "fallen snowflakes" appeared—so subtly, so fancifully flavored with rose-dew liquor, it was as much a relish of imagination as of palate. Crowning these were Fung-fa peaches and handfuls of Tsang Shing *lichi*, the ambrosial "suspended green" coming only from one small grove thirty miles northeast of Canton, its rarity reserved for the Emperor's table always.

Except for mountain mutton and stewed bears' paws, the other confections were Chinese. Likewise the five-hundred-piece Imperial orchestra played Chinese music during the meal, and for the langurous Dance of the Rainbow Skirt. Manchu tradition waited quietly in the background until the last velvety peach and the last dripping *lichi* had been peeled; and then, with a sudden tingling cry, men of the Plain Yellow Banner itself came dashing straight to the parapet edge. Jingling jade bridle buckles, they dismounted to salute the Imperial Cousin, and then mounted again—traditionally—on the right.

These elite of the Manchu military aristocracy traced decent from Yehonala clansmen who had founded the Ch'ing dynasty. Their equestrian training, their tests for rank were rigidly proscribed. But since billets were hereditary and six generations of Peking's effete luxury had sapped vigor and stamina, there were sad gaps between the theoretical complement of seventy-five hundred this Banner supposedly contained and the actual number of skilled horsemen they could muster. This year it was one hundred.

The afternoon grew older—with quail fights, with jugglers whirling rings on legs and balancing brimming goldfish bowls on chins, with magicians stringing pearls with their tongues, swallowing pellets and disgorging miles of paper ribbon, popping an asp into the mouth and waiting rigidly until it came crawling out through a nostril.

The Imperial Flower watched with robust cheerfulness and satisfaction, his heart fat with pride. He murmured, he clicked an approving tongue. He peaked scraggling eyebrows and waggled an astonished chin. And then, rhetorically, he asked the milling court whether China's sinews of war were as varied as life, and as abundant? Whether Chinese ingenuity, tricks, and combined skills weren't as prodigious as thunder and as awe-inspiring? The answering buzz of yeses turned the terrace into a wasps' nest.

Yi sat very still, wrapped in strangeness, hearing the blind complacency and parrot talk; but she couldn't respond, she couldn't gibble-gabble back. She could only smile a tailored smile and wait in agonized suspense for the afternoon to wane.

A rakish young captain of about thirty came riding by, close under the parapet, wearing the special yellow girdle of rank over his long loose linen gown. His jutting chin and high forehead marked him for a Tartar, yet he was exceedingly handsome. His eager, questing eyes found Yi, and fastened on her peony face in a sharp-set, asking stare.

Yi noticed his eyeplay; and she also was aware of the scowl gathering on the grooved and gray Imperial face, and that he turned and spoke hasty words to the Chief Secretary. But she neither withdrew nor turned away from the handsome captain. She merely raised her head on its lily-stem neck and fixed dream-struck eyes on the clean celestial blue above. Outwardly she was as detached as an islander watching a forest fire on the mainland. But inwardly she reminded herself again that life in this palace hive was as insecure as a swallow's nest in a tent. Inwardly she catechized herself with the words of the Diamond Sutra:

Like a dream, like a vision, like a bubble,
Like a shadow, like dew, like lightning.

The entourage of the Flower of Heaven strung out on its usual leisurely return towards Marble Bridge and the tilting terraces opposite which climbed to where West Flowery Gate crossed the moat into the Great Within. Instead of keeping step in the line Yi's four bearers broke pace, lagging slowly at first, and then dropping farther and farther behind. By the time they came to Big Fork, they had merged with the stream of litters turning away from Marble Bridge and heading homewards into the Imperial City. Unobtrusively Yi's anonymously curtained palanquin moved with this crowd into the streets of the pink city.

But the main stream gradually dissolved here—veering off, swallowed by a dozen radiating lanes or cavernous palace gates. Yi's bearers jogged on past a multitude of lanes—never hurrying, never varying their steady, persevering pace—straight across the full westward width of this city. The last slanting sun glare was in their eyes as they came to West Four Arches and passed into the Tartar City.

There they wheeled left on the broad way of Chun Chih-men Street, to be wedged in convulsive whirlpools of people, wheelbarrows, camel trains, and hooded Peking carts, all seething tumultuously towards the rearing mass of Chun Chih Gate and the corridor it opened into the Chinese City until sundown.

Once through the portal they were in the outermost of Peking's four cities—a checkerboard of narrow lanes, deep in dust and littered with chickens, broken wine jars, melon hawkers, and charcoal carriers. Yi's palanquin finally came to a halt in one of these, to squeeze itself quickly into the narrow courtyard before a dreary nondescript of a gray-stone house.

It wasn't a froth of hyacinth gauze which stepped from the chair, however. Instead a small beetle-brown drab got out. The coarse cotton of her robe hung in long, nun-like shapelessness to a pair of coolie sandals. Moreover, the face above it was straw-colored—a glistening monotone without mat of whitening and rouge. And the usual lacquered black gloss of hair was smudged now, and streaked with ashes.

A big countryman in coolie blues came running from the house as the big outer gate closed. He had no glance for the brown drab, but opened the heavy coin bag he carried and counted out two tens of large silver rounds for the impassive bearers.

Yi didn't wait for the paying. She kept on into the house with a quick, nervous step. In the first room Lan-fan stood waiting for her. He wore the sleazy black pantaloons and jacket of a fourth-rate scholar.

"My son?" Yi asked in a suffocating whisper. "Where is he?"

"Quite safe. He sleeps in the women's quarters," Lan-fan told her soothingly.

"I would see him with my own eyes," Yi pleaded, not waiting

even, but stepping to the open doorway which must lead to the women's quarters in the rear.

Lan-fan didn't seek to stop her. Without a word he led the way through two successive courtyards, along a porch to the left, and into a cell of a room. There on the half-curtained bed lay a small bundle in red cotton. Sitting beside on a stool was a girl of maybe fifteen keeping watch.

Yi leaned across the sleeping infant, adoring the placid little face with her eyes, and lifted one tightly curled fern bud of a hand to her lips. Then, in dizzy relief, she steadied herself against the bedpost.

Lan-fan was quick to motion the girl aside. He placed a chair near the bed for Yi and helped her into it. His voice was soothing-soft as he said: "This milk-mother I choose is young, perhaps. But her sturdiness and vigor are compensations, I believe."

Yi raised her head to glance at the girl now for the first time. Even in the twilight shadows of the room she could see that fresh, frank, country bloom, and the dewy girlishness. The girl met her glance with a smile of transparent friendliness.

"What of your child?" Yi inquired.

"Dead . . . of evil eye," the girl mourned simply, as a broken toy is mourned, and she picked up her stool and went out to sit in the courtyard.

Lan-fan's eyes were not on the girl, but on the weary droop of Yi's head. With a little signal to her, he went hurrying from the room. He was back moments later with a steaming bowl and a pair of bamboo foodsticks. "I had them prepare you this tonic of ginger boiled in vinegar," he explained quietly, handing the bowl to her, "that your body might have more strength for the days ahead."

A silent look of knowledge passed between them. But as she drank the broth and chewed the ginger bits, Lan-fan's deep-set eyes continued to watch her in troubled indecision.

When she looked up questioningly, he dropped to his knees beside her, to pledge devoutly: "You are blue heaven and white daylight to me. And I shall serve you until rocks decay! But—O Empress Mother . . . you leap from a pinnacle!"

Yi gazed at him with wise young eyes. "A pinnacle the worth of a fly's head," she whispered. "A pinnacle dizzy with capricious perversity. I saw it again today with the full court assembled. I saw it so indelibly . . . the Fates are bored with this empty shell of a Forbidden City! And I would keep my son from its tangled tomorrow." She motioned him up from his knees.

He rose, but still his eyes were troubled; and he murmured: "I ask myself—are we too precipitate in setting forth today?"

Yi stood then, facing him, calm and resolute. "Heaven was sweet today—granting us easy opportunity. We cannot ask Heaven to wait," she chided softly. "Besides—we journey in kind weather, before rain and snow hampers."

"But you yourself? Has childbirth left you strength enough for seven days in a jolting Peking cart? And then seven slow weeks southward on the Grand Canal?" Lan-fan persisted.

"My strength lies in my will," she told him steadfastly. "And that will has *faith* to support it—*faith* this new religion of God worship has taught me."

Lan-fan's lips trembled in a kind of prayer. "We leave, then, in half an hour," he told her, "that we may be out Nan Hsi Gate before it closes for the night. Three carts of us."

"They are God-worshipers, all?" Yi asked quickly.

"They are inspired to be," Lan-fan said simply. "They have read the translations of the scripture called the New Testament. And they have studied the Thistlemount sermons—secretly, even as you and I have studied them these past three months."

"They have forsworn idols and astrologers?" she wanted to know.

Lan-fan nodded.

"They know that when we reach the God-worship colony in far Kiangsi we shall each—without equivocation—deliver up whatever money we possess to our general treasury, and thereafter we shall all share alike—in food, in labor, in land?"

Again Lan-fan nodded.

Suddenly her lips quivered, and she stepped closer to ask: "None knows—*none guesses, even*—the identity of the boy child there?"

Lan-fan's lips parted in the suspicion of a smile as he turned and strode to the bed. "This boy child *here?*" he queried in fine surprise. "Why, whoever could he be except Little-Brother-Six-Pounds, First-Born of Itinerant Letter Writer Wei Lan-fan and his first wife, Yi?"

Yi listened to the fiction; not contradicting it, but waiting for Lan-fan to explain it.

"As we travel south, the name *wife* will be partial protection to you," Lan-fan said. He looked at the sweet appealing femininity of her unrouged face, at the sane forehead, and the willow-leaf arch of eyebrows. "Fate has decreed that you shall be eternally protected from me," he said. "But there will be other men along the way."

Yi agreed with her eyes, and turned to gather up Little-Brother-Six-Pounds.

Lan-fan stopped her. "Wait, Holder-of-Towels!" he commanded peremptorily, and then lowered his head in quick apology. "Forgive me. Calling you by the common name of *wife*—even in practice—is not easy. But . . . we must do something about your teeth. They are too conspicuously aristocratic for the household of an itinerant letter writer. We have need to disguise them."

He went out, and minutes later returned with brown paste in a bowl. "Tree-bark shavings and iodine," he explained, lightly painting a stain on her teeth with a brush, but daubing a second and a third time at the two front teeth to blacken them several degrees more.

He stood back to view the effect, and saw that some of her femininity had indeed fallen away; had changed for a new garment with less gender—a neuter, a crusader. He nodded, satisfied, and told her: "Now go join the others in the main house."

Yi wrapped Little-Brother-Six-Pounds in his red cotton shawl and took him in her arms. The girl milk-mother came carrying a basket stuffed with baby jars and ointments and diapers, and together they went to the main house.

Besides Lan-fan nine men and women were waiting there. As Yi went the rounds, bowing and inclining in calm dignity to each, she saw they were good, earnest people with humility and benevolence, and hope of God written on their faces. She felt a tide of contentment flow over her.

She handed Little-Brother-Six-Pounds to his milk-mother to hold and crossed over to the half-dead brazier. She stooped, blowing the ashes to life under the iron water kettle until it boiled. Then she brewed tea in an old earthen pot and poured it into plain white cups, which she offered—first to an elderly mother, and then to the others in the circle.

"Take comfort, sister. Take comfort, brother," she urged, serving all.

CHAPTER XX

HONG KONG,
October–November, 1839

DAYS PUSHED, shoved, and flashed by in a whirl-wind of weeks for Gill. It was the changing monsoon—when hot, wet winds from the sultry quarter wore away, and in their stead cool, sweet, dry winds from the northeast began to filter into the harbor—that he took actual count by the calendar, and found he'd been moored here in Hong Kong nearly five months. It had been late June when English merchants closed their Canton factories and moved to Macao so Chinese—but Lin Tse-hsu in particular— would feel the pinch of suspended trade.

It hadn't worked that way, though. Lin scorned compromise as stubbornly as he always had. He was still recklessly and ferociously adamant that British traders knuckle under to him, and he continued to hammer at them with increasingly coercive maneuvers.

In the August heat he marched a regiment to the Barrier Wall spanning Macao's slender stem of peninsula and closed the big gates there around the clock, thus cutting off vegetables and fuel from colony kitchens. Troops continued arriving to swell his forces until the yellow sandspit bristled with soldiers, and their incessant clamor of musketry and drill cries wracked Portuguese ears, and nerves, for a full forty-eight hours. Then, smiling vivaciously, Lin announced he intended paying the colony a state visit on the morrow, with complete military ceremony.

The skittish Senado sat in an all-night session—moody, tense, nail-biting, torn between physical and financial intimidation, and hysterically debating whether Chinese hurt would be greater torment than the hurt of stopped rent money if they expelled the English forthwith. In the end, fear of sword was strongest, and Governor Adriao Accacio da Silveira Pinto told the British that unless they left, all Europeans would be slain.

Next morning Captain Elliot had shepherded fifty-seven English families, and their baggage, aboard a hastily assembled fleet of schooners, lorchas, brigs, and sloops, which set off for Hong Kong harbor immediately. Two days later there was a second exodus of English refugees who joined the floating colony. And there, in the parching August sun, they had remained defiantly— men, women, and children, jumbled hodgepodge on tarpaulin- shaded decks and in oven-like cabins.

Lin was quick to issue a proclamation that all Chinese were permitted to arm themselves and fire upon any foreigner going ashore. He also forbade village folk from selling food or water to the outlaws. Yet after dark there were always several cheerful sampan smugglers hovering in the anchorage, and the evacuees would bargain over the rail for clandestine chickens and vegetables and kegs of sweet water from the Hong Kong falls.

Several weeks of this, and Lin commanded Captain Elliot to

order all his country's traders to sign indemnity bonds and return
to Canton immediately. When Elliot and the sixteen most influential merchants declined, Lin countered still more openly,
and still more dramatically.

He purchased five foreign schooners, moored them in the inner
bay up near Chuenpee, and then gathered five thousand assorted
fishermen and waterfront riffraff to practice assaulting and boarding the schooners from the windward side at neap tide. Lin paid
actual wages—not just promises—of six dollars a month for this
daily drill, and an additionally munificent six dollars for families.
Ultimate prizes were specifically listed on handbills:

Two-banked frigates	$20,000.
Merchant ship, three masts	10,000.
Smaller vessels, per gun	100.
Captain Elliot, alive	5,000.
Captain Elliot, head only	1,500.
Officer, alive	500.
Merchant, alive, black or white	300.
Merchant, dead, black or white	100.
Common sailors	50.

Meanwhile trade hadn't stopped. Supply and demand were
both abundant, and both had to funnel through neutral Americans who had signed indemnity bonds, as Gill had foreseen. His
receiving ship—which he'd renamed the *Crossroads*—was a thriving success. He was buying silk and tea in Canton, through
Gowqua, for Jardine's, and selling their Manchester cotton for
them at a straight two per cent commission. He was handling a
constant flow of similar orders for Launcelot Dent, Samuel Fearon,
and others. Coming and going, the *Dolphin* was stuffed with all
cargo she could handle, even to chests and boxes stacked ten feet
high on deck. Silk and cotton were bringing seven dollars a bale
—equal to the cost of sending it all the way to New York! And
still they hadn't got into the main tea season!

Gill's other mercantile ventures continued to mount. Coastal junks tied up to the *Crossroads* every day now, taking on cargoes of tortoise shell, coral, cotton shirtings, lute strings, woolens, pepper, rattan, gamboge, and betel nuts. A week ago he'd supplied a clipper for Philadelphia with pongees, cinnabar, indigo, quicksilver, kaolin, musk, ink, madder roots, hemp, ginger in jars, and whangees. He was stocking otter and beaver furs from Oregon sent by the trapper, John Jacob Astor; selling Formosa camphor and Fiji Island sandalwood; and meanwhile discovering the prodigal sums Chinese gourmets would spend on epicurean items —such as fifty dollars a pound for birds' nests, finest white, from Java; thirty-five dollars for a handful of whole-stem sharks' fins; and six dollars for a dozen dried sea cucumbers.

He had fixed himself a tidy office, along with commodious living quarters, aboard the *Crossroads,* with separate cabins for himself and Stacey, a collection of geranium boxes and herbs, and even got a milch cow to provide fresh milk. The friendly, good-natured boat-people brought them ducks, chickens, eggs, and vegetables. They drank Hodgson's Pale Ale, Jerez Sherry, and excellent La Rose; ate custard apples, melons, pears, bananas, and Swatow oranges in profusion.

Ah Lau was as capable a compradore, Gill found, as he'd been a Number One boy. And he had infinitely more scope—tallying cargoes, hiring transport coolies, contracting for guards against pirates, purchasing provisions, buying and outfitting the crew houseboat, combined with galley, which was moored alongside. In the course of this Gill shed any lingering delusions he'd had over the exact status of their relationship. Ah Lau, he decided, was tied to him by a very stout cord, but by this one cord only. The man functioned diligently and competently—around the clock if necessary—*not* out of gratitude, regard, or loyalty towards Gill, but out of pure and unalloyed faithfulness to Ah Lau.

Together with a salary of three hundred dollars a year, he could indulge himself in a compradore's fine prestige. Purveyors, coolies, guards, transient crews, all deferred to him; and he made *squeeze* on all services except cargo—and maybe on that too. As Gill's mercantile status rose, Ah Lau's respect and deference rose proportionately—for the substantiality of the job Gill provided. With this tacit practicality established between them, their alliance became staunch and cheerful.

Meanwhile opium had never been more golden. Calcutta and Singapore dealers, panicked over the news of Lin Tse-hsu's ultimatum, were offering new-crop Malwa for as low as two hundred dollars a chest. Andrew Jardine, the nephew of "Old Iron-head" William, quickly set up a branch office of the firm in Manila—with the cordial welcome of the Spanish government there—and bought enough chests to fill six schooners in Manila harbor. Once loaded, they sprinted up the China Sea, selling the little chests for anywhere from eight hundred to a thousand dollars each.

Matheson—still retaining his appointment as Danish consul—changed the name of several company clippers and ran up the Danish flag on them so they could get into the selling race. Other dealers used Swedish or Prussian flags; one chartered a Hamburg ship. The recalcitrant Innes did the very thing he'd done before —ran a load up to Whampoa under the noses of river guards, except that this time the price he received there was three thousand dollars per chest.

From the deck of the *Crossroads,* Gill watched the goings and comings without inner pangs. He found he was completely freed now from any hankering to get into the business. Often in the yellow dawn he'd see a couple, or even three, "scrambling dragons" come easing into the harbor, against tide and wind, as though being pulled on a rope. There was no mistaking their build—high-masted and low-hulled, their beam disproportionate with their great length, and with a crew of at least seventy manning the oars.

They'd hustle cargo—disguised in rice gunnies, tin ingots, or, maybe, copra meal—out of a Danish or Swedish or Prussian schooner in a twinkling; drift aimlessly around Stonecutters' Island to Green Point; and then, when the short dusk rubbed the peaks and coves and bays with its blue crayon, they'd vanish into the night.

The dodging, the dissembling, the clandestine, the furtive, the falsifying of ledgers and ships' logs held no glamour for him now. The adventurous part didn't begin to excite him as, say, assembling—from the *Crossroads'* own stock—a shipment of Peking rugs, scenic wallpapers, rosewood chairs, tables, settees, screens and lacquerware for Peru or Mexico by way of Cádiz, which was now the chief entrepôt for Chinese goods going to South America.

And there was the pride he began to derive now in the reputation he was building. Take that extraordinary example he'd had of it a dark night a week ago. A junk had cut in close to where he stood under the deckhouse lantern, and he'd heard a bump below him on the deck. When he'd stooped to investigate, he'd found a sack with fifty thousand dollars in it. No explanation. No name, even. Just a tally stick with notches cut in it. Three days later, in broad daylight, a junk owner who often traded with Gill produced a notched stick to fit the tally in the sack and asked for the money. He'd had reason to suspect several crew members, it seemed, of signaling pirates; and since he trusted Gill, he'd simply tossed his money aboard the *Crossroads* at Gill's feet for safekeeping.

Since summer was Hong Kong's rainy season, Gill had also had time to experience exasperating days which only dribbled and oozed by—days and nights of drenching, pelting, blinding rain when none of them could stir off the *Crossroads:* when they'd listen to the melancholy, discordant wail of sea gulls; and the damp smell of cockroaches, ants, and centipedes, filtered out at them each time a cupboard was opened.

Between downpours, though, Gill and Stacey had got into the habit of stretching their legs on the hard-trodden towpath running from West Point to East Point, where crews of trading junks, when wind and tide were unfavorable, tracked their junks along by a towing line attached to the foremast peak.

Once they'd got away long enough to take the cutter out to

the crooked slot of Lyemoon—the azure channel pushed between tumbled granite to give the harbor its second entrance. From here they'd walked up the ridge to the Punti village at Wongneichong Gap. But the sly, cunning, coldly venomous looks of these Punti farmers had persuaded them to return to the cutter before they'd had time to sketch even a simple map.

Actually today was the first he and Stacey had had the leisure, or the weather, for an all-day jaunt up over the Peak itself, and down to the shore on the opposite side. Their guide was a friendly, happy-go-lucky Hakka whom Ah Lau vouched for; and down at Shekpywan village, near the waterfall, a sailing-sampan was waiting to bring them back around to the harbor anchorage.

For Gill today's expedition meant infinitely more than satisfying his curiosity and need for exercise. The physical facts he'd pick up would be so much additional ammunition for the Hong Kong project he'd been formulating these weeks.

Tomorrow he was scheduled to call upon Captain Elliot aboard the frigate HMS *Volage,* which had lately arrived from India to bolster the China squadron. It wouldn't be his first talk with Elliot: they'd had several, for Elliot had been receptive to the idea from the first. But they'd dallied long enough on it, Gill felt now, and he wanted to talk realistically and succinctly enough tomorrow to convince Elliot he should throw full and immediate support amongst proper circles in London. The idea was simple enough—an international group of financiers would purchase the island outright from the Chinese government, and thereafter develop it into a free port where all nations could come to trade in orderly security.

Still—it sounded pretty grandiose, said in the crystal morning light here, halfway up the Peak. But Hong Kong itself was grandiose, Gill maintained to himself. He stepped off the path to part a ginger clump and look down on the stretching harbor below.

It was wondrous blue; and the scalloped Kowloon shores with rising crags and pinnacles behind were gems cut from the same precious blue. Around the solitary jewel of Stonecutters' Island the fifty British vessels and their two guardian frigates made a filigree chain of black and pyramiding white.

In swelling emotion Gill breathed deep as his gaze rounded back to the diving cliffs and green ravines beneath him. Would this dream of his persuade distant financiers in New York and London to invest dollars in this island? Would this evocative, tumultuous beauty ever become the actuality of home? Would this be the soil where Lael and he would put down roots, and build their love and hopes into the citadel of home?

His dreaming eyes roved the lower slopes, exploring, searching . . . *there,* that rounding little shelf, backed against solid rock, above the shore and looking wide over the whole sweep of the bay, that would be a spot to build on. That would be the place to build a secure and permanent house of granite for his children, and his children's children. . . .

Stacey's lugubrious sigh cut the skeining dreams. He stood peering over Gill's shoulder at the green wilderness below. " 'Hermitland,' they call it!" he groaned. "Dear suds, you know why when you look at the humbuggin' wolf's gizzard from here!"

Gill chuckled sympathetically. "You're liverish today, fella," he commiserated. "Probably that third helping of goose pâté you had last night."

"If I'd only had one helping—I suppose I'd be seeing an armload of beautiful blondes down there," Stacey jeered dolefully, "all strolling the waterfront, making peekaboo eyes. . . ."

"Yes, blondes by the bevy. And not alone, either! Just part of the everyday crowd," Gill declared in hushed, visionary seriousness. "I'll tell you other things you'd be seeing—bulkheads there, and over there, and further along, pushing shallow water back to make good, flat shore front for shops and warehouses and offices. Rows of stone houses, a barracks, a church, a club—why, fella, you see that duck swamp 'way over there behind Shakiwan village? Well, that'll be drained, and there'll be a banging fine baseball playing ground there instead. And—yes, of course, a regular racing track for our ponies! What do you think of that? And down here—directly below in that natural pocket there, what do you suppose will be there?"

"A diamond mine—most likely!" Stacey wagged his head in dizzy disbelief.

Gill's happy laugh rang out, sending a gaudy flycatcher to whirling out from a nearby bush with its long tail trailing behind like a yard of rainbow silk. "I hadn't thought of that one yet," he admitted. "I was merely going to say a reservoir. . . ."

Stacey threw back his head and howled like a wolf. "The sky leaks nothing but rivers of water for four months, and the man talks reservoirs! No, I want my diamond mine!"

"Diamond mine it is," Gill conceded generously, and released the ginger fronds he'd been holding.

A rufous partridge ran across the path, and then another followed, both crying out like croupy children. Their cry sounded for all the world to Gill as though they were saying the words: "Up the Peak, Pa-pa!"

He mimicked the cry to Stacey: "That's our motto—'Up the Peak, Pa-pa!' to more diamond mines."

They continued up the hard-trodden path which transport coolies had made through the years, carrying their loads in short cut across the island. It climbed leniently, but steadily. This morning, with the sun in their blood, they took it with eager, springing steps.

In time they reached a dividing gap where they looked out panoramically on green ridges falling away, leaping down, on both sides, to incredibly blue water. Off in the distance the fringing Ladrones floated between the wind tracks. Gill's mind registered pinnacle after pinnacle of perpendicular granite and turreting traprock on all sides, only sparsely layered here and there with red loam. He could see no meadowland, no fallow-lying fields, nor pasturage where farmers might take a living.

They stopped for early lunch under the shade of several massive camphors, where black-and-white swallowtail butterflies went sailing by, and occasionally a gold-spangled one whose wings flashed sapphire patches when the sun caught them. Off in the wild gardenias little barking deer kept up their asthmatic cough all through the meal.

Clouds drifted and massed about the Peak's bastion; and from a black lip below it water jetted forth in a white streak, arching over boulders, cascading right and left, in a gathering torrent. With their eyes Stacey and Gill traced its descent to the camphor grove where they sat, and then on and over and down. The Hakka guide indicated their path would follow it to the beach; and they guessed, from his jumble of gestures and lingo, that he was telling them this was the source of Fragrant Water itself.

Suddenly Stacey slapped his leg and asked: "What's come over me? Dear suds, I forgot to tell you the news I heard over at the British anchorage before we started—Jimmy Ryan and Joe Coolidge have resigned from Russell and Company for a go at our line. They're setting up, the word has it, same's you've done, and out after commission contracts now."

Gill wasn't excessively surprised. Others were bound to come into a venture as obviously successful as his had turned out to be. And there was room for competition.

"All thanks to Mister Lin," Stacey chuckled. "I hope you remember him in your prayers each night, Gill—for the more he obstructs the Canton trade, the more he hands us on a platter." He broke a chicken pasty in half, inhaling its robust flavor with relish. "Another little item I picked up this A.M. is that food prices have tumbled, and the supply's twice as plentiful these last three days since Elliot staged his ruckus over provisions."

Gill nodded. "That's natural—with three policing war junks disabled."

Stacey waggled his head. "Extra bunkum, you know—the cutter *Louisa* routing *three* Chinese men-of-war! Think, man! Five times the cannon, and yet nothing but cockeyed gunnery!"

Gill grimaced perplexedly. "That's what I can't fathom about this nation. No matter how hard I try! They're so damned smart—

and yet so fantastically blind about some things! For instance, they've a peck of adages about self-preservation and never cutting off an avenue of escape. Everybody says them—even school children. Then why doesn't somebody apply them today to ordinary acts of prudence—such as learning to fire a gun? Or investigating these new scientific facts we've brought with us? But instead they don't even exhibit intelligent curiosity about new threats and new realities!"

Stacey shrugged careless shoulders. "Too scholarly, perhaps, to descend to such unscholarly levels."

Gill made a rude sound. "That's another myth they eat regularly. 'Aristocracy of intellect,' my foot! What's intellectual about a parrot's memory? The scholar who passes with the highest mark here is the one with the best memory. The one who can quote the greatest number of classics. And what's he quoting—distilled wisdom? Certainly—but the distilled wisdom Mencius and Confucius worked out for living more than twenty centuries ago! How can these gems cover living in today's world?"

Stacey chewed thoughtfully on the last of his chicken pasty. "Still—if you pull Mencius and Confucius out from under the Chinese, wouldn't that wreck them? What would they lean on?"

"Logic. Judgment. Gumption—the same as anyone does," Gill reasoned.

"They require effort!" Stacey protested. "Much less fatiguing to lean on platitudes—even an outworn and dilapidated set."

"When you're homeless and starving?" Gill speculated.

Stacey smiled his irrepressible, boyish grin and reached for his fourth chicken pasty. "I wouldn't know," he confessed. "I may be next door to homeless, but I'm certainly not starving."

The downward path wound amongst pines, oak, pink laurel, and now and again passed the curious tallow tree with its white birchlike bark and waxen tallow berries inside a paper-skinned nut. They flushed pheasants constantly—some golden, others barred-tailed; and the fern pockets around small waterfalls bloomed brightly with the violet iridescence of thrushes who were singing mellow song one minute and at sudden sight of the three of them whistled raucously.

Occasionally they met a drove of transport coolies laboring up-hill with loads of dried fish, cabbages, grass, and charcoal—Hakka men always—who paused to shout jovially, stare, and roll eyeballs comically with the guide over the uncanny fair hair of these queer foreigners. But it was all kindergarten playfulness.

Their good-natured clowning reminded Gill of Ah Lau's explanations of these varying South China tribes . . . these Hakka were "strangers," he'd said explicitly, hardy, industrious, honest, and friendly migrants who'd pushed in here several generations ago over the northeastern Kwangtung hills from—nobody knows where. Because they found a way to thrive on rocky hillsides, and in swamps, where the native Punti settlers couldn't grow their traditional rice and buckwheat, the Hakka were gradually taking over. They turned willing hands to anything they could make a living at—cutting grass, burning charcoal, quarrying, even to becoming barbers, blacksmiths, and cooks.

As for the Punti—Ah Lau had scowled just speaking the name —they looked upon themselves as the real owners of Hong Kong since they'd been living in the place since early Ming days. They were cunning, adroit, dominant men with vastly different customs, language, and loyalties from the Hakka. And with all the smoldering, pent-up venom in their beings they hated foreign devils.

An hour of winding descent brought them to a narrow plateau where the stream veered right—away from Pokfulam village, Gill learned—and ran levelly for several hundred meters through bamboo grass until it dived again into the deep crevice of a ravine. When they reached the lip and crept down its abrupt walls, they found the place delirious with the scent of white ginger crowding every inch of bank on both sides. Below them the stream gathered torrent force over a bed of blue rock, but only for a short interval. Then it jetted out dramatically into nothingness.

It was not until minutes later, from an adjoining shelf where the path circled and switched downwards, that they could look across and see the crystalline arc of the stream as it fell clear for a full hundred feet into a sandy pool. It was only a small shallow pool the tide would cover when it came in, and then the fragrant scent of white ginger would be raining onto the sea itself all through the night.

Shekpywan village turned out to be a sty of mat sheds and mud shanties bordering a sheltered inlet. The channel was lined with a crazy patchwork of black nets hoisted high on the masts of more than a hundred junks. Huddling thick along the shore were twice as many rickety *tangkas* and dilapidated sampans. It all spoke of molder and decay, scraggle-boned poverty and impotence.

"Shekpywan." Gill said the name aloud in dismay, remembering that everyone he'd talked to had assured him it was the island's most important settlement, housing at least two thousand ashore and Heaven only knows how many more afloat in its permanently transient boat population. "Well, if Shekpywan is this kind of a blot," he told Stacey, "it's dollars to doughnuts the other two villages farther along—Shek-Chuh and Shek-O—are even more squalid. Lordee, think what a boon a trading depot would be to these scarecrows . . . regular employment, decent food!"

He pointed to the black-pantalooned and jacketed Hakka men and women shaping little dabs of fish and seaweed into a sort of pemmican cake which they put on the rocks to dry. All were skin and bones under those curious tribal hats as broad as straw parasols. The only luxuriance about them was in the thick, braided queue of black hair, hanging as invitingly as a bellpull from under each hat.

Gill and Stacey were as droll as circus freaks to the Hakka. They doubled with convulsive mirth, they guffawed raucously, repeating: "Tiger eyes! Tiger hair!" They ran up to offer each a taste of the pemmican they were shaping, and laughed just as uproariously when it was declined. Gill thought he could read a kind of docile and unresisting patience in their faces, and he had the feeling that behind this there was neither yearning nor sadness nor anticipation of more than they'd been born to. They were curiously appealing, and very likable.

Gill spotted the vivid green of seed rice being planted beyond the village, and he and Stacey strolled out to a scattering of paddies which had been scratched from crumbling granite. But it was Punti folk planting the rice, they found, and Punti hoeing the meager fields of buckwheat and yams nearby.

Gill tabulated them as a poor, weather-raddled lot, who had little burning within them besides animosity. They watched every step, every movement Gill and Stacey made—not openly, but with the pinched, sidelong glances of caged creatures. And their eyesore children came trooping in yapping packs, to nip around the strangers' heels, throwing dirt clods, then mud, fish heads, and offal at their shoes.

Both men wanted to smack several nasty little faces as a lesson. But instead they both spoke at once, cautioning each other not to start a ruckus in this God-forsaken hole, and turned and got themselves away at a quick run before they lost temper entirely.

It was a relief to abused nostrils and straining muscles when they reached the sailing-sampan Ah Lau had hired and could step aboard. The boatmen pushed out through garbage-strewn water, through a welter of stinking food rafts and floating kitchens, through the nerve-shattering din of filthy *tangka*. And yet facing them there—as they rounded out of the nauseous inlet— was the divine purity of a descending white plume of ginger-scented water.

Gill was early for his appointment next morning with Captain Elliot; and as he stepped aboard the double-banked HMS *Volage*, he was directed to the forward spar deck. In the middle of it, attached to the rigging, he saw an umbrella of potentate proportions. Under it the Captain sat painting.

He was doing a water-color sketch of Hong Kong—the morning sun shining full on its blue turrets and grooved ravines—and he was doing it with considerable feeling and talent. Gill thought he'd never seen the harassed naval leader so relaxed, and so thoroughly happy.

He stood silently watching until Captain Elliot grew conscious of his being there and looked up. Elliot smiled penitently: "You've caught me stealing . . . what I can of it. It's quite extraordinary in this golden light."

"In any light!" Gill intoned devoutly, and then acknowledged his persistent fervor with a mocking grin.

From little Chinese packets Elliot shook out several brittle chips of red and of blue paint, and dribbled water over them. Waiting for the color to dissolve, he said: "I've dug up an item that's certain to encourage you. Yesterday, when I was quizzing my linguist, he told me that six generations ago, when these 'Manchu horse dealers,' as he called them, drove the Mings off the throne, they, and the remnants of their government, set up shop here in Hong Kong."

Gill was surprised. "A Ming capital, imagine!" he exclaimed.

Elliot smiled quietly. "Yes, they even rallied an army and preached the doctrine of returning to recapture the mainland. Nothing came of it, however, because they ran out of money. Their resistence finally petered out after four years, and when the Manchus sent a fleet down to blockade the island, they scattered farther south into Indochina. But this is the point, as I see it—in two hundred years no Ch'ing emperor has cared enough about the island to even appoint a visiting magistrate to it. 'Too utterly worthless and unproductive,' they say in Peking."

Gill's eyes glowed. "Might be bought at a bargain, eh?" he prodded softly.

Elliot laid his brush down, and then—a small tremor of wistfulness tugging at his lips—he confided softly: "You know, Bennett, I've a notion the island is witching me too. At first I thought it was merely twitching my imagination. But now . . . *now* I've a feeling it's bound itself, insidiously, around my heart."

Gill knew this was no ordinary confession. The man was revealing himself. He saluted, in quiet undertones: "I'm in good company then, sir."

Elliot quickly snatched up his brush. "That's only for your ear, my friend. See you don't let it get abroad! 'Twould only be another thorn added to the crown 'that controversial Captain Elliot' wears already. How they'd relish bandying it about that I made a game of selecting a commercial depot out of sentimental reasons!"

"There are plenty of practical ones for the choice, sir," Gill defended hotly.

With his brush Elliot touched the paper mountains with purple shadows. "Remember," he reminded, *sotto voce,* "Jimmy Matheson is plumping mighty hard for Lantao."

In unspoken accord they both turned to stare off the starboard quarter—past the wooden castles of two nearby Indiamen and the skeleton spars of clippers beyond, to the walled decks of the *Hercules,* for this opium ship was Matheson's company office now. Junks still clustered both sides even at this midmorning hour . . . suspiciously long and narrow junks, ranked with many oars. Pinnaces, cutters, jolly boats and *tangka* were busily coming and going from it, churning the water like sea gulls after sardines.

"A man gathering in a fortune that rapidly demands substantial facts," Elliot observed dryly. "Suppose you school me in the *practical* roster again—*Hong Kong versus Lantao*—to make certain I've forgot none." He touched his brush with blue and purple and green for a distant cliff, and prepared to listen.

Gill plunged in resolutely. "For the life of me—I can't make out why Matheson harps on Lantao," he declared. "I took the *Dolphin* over there and did a circuit of it. Then I went back a week later and did it a second time to make certain I hadn't missed any opening anywhere in all that cliff mass. But no—I could only find three coves! Mud flats at low tide, mind you. Not even a single decent small harbor. Our ships would have to load in the open roads—and in blowing weather that's dicey. Does that sound comparable with the size and protection this deep-water anchorage gives us?"

Elliot didn't answer, but continued painting.

Gill's question had been rhetorical, so he didn't wait for a response. "Secondly—Lantao's equally dicey on the human side. It's obviously a pirate haunt. Hoklos people everywhere—all from Swatow way. They're a different breed from the amiable Hakka folk who predominate here. Hoklos are born raiders, I'm told. Fierce, daring, ruthless devils looking for a way to snatch five coppers, or anything else they can lay hands to. They've no stomach for law and order. No heart to obey. They're a band of cutthroats who'd be generating constant trouble for us. And on Lantao they've got twice as much territory to be troublesome."

Still Elliot painted on, thoughtfully and minutely.

Gill had argued these points so often, so hotly, with himself and with Stacey, that they welled now from fluent memory. "The very fact that Lantao is twice as large, and has good crop land, is bound to run its price up. Yesterday, from up on the Peak, we calculated the whole of Hong Kong doesn't cover more than twenty-nine or thirty square miles. Practically all perpendicular! And farmland can't be hacked out of granite or these poor, patient Hakka would have broken their backs doing it long ago."

Gill paused, and to leash the ardor creeping into his voice he strode across the deck. But he was too wound up to stop talking, and he came back to the easel, spreading his legs and swaying in a sort of rhythm to the words he was uttering. "The settlers this island can attract are—merchants! That's the sort we want—practical businessmen who respect law and order, because that's what they thrive on."

He smacked one hand against the other. "Oh, I tell you, we'll make a beautiful thing out of it here. Everything proper—houses, shops, warehouses, barracks, everything, of stone. Good, solid unresisting stone, so we'll never be devastated by a fire like that I saw in Canton last winter. We'll offer safe, and unrestricted, liberty of trade. A free port. We'll have government by r-i-g-h-t-s

—and not by r-i-t-e-s! Under some sort of international flag. Don't ask me now *what* international flag, sir. Most probably we'll have to invent one. But we can do that too!"

Elliot's brush stopped abruptly in mid-air, poised there as he turned with portentous deliberation and fixed Gill with steady blue eyes in which there was the premonition of withdrawal. "I fear I must interrupt you at this point," he said with icy impersonality. "The flag will *not* be international."

"Not international! But, sir, the other day you agreed on that vital point. I believed I'd won you as a strong ally." Gill was pleading now. "Do allow me to——"

Elliot interrupted. "Until eight o'clock this morning I *was* in full accord with you on the international ownership of Hong Kong. However, precisely at eight I abandoned that phase of possession."

Gill stared in stricken amazement. "Why?" He pushed the hateful word out.

"Because"—Elliot's gaze now swung around to include the smartly rigged frigate lying beyond— "in another hour I shall give the command for HMS *Hyacinth* and HMS *Volage* to prepare to engage the enemy."

"*Fight* to secure Hong Kong!" Gill was rocked.

"No! Fight for the right of free trade!" Elliot declared in ringing rhetoric. "And when the victors of Trafalgar and Abukir have finished with this navy of worm-eaten, waterlogged, sixteenth-century junks, Peking may be very glad to *give* us Hong Kong!"

Gill felt as though the breath had been kicked out of him. "*Why fight? Why*, when we might buy it peaceably as a straightforward business deal?"

Seeing Gill's misery, Elliot's eyes softened, and when he spoke, the commander's voice was quiet with incisive and dreadful reasonableness. "I have no other choice. Lin Tse-hsu has now exceeded himself. Three days ago he demanded that I execute Matheson, Dent, Fearon, and Innes forthwith as outlaws. I declined. His answer was delivered to me at eight o'clock this morning. *It banishes all British trade with China forever!*"

"Oh, the crazy, hindering madman!" Gill cried out. "The monster of ego!"

Elliot nodded in accord. "Lin's ultimatum is explicit—with ritualistic rudeness he says, 'My navy shall defeat you in the morning and decapitate you in the afternoon! Submit, or be annihilated!' Neither prospect entertains me. So—since I learn they have secretly strengthened their battery here at Kowloon, and are assembling an attacking fleet of fireships at Chuenpee under Admiral Kwan—I have no alternative but to attack first."

Gill stood wrapped in gloom, unable to speak.

For a long moment Elliot remained motionless, staring up at the awesome loneliness of the Peak as though it were an altar. Then he picked up his brush again, to stir it in a yellow wash. "And now, Bennett, if you'll excuse me," he said with precise deference, "I've a mind to commit this cherishing reality of Hong Kong to paper as I see it in this hour before we engage in the histrionics of war."

Admiral Kwan bent to pick a fat caterpillar off the leaf of a tender herb he was growing in a tub outside his cabin door and flicked it into the river. His eye was caught by sheets of white light out in the bay, and he stared at them in nettled surprise. Two barbarian frigates—double-banked ones!—rounding under full spread of sail a mile off Chuenpee battery! What were the unsophisticated cutthroats up to now?

Was it, he asked himself leniently, the clear, bright November sun rousing prankish spirits in the barbarians? Or were those top-heavy gewgaws with their childish rigging merely spending sail in a sort of minor splurge before the eyes of those ten English merchantmen anchored nearby—to further their nefarious offside trade after dark?

The pucker cleared, and a cherubic smile came instead to crease his bland face. H'm-m, this exuberant sun! This very ex-

uberant sun! Warmed his veins, too, didn't it? As for *splurge* . . .
Great shade of his ancestor! Could it be said that a Kwan descended directly from the God of War was unable to engage in
byplay? In adroit byplay? *Ai-yah*—his bright eyes pinched shut
in calculating thought—mightn't this be the ordained moment
to *splurge*, say, to the accompaniment of a little simple arithmetic?
He thought it was.

He tapped the rail with his brass spyglass, sang out sonorous
orders to the officer who leaped to his side, and then stood admiringly as the new serpent ensign was hoisted on the mainmast.
He watched it writhe out its signal in the easterly breeze and
observed the ripples of activity it stirred throughout the flotilla
moored in the Pearl River around him.

He still watched, revolving slowly, and his chest expanding
elastically as his gaze traveled from one mass of stout teak to
another. Fourteen war junks, each pulling sixty oars in the classical image of destruction! Fifteen fireboats! Floating thunderbolts
loaded with fire physic enough to render the night hideous—with
spewed fire arrows, whizzing rockets, catapulting balls of wild-
fire! And flying from twenty-nine masts the armada's glorious
emblem itself—a dragon swallowing the moon in unconquerable
invincibility!

Admiral Kwan's head continued to rotate in tremulous appreciation as the squadron transformed itself. Simultaneously enormous batwing sails heaved and opened, oars ran out, wooden
anchors splashed up on rattan cables from the mud, battering-
rams jutted from sterns like bristling tail feathers, and the snub-
nosed prows turned downriver towards the bay.

They came sweeping out into it with flourish and importance,
the great staring dragon eyes of the Imperial insignia painted on
each bow, and each mast flying its proud black dragon. With the
Admiral leading, they circled in majestic formation, to string out
southward, one after another, in a diagonal line from Chuenpee
across the entire river mouth. As each took position, anchors
splashed and sails thudded down into cradles. Last of all the

Admiral's serpent ensign slumped obliviously into a silken heap on deck.

So-o-o . . . Admiral Kwan clasped one plump hand in the other as he prudently summarized facts. Yes, action had been explicitly framed to the exigencies of the moment, *Manual of War,* page twelve. Twenty-nine absolute ships of war had been paraded before two prosaic frigates and ten inconsequential merchantmen. A neat, pithy, and conclusive lesson in the arithmetic of destruction had been provided—establishing the robust ratio between three hundred guns manned by three thousand seamen and forty-six guns with a muster of not more than four hundred. By mooring he had clearly indicated that he wasn't attacking, and also that he didn't expect to be attacked.

Moreover, potentials were exhilarating. With the right tide abetting—which it would at midnight—loosened fireboats would drift silently, secretly, devastatingly amongst those merchantmen and their sleeping frigates. Or, at least, create crippling delay until tomorrow's flood tide, when Commissioner Lin's five thousand fishermen brigands could converge and swarm over the Abominables like ants smothering a cockroach. Yes, the potentials were diverting.

He phrased a prayer for the midnight tide, and then, in added precaution, took a cup of his favorite peony-petal tea to the small deck shrine. It was dedicated to Teen How, the Virgin Queen of Heaven, who was also the patroness of sailors. A small bean-oil lamp burned steadily before her image. The Admiral lifted the cup to his lips, repeated his prayer aloud, and placed the tea for Teen How's spirit to quaff.

Kwan's empty stomach rumbled; and he patted it tentatively, glancing up at the sun. *Ai-yah,* already an hour before midday! Time enough for small chow. H'm-m, a few shrimp dumplings, a flaking pastry, and . . . and what? Silver-thread noodles? Wild-duck pâté? Fried dough rings in crisp blisters with——?

But—what was happening out there? What bluster was this? What monkey trick? The barbarians hadn't furled. They still maintained commanding sail. Why behave so uncandidly? What were they waiting for?

They weren't waiting. *They weren't waiting!*

He couldn't believe what he saw. Snatching up his spyglass, he trained it on the two frigates. It was true: they were standing south, their topsails spread to the freshening easterly breeze. Not running away exactly. No, they seemed to be circling . . . circling west to . . .

Merciful Buddha! To come up fast towards the Chinese line! Aiming at the flagship itself. Not flying the white flag of truce. No! The red flag of war. That is, their adaptation of it, confused in some outlandish way with diagonal blue bars. But—red enough to warn any fool they were attacking!

Kwan's knees trembled in surprise. These nincompoops chose annihilation, did they? *Two ships charging twenty-nine!*

In a daze he stumbled to the battle gong and beat a tattoo which quickened into frantic summons. He clung to the big baton while the screaming-eagle banner ran up to rouse the flotilla to battle stations, and then he flung it from him and went running pell-mell to the cabin for full battle regalia.

His hands groped ineptly when he reappeared, fumbling at tying the court sash, dropping the *Manual of War,* until he reached the mizzenmast and could steady himself against the pike rack which sheathed it. Before him on deck he saw faces lifted in consternation, panic, apathy, and bravado.

Next minute he snatched the longest pike from the rack and waved it aloft in symbolic thrusts. The red cow hair on his rattan helmet flamed in the sun and bounced with each thrust. Then, throwing his head back, he screamed stentoriously: "We enter the Dragon's jaws! Remember—the prime art of warfare is to confuse and intimidate. The time has come! Ready . . . *Strike terror!*"

His crew howled like wounded wolves; they beat drums, clashed gongs, and set giant firecracker baskets to exploding. The wave of sound multiplied and mounted to crescendo, for each ship in line was contributing intimidation now.

Still the northing frigates stood on with the easterly wind on
their starboard beam—the 28-gun *Volage* leading resolutely, the
18-gun *Hyacinth* following in close order.

"Assemble fire physic!" Kwan ordered.

His crew sprang into lines which descended into the hold, and
in a sustained rush they handed up apothecary jars filled with
gunpowder and stacked them on the forward deck between the
two jingals named *Subduer of Barbarians* and *Robbers' Lament*.
In the same grim haste they grabbed the jugs of fresh garlic water
the two kitchen boys lugged up on deck and sprinkled each other
thoroughly for protection against shell shot. Then they ran to
battle stations.

The excited gunners manning the *Subduer of Barbarians*
loaded forthwith, and were on the rash point of firing when
Kwan caught them. He shrieked wrathfully: "Hold fire, idiots!
Never attack from the north! It's inauspicious!"

He turned to watch the doomed imbeciles sweep nearer,
nearer. Pitiful, crazy martyrs! But doltish incompetents too.
Couldn't even manage their own vessels. Miscalculating the
range! Closing in, closing in to a hundred yards! No, closer,
closer! Still they came. Queen of Heaven, only observe them!
Coming up with studding sails set alow and aloft to fifty-yard
range. They'd botched. They'd violated all principles of naval
warfare. Waging at this ridiculous range. Guns wouldn't bear.

But—perhaps they didn't mean to attack? This was their version of intimidation? Of harrying? Certainly, why hadn't he
guessed earlier? Through rigid throat muscles he chuckled like a
hoarse crow. Hah . . . that low-class bravado deserved its own
answer. Through cupped hands he shouted: "Expose backsides!
Make the indecent gesture!"

To a man, the crew obeyed.

As the towering *Volage* swept abeam, Kwan danced in tiptoe
anxiety—would the audience comprehend? He squinted at the
idiot figure sitting there leisurely on deck under an umbrella and
watching with such stoical calm. It was Elliot himself! Kwan

chuckled wholeheartedly. Capital audience! And—up forward there, that would be the vessel's commanding officer—Captain Smith, no doubt—viewing the ranks of backsides through a spyglass. Kwan laughed so hard he couldn't see well through his tears . . . but the English Captain was doing something. He'd flung his spyglass aside and was grabbing up a fowling-piece.

Bang! A charge of snipeshot peppered the assembled backsides!

The yowls of pain and surprise were never heard, though, for at that second the *Volage* thundered a starboard broadside of fourteen guns.

It was the clap of doom. The sea, the heavens, the deck shuddered with the impact. Seamen fell every which way on deck; the Admiral clung giddily to the pike rack to keep upright. He saw one ball shatter the foremast and topple it in a tangle of cables and bamboo splinters. He heard cabin housing crashing behind him. Then the adjacent fireboat disintegrated in a roaring, flaring sheet of flame.

Dazed, deafened, incredulous, the Admiral shouted a word which had congealed on his lips: "Fire!"

The flagship's seven larboard gunports spat flame. Iron whined through the air into empty space above the *Volage*.

"Fire! Fire!" The Admiral choked in anguish, knowing his guns were immovable, knowing they couldn't be lowered to bear at this idiotic range.

The *Volage* swept on.

Then the *Hyacinth* was upon them—blasting point-blank at the same murderous range, gashing his bow, breaching his hull . . . splintering, smashing, destroying.

He ordered a salvo at the *Hyacinth's* flat stern with those formidable forward jingals. The *Subduer of Barbarians* blew up. The *Robbers' Lament* fired wild.

"Cut anchor cables! Up sails! Pursue!" Admiral Kwan panted. His head spun, his ears drummed, and his heart cramped with stupor.

But by the time torn sails were braced, by the time they'd rounded north, he saw water seeping through a dozen gaps into the hold. He dispatched the crew to plug the holes with mattresses, rice bags, themselves, anything, anything!

It was useless. They could only lie where they were, wallowing inertly. In stricken incredulity he stood on the rocking poop deck to watch the two frigates run their lethal course northward, inflicting calamity with every broadside, but passing unscathed under—always under—the Chinese cannon.

Four war junks settled beneath the brown water. Another two fireboats filled the horizon with flame and debris. Others were holed or dismasted, and crews were panicking.

The frigates reached the last ship in the Chinese line, turned sharp, and came running back down the same path of destruction, blazing away now with larboard broadsides.

But the line was gone. Admiral Kwan moaned a dreeing keen, seeing fragments of ships and crews scattering, weighing, slipping anchor, abandoning remnants, and rowing for shore with fear devils whipping them. Only his waterlogged derelict remained, wallowing in the gentle swell; too crippled to limp away; too dominated by his agony of unbelief to be abandoned.

The white-winged frigates bore down in inexorable doom. Kwan thought they meant to cut him in two, they held so sharp on his bow. Only at the last second did they veer aside—the *Volage* all but scraping his starboard rails, the *Hyacinth* passing to larboard with the same tight margin.

He stared at the passing decks—no evidence of blood, no wounded stretched out on them; no visible damage except for trifling slits here and there in the shrouds. And there—under that contemptible deck umbrella Captain Elliot still sat viewing the carnage with the same stoical calm he'd exhibited when he'd passed here forty-five minutes ago.

Straddle-legged, the Admiral stood a lone figure on the high poop deck. His purple court sash flared bright in the noonday light, his eyes glittered hate, and the sun kindled the pike head he raised in loathing defiance before they butchered him with cross fire.

But no guns sounded. Not even a breech block clicked aboard the two encompassing vessels. No cutlass, no sword was brandished, and he saw Captain Smith run up a commanding signal.

The red flags of war, cross-barred with blue, dipped in strange salute—to *him*, it seemed, for his living crew were flat on their faces amongst the dead. That was all. Except for the hissing rush of water and the singing sails the frigates skimmed by in masterly silence, to round away and stand north until they rejoined their merchantmen at Chuenpee anchorage.

Kwan dropped the pike and groped for the parapet—to cling there with both convulsive hands, to cling to the substantial, to lucid reality. What uncanny weakness had possessed them at the last moment of all? Why hadn't they fired? Why hadn't they cut him to ribbons?

By and by he shrieked his questions into the clear, bright air. He asked the shadowless sky. The quivering glitter of sea. For he had great need of help. He couldn't fathom the mystery himself. He had no inkling. He could only speculate within the realms of reasonableness and experience . . . Had they spent all ammunition? Were they too exhausted? Or had this one, small, fortuitous, and inconsequential success utterly deranged their poor brains? Was that the reason?

CHAPTER XXI

CANTON,
November 1839

THROUGH THE clouded transparency of pearl-shell panes Mei-deh saw the afternoon light fading to fog gray. She crossed to one window, and then the other, releasing rolls of woven bamboo fiber to cover the staring blankness. These were the winter-season blinds she'd painted with tranquil pines hugging snowy crags, to remind herself of the sturdiness of one and the provocative loftiness of the other.

With the windows covered, she lit the candles—red ones all, in the several wall niches, on her desk, at the altar table, and by the bookshelves. She lit almost as many more in her sleeping alcove, where the high Nanking bed stood with drawn curtains; and still other candles in her dressing-room beyond. The apartment became bright and candid and frank with light. There were no dissembling shadows: no concealment, or evasion.

She went the rounds a second time, snipping guttering wicks so they'd blossom into bright flame and dousing the smelly smoking bits she cut off in a bowl of water E-ling held for her with priestly precision. There were no words between them: each understood the other. E-ling moved soundlessly across the tiles and Peking rugs—her feet and legs and spirits schooled in quiet hush.

As Mei-deh passed the long dressing mirror, she was caught by the unfamiliar reflection of herself. Not the gown of muted carmine with its sea-colored jacket, for she'd worn them before. It was her hair that was different. It no longer hung in maiden plaits, but was drawn back smoothly from her forehead into a coil on her neck and fastened there with bodkins of gold. It was the married style.

E-ling stood behind her, gazing at this change in the same absorbed reverie. Their musing eyes met in the mirror, to smile, to bolster and give comfort, to hope.

Sounds came from the outer corridor. E-ling murmured a small prayer and glided quickly to the antechamber door. She opened it upon Gowqua and, as he stepped in, closed herself outside.

"You asked for me, Piece-of-My-Heart?" Gowqua asked gently.

Then Mei-deh stepped forth from the curtains of her dressing room, and he saw her hair. He stared long at it, his eyelids, his lips, his jaw muscles graven in stone.

In the clutch of crisis Mei-deh neither lowered her head nor blushed nor opened supplicating hands. She stood straight and proud and impenitent . . . except for her eyes. They brimmed with tenderness for her father, with compassion and love for him. Softly she said: "Please sit, my parent, while I tell you of my imperfection—which I have hidden by subterfuge until now."

Gowqua's steps were those of a burdened man as he crossed the room and sat himself. He chose a straight-backed, formal chair without cushion.

Mei-deh did not move. She stood, a bright carmine figure in the center of a rug of spring green, facing her father. "You guessed I was harboring a secret," she ventured, "since you have not pressed me for reasons or explanations."

Gowqua nodded quietly. "When you mewed up in your apartment too continuously, I guessed—something. I have waited—knowing you would tell me when you were ready."

Mei-deh clasped one hand in the other within the sleeves of her jacket to steady herself against pity for the heartbreak she was dealing, and in a clear distinct voice said: "I met a *stranger*, said three words, and tore my heart out for him. I shall bear his child."

Gowqua's eyes sought empty space above her head, regarding it steadily, never wavering, never blinking. After an eternity he let breath out slowly and observed: "The word passion can be more malignant than arsenic."

Mei-deh's red lips parted in gentle denial: "Not malignant, my parent. Call it easy blindness, for in our moment we were heart-tied. We neither of us thought of nights and days and years to follow . . . and I shall love him until rocks decay."

Gowqua's gaze dropped to his hands, which were trembling. "You desire marriage to him?"

Mei-deh's back stiffened, and she raised her head with infinite sadness. "No, that can never be."

"Would you have me guess this *stranger's* name?" Gowqua asked, a sudden obstruction in his throat.

Mei-deh shook her head firmly. "No. He neither knew my

name nor who I was. I would leave it that way. As for me—I knew his name. But nothing will ever make me reveal it. I shall not whisper it—even to an ant."

There was aching silence while Gowqua contemplated the years ahead. He tapped the tabletop in sudden decision and said: "We shall not mention him again! However, I would protect you from slander . . . therefore I shall negotiate the *semblance* of marriage for you immediately, with a Chinese."

Sorrowfully Mei-deh said no again. "Not even that, my parent. You see, in my heart I am married to this *stranger*. It does not matter whether we burned incense over mumbled words. Or whether we quaffed the bubbles of champagne to solemnize it. I pledged him my heart, and my fidelity, in the *act* of marriage— and he shall have them always."

Silence grew thick between them.

Mei-deh opened her hands in appeal. "There are women who marry, only to say farewell to soldier husbands who ride off to battle and never return. I would have you regard me henceforth as such a widow—for I bear this man a love as high as the mountains and as deep as the sea, and shall continue to bear it until I am called to the Nether Springs."

Gowqua bowed his head in acceptance and asked her what she proposed. For he sensed now that she had a "planned adjustment" in her mind.

Because it was a thing of the mind, Mei-deh was scrupulous not to touch her father or seek further appeal to his emotions. She seated herself quietly in a chair opposite him and asked that he give her, in a lump sum, the marriage dowry he would have paid to a bridegroom she might have married according to custom. Immediate cash would be needed, she explained, to buy a way around restrictions preventing two Chinese women from voyaging out of China.

"Two?" Gowqua queried.

"E-ling will accompany me," she told him. "The remainder of

the dowry I shall use to set myself up in some commercial business."

"Where do you think to go?"

"To Macao first—because it is the transfer point to Manila, or to Singapore. Ultimately, perhaps, I shall seek the land called America."

"You think to outwit destiny in a foreign land?" he inquired.

"I would outwit Chinese destiny, if I can," she told him tersely. "I would make life less thankless and unprofitable by living in a country where law and order prevail, where perpetual *squeeze* is not the code of life."

Bouncing the fingers of one hand against those of the other, he regarded her thoughtfully, agreeing that China's need for reform was grievous.

Mei-deh exclaimed in earnest conviction: "It pains me to confess it, my parent, but I have come to regard Confucianism as a mental disease! It is paralyzing Chinese minds, and drugging them far, far more hideously than opium!"

She drew breath and hurried on: "You see, during my weeks of quiet isolation here I have read and thought much. It is from this thought that I speak now. Confucius' wisdom was an estimable code of behavior for a small nation of small clans. But today—we are unwieldy millions adhering only to the past."

To encourage her Gowqua nodded in what passed for thoughtful agreement.

"For instance," she said, "Confucius extolled loyalty to family above loyalty to nation. Yet, I observe, these English and Americans of today place loyalty to country, and civic consciousness, above all. They care whether children starve, whether city streets are pigstys, or a flood destroys neighbors. We Chinese don't. By Confucian mandate we provide the best possible within our family gates, we enhance the family home and the family tomb, even stealing to do it—in the name of filial piety. We ignore those from whom we steal."

She sighed perplexedly. "I realize we can't change centuries of habit suddenly. But there must be a start—and when shall that be? In my lifetime? I tell myself these Ch'ings will disappear . . . assuredly their mandate from Heaven exhausts itself. Yet when they go—will the new order be better?"

Her question struck cords deep within him; and in his reluctance to relinquish her to foreign shores, he told her of the whisper of a good new order already stirring in a neighboring province. He described the good and high-minded "God-worshipers" collecting farmers and scholars and artisans into a model community of selflessness at Thistlemount. He did not ask it of her, but there was the hope implicit in his words that this movement in her native land might be the thing to win her.

She understood, and shook her head in slow negation. "I do not advocate in the name of religion. I would have law and order because they are basic moral principles."

"Perhaps you merely reach towards a fond and insubstantial dream. I suggest you remember that, as an exile, you will sit opposite your shadow for companionship."

She smiled comfortably. "At night there will be the moon for companion—and dancing flower shadows. There will be the assuaging contentment of painting, which you have encouraged me to discover in your home. And . . . I shall have my son."

"Son?" he queried in mild skepticism.

She nodded brightly. "I ask that kindness of Fate. That my child be born a son, so that I may rear him in the best of two worlds—in your likeness, and in the *selected* likenesses of Westerners."

Gowqua closed his eyes in abject sorrow. "Mencius has said—'The greatest sorrow is the death of the heart.'"

Mei-deh's surprise was in her voice. "Indeed, my heart is not dead."

"*Mine* is," her father told her through gray lips. "Of my three dearest . . . one is now dead, one irresponsible, and one about to become a self-imposed exile."

Mei-deh slid out of her chair, running to kneel before him,

clasping his hands in hers and resting them against her warm cheek, too overcome to speak. She promised brokenly: "You will live in my son."

Gowqua gazed at her dear bright face. " 'Twill be comfort for my mind, but not heart's ease."

She had no answer, but she did not release his hands; and she stayed pressing her cheek against his knee.

He told her: "We say 'Daughters are merely pretty guests in a household during the short span between birth and marriage,' but I say—you, Mei-deh, have been infinitely more to me than a guest. You have been a living part of my mind and my heart. I do not let you go without suffering a measure of death."

Mei-deh's face bloomed in a tear-glistened smile that was full of promise and salvation, and she spoke the thing that had been there in her heart all along. "My parent, I shall go to put new roots down in a new life. When they prosper and grow foliage, I would have you come and sit in their shade with me . . . and with *our* privileged child of two worlds!"

Lin Tse-hsu favored the "dragonfly method" of writing, and his brushstrokes skimmed as lightly over the parchment as a winging insect over water—dipping, darting, thrusting, and never hesitating. He stood the brush in its soapstone holder and held the page at arm's length, squinting critically through half-closed eyelids at its compositional balance. Symmetry . . . ? Yes. Harmonious vitality . . . ? Yes. Elegant delicacy . . . ? Umh, enough certainly for a twenty-year-old queen, a tributary sovereign so illiterate she couldn't even read the Universal Monarch's language.

Then he brought the pliant parchment close under the circle of red lantern light to reread his exact words to Victoria, of the Outer Isles.

"Poor Queen—Your savages of the Further Seas have waxed so bold, it seems, as to defy and insult our Mighty

*Empire. Of a truth it is high time for you to flay the face,
cleanse the heart, and amend your ways. If you submit
humbly to the Universal Monarch and tender allegiance,
it may win a chance to purge yourself of past sins. But if you
persist, and continue in your path of obstinate delusion, your
three puny islands will be laid waste and your people
pounded to mincemeat so soon as the armies of his Celestial
Divinity set foot upon your shores."*

Yes, 'twould do for the queen of pilfering dogs. He handed the
page to the translator and turned to regard the gray ghost of light
fingering the windowpanes. There'd just be time to hear the diverting account of another trifling brush with the Abominables
before breakfast. He called for the Captain of the sampan fleet,
who was waiting to report.

Lin fastened the grape-colored jacket with its warm lambskin
lining more tightly across his chest and settled himself in a
straight-backed audience chair. His eyes were bright with reflected fire from the red lanterns, and he stroked his philosopher's
beard with lingering fingers in amiable anticipation. H'm-m,
where had the imbroglio taken place? Off Chuenpee in the river's
mouth, hadn't someone said? Poisonous vermin—probably trying
to creep upriver after nightfall!

The sampan Captain was a round-faced stalwart with bristling
black hair and a fierce mustache. But his manner was neither
stalwart nor fierce now as he came treading softly on bare tiles.
His jowls sagged, and his eyes were like captured sparrows darting
from doorways to rafters to windows.

The man's foreboding look graveled Lin. He jerked his head
up and demanded resonantly: "You annihilated the vermin?"

The Captain's eyes slid sideways before he temporized: "Not
exactly, Sire."

"You annihilated half?" Lin's voice teetered between rumble
and roar.

The answer was a hoarse whisper: "Not exactly, Sire."

Lin's face became a bare knife. "With five thousand men, you couldn't annihilate five hundred English?" he demanded.

The Captain threw up both hands, wailing dolorously: "The tide was wrong. We couldn't move the sampan fleet out the creeks at low tide. These English surprised us twelve hours before we planned to surprise them!" His words came fast then, tripping over each other, as he told the tale of complete rout of the war-junk fleet in forty-five minutes.

Lin sat stunned, his hate making a bonfire of all there was in him. "Bah!" he roared, and the timbre of his cry shivered a dozen lanternpanes. He clutched up the baton on the gong rack and beat a furious tattoo.

Guards with clanking swords, with spears and pikes, flung open the doors and came rushing in. Lin pointed to the cringing Captain. "Sew him in a sack and turn him into the river!"

Squirming like an eel, the Captain threw himself at Lin's feet, kissing the morocco boots, groveling, slobbering, beseeching abjectly: "A coolie's death! Spare me! Me, Captain of the greatest sampan fleet in history. Me . . ."

Lin interrupted. "Sew him in a *velvet sack*—and throw him into the river!" He kicked the supplicating hands aside in abhorrence, turned his back, and strode towards his desk.

The guards dragged the sobbing wretch from the room; but even before his wails had ceased echoing in the corridor, Lin's secretary had scurried out with a dozen new orders. First of all he saw to it that the Commissioner's breakfast was postponed, and that a more bounteous and more comforting one was put on the fire. Then he came to open the ingeniously hidden door of a secret antechamber.

Two oddly assorted men stepped out. One wore the flapping black pantaloons and jacket of a sampan coolie; the other, farmer's blue covered with a dirty sheepskin jacket. Both faces were browned, but not etched and patterned by a lifetime of daily association with the sun. Nor, as they crossed the room towards

Lin's desk, were there steps lowly and subservient enough to suit their clothes.

Lin greeted them with neither word nor gesture, but sat twisting a writing brush between two taut hands. It broke suddenly with a splintering pop. He threw the bits to the floor in a spasm of bitterness, scowled up at the two men, and said in the Mandarin dialect of educated men: "For one moon you have spied for me aboard each and all their ships. You are both officers, naval and military. Tell me, as experts, how this could happen? *How?*"

An answer came quickly in Mandarin from Chen, the one in sailor pantaloons: "Their vessels command more speed."

"How?" Lin stormed. "Our naval reports list them 'slow, clumsy, five to eight hundred tons'!"

"Outdated reports of ten years ago! Westerners aren't traditionalists. They have the faculty for rapid change." Chen shook his head bleakly. "It's true their heavy tea wagons filled Lintin Roads ten years ago. They were survivals which took forty-five days from Calcutta. But not today! Today they're using long, low, flush-decked frigates with little or no sheer. They're copied from American privateers. Likewise their clippers, which make the Calcutta run regularly in eighteen days. They can be driven straight up the China Sea into the teeth of the northeast monsoon."

Lin put hands to his head, to rock it in moaning affliction. "Every loading coolie, every sampan rat could know this," he grieved mightily. "Why doesn't the frog chorus reach Peking?"

Chen fixed inexorable eyes on the wall above Lin's head and said: "I'm told Peking doesn't want to hear of change. You will recall—Minister Ho reported repeatedly on the merits of foreign ship design. His reward was the gift of a foreign dog."

Lin's hands jerked from his head, and for a minute his eyes talked death. But Chen was not looking at them, and did not quail.

It was then that Feng, in farmer's blue, cleared his throat and said calmly: "Western weapons have also altered, and improved."

Lin scowled in monumental disbelief.

Feng drew wadded paper from a slit in the lining of his shaggy sheepskin and unfolded it before the Commissioner. "A drawing of their swivel gun, with four times the range and velocity of any weapon we possess. Their cannon exceed our largest jingals, and none are made of *wood!* Their weapons are for use, not intimidation. They have a Congreve rocket—a most deadly weapon, especially with combustible materials to act on. And—their guns can be depressed or elevated, according to combat necessity."

Lin snatched up the drawing in trembling hands, but he scarcely glanced at it, for his mind had leaped ahead. In a resounding thump he smacked the desktop and screamed: "Collect me every book, every pamphlet, every journal these verminous English and Americans have describing *their* tactics of war, *their* strategy of maritime defense, weapons, and training—that I may set a staff of linguists to translating each and every word!"

He strode out from behind the desk and down the length of the long room, waving hands above his head in an apoplexy of commands: "Get me Admiral Nelson's account of Trafalgar! Obtain his record of the Battle of Abukir off Egypt's coast, where he sank Napoleon's fleet. Steal them! Buy them! Question their old storytelling devils—the missionaries! Ply their born-in-cheap-wombs seamen with humble words and rich gifts to *obtain these manuals!* This is the immutability of my will!"

It took a full breakfast, and after that an hour's solace in the stone garden, before the muscles of Lin's face had stopped twitching. By then he felt composed enough to address himself on paper to Tao Kuang. Today's report would be scrupulous labor, for it would require a *finesse of wording,* he acknowledged to himself, that he'd never had the necessity to employ before.

Thoughtfully, painstakingly he warmed the brush between his lips as he considered each syllable. Then he dipped it in newly rubbed ink and wrote in his delicately skimming dragonfly style:

"I, with most assiduous heedfulness, hasten to report that British sampans, in an uncivil breech of peace, earnestly begged to pass upriver. Admiral Kwan did not grant their prayers, and they meanly attempted to sneak through. The intrepid Kwan ordered cannon fire, and killed many tens of their crews in the Volage and Hyacinth. The remainder should have fled, but instead that poisonous sprout, Captain Elliot, dared to return fire, which, of course, was like beating an egg against stones.

That clearheaded Kwan, as masterly in tactics as his esteemed ancestor, stood directing the entire action, which circumvented the English passing upriver. As a consequence he was wounded by splinters, four of his sailors lost their footing and fell into the sea, and were drowned. Kwan cheered his men, displayed the terror of his name, and firing a broadside, killed many tens of barbarians, thus ending the battle. Once again the Chinese have been a stalwart avenging host, and have punished the boisterous instincts of these foreign devils.

We shall continue to soothe and admonish these would-be tigers. Daily I ransack my dry intestines to cope with their fractiousness. But be assured the accumulated virtues of our dynastic line are a bright and powerful beacon of Righteousness."

He read the text aloud, testing the ring of truth in each word. Then he held the paper off, examining it meticulously from one angle and another. Yes, happy symmetry in the balance of each spider-stroked column. Yes, harmonious vigor . . . and delicately turned, that double allusion to righteousness in the final word. . . .

Lin rolled the parchment, fitting it into a bamboo cylinder, and sealed the grooved lid. When he'd stamped the congealing wax with his jade name-chop, he handed the cylinder to his aide. "This goes by express messenger to Peking. The fleetest! Direct him to cover more than one hundred and thirty miles each day."

CHAPTER XXII

HONG KONG,
February 1843

IN THE giddy, stinging morning air his two little redheaded daughters frisked on either side of him, pinafores flouncing and plaits flying, as Gill crossed the trellised courtyard. Each tugged at a hand, straining him forward to the delicious adventure of farewell beyond the big gate. They'd got to the glossy clump of sealing-wax palms framing that portal when Lael called in alarm from the upper veranda. She came running along it in a ruffled peignoir to the nearest arch, waving a batch of papers at Gill. "Your speech!" she wailed in dismay. "I feared you'd gone without it!"

Gill clapped an admonitory hand to his forehead in thoroughly mortified chagrin.

Lael laughed now, understandingly. "*Amah* will bring it down to you," she told him.

And then, in the interval of waiting, she rested both arms on the stone ledge and leaned out cozily towards him, to counsel with wifely gentleness: "Mind you don't allow yourself to become excited and take to galloping. It's a beautiful and proud speech, darling. It melts me much. And I would have everyone at the dedication hear, *and feel,* each word."

Gill crossed his heart and raised his right hand in the gesture of dutiful submission. But his eyes continued feeding on that lovesome face above, with ruffles slipping away from the white neck and the thick russet-red braid hanging over one shoulder. The fathoms she continually plumbed in him, he marveled. The welling sense of harmony, affection, alliance, and enchantment she stirred up a dozen times each day.

He blew her a kiss and turned to the small redheaded pair, so preciously like her, who were prancing now on tiptoe to be out and away to the rapturous daily pageant on the Peak Path.

"Camel, Pa-pa!" young Samma piped. "Hurry—or we miss him!"

"Camel! Camel!" baby Melissa caroled in boisterous treble.

The hovering *amah* clucked her tongue reprovingly, *amah* fashion. "No makee flute! Talkee plop-ah!" she scolded dotingly.

But the redheaded chorus went on warbling and skipping in irrepressible excitement towards the green viewing knoll at the first bend. It was the outermost boundary, the frontier between home and that vast unknown realm below. Here each morning there was the distracting spectacle of a haughty two-humped camel swaying upwards in gurgling complaint, contemptuously carrying charcoal and vegetables for the householders who lived above. Here a serpentine of shoulder-pole vendors came clacking or fluting or belling their dazzling wares. Here they'd see a harlequinade of coolies and carpenters and necromancers clearing ground for another new bungalow. And then the climax, the fond drama of a dozen smothering good-by kisses before *amah* clucked them back inside the walled garden for another lifetime of twenty-four hours.

Gill stood watching until the gate door banged shut behind them, and then continued on the downward path towards town. Tatters of milky mist were still caught on the pinnacles above, but it was gloriously clear below. A bright and shining day. Gossip birds were busy in the sweet olive and fig trees, tiger beetles scurried this way and that across the patterned moss, and from a laurel branch he brushed with his shoulder two golden orioles flashed out in a yellow blaze.

At the fork he turned left, away from his habitual route, which circled down past Scandal Point and the parade ground adjoining Murray's Barracks. He had a business errand this morning which took him over into the Tai-top-pei district before he was due at the dedication of the new Courthouse.

Other trails threaded away intermittently from the path, but Gill kept to the main westerly one, which wound through spraying plumes of wild spirea and around gardenias white with bloom as it ran along the small plateau above the spot where foundations were being laid for the new Government House on Caine Road.

At the nullah beyond he quickened his step to plunge under dripping tree ferns and across the soaked footbridge straddling the noisy, spilling torrent there. The fissure was always strident with cicadas and incessant frog croak, always foggy with spray. But in a few more steps he'd spanned it, and was skirting an obscuring granite outcrop which rounded away from the cleft and looked down steeply on the city spread below.

It wasn't often he came by this longer path, so when he did and reached this lookout spot he always caught his breath in unbelief. Each time there was another cluster of bungalows, another row of substantial stone-walled shops. Today's view seemed even more incredible. For there, winding along the narrow shore from West Point to Wanchai, was two full miles of city!

The figures of that informal census taken last month came back to him, and he remembered they'd estimated then that the colony had grown to twenty thousand. But still this incredible visual reality of two crowded miles of terraces, of houses climbing the green cliffs . . .

Queen's Road meandering lengthwise, with Wyndham, D'Aguilar, Duddell, Ice House, and a dozen other streets leading into it . . . the big airy seamen's hospital a Parsee merchant had donated; the magistry and jail; the church; the busy Central Market; Peddar's Hill, with the harbormaster's office on it; the Arab mosque; the dozens of wharves; the handsomely pillared new Courthouse being dedicated today . . . all, *all* monuments to equity!

Gill drew breath from deep within his being and murmured thanks for the occasion which had brought him along this path today so he could reaffirm with his eyes, and his consciousness, what law and order and impartiality had wrought in two cramped years.

Inevitably his mind scanned back to '41—Lin exiled in disgrace; the suave and astute Ki-shen succeeding him; the Convention of Chuenpee, which Captain Elliot formulated with Ki-shen, who was quietly sure he'd struck a dandy bargain with unwary foreign devils in foisting off what he described in court records as "a worthless, barren rock."

So Ki-shen had cheerfully signed the convention of January 20 . . . ceding to England, *in perpetuity,* this granite speck far to the south in exchange for China's two captured forts on the Pearl River, and for the evacuation of Chusan Island, so threateningly near the Yangtze estuary. Furthermore, Ki-shen reported proudly to Peking, he'd been able to pare indemnity money down to a paltry six million dollars, which they owed the merchants anyway for Lin's wholesale confiscation of opium stocks back in '39.

Six days later the Union Jack had gone up on Hong Kong's northern shore; and men of the 18th Royal Irish, the 26th Cameronians, and the 49th Bengal Volunteers broke ground with their tent pegs.

That first agonizing and calamitous summer! Gill groaned aloud even in memory of it now . . . when young Victoria had indignantly removed Captain Elliot from command for "*trying to get the lowest terms he could*" and accepting such a booby trophy as Hong Kong; when Sir Henry Pottinger, the present Governor-General, had lived in a pitched tent; when the smothering southwest monsoon had brought a persistent plague of green hoppers, mosquitoes, lizards, and centipedes to crawl on walls and under nets and pillows; when, out of six hundred men in a regiment more than three hundred and fifty were in hospital at one time with what everyone called "Hong Kong fever," but which was actually malaria; when sentries were fortified for two-hour duty with tots of sherry and bitters, and, even so, keeled over and died like flies; when doctors said the carbonic acid in the soil made the air unfit for human respiration . . .

When a July typhoon snatched roofs off; recurved next night and blew the remnants of their Happy Valley settlement to shreds in shrieking darkness; when many Britishers shook their heads and openly said: "No one can approve the selection of Hong Kong for a colony"; and when the only Chinese who'd come flocking from the mainland were washerwomen and carpenters. . . .

Not that the Chuenpee Convention had reconciled Chinese animosity and rancor and abhorrence. Tao Kuang ignored it almost immediately; mandarins reneged on its provisions; Chinese mobs ransacked and burned foreign agencies in Canton; and fishermen up and down the coast, when they weren't tossing oilpots aboard foreign trading vessels, were loosing fire rafts against them at night.

It was not until Pottinger and the new Admiral of the China Squadron, Sir Gordon Bremer, captured Amoy, reoccupied Chusan Island, vanquished Manchu troops defending the two cities of Chapu and Chinkiang, and were moving onto Nanking that Tao Kuang announced he would "soothe the foreign devils so the nation's situation would ease."

The Treaty of Nanking, subsequently signed in August of '42, had indeed soothed many. Not only the foreign devils, but thousands of Chinese also, for it opened China's door, at last, to a modern world of trading.

It abolished the co-Hong system of trading. It paid British merchants six million dollars for twenty million dollars' worth of opium they'd surrendered three years ago to ransom their lives, as they now claimed. It scheduled fixed harbor fees, and limited customs duties to five per cent. It ceded Hong Kong forever to the British Crown and its heirs. It declared the ports of Canton, Amoy, Foochow, Ningpo, and Shanghai permanently open to foreign traders, who might reside in them with their wives and families. Also, foreign consuls could come and set up their own courts of justice.

"Justice!" Gill half sang, half cried the word, and the timbre of it went spilling over ferns and lilies and speckled iris until the yellow sunshine swallowed it.

He'd chosen the word—and the fullness of its concept—for his speech today because he'd watched its seed flourish and had learned in these two pioneering years that it was the very nucleus of citizenship.

He fingered the written draft of his speech, taking it from his pocket and running through it, paragraph by paragraph, repeating a sentence, and another, for the sound, for the feel . . . Was he chewing too many words, for instance, over the controversial hubbub being raised in New York and Washington over establishing American courts in China's treaty ports? Extraterritoriality, it was called. Well, he used its real name. He said it "wrapped every American in China in the shining armor of impartiality!"

Not a new notion, exactly. History said the Egyptians granted it to a Greek colony at Alexandria three hundred years before Christ. Common practice for Christians in non-Christian countries during the Middle Ages, it seemed. As for China—precedent for it had been firmly set by Arabs back in ninth-century Canton when they installed a Moslem magistrate for their community. . . .

He couldn't omit any of that. No! He had to say each word. He had to advocate extraterritoriality in China to the utmost—remembering Macy's headless body! Remembering that hideous farce of courtroom justice!

He stuffed the speech back into his pocket and walked on. The path bore downward now—leveling through mounds of wild roses and thick-growing holly bushes which reached out with spiny leaves to snag at his sleeves—and then broadened as it passed Widow Wong's house. She was Hong Kong's woman of mystery: a widow, obviously wealthy and making more in business every day, who'd never been known to appear anywhere in public. No one knew where she'd come from, or exactly when.

But everyone knew her red-brick house, its roof and curling eaves glossy with green tiles, surrounded by a high, blank, convent-like wall. The two-storied mansion was handsomely ornamental in a colony of utilitarian bungalows—a showplace, really. Outside, that is, because no one of them had been invited to see inside yet.

Widow Wong conducted business—buying and reselling Crown sites; building and leasing stores and offices; purchasing marine engines and two complete steamers for the Canton run— with acumen and scrupulous integrity. But, always and invariably, through the intermediary of a female compradore—a hushed woman, as quiet as a shadow, with a biddable and enduring face, who was always calm, always detached and impersonal, no matter how involved and drawn-out negotiations became. The story was that she wore the brass ring of a maidservant on her arm, high up under her drab-gray sleeves.

Gill had gone into one of these three-party deals with Widow Wong recently, and he chuckled now, remembering its odd circumstances. He'd sent around—to this agency the Widow had obtained from the manufacturers in England—an order for a middling lot of chintz piece-goods he intended selling for Chinese bedspreads and curtains. Back had come his order that same day with a cramped notation—"Cancel house, bird, beast, and stripe patterns. Chinese unappreciate. Double order of bright flower prints, lilacs, roses, tulips, wisteria. Chinese appreciate." He'd followed the advice, except that on sudden hunch he'd trebled it. He'd made a killing! Chinese women came flocking to buy the chintz for dresses!

He glanced up curiously now at Widow Wong's hermetical wall. Higher, by at least a meter, than ordinary garden walls; secret, seclusive, and bristling at the top with hostile shards of broken bottles. He wondered—was the life within it equally hostile, or merely indifferent to others? Was it lived in frigid impassivity? In lukewarm and humdrum repression?

He'd passed half the wall's length when, suddenly, a ball came sailing over it and landed at his feet—a brightly painted child's ball. He heard an exclamation of distress from a youngster inside, and the next moment there was the grind of a lock being turned in the big iron-studded gate several paces ahead. Gill caught up the ball and strode to the medieval panel swinging back on its dowels.

A three-year-old ran out onto the path—a bonny, smiling, fair-skinned boy with curly blond hair and bright brown eyes that brimmed with fun. There was nothing Chinese about him, even his clothes.

Unafraid and friendly, he made directly for Gill. When the lad was close enough to catch the ball, Gill tossed it to him in a slow, easy arc. The youngster caught it agilely and, in impetuous playfulness, volleyed it back in a high swoop. His merry little laugh exploded admiringly when Gill stepped into position and the painted sphere descended into his cupped hands.

"Show me!" the boy demanded eagerly.

Gill tossed the ball in a steep arc this time, and then stood demonstrating how to gauge its fall.

After the third try the boy had the knack of it. "What's your name?" he asked in lively curiosity.

"Gill. What's yours?"

"Robert."

"That's a first-rate name!"

"I like it very," Robert agreed candidly.

Gill thought he'd never seen a more winning lad. That open frank look! That bonny, embracing smile! The strange thing, though, was that he was speaking pure English without a bamboo accent, or any pidgin lingo scattered in. Whatever could he be doing here in this Chinese household?

A quick movement at the gate drew Gill's attention, and he turned to see a Chinese manservant come striding out. He swept towards them, chiding in rapid Cantonese.

Robert shook his head in vigorous, and imperious, negation to the Chinese, and then swiveled around to Gill with a drollery of apology on his face. "Ah Lam's a goose—he doesn't know you're my friend."

"Some people can't read hearts," Gill commiserated gravely, "so they need words to tell them."

Robert nodded in grave agreement. Then, with the same earnest preoccupation, he stepped nearer and faced Gill squarely. "Will you play ball with me another day, Gill?" he asked.

"I will," Gill told him, making the words into solemn promise.

Robert made a funny little decisive gesture with both hands in unison and beamed triumphantly. "I knew it!" he crowed. "I read your heart, didn't I?"

"Yes, I believe you did," Gill said aloud out of his own strange conviction.

The Chinese harangued a sober sort of counsel.

Robert nodded his head in agreement, and then capered about in coltish high spirits. "I have to go inside now to make ready for August Grandfather's visit. Come with me—to my gate. Only there—no farther!"

At the threshold Robert's good-by was sedate and poised. He composed his small body in an instant of tranquillity, grasped one hand with the other—Chinese style—and bowed.

Gill returned the bow in kind.

Before the gate closed, Gill caught a glimpse of exquisite garden beyond . . . with rainbow begonias, butterfly orchids, peonies, and flowering pomegranate growing in eye-fetching vistas. At the far corner he saw the chaste sphere of a moon doorway leading onto a belvedere which looked over cobalt water by day. And at night it would become a moon-viewing pavilion, for over the wondrously serene doorway was an inscription in fluted characters—which Gill had now learned to read—that said: "Place to cultivate the friendship of the moon."

The sun was a good hour higher, but still a friendly, tender yellow when Gill veered down through the turpentine-scented green shade of a mango clump and came out at the upper level of Gutzlaff Street. It tickled Gill that this new one had been named for the old Pomeranian Bible seller and pill doctor who was ensconced these days in government under the aureate title of Chinese-Secretary. He had become a bridge—compounded of dexterity in six Chinese dialects, and enduring compassion—between amateur government and growing hordes of amateur citizens.

It was a short, tilted, knife slice of a street, cut from gray granite, but already the wares of a double row of shops bulged out onto cobbles, and the two- and three-story verandas above were motley splotches of multiple family laundry strung on bamboo poles. Flowerpots were everywhere, but only a single tree remained in the stretch—a kapok at the lower end, layered with blossoms today, which burned in crimson brightness against the blue enamel of the sky.

Something in the burgeoning new street made Gill think of the three men who—in odium, suave bargaining, and sensitive perceptivity—had been prime creators of this colony and these city streets. The exiled Lin Tse-hsu, now eking out his days in the white north above the Amur River, by writing treatise after treatise on Western weapons of warfare, Western maritime defense, Western geography and sciences. The polished and tactful Marquis Ki-shen, taken to Peking in chains, stripped of all rank and a fifty-million-dollar fortune, and condemned to death, only to receive at the ultimate moment an empty appointment which took him into the distant exile of Tibet. And the ill-starred Captain Elliot—punished for accepting the very object Ki-shen paid so dearly for having given—now serving the equivalent of exile for an English naval officer as consul-general to Texas.

Gill swung around the bend into Queen's Road near Central Market and came upon an unholy commotion outside Lum's Bake Shop—the principal baker for the colony. Cobbles were white with flour, a grinning crowd was dusted with it, and the plaid slacks of the Cameronians were a frosty white as the soldiers moved rapidly in and out of the shop—sluicing water over spilled flour until gutters ran soggy with dough, stacking golden loaves on wheelbarrows they trundled to the Bund and dumped into the sea.

Gill spotted Major-General d'Aguilar, General Officer Commanding, standing apart with a group of Cameronian officers, watching the strange proceedings, and he made his way over to them.

"Arsenic in today's batch," they told him with stoic calm. "Both the bread and flour—loaded with it! Twenty dead already. Lord only knows how many more to go!"

An aide came hurrying up just then from the direction of the jail to report: "Lum's in the clear. The villain's his new chief baker, who's confessed. Seems he's a dedicated killer. Took the vow in some secret-society rigmarole when Lin went into exile. Been biding his time ever since for the means of doing a wholesale job of it."

Gill turned away, walking very fast as horror washed over him. "The brutish hate!" he kept saying over and over again. "The mad, savage hate! Hatching mass murder!"

Faces traveled past him in an anonymous blur as loathing mounted within him, and mounted . . . until a familiar round one edged into focus, smiling insistently in trusting friendship. It was Kwok Hon-chu, the kindly, intelligent rattan wholesaler who traded regularly with him. Gill forced himself to nod a plausible greeting, and strode on.

There was neither hate nor venom in Kwok. He was upright, honest, industrious, genial . . . Gill hammered at himself for control, for perspective. He forced himself to look deep into those other faces around him, the faces of those Queen's Road merchants intent on the morning's business. . . . They belonged to healthy, active, hard-working, frugal, law-abiding, and tolerant men.

And, gradually gaining the upper hand over triggered emotions, he spent the last hundred yards before he reached the new Hong Kong Club on D'Aguilar corner in reminding himself . . . hadn't he learned in five years' association that Chinese weren't all one color? That they were an intricate and complicated mosaic of many colors and varying hues?

Passive, calm in affliction, cheerful in disaster, yet eager for venture and doing. Abundantly imaginative, abundantly full of theatrical flourish, yet excruciatingly meticulous artisans. Warmly, overwhelmingly generous in hospitality, they'd let a starving waif lie where he fell. Outrageous liars, inspired gamblers in one mood, and in the next would put their elegant, talented fingers to creating infinitesimal beauty for the eye. And—always the instinctive reflex to save face, shift responsibility. Always a wily maneuvering for an inch more—even a half inch—of temporary advantage.

Except for the shadowy, silent-footed houseboys moving about their chores the club seemed to be deserted. Gill guessed everyone had already gone on to the Courthouse. He'd stepped in only to make sure he'd get the New York *Tribune,* which Joe Coolidge was loaning him.

He found the journal in his box—a year-old issue which Coolidge had written to New York to obtain because it contained the full text of John Quincy Adams' lecture in defense of what people at home were beginning to call the "Opium War."

He ran a quick eye over the lengthy text, knowing he couldn't spare time to read it now. Then clarion words jumped out at him, holding him while he read the entire paragraph: "'Opium War' is a misnomer. It is a trade war. Opium is a mere incident to the dispute, but no more the cause of this war than throwing overboard the tea in the Boston harbor was the actual cause of the North American Revolution. The insistence on *kowtow,* in all its forms, caused this war. . . ."

Reading the words, Gill gave thanks. Sober, honest truth every captain, every trader in the performance out East knew. But it was heartening to have a man on the other side of the globe, a man of Adams' stature and acumen, declare it. History books, he told himself with a quizzical grimace, might—they just *might—*

agree with the facts of this turning point instead of with popular prejudice.

He folded the journal and slipped it under his arm, stepping to the bulletin board to skim through several new notices posted there. He read:

THE COMMITTEE OF THE SOCIETY FOR DIFFUSION OF USEFUL KNOWLEDGE (formerly Canton) OFFERS $300 FOR THE BEST ESSAY ON TEA

Below that was:

CHU-KO'S MILITARY EXPEDITION POWDER

Best medical preparation for sunstroke and dysentery. Recipe formulated by the famous statesman Chu-ko Liang of the Han dynasty, and dates from his expedition to Yunnan in 225 A.D. Administered as snuff, it causes sneezing; and thus opens the 7 outlets of the skull. Or can be swallowed. Sold in small, handy porcelain bottles, tastefully decorated.

Messrs. Cudlipp and Bascombe, Ltd.
Old Bailey Street

Two men came in from a side portico to stop at the board, and Gill turned to say hello to William Scott, the Edinburgh trader he'd known since his first Canton winter, and to Richard Gilman, the newcome merchant who'd opened a trading agency.

"Heard the news about Widow Wong?" Scott asked breezily, and seeing the query in Gill's look, went on to say: "She's just donated fifteen thousand dollars for a foundling home. Wants it built over Pokfulam way with plenty of garden space. But refuses point-blank to be on the committee. Appointed old Gutzlaff in her place." His chuckle rumbled comfortably. "Rum old gal, what? That is, *if* she is old. Who knows? Still and all, she measures up to a Number One citizen, by Harry, so we shouldn't ask her age."

Gill's mind was up and away with the bonny youngster he'd met this morning when Gilman pulled him back to here and now by asking: "What's your opinion of those sites, Bennett?" He motioned to a government notice on the board announcing Tytam building sites for marine-front villas would be offered for auction on March 25 next.

Gill felt an inner wrench as he put the scene at Lum's Bake Shop behind him and answered as he would have yesterday, and as he hoped to on succeeding morrows. "I intend bidding on one."

"For investment?" Gilman pried smilingly.

"No. For breezy summer living," Gill told him. "For sending my family out there during the sticky months on this side. Plenty of sweet water from the upper Tytam ponds now on the sites—thanks to this ingenious bamboo aqueduct the Hakka folk have tied together. And, come June, I expect we'll be whipping out there—very macaroni—in basket carts, now that the Bengal Engineers are completing that stretch of broad, hard road around the island."

Gilman quirked his mouth in deliberation. "You make it sound very reasonable. I might attend the auction. *Might* even be a bidder," he allowed, a glint of quiet humor showing in his gray eyes.

"Not me!" Scott humped shoulders in amused skepticism. "I intend biding my time on this side. Who knows, the ladies—bless 'em—may succeed in persuading Colonel Lugard to drive a tunnel clear through Victoria Peak so's to let the breezes cool us on our own verandas."

He sauntered towards the door to the bar, and then turned to include both men in a gesture of invitation. "Time for a quick one—to get us in a dedicating mood, eh?"

Gilman said he'd willingly dedicate himself to dedication, but Gill excused himself on the grounds of being the speaker today for the American community, and took himself off by a side door.

Peddar Wharf, and the beach around it, was stacked high with cargo, he saw as he crossed the Bund, which was coming ashore from the fleet of clippers, brigs, and schooners at anchor beyond. Amongst them he recognized the beautifully raked masts of the *Falcon*, her unfurled sails falling in cloudlike folds over her massive yards and spars. She was the newest of the new Jardine Matheson clippers, and already famous for the driving speed she got from beam spread rather than hoist. The men who sailed her said "she was witchy with response, or rebellious and sulky at the least mishandling, and could do everything but speak."

"Perfection!" he murmured, allowing himself another look at those towering masts as he hurried along. And then had to side-step quickly to avoid the flailing fist of a Chinese girl in a bright-flowered chintz gown who was dickering in lively vituperation over the price of crystallized ginger a street hawker had on a tray. But he wasn't quick enough, and the fist thudded against his shoulder. The girl spun around indignantly.

But next second she was beaming happily. "Hallo, Mas-tah! Hallo! Hallo!" she cried.

It took Gill a moment to recognize Su-ling in this gaudy gown, and without her cart-wheel hat.

His surprise delighted her. "You no know my?" she cried. "My so-fashion belong Number One plitty, yes?"

Gill nodded in amused accord. "That's right, Su-ling, belong Number One pretty now."

She preened with head and shoulders and provocative hips; rotated both hands slowly, and with princess aplomb said: "Suppose you plen-tee wantchee my sleep you—my no can do! No! My have catchee plop-ah mas-tah now. He wantchee my allee time!"

Gill's laugh was token for rejoicing; and the look on his face a pious invocation, even though his words were: "And yet they say persistence is a virtue!" He waved his hand in small salute and started on.

But she was after him pell-mell, catching at his sleeve, pulling him to a stop, her face puckered like a baby about to cry. "Whassa malla you? No pay Su-ling cumshaw?"

Gill tried to figure what in the world she meant.

She told him. "Before time my no sleep you, you pay my two dollah. This night allee samee. My no go, must wantchee cumshaw! Must!"

Gill shook his head in chiding surrender. "I should have known your dress was the only thing you'd changed." He dug two dollars from his pocket for her. "Here's your 'golden sand'—you unregenerate leech!"

Su-ling snatched the money with a cackling "Hi, tank-oo! Tank-oo! My chin-chin you!" and was back in a jiffy haggling in abusive screams with the candy vendor before Gill had even taken three steps.

The rolling roar of salute came from the three .74s in the harbor—the HMS *Wellesley, Melville,* and *Blenheim.* Ceremonies were about to commence.

Gill pressed forward at a run, dodging his way through street crowds in the last intervening block. All around there was the popping of firecrackers, the blowing of trumpets, and the Chinese shout of "Ten thousand, thousand years!" As he reached his designated chair on the broad stone portico of the Courthouse, the naval band struck up "God Save the Queen"; and he stood, hat on heart, singing under his breath the words of "My Country, 'Tis of Thee" to the selfsame tune.

When it came Gill's turn to step up on the flag-draped speaker's dais, he found himself glancing quickly out at the wide blue of the harbor, up at the glory of the Peak, and he felt a strange impulse of futurity, a germinating perception, something bigger than himself, as though he were gazing through today to a distant tomorrow, seeing this port thriving, blessed, a haven . . . and he began his speech on man's eternal need for the bulwark of justice.

ADVENTURES OF HSI MEN	*Chin Ping-mei*
AMERICAN MERCHANT SHIPS	*W. J. Abbot*
ANNALS AND MEMOIRS OF COURT OF PEKIN FROM 16TH CENTURY	*Backhouse and Bland*
ANNUAL CUSTOMS AND FESTIVALS IN PEKING	*Tun Li-ch'en*
AUTOBIOGRAPHY	*Sir William des Voeux*
BIRDS OF SOUTH CHINA	*Caldwell*
BITS OF CHINA	*Tcheng Ki-tong*
BITS OF OLD CHINA	*H. Lindsay*
BITS OF OLD CHINA	*W. C. Hunter*
BOOK OF POETRY	*James Legge*
BOOK OF SONGS	*Arthur Waley*
BRITAIN'S FOLLY AND AMERICA'S GUILT	*Chester Holcomb*
BRITISH MERCHANT ADVENTURER	*Maurice Collis*
BRITISH TRADE AND THE OPENING OF CHINA 1800–42	*Michael Greenberg*
CAMPAIGN IN CHINA	*G. G. Loch*
CANTON CHINESE	*O. Tiffany*
CANTONESE LOVE SONGS	*Cecil Clementi*
CANTON REGISTER	*1827–1838*
CHATER COLLECTION 1655–1860	*J. Orange*
CHINA	*P. Auber*
CHINA	*R. M. Martin*
CHINA	*W. H. Medhurst*
CHINA AND THE CHINESE	*Herbert A. Giles*

CHINA CLIPPERS, THE — Basil Lubbock

CHINA AND THE MANCHUS — Herbert A. Giles

CHINA OPENED, Vol. II — Rev. Charles Gutzlaff

CHINA REPOSITORY, QUARTERLY, Vols. 1–12, 1832–43

CHINESE, THE, 2 vols. — J. F. Davis

CHINESE, THE — K. Latourette

CHINESE ACCOUNT OF THE OPIUM WAR
   Trans. by Wei Yuan of 2 chapters of Shen Wu-ki — E. H. Parker

CHINESE AS THEY ARE — G. T. Lay

CHINESE BIRDS AND BEASTS — George Lanning

CHINESE MORAL MAXIMS — J. F. Davis

CHRONICLES OF THE EAST INDIA COMPANY TRADING TO CHINA 1820–34, Vol. 5 — H. B. Morse

CLIPPER ERA, THE — A. H. Clark

COMMERCIAL PRODUCTS OF INDIA (Opium), pp. 845–61 — Watts

COOLIES, PSYCHOLOGY AND SONGS — A. N. J. Whymant

COSTUME OF CHINA — G. H. Mason

COSTUME OF CHINESE — William Alexander

CRITICAL STUDY OF FIRST ANGLO-CHINESE WAR — P. C. Kuo

CULTURAL HISTORY OF CHINA, A — Fitzgerald

DEVELOPMENT OF CHINA — K. Latourette

DIARY 1828–1851 — P. Hone

DOINGS IN CHINA — Lt. Alexander Murray

EARLY DAYS IN CANTON — G. Nye

EARLY RELATIONS BETWEEN U.S. AND CHINA, Vol. XXII — K. Latourette

EMINENT CHINESE OF THE CH'ING PERIOD, 2 vols. — Arthur Hummel

ENGLISH IN CHINA — William C. Young

ENGLISHMEN IN CHINA — Michie

EXPEDITION TO CHINA, 2 vols. — J. Elliot Bingham

FAN KWAE IN CANTON BEFORE TREATY DAYS 1825–44 — W. C. Hunter

FAN QUI IN CHINA 1836–37, 3 vols. — C. Toogood Downing

FENG SHUI — E. J. Eitel

FIFTY YEARS OF PROGRESS, 1891	Hong Kong Government Publications
FIVE YEARS IN CHINA 1842–47	Lt. F. E. Forbes, R.N.
FLORA HONGKONGENSIS	G. Bentham
FOREIGN MUD	Maurice Collis
GOVERNMENT AND PEOPLE OF CHINA	T. T. Meadows
GREAT BRITAIN AND CHINA 1833–60	W. C. Costin
GREAT WITHIN, THE	Maurice Collis
HISTORY OF AMERICAN SAILING SHIPS	H. Chapelle
HISTORY OF HONG KONG	E. J. Eitel
HISTORY OF SUMMER PALACES	C. B. Malone
HONG KONG 1839–44	W. Tarrant
HONG KONG ILLUSTRATED	M. Bruce
HOUSEBOAT DAYS IN CHINA	J. O. P. Bland
INTERNATIONAL RELATIONS OF THE CHINESE EMPIRE	H. B. Morse
INVASION OF CHINA BY WESTERN WORLD	E. R. Hughes
JOURNAL OF THREE JOURNEYS ALONG COAST OF CHINA 1831, 2, 3	Charles Gutzlaff
LETTERS	Wells Williams
LETTERS FROM FAR EAST	Sir Charles Eliot
LETTERS FROM HONG KONG AND MACAO	A. R. Ridgeway
LIFE OF TAO KWANG	Charles Gutzlaff
MAP OF CITY AND SUBURBS OF CANTON	D. Drooman
MEMOIRS, 3 vols.	William Heckie
MIDDLE KINGDOM, THE, 2 vols.	S. Welles Williams
MORNING OF MY LIFE IN CHINA	Gedeon Nye
MY MOTHER'S DIARY	Mrs. Hellyer
NARRATIVE OF EXPLORATORY VISIT TO HONG KONG	G. Smith
NATURALIST ON SHORES AND WATERS OF CHINA SEA	Cuth Collingwood
NEMESIS IN CHINA, THE	R. D. Bernard–W. H. Hall
OLD CHINA TRADE, THE	F. R. Dulles
OLD COUNTRY TRADE, THE	W. H. Coates
OPIUM	S. Warren
OPIUM—Encyclopaedia Britannica	E. M. Holmes
OPIUM CLIPPERS	B. Lubbock

OTHER SIDE OF THE LANTERN	*Sir F. Treves*
OUTLINES OF CHINESE SYMBOLISM AND ART MOTIVES	*C. A. S. Williams*
PERSONAL REMINISCENCES	*Robert B. Forbes*
PIDGIN ENGLISH SING-SONG	*C. G. Leland*
PIDGIN ENGLISH VOCABULARY	*A. P. Hill*
PIDGIN INGLES TAILS	*F. W. I. Airey*
POINTS AND PICKINGS ABOUT CHINA	*George Mogridge*
RESIDENCE IN CHINA 1830–33	*David Abeel*
SCENES IN CHINA—1820	*J. F. Davis*
SERIES OF VIEWS IN CHINA, A	*Allom and Wright*
SERVICE IN CHINA, 2 vols.	*Cunynghame*
SHORT HISTORY OF CHINESE CIVILIZATION	*Ts'ui Chi*
SKETCHES OF CHINA	*J. F. Davis*
SOME TRUTHS ABOUT OPIUM	*H. A. Giles*
STRANGE STORIES FROM A CHINESE STUDIO	*Pu Sung-ling, translated by H. A. Giles*
TEN THOUSAND THINGS ON CHINESE	*W. B. Langdon*
THES FROM THE LAND OF SINIM	*Robert Hart*
THREE YEARS' WANDERING IN CHINA	*R. Fortune*
TRAVELS IN CHINA	*John Barrow*
TRAVELS IN CHINA	*M. Huc*
TRAVELS OF AN ALCHEMIST	*Arthur Waley*
TWILIGHT IN THE FORBIDDEN CITY	*Reginald F. Johnston*
UNDER THE PEAK	*W. T. Mercer*
UNDER TOPS'LS AND TENTS	*Cy. T. Brady*
VISIT TO INDIA, CHINA	*B. Taylor*
VOYAGE AROUND THE WORLD 1835, 6, 7	*W. S. W. Rushchenberger*
WANDERINGS IN CHINA	*R. Fortune*
YANKEE SHIPS IN CHINA WATERS	*Henderson*